Hold Still

ARELL RIVERS

Hold STILL
Book 2 in **A HOLD SERIES SPIN-OFF**
ARELL RIVERS
Copyright ©2018 Tarnished Halo Publishing LLC
Published by Tarnished Halo Publishing LLC
2018 Edition

isbn digital: 978-0-9980316-0-6
ISBN print: 978-0-9980316-1-3

Editing: Sarah Murphy, www.sarahmurphyeditor.com
Proofreading: Virginia Tesi Carey
Formatting: Cassy Roop, Pink Ink Designs, www.pinkinkdesigns.com
Cover design: Cassy Roop, Pink Ink Designs, www.pinkinkdesigns.com
Author photo: Elzbieta Kaciuba Photography LLC, www.elzphoto.com

Dedication

For Gram, in heaven

She was my guiding star that dimmed even while she was alive. Her long good-bye ended about a year ago, at 99 years. I miss the woman she was.

Hold Still

One

OZZY

I HOLD THE KEY UP TO MY FRONT DOOR, but voices inside warn me it's unlocked. *Crap.* Running my hand across my forehead, my after-sex buzz with Jenna seeps out of my pores even while remembering her shouts as she came. Hell, everyone in the Jade probably heard her. But now I just want some peace and quiet.

Opening the door, I whistle for Bans. She comes scampering over, tail wagging. I bend down to accept her kisses, which erase those from Jenna. I'm fine with that.

I extend my hand. "How're you doing, girl?"

The golden retriever puts her paw in my calloused palm, barking her hello. At least one living soul in this house is genuinely happy to see me.

"Ozzy. There you are." My rep from Platinum Records walks into my foyer, all legs and hair and makeup. Her skirt lands above her knee by maybe an inch. Respectable yet somehow *not*.

My eyebrow raises as I stand. "Ginger. Baby. How's tricks?" I extend my tongue and wiggle it. Gotta keep her off-guard. Especially since I know exactly why she's here.

"You," she half-laughs, half-scolds. "I caught most of your show last night."

My eyes slant to the other person in the house, my PA, Aiden. Why didn't he tell me Platinum was at the show? Averting his gaze, Aiden snaps his fingers. Bans walks to him and rolls on her back. Traitor. As he rubs her stomach, I reply, "It was a good night."

Ginger approaches me. "You had the audience eating out of your hand." Smiling, she hits my pecs.

I grunt as if her puny tap hurt, which puts an even bigger smile on her face. "Glad you enjoyed."

"So, I must have missed the part where you played your new stuff." She crosses her arms across her ample, doctor-enhanced chest. "Right?"

No wasting time with this one. Directly for the jugular. I shrug. "Aw, Ginger. I haven't seen you in what? A few weeks? And you don't even kiss me hello before jumping right to work shit?" I grab her hand, making a show out of kissing it. "That's better."

She fans her slightly-pink face with the hand I just had my lips on. Not immune. Yeah, I can finesse my way out of this. Again. I start toward my kitchen. "Come on in, stay for a while. Hey Aiden," I toss over my shoulder. "We're all stocked up on prosecco, right?"

Behind me, Aiden clears his throat. "Of course. Top shelf of the wine fridge."

"Let's go out to the patio and talk like civilized folks. Mimosas for everyone," I say, hitting my thigh twice for Bans to follow. Unlike all of the other women in my life, she follows my orders immediately.

"Ozzy, we have work to discuss," Ginger reminds me. As if I could forget.

"And we shall. With prosecco and orange juice. Nothing says we have to talk business sitting around a stuffy conference table dying of thirst." I grab a bottle of OJ and dig into my wine fridge, pulling out two bottles of bubbly. One for me and one for them. I nod for Aiden to take the glasses and head out.

On the patio, I pick up a ball, while Aiden makes the drinks. Bans barks and runs around, retrieving the ball and dropping it at my feet. I'd much rather play with her than deal with Ginger.

"Here you go." Ginger hands me a glass and clinks hers against it. "To making more music together." Emphasis on the word "more."

My eyebrow quirks up. Last I checked, I was the one in charge of writing songs. Ginger's only here to protect Platinum's investment. Make me happy so I produce more songs that sell and make everyone—especially the label—more money. I know the game. Downing my glass in a couple of swallows, I hand it back to Aiden for a refill while tossing the ball for Bans.

Ginger's eyes follow my dog's progress, her face now pinched in annoyance. Maybe she'll leave me alone if I keep playing fetch. "So, tell me, how's the writing going?"

No such luck. "It's coming along." I offer Ginger the ball, but she shakes her head so I throw it deep into the yard. Bans races toward it, totally oblivious of my inner turmoil.

Ginger puts her half-full glass down on the table. "I'm here now. Let's hear a new song. I'm excited to hear how your writing has changed since your last album."

I smother a snort. It's changed alright. I no longer have a writing partner. Nor do I have anything to show for my well over one-year break. That is, if you can call performing five shows a week at the Jade a hiatus. "It's a different sound now. You know, reflects the current times."

She claps her hands. "Great. We at Platinum want our talent to stay on top of, or even ahead of, the trend."

"Yeah." Bans drops the slobbery mess of a ball at my feet again, tail wagging furiously. Bending down, I flex my thighs and then my arms, and stand. Ginger's eyes are somewhere south of my face. Time to change tactics.

Stepping away from my rep, I head toward the pool. This will work nicely.

"So, a new song? Your deadline's right around the corner."

Knowing full well the label expects me to record my next album in a couple of months, and my muse is buried in an iceberg in Siberia, I do what I always do when I don't want to answer a question—deflect. I toss the ball toward the nearby pool, which Bans dives for and catches in her mouth before hitting the water. A huge splash ensues, to which I position myself to get drenched for my efforts. *Perfect.*

"Bans! Good girl!" I whip my now wet head from left to right, causing water droplets to fly everywhere, including on Ginger's no doubt million-dollar outfit. "Did you see that catch?"

She wipes the water off her blouse while I strip off the shirt that's now clinging to my torso—unsnagging it from one of my nipple rings—and drop the wet material over the back of a patio chair.

Ginger licks her bottom lip when Bans jumps out of the pool and shakes the water off her body. "Oh!" She jumps back to avoid being sprayed again.

I smile at my rep, amping up the wattage. "Sorry." Yeah. So *not*.

Bare from the waist up, I accept my refilled glass from Aiden with a thanks. He rolls his eyes, knowing exactly what this play is all about.

As I take a sip, he says, "I don't want to interrupt, but Ozzy's plane leaves in an hour for Cole and Rose's wedding."

Any annoyance I felt toward Aiden for letting Ginger in dissipates. "Oh, right." I make a show of looking at my watch. "I didn't realize the time."

Ginger sighs. "It's been a pleasure as always, Ozzy. Are you all set for the wedding?"

Now, that's two times in under a minute that the "W" word's been used. The mimosas threaten to make a second appearance. Breathe, man.

"Yeah. Packed yesterday." Trying to forget where I'm headed today was the main reason I kept Jenna up all night. I run my fingers through my damp hair. "I appreciate Platinum letting me use the private plane."

"Of course. Besides, Cole's also a Platinum family member. We'll do anything to keep our talent happy."

Cole's one of my best friends and a fantastic musician. I've enjoyed rocking with him. Yet, he's put out three albums to my one, with another in the works. Writing never slows him down. Unlike my current Sahara Desert status....

Ginger brings me out of my musings when her eyes run the length of my naked chest, lingering on my V. "Anything."

Play it cool. "Got anything to take the edge off having to get into a penguin suit?" At least my request is genuine, if not the reason for my nerves.

"What do you need? I'll make it happen."

Now she's talking. Something to help me get through the upcoming ordeal. "How about some Molly?"

"There'll be some waiting on the plane for you." She takes a sip of her mimosa. "As long as I hear your new song when you return."

Ignoring the last part, my lips tip upward. "You're alright, Ginger. No matter what Aiden says about you." I offer her a wink and escort her out to her car.

Back on the patio, I take a deep breath. "Hey Aiden, thanks for helping me get the suit out of here. You texted you wanted to talk about something before I leave?"

He pats Bans and stands. "Yeah. You're not going to like it."

Great. What's new? I swallow the rest of my mimosa and hold out the glass. "No OJ this time."

"You might want a clear head for this, but fine." He refills my glass without the juice and says, "Let's go to your office. I put the papers there."

Papers. That can mean only one thing. My heart starts to pound. "It's done?"

He nods and I follow him inside. Walking directly to my desk, a nondescript manila package sits front and center. I pick up the opened envelope and dump the contents on top. "You looked at these?"

"Yes."

My eyes search his face, but I can't read anything in it. I take a deep breath and dive in. The words in Spanish flash before my eyes. It's done. I flip through the pages, noting everything that we agreed to is in here. I get to the next-to-last page and stop.

Pago. SRTA. ALFONSO acuerda aceptar un pago único del SR. MARTINEZ por un monto de $10 millones.

Translation—I pay the bitch ten million dollars and she goes away. In any language, that's a shit ton of money. I suck in my breath. "Once I pay her off, it's over, right?"

Aiden doesn't say anything but hands me a piece of paper with "Wire Transfer" written across the top. Fuck. Me. "I have everything arranged with the bank. Sign here and here." He points to two spots.

I swallow. She's totally wiping me out. *Bitch.* I grab a pen and write "Osvaldo Martinez" in the two places Aiden marked. Exhaling through my mouth, I drop the pen to the desk. "Done."

Aiden picks up the wire transfer paperwork and points to one last place for my signature. Right above Teresa's on the last page.

"Gladly." I scrawl my name across the final divorce papers and stalk out of the office, straight to the liquor cabinet. Enough with the prosecco shit. I don't care if it is before noon. I need a shot—or ten—of whiskey. Neat.

Pounding my first, I slam the shot glass on the counter. Married for four, finally divorced after three. "Fucking bitch."

Aiden enters the room. "It's over."

I pour another one. "Thank fuck. I can't afford another day and another million for that whore." I take the second shot in one swallow.

"I'll make sure the wire gets processed." Coming up next to me, he deposits the wedding invitation on the counter, showing the date for tomorrow—November nineteenth. Ice runs down my spine. Cole's getting married. Besides my family, my label and my PR team—who've kept even a whiff of my marital status top secret—he's the only other soul who knows about my failed marriage. And now I'm going to *his* wedding the day after the final curtain dropped on my own. I shake my head.

As if reading the direction my thoughts veered, Aiden says, "Rose isn't anything like Teresa."

My assistant is a good guy. He knows me, my moods and my preferences.

And he's right—Rose seems to be a good woman. But then again, so did Teresa.

Right now, all I want to do is throw something against the wall. Break every fucking piece of crystal in this place. "Whatever."

"You have to get going." He grabs the leash off the counter.

"I'd rather stay here with Bans," I mutter. Aiden taps his lip and I trod to the bedroom to grab my luggage while he heads to the kitchen for her bowl and dogfood. My thoughts bounce off the walls and land squarely on the ridiculous institution of marriage. I'll never get caught up in that trap again.

The next twenty-four hours are going to suck.

Without warning, the maid-of-honor's face flits across my brain. McKenna is a freak in bed and never pushes for more.

Yeah. Banging McKenna's brains out is just what the matchbreaker ordered.

Two

MCKENNA

I TUG ON THE SIDE ZIPPER OF MY DRESS, but no matter what I do, I can't get it to go up. Rose is over in the corner putting the finishing touches on her wedding ensemble. She looks magnificent, as usual. I, on the other hand, am about to be the slumpy maid-of-honor if I can't get my dress zipped. I've tried to lay off the pastries, but I needed something to help me get through all the uncertainty with Mom. *Sweets are better than a crack habit.*

The door opens and Emilie Dubois, the French supermodel with a heart of gold that prevents me from hating her, floats into the room. Of course she floats. What self-respecting supermodel wouldn't float? She heads toward Rose with an envelope in her hand.

Knowing my dress is a lost cause, I admit defeat, scrunch the fabric in my hand and head over to the pair. "Emilie, can you please help me?"

"Sure."

I point to the window and we leave Rose alone with her envelope. "I put on a few pounds since the final fitting."

"No worries. Let me see what I can do." After several attempts—I hold my breath as she pulls the zipper up with surprising strength—she manages to get the dress zipped. "There. How does that feel?"

I inhale. Oh. My. God. I better not eat anything during the reception. Or breathe too deeply. Can't let on, though. It's not her fault I've been overindulging. Moving back home will do away with anyone's food resolutions. Not that mine ever were too strong.

"Good. Thanks so much!" I flip my hair—the only part of me that doesn't feel like it's about to pop off my body.

Ignoring the mass of dark brown hair falling around my shoulders, Emilie traces the part I dyed specifically for the wedding. "White?"

I nod. "I needed something demure for the occasion." Knowing demure isn't in my vocabulary, we burst out laughing.

From the other side of the room, Rose lets out a sob. Emilie and I look at each other and rush to her side. She waves a handwritten note—the opened envelope Emilie gave her in her other hand.

My eyes bounce from the letter to Rose's face. "No crying! It'll ruin your makeup!"

"He's so," sniffle, "amazing! Listen to what he wrote." After Suzanne—holding her little daughter, Emma, who's serving as the flower girl—joins us, she reads, "My dearest Rose, you are making me the happiest man today. I can't wait to go to bed and wake up together for the rest of our lives, sharing the happy and the sad. From our night in college to today, you have been there for me, even when I was too stupid to realize it. I impatiently wait for you at the altar to declare to the whole world that I am yours. All my love, Cole."

My hand covers my mouth and I realize I'm mirroring Emilie's and Suzanne's postures. What would it be like to find someone who loves me like Cole loves her? My reality tamps down such sentimentality. Who am I kidding? After Matt, true love isn't in my vocabulary, either.

Rose's eyes fill with tears again. I reach into my pocket—the reason I bought this dress—and wave a tissue in front of her face.

"Here. Let me." Emilie grabs the tissue and dabs the tears, then fixes Rose's makeup. Having a supermodel around sure is handy. After a few more touch-ups, Emilie declares, "There. Perfect."

Rose smiles like everything is right with the world. I truly am happy for her—even knowing her happiness won't ever be mine. Matt made sure of it. At least he's locked away in prison.

Emilie clears her throat. "I think my work here is done. I will go take my seat and await your perfect day." Emma races around in a circle and claps as Emilie leaves us for our final minutes of Rose's singlehood.

Looking at my beautiful bestie, I say, "You're so lucky, Rookie."

She smiles at my use of her college nickname. I pluck the tissue out of her hand and dab at her cheeks. On a sigh, she says, "I know. I can't believe this is really happening. Pinch me."

I tweak the soft, fleshy part of her hand, and then wink. Leaning in, I whisper, "I think it's real." We both giggle.

"I would say this is your last chance to back out, but you're a lost cause. I knew you were a goner when we reconnected in that suite in Las Vegas"—I leave out the part about the suite belonging to the utterly off-limits Ozzy Martinez—"and now you're a bride."

"I know. Can you believe it?"

Suzanne joins us, keeping one eye on her adorable, yet rambunctious, two-year-old. "I've never seen Cole like this with anyone, Rose. You saved him from living the whole shallow rockstar life."

"He saved me, too. He made me live again."

The wedding coordinator enters the room and announces it's time for us to line up. Since I'm the only attendant besides the flower girl, I'm up first. I turn to Rose. "I'll see you at the altar. I'll be the one next to your man with the big, sappy smile on my face." As we hug, I whisper, "So happy for you."

I mean it. I am ecstatic for her. Because this won't happen for me doesn't mean I don't want my friends to find and experience love. And Rose deserves all this happiness after everything she's been through. I grab my bouquet of roses and lead us to the double doors.

The music changes and the sound of people turning in their chairs indicates it's time for me to make my entrance. "See you on the other side, Miss Bloomer."

I strut my stuff up the aisle, carrying my bouquet at hip level just like the coordinator told me to do. My nude stilettos are killer with my midcalf deep orange dress, if I do say so myself. Even if it's a tad too small. Trying to forget how the dress feels—it's better to look good than to feel good—I smile at friends I haven't seen in a while and new ones I've met.

Better soak in all this happiness. It has to last me a lifetime as well.

Everything's going great until I get up near the front. There *he* is. In an aisle seat. Of course he's here—why did I think his non-appearance last night at the pre-wedding party open to all early-arriving guests meant I was out of the woods?

My cheeks deflate as my eyes lock onto the dark brown ones belonging to Ozzy. The ultimate bad boy rocker. The only man I've hooked up with since Matt. Too bad his wild streak can no longer fit into my recently re-prioritized life.

He's wearing a tux that's molded to his broad shoulders and trim waist. Dayum. His back straightens, and he nods at me.

Stay strong, McKenna.

I force my feet to keep a steady pace forward, my smile returning in full-force once I get past the man who makes my heart race, panties drop and heart break. Emilie's nearby, next to her fiancé, Wills. I give her a little wave and take my place at the makeshift altar, across from Cole. He looks so calm. So sure of himself.

From the doorway, Suzanne urges Emma forward. She starts up the aisle, throwing rose petals all over. Literally. I shake my head at how cute this little girl is.

The music stops. Cole strides over to a piano and begins playing 'To Have and to Hold,' his latest hit that he co-wrote with Rose. As we practiced, when he sings, "You're my heart—I'll fight for us both," Rose appears.

All the guests stand.

Rose is glowing as she glides up the aisle, carrying an overflowing bouquet of multi-colored roses. She stops a few feet away from me and when Cole finishes the song, he joins her, kisses her hand and they complete the walk together. Their eyes never stray from the other.

I breathe in their love.

The celebrant begins, "Dearly beloved...."

His voice becomes background music.

Do not look past the couple. Do not tear your eyes away from your beautiful best friend on the most important day of her life. Do not even think about glancing at. *Shit.* Ozzy's eyes are squarely on me. His kissable lips tick upward. Look away! Look away! His tongue swipes his lower lip. My nipples harden. Stop. Focus on Rose and Cole.

I rip my disloyal gaze from the tatted and pierced Latin rock god and focus on the shiny new couple standing at the altar. The celebrant says it's time for them to exchange their vows and hands me Rose's bouquet. It's really gorgeous. And heavy.

Cole takes the mic. "Rose, before you came into my life, again, I was empty. Mom recognized you were meant for me long before I did. I can't believe you so patiently waited for me to wise up, but I am forever grateful you did. You taught me how to open my heart and how to love. You brought meaning into my life, and have been my steady hand in the crazy rock and roll world. We've already been through so much, but I vow to love you more tomorrow than today, and to keep your needs above mine always. Because without you, I have no music. I am honored that you will call me your husband and will strive to deserve this title every day for the rest of my life."

My mind goes to mush at his words. They truly have survived hell and deserve this happiness.

Cole hands the microphone to Rose, and wipes a tear off her cheek with his thumb. In a breathy voice that gets stronger as she speaks, she says, "Cole, I didn't want to let myself go and trust you, after living in the background for so long. But you refused to take 'no' for an answer and kept pushing me to be a better person. And I am better because you're in my life. You bring music to my soul and love to my world. I look forward to spending the rest of our days together and to facing whatever is ahead as one. I vow to put you above all else forever. I love you so much."

When she finishes, a collective sigh raises to the ceiling from all of the guests. It's obvious they have found their soul mates in each other, and it is truly special.

The celebrant calls for the rings and Jayson, Cole's brother and best man, reaches into his pants pocket. And then the other pocket. "I know I have them somewhere," he says, smiling at his big brother while tapping his chest. He reaches into his blazer pocket and pulls out two ring boxes, holding them up high for everyone to see.

I snort at his antics, which I'm sure he planned. Looking out to all the guests, I'm not alone. Leave it to Jayson to inject his own brand of humor into the ceremony.

The celebrant swallows, then he blesses the rings. Hers is a beautiful diamond band, while his is a huge platinum one every fan will be able to see, even from the back rows. Nice.

After they slide the rings on each other's fingers, the celebrant raises his voice. "By the power vested in me by the State of New Jersey, I now pronounce you husband and wife. You may kiss—" Before he can finish his sentence, Cole plants his hands on Rose's cheeks and brings her in for a long, delicious, swoon-worthy kiss to end all kisses.

My eyes stray from their very public display and venture down the aisle. Toward the one man whose kisses make my own toes curl. No! Do not do this again, McKenna. Before they reach their traitorous destination, I force my gaze to return to the embracing couple.

When Cole releases Rose, they smile at each other as if they're the only two people in the world. They know how lucky they are to have made it to this point. Rose's beaming face confirms they're reveling in their good fortune.

"Let me introduce to you, for the first time ever, Mr. and Mrs. Cole and Rose Manchester!"

Guests clap. Grinning, I return Rose's bouquet to her and watch her join hands with the man who will hold hers for the rest of her life. The happy couple strolls down the aisle and for a moment, I feel the emptiness at being left here alone. It passes when Jayson offers me his arm to follow them. I even manage to ignore the oversized rocker as we pass.

When we get to the back of the room, I grab Rose and give her a big hug. "You did it, Mrs. Manchester!"

"I did, didn't I?" Her smile radiates from her whole body. Now I understand why everyone wants to touch the bride on her wedding day—to soak up some of that giddy love.

I turn to Cole. "Come here," he says, grinning.

Exchanging places with Jayson, I rush into his embrace and kiss his cheek. Raising on my tippy toes, I whisper in his ear, "You better make her happy for the rest of her life, or you'll have to answer to me."

He winks.

After everyone says their congratulations to the newlyweds, and the photographer has her way with all of us, I end up in the cocktail reception. My dress has adjusted to my somewhat fuller frame, so I pilfer a pig in a blanket from the server. I wonder what Cole promised Rose so she'd allow this delicacy to be served? Biting into the phyllo dough, I don't care. Whatever it was, it was worth it.

"There you are, McKenna. I love your dress."

Swallowing, I turn around and greet Rose's friend-slash-PR client-slash-television star Jessie Anderson and her girlfriend. "Jessie! Amanda!" We exchange hugs.

Jessie asks, "Didn't Rose look beautiful?"

"I know. She's so gorgeous." After gushing over the wedding, I can't stop myself from prying. "So, how are things going with your show, Jessie? Care to share any secrets? I promise not to tell anyone." I make an "X" over my heart.

"We wrapped last week until the new year. It's a blockbuster finale, that's for sure. Lots of pyrotechnics going on. But I can't say anything more—I've been sworn to secrecy."

A server walks by with a tray of champagne, which I snag for the three of us. After handing a flute to Amanda, I ask her, "Did you get any more out of her than this?"

She shakes her head. "Nope. Guess we have to wait like the rest of the world."

"Geez. So much for insider info." I raise my glass. "To the happy couple!"

The champagne goes down smoothly, washing away worries about where *he* is, even for a moment. Before I know it, I've guzzled the whole glass. Holding up the empty, I say, "I'm going to the bar. Anyone want anything?"

When they say no, I head off to one of the three bars set up around the perimeter of the room. Coming to a halt next to Grandma Gertie—Rose's old neighbor, now her live-in cook cum confidante—I order a mojito.

"McKenna! Give me some love!"

I hug this woman with all I have. She's my savior and doesn't even know it. "Hi! How did you like the ceremony?"

"It was beautiful, don't you think? The way Hot Stuff radiated his love for my little Rose nearly made my heart explode."

I giggle at her very expressive, yet apt, description of Cole, and accept my drink from the bartender. Clinking my glass to hers, I agree. "Yes, they're a fantabulous couple."

Scanning the room, I find Ozzy over by one of the carving stations. "Come on, let's catch up over here." I indicate a sushi bar on the other side of the room from him.

We walk over and watch as the chef prepares a tuna roll. "Now this is something I'd never try to make. Give me a vegetable tray or some high-faluttin' finger sandwiches, and I'm good to go. But this? No way." She shakes her grey head.

Putting a California roll on my plate—how many calories can this have anyway?—I nod in agreement. "Or a dessert bar. You'd rock that."

Grandma Gertie preens and leans in. Even though we're both five-foot-nothing without shoes, I have to bend down due to my heels. "I may have had something to do with the desserts."

"Oh my God! I can't believe Rose let you lift a finger for her wedding."

She tosses her nose in the air. "Pfft. She tried. But I have my ways."

I giggle and pop the sushi into my mouth. As I chew, her eyes widen a fraction, then her smile grows. Over her head, I search the room, but the buzzing of all the hairs on my body tells me all I need to know. *It's him.*

A deep baritone wafts from behind me. "Two of my favorite ladies."

Crap.

I stand stock-still while Grandma Gertie taps Ozzy on the chest before he pulls her up into a bear hug, lifting her feet right off the floor. I make sure mine are firmly planted and suck in a breath before turning around. Be strong, McKenna.

He puts her down and opens his arms to me, his tats covered by his tux. It can't hide the muscles underneath, though. "Babes."

At his use of the endearment, my heartrate picks up speed. *Down!* My traitorous body remembers the times he called me that as he was thrusting into me. No, no, no. Inhaling, I say, "Ozzy."

My eyes travel up his torso and land somewhere around his chin. Danger ahead! Don't look any higher.

Not noticing—or ignoring—my body language, he steps forward and his arms crush me to him. Due to our height difference, the top of my head reaches his pec, and I'm treated to the mouthwatering scent of the man. All musky with a slight hint of citrus. As I fight my pheromonal attraction to him, he whispers, "Let's make this a real good time." And then he nips my earlobe.

Every muscle in my body clenches, screaming out for him.

Once his arms become slightly lax, I step back and look directly into his eyes. His pupils are pinpricks. And his cheeks carry a light flush.

What the?

I know these signs—he's high.

No. Freaking. Way.

My chin raises. "What are you on right now?"

He breaks into a wide grin. "Some Molly. Got some here for you, too."

He flicks his long, very talented fingers down toward his trouser pocket.

I recoil. Why does he think I'd touch the stuff? Before something awful spews out of my mouth, the wedding coordinator approaches me. "McKenna, we're getting ready for the grand entrance. Please come with me." Excusing myself from Grandma Gertie and ignoring the high rocker next to me, I turn on my heel and follow the coordinator out of the room. Fuming with every step.

I don't care that he sets my blood ablaze from the inside out with his touch.

He's not who I want. He can't be. Especially now that he's strung out. I don't remember him using drugs in the past, but I wasn't around him too often. What brought on his using now? Or is it a new lifestyle choice for him?

No matter what, I can't have that back in my life again. Drugs took away Daddy and landed me back home with more responsibilities than ever. Mom is my priority now. No way will I ever go down that road again.

Oblivious to my inner thoughts, the coordinator leads me into a room where Cole, Rose, Jayson, Suzanne and her husband Dan plus Emma are standing around. Cole's dad and Rose's mom—oh, joy—round out the rest of the group. The coordinator asks us all to wait here while she lets the band know we're ready for introductions.

I head toward Suzanne but don't take more than a couple of steps before Rose's mom intercepts me. I force a smile. "Ms. Bloomer."

She waves her hand. "McKenna. How long have you known me? Please, call me Lynn."

Wishing I had my mojito so I could swallow the whole thing in one gulp, I repeat after her while gritting my teeth. "Lynn."

I haven't been on good terms with *Lynn* ever since Rose and I were college roommates. She thought I was flighty. A bad influence. All because I changed majors a few times and dated a few guys—at the same time. Well, I guess I was a bit of a head case back then. Life has a way of smacking that right out of you. At least she doesn't know about what happened after graduation. I've worked hard to make sure few people know. Besides, so many years have passed, it's old news.

"I wanted to tell you that I love your dress. Rosie told me you picked it yourself. You have such great style."

Opening my clenched fists buried in my pockets, I reply, "Thanks."

"And all of the wedding papers, especially the programs, were gorgeous. Rosie told me you designed everything."

My limbs relax. Her words aren't what I expected. They almost soothe the pain left throughout my body from Ozzy's hug. Almost.

"Why, thank you so much. Coming from you, it means a lot." I offer her a genuine smile. This was some of my best work in recent memory, but I still can't label them gorgeous.

Rose's diamond-studded hand lands on my arm. She, above everyone else, knows my history with her mom. As she looks between us, she licks her lips. "Everything alright here?"

"Of course, Rosie. I was just complimenting McKenna on the job she did for all of your wedding stationery. She's really grown up."

Rose looks at me for confirmation. Ignoring her final snarky remark, I nod. "I'm so happy she likes them. And you, too, Rookie."

"The design was so different. Even my wedding coordinator asked me who did them."

I force a laugh. "Well, if my work with the Artist Avenue Adventure Project goes south, I'll look her up." It better not. I'm counting on winning their regional contest next month, and going on to the Consortium's national competition. I have to—Mom needs the purse. Just hope true inspiration hits my graphics. Somehow.

Our conversation ends when the coordinator returns to the room and says everything's ready. I take my place next to Jayson, right behind Cole's dad, Ken, and Lynn. The MC introduces them first.

Jayson bends down. "Ready to set the room on fire, McKenna?"

Oh boy. What does he have in mind? I shrug. "Do your worst!"

"Oh, I plan on it. Follow my lead."

The MC says, "The groom's brother and best man, Jayson Manchester, together with maid-of-honor McKenna James."

Hoots and hollers greet us as the doors are opened. Jayson grabs my left hand and tugs me forward, then raises both of his in the air. Since I'm connected to him, my left one goes up with his, and I lift my right one with my bouquet, too. Halfway across the dancefloor, he stops, drops to the floor and does the worm. The worm! I do my fancy kick move when he jumps back to his feet. He twirls me around, ending by dipping me down to the floor. I suck in my breath as the zipper pinches my side, extend my right arm and hold the pose. The MC says, "Well, that certainly was an entrance."

Standing upright, I hug my partner and offer a silent prayer that the zipper held. We walk over to the parents. Ken shakes his head while Lynn looks only slightly horrified. Standing next to Cole and Jayson's father, I clap for Emma as she makes a beeline to her dad, who scoops her up.

"And now the couple of the hour, please make some noise for Mr. and Mrs. Manchester!"

"Woo-hoo!!" I scream while Jayson whistles and guests clap and stomp. The couple walks out to the center of the dancefloor and does a full circle. The MC announces their first dance and everyone crowds around.

Rose and Cole dance to "Unforgettable," performed beautifully by the band. After a minute or so, the MC invites us all to join them. Jayson pulls me forward and we assume a formal dance posture as he waltzes me around. I didn't know he had these moves, but I'm thankful to be—at least momentarily—swept away from the man I know is in the crowd and who I'll have to face again before the night is through.

When we approach the bride and groom he says to his brother, "Guess we shouldn't show up the happy couple," and whacks him on the shoulder. Cole replies, "Not a chance, baby bro," and whisks Rose away with some fancy footwork of his own. I laugh at their antics.

When the song ends, Jayson leads me over to his boyfriend, Carl. Kissing him, Jayson says, "You're all mine now." He turns to me. "Of course, feel free to drag me out to the dancefloor if your date isn't up to snuff."

I high-five both men. They don't know I came alone. Perfect. It's not like I need a partner to dance with anyway. I make my own dances, thank you very much. I hope Ozzy doesn't figure out I'm here sans date. Although he didn't seem to care when he was offering me a good time, washed down with drugs.

After Cole and Rose dance with their new in-laws—the traditional pairings can't be made—everyone is invited to take their seats for the toasts. Which means I'm up first.

Grabbing a champagne flute from my place setting—far away from the man I want to avoid, thank you Rose for honoring my seating request—I walk over to the MC and grab the mic. Pulling my notes out of my pocket, I start, "Can you believe the day has finally arrived?"

One-hundred-plus wedding guests laugh and clap. Encouraged, I continue, "I've known Rookie since we were freshmen roommates at NYU. She had this huge crush on the star of all the musicals on campus, and dragged me not only to Cole's shows, but also to all of his solo performances around the City. I thought it was cute, since half the school had the hots for him. Myself excluded, of course."

Laughter bubbles up from the crowd as Rose blushes. Cole grabs her hand. If only I could bottle their love, I'd make a fortune. My money worries would be a thing of the past.

I clear my throat. "Now, Rose and Cole met up much later and that's where their real romance started. We all know what they went through to get to today." I pause. "And I want to say I've never seen two people more in love than they are. They love each other, yes, but they also like each other. And treat each other with respect and kindness. Their relationship is one love ballads aspire to capture." The several musicians in the room show their appreciation with applause at this line. I refuse to check if Ozzy's one of them.

"It doesn't matter that Cole's an international rockstar or that Rose is a totally up-and-coming PR guru. Together, they are the perfect combination."

I raise my glass. "So, please, let's give a toast to my best friend and her husband, the newly-minted Manchesters. May they have a long, happy and joyful life together."

I take a sip and then rush over to them. Hugging her, I say, "I love you, Rookie." And she whispers the same back to me. After kissing Cole on the cheek again, I return to my seat.

The reception continues and I dance with people I know, people I don't know and by myself. Emilie's fiancé Wills even took a turn on the dancefloor with me.

Eventually, I need to come up for air, so I head to the bar. Taking a spot near the end, my eyes skim over the crowded dance floor. Ozzy's nowhere to be found.

"The lady will have a mojito, and I'll take a Cuba Libre."

My back stiffens. Muscular arms bracket my body while we wait for the bartender to make our drinks. I remain ramrod straight. No, I'm not going to lean back into his hard body. One I remember so well. One that has given me more pleasure than I ever thought possible. *He's high.*

"Still know your drink, babes," he says directly into my ear. Hot puffs of his breath skid across my sensitive skin.

"Yes," my voice croaks.

"I also know what else you like. To swallow." He punctuates his last sentence with a nip to my lobe.

My breathing hitches. He flexes his hips into my backside, his size XXL cock making contact with my butt. Stay strong, McKenna. I don't move a muscle. That he can see. Kegels on the other hand....

The bartender brings our drinks and I gratefully grab mine and slip away from Ozzy's quasi-embrace. From a few steps away, I chug a quarter of it and lift it to him. "Thanks."

He closes the gap I created. "I know how you could thank me." Running his fingers down my bare arm, he continues, "I couldn't stop thinking about you on my flight over here from Vegas. It was so lonely on my plane."

"I bet the flight attendants and other passengers in first class kept you entertained."

He wraps his large hand around my wrist, overlapping his fingers. His size dwarfs me. Makes me even feel small. "Nah. Flew private."

Nice life. I had to save for months to afford my flight from Vegas. I rip my arm from his grip. "Yeah, well, us commoners fly coach."

"Aww, c'mon. Don't be like this." He traces my jawline with his finger, causing me to purse my lips. "You know we're fucking amazing together. I could take you over there," he juts his chin toward a closed door, "and make you feel real good."

Looking into his tiny pupils, my resolve to push him away strengthens. Even if he's my drug of choice, I will not give in to the desire swirling low in my belly. Too much rides on my shoulders now. I promised Daddy I'd take care of Mom, and she needs all my attention. "Not going to happen, Ozzy."

He bends down and puts his nose in my hair, inhales deeply, then trails his lips over to my mouth. Kissing me, he says, "Sure there's no way I can tempt you?"

He's a living, breathing walking temptation. To me and to every female on earth. Okay, maybe not to Rookie, but still. I raise my chin. "No." *Shit.* Why did I sound breathless?

My cell phone vibrates. I place my half-full mojito on a nearby table and reach into my pocket. My stomach clenches when Becky's name shows on the screen. Turning away from him, I accept the call.

Three

MCKENNA

Sucking in a breath, I say, "Hi, Becky. Is everything alright?" Thoughts of Ozzy pushed to the back of my mind, I pray Mom's okay.

"I'm so sorry to bother you, but I caught your mother wandering around the neighborhood in her nightgown. I brought her home, but now she won't quiet down."

My eyes slam shut. This is my worst nightmare. I only wanted two nights away. *Two*. Not the full week Rose hoped for. And Mom's been doing so well lately. Inhaling, I reply, "Did you try some hot tea? Or knitting?"

"Yes, I tried all the usual tricks. She's very agitated and I'm not sure what I can do to calm her down, short of restraining her."

"No, please don't do that. Can I speak with her?"

"I'll try to give her the phone. Not sure how receptive she'll be."

Biting my lip, I stand helplessly thousands of miles away amongst wedding guests while my neighbor and lifelong friend tries to coax Mom to pick up the phone. My vow to Daddy burns in my mind. Lying on the pavement, he whispered, "Promise me you'll take care of Mom. Never put her into a nursing home." Mom already was showing signs of forgetfulness at that point, but Daddy had no idea what was coming.

On my knees, trying to staunch the blood flowing from his abdomen, I'd cried, "Of course, Daddy." *Please stay with me.*

He reached out and placed his hand on my cheek. Then it dropped away. Six years later, the pain is still sharp. I wrap my arms around my middle, trying to maintain my composure in such a public venue, and do the mental exercises my therapist taught me. My breath already was constricted from squeezing into this dress and now it's hitched up a few more notches. Thank God it has a scoop neck, or I'd pass out.

Noise from the phone signals Becky's return to the line. "I'm sorry, McKenna. She won't take it."

When my teeth pierce my inner cheek, I run my tongue over the spot. This is one of her worst episodes yet. "That's okay. Thanks for trying." Think, McKenna. "Have you tried putting NatGeo on?" That's my last resort, which soothes her. Usually.

"I haven't. Wait a sec." The sound of the television turning on comes through the headset. Then, nothing. I count backwards from ten. Finally, Becky comes back on. "As soon as she saw the lions, she sat down in the chair."

I exhale, my entire body slumping. "Thank goodness. Listen, I'll move up my flight home. Please call me if you see her leave the house again. I really appreciate your keeping an eye out for her."

"Not a problem. I'm so sorry to bother you at the wedding."

I stifle a sigh. "I'll text you when my flight lands."

Disconnecting the call, I pull up the airline's website to check available redeye flights out. Given the time, though, there's probably nothing left for tonight. What was I thinking when I booked an early evening flight back to Vegas tomorrow?

"Can we please have everyone to the dancefloor?"

Ignoring the MC, I press search. The next available flight leaves at six-thirty in the morning. Nothing earlier.

"The bride and groom would like everyone on the dancefloor."

Crap. I'm one of two people in the bridal party, and the other's a two-year-old. I have to go. Schooling my face into a party-girl expression, I run onto the floor and hip-check Shari, Rose's partner at RM Publicity. Her boyfriend catches her, and they both laugh. I force myself to join in. Can't have people asking questions. This is Rose's day and I won't let anything take away the attention from her.

We all crowd in, looking for Rose and Cole, but they're nowhere to be seen. Suddenly a door on a second floor opens, and they step out onto the Juliet balcony. They've changed. She's now in a beautiful teal shift dress, and he's wearing a white button-down and khakis. They make such a striking couple.

From the balcony, Cole says, "Thank you all for coming to our wedding. I'm whisking my beautiful bride away on our honeymoon—she doesn't even know where we're going—but feel free to stay and party for as long as you'd like."

Rose nudges Cole in the ribs. He bends down and kisses her. Their love is something of fairy tales. A rarity. Before my brain goes down the wish-laden road again—because I know that road is a dead-end for me—Rose steps back and holds up a small bouquet. She catches my eye before turning her back to the crowd. I take a few steps backward, and the crowd fills in the gap.

A drumroll punctuates the bouquet toss, which lands in Emilie's hands. Tears well behind my eyelids when she and her fiancé share a kiss. After a few more waves, Cole and Rose disappear from the balcony and the band starts to play another set.

Now that the newlyweds are gone, I need to focus on getting back home. I head in the direction of the ladies' room, but veer to the right and down a hallway. Ducking into what appears to be an old-fashioned library, I take a seat and pull out my phone.

My search confirms that all of the earlier flights are sold out. *Of course they are.* Under my breath, I mumble, "Daddy, I'll keep my promise. I'll get back to Mom and keep her safe at home." But how? By giving up my nights to stay in with her from now on, that's how. She's deteriorating and I need to step up.

Ozzy walks past the half-open door. He came here on a private plane. He told me so himself. I really don't want to owe him anything, but desperate times and all that. I race out of the room and follow him.

Rounding the corner, I find him in the courtyard by a fountain. A server is near him, and he's flirting with her. Great.

He's my only hope of getting home to Mom sooner than tomorrow evening. Swallowing my pride—which, for the record, is not among the things I like to swallow—I put my shoulders back and march in his direction. As I approach, the server giggles at whatever he's saying.

When I walk in front of him, his smile widens. "Knew you couldn't stay away for long."

What? Does he think I'd join in and make this a threesome? Well, I might have done so years before. But not now. Too much has changed. "I need to ask you a favor, Ozzy."

"Sure thing." He pats the server on the butt, eliciting a squeal of delight, before she leaves us alone. He gives me his full attention. "What's up?"

"I want to take you up on your offer for a ride." That came out wrong.

Ozzy's tongue swipes his lips. "I'm always up for a ride with you."

The last time I climbed aboard the Ozzy-train was last year, and I loved every second. His cock is huge and he certainly knows what to do with it. And then I had to face Mom's reality. Shaking my head to clear the images—and reminding myself he's high—I say, "You mentioned you flew out here on a private plane."

"Sure did. Want to join the Mile High club?" His eyebrows wiggle.

My spine tingles at his suggestion, but I tamp it down. I'm doing this for Mom. "When are you flying out?"

"I can leave whenever." He waves his hands. "Figured sometime after brunch tomorrow, since my next concert at the Jade is tomorrow night."

"Think you could disappear with me any sooner?"

"Now you're talking."

"How about now?"

Ozzy takes a step back. "Now?"

I shrug. "Yeah. Got something to attend to at home and I figured you could set your own flight schedule." Not a lie.

A slow grin lights up his face. "Well, sure. Vámonos. Give me a minute to call the pilot and we'll be thirty-thousand feet up in no time." He pulls out his cell. "I knew you'd see it my way."

More like the other way around, but I don't correct him. "Great! I'll say my goodbyes and get my things." I point my head toward the ballroom.

Leaving him to make the arrangements, I hug the warm, wonderful people who came to celebrate with Rose and Cole. None of whom have to deal with a family member with early onset dementia or a small business on the brink. Since the newlyweds already had their grand exit, no one questions why I'm ducking out.

When I'm done, I race back to my room and grab my purse and luggage. I open my bag and quickly switch out my stilettos for a pair of ballet flats. Taking another few minutes, I exchange my tight maid-of-honor dress for a pair of black yoga pants and a long, purple top, and inhale deeply for the first time all day. After doing a quick sweep around the room to ensure I didn't leave anything behind, I return to where I left Ozzy. He's still on the phone so I take a seat and text Becky to let her know I should be home in the middle of the night. She says Mom calmed down after watching TV and is now sleeping. Good. I'll be by her side before Elaine starts her morning shift.

"All set, babes."

Ozzy saunters toward me then drops to his haunches at my side. I look down at his upturned face. With full lips and long eyelashes I pay to get. But his pupils are still dilated. He places his overly-large hand on my thigh and squeezes. "We'll meet my pilot at the airstrip in a half hour."

My pilot. Yeah, he's never had a shred of worry about money in his life. Bouncing my thigh to dislodge his grip, I reply, "Great. I've already said my goodbyes. How about I call an Uber while you do the same?"

He stands and strokes the back of his hand over my cheek. My heart races and my cheek tingles where he touches me. "I can't wait to get you alone up there. You know, there's a shower on board."

Stop it, McKenna. Do *not* get sucked in again. "At least you'll be clean!"

He chuckles. "Oh, I think we'll both be clean by the time we land. Or very, very dirty." He strides back into the ballroom.

I spend the next five minutes wrestling my heartrate back to normal. Five hours trapped alone on a plush plane with my kryptonite—how hard can this be?

Four

OZZY

WE PULL UP TO THE DESERTED AIRSTRIP in New Jersey. No planes are lit up except for Platinum's, which is waiting for us at the end of the tarmac. My high is waning, but it really helped me get through the wedding. And sex with the spunky brunette sitting next to me will see me through to Vegas.

Damn but Cole looked happier than I've ever seen him. Maybe Rose won't do him dirty. Though that's what I thought about Teresa, too.

Diverting my thoughts, I look at my travel companion. Even though she changed out of her orange dress, she's totally hot. Well, not in the stick-thin model way, but in the let-me-grab-your-hips-and-rock-your-world way. My cock rises to the occasion. Yeah, this is going to be a much more enjoyable flight home than it was coming out here.

I get out of the SUV and pick up her luggage. Hefting the oversized bag out of the back, I get it to the pavement and pull up the handle. "Geez. How long have you been out here?"

"Got in yesterday."

This is what she packed for two nights? Holy shit. "Were you thinking of moving in?"

"Nope. Just need options." She laughs and my balls tighten at the melodious sound. Something unlocks inside my blackened heart, which I promptly quash. No. I need to get her alone pronto, so I head for the plane.

From somewhere behind me, I hear her call out, "Don't you have any luggage?"

"The crew brought it with them to the hotel, so it's already on the plane now." Condoms. I only have one on me, but I put more in my duffel bag. Signing the divorce papers—turning over all my money—Cole's wedding. I need to bury myself inside her and forget the hell of the past twenty-four hours.

At the foot of the stairs, the crew takes her luggage from me, and I ask for my duffel. "Go on ahead of me, I'll meet you up there in a minute." I watch as she climbs the staircase, admiring the way her round ass sways as she ascends. Yup. She'll definitely help me forget.

Grabbing a handful of condoms from my duffel bag, I wink at the flight attendant and bound up the stairs. Inside, McKenna runs her hand over the light beige leather seats, but I go straight to the sofa. Throwing myself down on it, thighs splayed wide, I pat the cushion next to me.

McKenna crosses her arms over her tits and stares at me from across the plane. Damn. What I want to do to her body. And I know, from experience, she's a total wildcat in bed, always up to try anything. "Take your seat and strap in." Smirking at my not-so-subtle inuendo, I pat the sofa again.

She shakes her head and sits in a chair across the way.

I poke my tongue against my cheek. "Why are you playing so hard to get? You know you're going to love it, babes. You always have."

Her lips thin. "I only needed a ride, Ozzy. I'm not going to sleep with you. Think you can handle doing someone a favor without expecting anything in return?"

"Who said anything about sleeping?"

"I'm serious." She crosses her legs. Only now do I realize she swapped her sexy-ass heels for flats, too. Oh well, they'll be off soon enough.

The flight attendant who saw me grab the condoms walks into the cabin with a tray, offering us champagne with a smirk. I stand and take two glasses. Handing McKenna a glass, I sit down on the chair next to hers and lean in. "We'll see. We have five hours to kill."

She opens her mouth and yawns.

"Good try. You told me you flew out yesterday, so you're still on Vegas time. It's only seven o'clock according to your body clock."

"Ozzy, you don't know anything about what my body needs right now." She turns her head away to watch the safety demo. I'm sure she pulled a face. What's with her? Concern floods my brain as the remnants of my buzz dissipate. Her body language screams she's upset. No, more like anxious. Is she afraid of flying?

We're soon airborne and the pilot says we can unbuckle our seat belts since he doesn't expect any turbulence. Undoing hers first, I get out of mine and swivel to face her. Reaching out, I grab her left foot and place it on my lap. After discarding her shoe, I massage her instep, hoping to relax her.

Her gentle sigh clues me in about how much she's enjoying what I'm doing. In silence, I switch to her right foot. Some of the anxiety has drained from her eyes, which now take on a deeper hue.

Without saying a word, I place both of her feet on the floor and skim her arms. Her eyes slam shut and her breathing hitches. I trace her shoulder and place my index finger on her cheek, pulling her closer to me.

She's exactly what my body needs right now. And despite her comment, I believe I'm what she needs, too.

Our breaths mingle, our lips almost touching. "Open your eyes," I demand. I want to confirm I'm right.

McKenna's eyelids flutter open midway, unfocused. Her breathing comes in rapid pants.

I move to seal the deal when her eyes fling wide open and she plows backwards into the chair, words flowing from her kissable mouth. "So, how's your new album going? Almost finished with it? Your residency is ending soon, right?"

I close my eyes to shut out her rapid-fire questions. I don't want to talk about my nonexistent writing. When I open my eyes again, I play with the stripe of white hair amongst the dark brown. "I like this."

She huffs out a small breath. "I thought it would be good for the wedding. You know, festive and all."

I twirl a white lock around my finger, bring the softness to my lips and kiss it. She shakes her head and leans back even further into the soft leather seat. Sighing, I retreat. "So, ah, what have you been up to lately? Haven't seen you around Vegas." Hmmm, at all. Has she been avoiding me?

"I've been keeping busy. Working on the Artist Adventure Avenue Project, you know."

"Oh, right." How could I forget? They've been hounding me for songs for their exhibition. Of course, Platinum insists that they be my *new* songs. "How's it coming along?"

She twists and puts one leg under the other. Damn. What I want to do with those legs.

"It's good, actually. I've finished up the part of my presentation for all the other artists but you." Her eyes bore into mine.

Fuck. "Oh. How many were there?"

"Sex." Her mouth forms a perfect circle and eyes grow wide. Clearing her throat, she says, "Six. I meant six." She holds up six fingers. "And I know Felicia, my contact at the Project, has reached out to you for your songs, but I haven't seen them yet. Did you send them to her? I'd like to dive right in when we get back."

"Freudian slip?" I chuckle and reach out to skim her bare arm. No need to keep talking about such an unpleasant topic.

She pulls her arm back. "Ozzy. I told you I'm not sleeping with you. I only needed a ride back tonight."

Something in her voice clues me in that she's none too happy with her decision. "What's the hurry? Didn't you have a flight booked?"

She turns her head toward the windows, but since it's dark out I know she can't be admiring the view. For the second time tonight, I want to know what she's hiding.

"Something came up at home that needs my attention right away. I could've waited for my flight, but since you had this at your disposal, I thought I could get back sooner. Must be nice to have a private plane on speed dial."

Yeah, right. I stifle a snort. If she knew my now ex-wife cleaned me out right before I hopped onto this borrowed plane, maybe she wouldn't be busting my balls about it. "Looks can be deceiving."

She faces me again. "So, I'll be ready to start in on your music tomorrow. It takes me about a month to do the graphics per artist, and as the final deadline is year-end, I don't have any time to waste. And, not that I want to feed your already galactic ego, but your new songs will be the highlight of my submission. If I win, it could make a real difference in the lives of people who depend on the proceeds from this event—disadvantaged youth who need a creative outlet." She plucks at her top. "It could make a real difference in my life too, Ozzy."

Yeah, like I need this kind of added pressure. Instead of continuing the conversation, I stand up and head over to the bar area. Opening the rum, I hold it up to her with a can of Coke. "Want some?"

"I'll take the Coke, straight."

"Ah, c'mon. If you won't let me have my wicked way with you, at least let me make you a real drink. You've got to tolerate me somehow for the next five hours."

She tilts her head. Something passes across her eyes and she says, "Well, alright. Just one."

"There's my girl." I busy myself making our drinks. Walking over to where she's sitting, I hand her the glass and clink mine to hers.

"Thanks." She takes a small sip and puts the glass down into the cupholder. "So, really, I can't wait to hear your new stuff. Want to give me a preview?"

Her latte-colored eyes bore into mine. How long can I keep the truth from her? I swallow the last of my drink and deposit the empty into the cupholder at my seat. "Yeah, well."

"Pretty please with a cherry on top," she says, batting her eyelashes.

Shit. She's so fucking cute. And she's going to find out that I'm empty as an old guitar case soon enough. I inhale the recycled air and force myself to expel all of it. Here goes nothing. "You see, McKenna… I've been having a bit of a dry spell."

Her eyes slant. "And by dry spell, you mean—"

Her sentence hangs there. I clear my throat. "I mean that I haven't been able to write any new songs."

Silence.

"Any?"

I shake my head.

Her voice takes on a hard edge. "At all?"

I can't look at her any longer, so I walk over to the bar for a refill. Within seconds, she joins me.

"Please tell me I didn't hear you right. You've been at the Jade now for well over a year. During this time, you were supposed to be doing shows and writing the songs for your next album. Remember, I was at the dinner when you and Rose came up with this plan. You really don't have one new song written?"

I dump ice cubes into my glass. "No."

"What the hell have you been doing? Oh wait, let me guess. You've been *doing* every vagina in Vegas rather than actually working."

I bang my glass on the bar. "You don't know anything about it."

She stomps her newly-massaged foot. "I can guess. You get up on stage, sing your *old* songs and choose which bimbos you want to take backstage after. You're too busy getting laid—and *high*—to do actual work."

"I have a penthouse, thank you very much." And I rarely touch drugs. However, having to attend a wedding the day after finalizing a three-year-long divorce certainly was a valid reason to do so, but she doesn't deserve to know this. I pick up the rum and pour a very healthy splash into my glass.

Through clenched teeth, she responds, "Whatever. Your songs were contracted to the Project a year ago. Your *new* songs."

I add a second pour of rum and whisper some Coke into it. Before taking a sip, I face the woman I wanted to fuck five minutes ago, and now just want to throttle. "It's not your problem."

"Not my problem! Are you kidding me? While you've been fucking your way through Vegas, I've been working my ass off on this project. Getting actual deliverables ready. Yours is last on my list and then I can hand it in."

I raise the glass to my lips and take a sip. Shit, it's strong. My eyes stray to the woman next to me and I take another swallow. Turning my back to her, I head to the bedroom. "I think we're done here. Since we're obviously not going to *fuck*, which is the only thing you think I enjoy doing, I'm going to sleep until we get back to Vegas."

"Ozzy—"

If I wanted nagging, I would've stayed in Vegas and listened to Ginger. McKenna's not my boss by any stretch of the imagination, so I don't have to take this. Slamming the door behind me, I collapse on the bed.

If I could snap my fingers and create a whole new album, don't they think I would've done so before now? It's kind of hard to create fresh material when your own life is in the fucking shitter. Ducking deadlines from my label is exhausting. Getting hounded by all of these women is getting old.

I take another huge swallow of my drink, the ice cubes clanking against my teeth. A knock sounds. "Leave me alone."

"Can we talk?"

I'm done talking about my failures. Failure as a husband. Failure as an artist. Failure as a client. Failure with this woman who flitted into my life and brightened it up. Finished. Through.

"Go away." My glass sails through the air and crashes against the closed door.

Five

MCKENNA

"THANK YOU." I CLOSE THE DOOR TO the Uber and rush into Mom's house. Well, my house again, since I sold my condo and moved back in so I could afford a day nurse for her. The flowerbeds under the window could use some TLC, not to mention the grass needs to be cut. At least it's green. Mostly. I never seem to have enough time to keep up with everything.

Opening the welcoming red door, I wheel my luggage into the living room. Mom's rocking chair is still and the television is off. Well, it is four in the morning. Not seeing her up is a good sign.

I roll my bag into my room and go to check on her. Quietly, I open her bedroom door. The light from the hallway illuminates her sleeping form. With a smile, I exhale, close the door and make my way back to my room.

Changing into my nightshirt—a concert T from one of Cole's shows—I go into the bathroom to clean up from the flight. Tears mingle with the water as I wash off the wedding makeup.

I can't get my final payment until the project is completed, and it won't be done until I create the graphics for Ozzy's new stuff. Of course, now he's not speaking to me, which is awfully convenient for him and his dearth of songs. Why can't anything be easy?

Toweling dry my face, I look at myself in the mirror. Thirty. I'm thirty-years-old, live with my mother, don't have a husband or boyfriend. I emit a humorless laugh—Matt quashed those ideas. He broke me. I clearly have really bad judgment when it comes to men, so staying away from all of them is best. Besides, Mom is now my number-one priority.

While I put on moisturizer, I continue the litany of my failures. My career is hanging by a thread. It could be much better if only that asshole Ozzy Martinez would get off his ass—rather, get his cock out of some bimbo long enough—to actually do some work. I know the Project's graphics I've put together for the other artists are better than most of the routine stuff I've been doing for my other clients lately. Working on Rose's wedding stationery boosted my creativity. I was banking on Ozzy's new songs to level me up, dammit.

Brushing my hair, my mind drifts to Mom. Her medical bills are piling up. I need my submission to the Project to carry me into the national competition so I can forge a name for myself. One-off paydays doing casino graphics won't cut it much longer. Which means I need to jumpstart Ozzy into writing more songs. *Damn.* I hate having my career in someone else's hands. Even if his hands still make my panties wet.

Hanging my towel back over the bar, I trek back down the hall and face-plant into my pillow. Maybe things will look better in the morning, like Daddy always used to tell me.

Yelling wakes me from a deep sleep. I jump up, only to find Mom screaming from my open doorway. Maybe things won't look better. Ever. I take a deep breath and regulate my voice. "Mom, it's me, McKenna."

She quiets but wraps her fingers around the doorway. In a calm voice, I continue, "I got home last night but didn't want to wake you up. You were sleeping."

Her hands drop to her sides. "I was sleeping. Oh, right. I was sleeping."

Like I was minutes earlier. "Yes, you were." I drag my tired body out of bed and shuffle over to her, slipping my feet into my slippers as I move. "How are you doing today?"

Cloudy brown eyes greet me. "I'm fine. I think." She looks down to the floor, then her head pops up. "McKenna." Her eyes clear.

I smile and open my arms for her. "Yes, Mom, it's me."

She gives me a hug. "Want me to make breakfast for you? I could make French Toast. I know it's your favorite."

"Nah, I'm still a little tired." I check the clock. It's only eight o'clock. "I think I'm going to go back to bed for a while, okay?"

"Sure thing. Come out when you're ready."

She leaves me and I return to bed. Getting back under the blankets, I try to fall asleep. After tossing and turning for an hour or so, I give up. I need to light a fire under Ozzy, and pronto. Sleeping in won't get me a much-needed paycheck.

I ENTER THE Jade's lobby, one of the newest casinos in Las Vegas. Although it's barely after noon, the place is jumping with tourists and gamblers trying their luck. A huge crystal chandelier tinted green watches over everyone from high. I take the escalator past a mammoth digital billboard advertising a male strip show featured at one of the theaters here. *I would've used a more legible font.*

As I go up, the photo changes from a group of hot men, their ripped chests oiled up, to a close-up of Ozzy. His eyes are closed and he's singing directly into a microphone, sweat beading around his forehead. My stomach clenches with want, but my brain engages right away to shut that down. No. More.

Crossing the expanse of the upper lobby to the concierge, I hope Shelia's on duty. She and I went to high school together, and she's often given me the inside scoop around here. Nothing to get her into trouble, but tidbits of info that make my life easier.

Two other people are at the desk, so I take my place in line. Shelia nods at me—thankfully, she's here—and I wave. Good. I'm sure I'll be up in Ozzy's grill in no time.

While I wait, I pull out my cell phone and see I missed a text from Rose.

I can't thank you enough for all of your help yesterday! It truly was the best day of my life, and you are one of the main reasons. I couldn't have asked for a better maid-of-honor, or best friend, than you! I promise to call you when we get back from our honeymoon. I love you so much!! ~ Rose Manchester (couldn't resist! :-)) PS-saw you with Ozzy last night. Don't think that got past me.

Rose's joy practically jumps off the text. She's such a sweet person, and I'm so happy she found her happily-ever-after. I reply by wishing her a wonderful honeymoon and ignore her reference to Ozzy.

"McKenna, come on over! What brings you to the Jade?"

Dropping my cell back into my bag, and leaving all improper thoughts of Ozzy with it, I walk toward the desk. Injecting my voice with a layer of positivity, I reply, "Hi, Shelia! I'm so happy you're here!" I run around to the side and give her a quick hug.

"What's up?" she asks as she returns my hug.

Back at the front, I put my elbows onto the counter and lean in. "I need a tiny favor." I raise my hands up, close together, indicating how small.

She laughs. "Sure thing. Do you want a dinner reservation at our sold-out restaurant? Or theatre tickets to *Men Gone Wild*? I wouldn't judge you."

I lick my lips. "Well, have you met any of those guys? I'm sure they could make an afternoon go by really quickly." I throw in a wink for good measure.

She shakes her head. "I wish. They stay in the back of the house. I caught their show a couple of times, though." She fans her face.

I laugh. It's my first real laugh in a long time, and I almost forgot how good it feels. "Nah. Nothing like that. I only need to know where Ozzy Martinez practices. I'm working on a submission for the Artist Avenue Adventure Project and I've been waiting on him for months."

"Well, he's got his own wild thing going on, if you know what I mean." She waggles her eyebrows.

Yes, I do know. Intimately. I give her a fake scowl. "I'm here for business, Shelia."

"Right." She types on her computer. "He's such a monster on the eyes."

"If you like the Latin type."

She continues typing so she doesn't see my hands flex into fists. I open them out before she catches my reaction. The Latin type is what got me into the position I'm in now and I can't revisit it. *Won't.*

Shelia stops typing and looks at me over her computer monitor. She motions me forward. In a whisper, she says, "He practices in the conference room off the back of the stage where he performs. He also has a suite for the duration of his show, Penthouse Room 8H."

"Conference room and 8H. Got it."

"You won't be able to get onto his floor without an elevator pass, though. And I can't give one to you. I wish I could."

"I totally understand. I'll go check out the practice room. Hopefully, he'll be there. What time is his show tonight?"

"Starts at eight."

"Thanks so much. I really appreciate your help. When do you have a break for lunch? Maybe we can grab something."

"I just started, so I don't get my break until four."

"Oh. I'll probably be done well before then. Let's do dinner, soon. Text me."

"Will do."

I reach over and give her another quick hug, then scurry away toward Ozzy's conference room. He has a penthouse here. Must be nice never to have to worry about money.

After cutting through the casino, I walk past a beautiful display of humongous origami of all different shapes in shades of green. The color reminds me of Daddy's eyes—such a distinctive shade. I smile picturing his face, and continue my trek. Finally, I end up at the hallway that leads to Ozzy's stage. I try the main doors but they're locked, so I wander down another hallway that appears to mirror the stage area.

Stopping in front of double doors, I reach out but the handle doesn't budge. Shit. I look around and go down a smaller hallway and it dead ends with another door. I try it, but it's locked too. I press my ear against the door and don't hear anything, which means Ozzy's not there. Turning, a tall guy with glasses and a clipboard walks toward me. Maybe he can help?

I meet him at the set of double doors I tried before. He has a key in his hand. "Hi!" I shout before he can slip through.

He looks at me, a smattering of freckles covering his nose. Pushing up his glasses, he returns my greeting in a wary voice.

I stick my hand out. "I'm McKenna James. I'm working on a project with Ozzy Martinez. Are you with him?"

He places the key into his back pocket and shakes my hand, eyeing me up and down. "Hi, Miss James." He chuckles. "That's a very good introduction you got there. Much more creative than most."

I place my hand over my heart. "Goodness, what you must think of me. But you've got it wrong, I can assure you." Been there, done that. Wouldn't mind the T-shirt. I shake my head. "No, I'm with the Artist Avenue Adventure Project and I need to start collaborating with Ozzy about his part."

"Oh." He runs his hand through his ginger hair. He's kinda cute, in an overworked sort of way. "Sorry. I didn't mean anything by what I said before."

I wave my hand. "No worries. I bet you dodge this kind of thing all the time. Now, you're with him, right?"

He pulls out the key, opens the doors and ushers me inside. "Yes, I'm his personal assistant. He was out of state yesterday, so he hasn't arrived quite yet."

I don't feel the need to share that I was with him yesterday—this morning, actually. "This is where he practices, though, am I correct?"

He nods. "Yes, but I don't expect him here until closer to showtime today."

I sigh. "Really? I have to start working on the project with him and was hoping to do some prelims today."

"Give me your card and I'll pass it along to him."

In other words, time to get rid of you. Needing to play this to my advantage, I raise my chin. "I didn't catch your name?"

"It's Aiden. Aiden MacQuade."

"Well, Aiden, as his assistant you must know the Project's deadline is next month. Is he here in the hotel somewhere? I only need a couple minutes with him. No biggie."

He looks around as if the answer is written somewhere on the four walls. Giving up, he says, "He's not at the Jade."

"But I understand he keeps a penthouse here?"

He rubs his hands up and down his jeans. "He does, but that's not where he sleeps."

Okay, I'm going to process this statement later. Right now, I need to talk with Ozzy. "Alright, I'll bite. If he doesn't sleep here, where does he sleep?" I nudge him in the ribs. "He's not a vampire or anything, is he? I never noticed sparkles around him." I smile broadly.

He chuckles. "I haven't seen any coffins around, if that's what you're asking."

"Oh, Aiden." I tap his shoulder. "C'mon, help a girl out. I promise not to tell him how I found his lair." I cross my fingers over my heart.

He runs his hand through his hair again. I'm winning. He's going to cave any moment now. "I can't give out his home address."

"It's not like I'm some groupie or anything. I only need a few minutes with him." I drop my voice. "He told me he doesn't have any new songs yet, and I'm hoping to help him out."

His shoulders dip. Bingo! He gives me another once-over. "Don't tell him I gave you his address, alright."

He walks over to a desk and writes something down on a scrap of paper, then hands it to me. I kiss it. "Thanks, Aiden. You're the best!" I turn and scamper out the door before he changes his mind.

I walk double-time through the expanse of the Jade, and hop into my car. Opening the crumpled piece of paper, I plug the address into my phone's GPS and drive away from the Strip. The directions lead me to an upscale residential neighborhood, but it doesn't scream "celebrity." The lawns here are well-manicured and lead up to sprawling contemporary houses, which are modest for millionaire-plus-status. This is a place someone would live if they wanted to hide.

I pull to a stop in front of number 1785. This is it. Ozzy's somewhere inside. All I need to do is talk with him about the status of his new songs. He must've been overstating things on the plane—I'm sure he has several written. His prior songs were megahits. He couldn't have lost the ability to write them simply because he was banging every groupie who came his way. *If anything, that should have given him even more creative inspiration.*

Because there's no fencing, I pull into his driveaway, next to a shiny motorcycle. Of course he has a bike. Taking a deep breath, I march up to the huge wooden front door and ring the bell.

Nothing.

I ring it again and wait. Still no response.

He has to be in there somewhere. I peer through a window but don't see any movement. Perhaps he's in the backyard?

Heading off toward the fenced in backyard, I curse myself for wearing my strappy, high-heeled sandals. They complemented my skirt and top so well, though. Oh well, the price of fashion.

At the gate, I raise my face toward the sky. "Please let this be unlocked." Other than cameras by the front door, I haven't noticed any security, so maybe I'll get lucky. I test the latch and it opens. Score!

I slip into the expansive backyard, taking in the grassy area and pavers, leading to an outdoor kitchen and Olympic-sized swimming pool. Ozzy has it so hard. He probably wouldn't know a money problem if it bit him on his nice, tight ass.

Stop! I'm not thinking about any of his amazing body parts.

All of a sudden, Ozzy's head pops up of the pool—he must've been underwater when I came in—and he hoists himself out, muscles flexing on his arms and legs. The top of his curly hair is wet and slicked back.

The sun catches on his pierced nipples. Black ink all over his body stands in relief to the water rivulets coursing down his toned abs. I follow their path down his naked body. His *entirely* naked body. Complete with a pierced cock.

Oh. My. God. His Prince Albert is *new*. Saliva pools in my mouth.

And a gasp escapes my lips.

Six

OZZY

As usual, I finish my workout by trying to swim the entire length of the pool underwater. When my lungs feel like they're about to burst, I break the surface, gasping for breath. Hard session. So much so, I almost forgot all about Teresa. Once again, I send praises through the universe to my PR team for burying the story—both its beginning and end.

Swimming over to the side, I place my hands on the deck, heave myself out of the water and stand. A gasp swings my attention toward the side entrance to the backyard. A short, curvy woman with black hair stares back at me. I wipe the water from my eyes.

McKenna?

A slow smile spreads across my face. Instead of grabbing my towel off the back of a nearby chair, I saunter over to where she stands. Her only movement is her hand flying to her mouth.

Stopping feet in front of her, I lick my lips. My exposed cock starts to stir in recognition—swimming in the buff has its benefits.

I raise my eyebrow. "Babes."

She finds her voice and looks to my left, where Bans has entered the backyard through her doggie door. I was lucky to find a rental with both a pool and easy backdoor access for her. I refocus on the woman in front of me.

"Ozzy. I'm sorry. I didn't know you'd be naked. I mean, here. Well, of course I thought you'd be here, but not naked. And you have a dog. A very big, not naked dog. Oh my God. I'm going to shut up now."

Bans bounds over to me carrying a stick this time, barking and wagging her tail. Some attack dog. But McKenna doesn't seem to realize this, as she steps back with each advance Bans makes.

"She's harmless." I reach down and scratch her ears.

"Oh. Okay." McKenna wraps her arms around her middle, now refusing to look at either my dog or me. "Would you please put some clothes on?"

I take the stick from Bans's mouth and toss it over my shoulder. She scampers away in hot pursuit. "I don't know. I'm pretty comfortable. And I'm at my own house, after all. Maybe you should consider getting a little more comfortable, yourself. I can only assume you're here to finish what we started last night, although now that we're back on solid ground, we won't be able to join the Mile High club. Pity."

She raises her chin and looks directly into my eyes for the first time. In an even voice, she says, "You must be a Mile High if you think that's why I chased you down. Let me be very clear, I'm not here for *that*." Her eyes travel down my torso, causing my cock to stir even more, then zoom back to my own. "But you're correct, I do want to finish what we started last night. I need you to write the songs for the Project, and I'm damn sure going to keep hunting you down until you produce."

I scratch my two-day stubble. "I'm not sure what you mean. But I do know I can produce," I look southward. "Well, given a little more—stimulation."

She exhales and walks around me to the chair and snatches up the towel. Holding it out to me while keeping her head facing away, she orders, "Put this on."

Bans decides McKenna wants to play a new game. She drops the stick and races for the towel, latching onto it and shaking her head with a growl. McKenna shrieks and drops her end.

Laughing, I say, "Looks like Bans doesn't agree with you."

McKenna stomps her sandaled foot. When Bans tries to get her to play again by running at her with the towel in her mouth, she races around the table, the dog hot on her heels. En route, McKenna shouts, "Get her to stop!"

Bans wouldn't hurt a fly, she just wants to play. But McKenna obviously didn't get the memo. Deciding to put her out of her misery, I call out, "Bans, come."

The dog stops on a dime and trots over to me, taking her place at my heel. "Good dog." To McKenna, I say, "She's playing."

"Yeah, well, I didn't come here to play!"

Petting my dog, I repeat, "Then I don't know why you bothered to come at all."

"I'm going to go inside and wait for you to get dressed. Then, maybe, we can have a civilized conversation." She turns on her heel. "And leave the *playful furball* out here." She takes a couple of steps. "Please."

She opens the French doors and enters my rental. Looking down at Bans, I say, "I don't know what got into her, girl. She used to be a lot more fun." Walking over to the stick that we were playing with before, I proceed to play fetch with her for a good fifteen minutes, sans clothes. Let McKenna stew. She came to my house.

When Bans flops down in the grass, I know she's done. I scratch her belly and pick up the discarded towel, shake it and wrap it around my waist. Sighing, I walk into the house.

McKenna stands up from the sofa, a glass of prosecco in hand.

"Help yourself."

"I did."

"McKenna, this is my time. You came to my house and ordered me around. You clearly don't want to go a few more rounds in bed with me, which I still can't understand, so what gives?"

She sighs. "Here, I poured you one."

She gives me a glass of bubbly. My hand slides over hers, causing electricity to scream up my arm. Her eyes widen, so I know she felt it too.

With a shaky voice, she starts, "Don't you want to put something on?"

My hand falls to my waist and cinches the towel wrapped around it. "Why? It's nothing you haven't seen before. And tasted. And—"

Her hand flies up. "Stop it. I get it. But I'm not here for sex."

I take a swallow of the prosecco and hold her gaze.

She puts her glass down on an ottoman and wipes her hands on her legs. Ones that could be put to much better use wrapped around my shoulders.

"I need to talk with you about your new songs."

My fingers tighten around the stem of my glass. To prevent me from hurling it—again—I cross the room and deposit it next to hers, collapsing down on a chair facing her. "There's not much to say."

"Last night you said you don't have anything new written."

I nod.

"At all?"

I nod again. This is getting tiring. Restless, I stand and tower over her. "If you came all the way over here to yell at me to write more or faster or whatever, you wasted your fucking time." I start toward the main hallway and the stairs. Might as well as end this farce before it escalates. One thought stops me short. I turn to face her. "How did you find out where I live?'

She worries her bottom lip. "I really need you to get writing."

So does my bank account. My residency at the Jade is up in a month— and with it, my paycheck. "Yeah, well, telling me to sit down and take out a pencil isn't doing it for me."

We stare each other down.

"Can I talk with you?" She motions toward the living room. "Please?"

Fuck. She looks so sincere. Without saying another word, I return to the living room and sit down. "Talk."

Sitting opposite me, she starts, "You know I was one of the graphic designers who the Artist Adventure Avenue Project hired to do the new designs for the music show."

This again? I nod.

After a beat, she continues, "You also know you're the final artist I need to work with before my presentation is completed."

Nothing new here. "Okay?"

She reaches for her glass again but stops and drops her hand to her lap. "I need to finish this project, Ozzy. It means a lot to me and for my firm. The Project is a part of the national consortium of charities that raise money to foster youth programs for art. If my submission is the Project's best, they'll enter it into the national competition. Going on, and hopefully winning, the nationals has the potential to change my life." She swallows. "I'm not like you. I'm not independently wealthy, living with private planes and humongous houses and my name in lights on the Strip. I need this project to make a name for myself."

As she's talking, it's all I can do not to snort. Yeah, right. Independently wealthy, my ass. More like that bitch of my now ex-wife took me to the cleaners and if it weren't for having prepaid my rent through the end of the year when I took the residency, I'd be living in the suite at the Jade. And private planes? Platinum let me use it so I would get back here for my concert tonight. And as an incentive to write more songs. But I'm not about to share all this with her.

"Listen, McKenna, I'm not holding out on you. I really don't have any new stuff."

Her eyes turn to slits. "Have you really been partying it up so much that you haven't bothered to sit down and write?" She looks away. "At least your cock has been getting a workout."

"Who I sleep with is none of your concern." I finish off the rest of my drink.

Neither one of us speaks.

When McKenna and I hooked up before, she was a good listener in addition to being a standout sex partner. Maybe she can help me get through this block? If I want to turn this train around, something has to change. What have I got to lose? "For the record, I *have* been trying to write."

She stares into my soul. "You have writer's block?"

I cross my ankle over my knee, the towel flipping open to reveal my hairy thigh. "I guess you could call it that."

"Oh."

"Yeah, oh."

She runs her hand down her arm, which draws my attention to her nice-sized tits. Too bad she's turned me down. It would have provided a nice diversion rather than admitting my failure to her. One of them, anyway. "But you had six number ones on your first album."

"That was then."

"What happened?"

She's the first person to ask me this question. Usually conversations like these go from "what have you written lately" to "we need your songs by the end of the year." No one ever goes any deeper. Not even Aiden. Am I ready to share? I scratch my knee. Shrugging, I start, "Actually, a lot."

She leans forward. "Tell me. Maybe I can help."

"I doubt it."

"Let me try."

Suddenly I feel naked before her. "Let me go change and we'll talk, okay?"

"Sure."

I bound up the stairs to my bedroom. Tossing the beach towel off my body, I hop in the shower and try to calm my nerves with liquid soap and shampoo. I change into a pair of shorts and a Jade T-shirt, then walk down the stairs. It has to be a good idea to share some of my truth with McKenna. Nothing else has worked.

Before I turn the corner, I hear her sweet voice. "I'm going to stay over here, and you stay over there. Got it?" In response, Bans barks. McKenna now pleads, "Please. I never did anything to you. Well, I did kinda invade your house, but your master invited me in. Sort of. Oh, I know." Rustling from inside the room makes me wonder what's going on, and then a doggie toy sails past me and lands in the kitchen. "Go get it!"

Bans races out of the living room to get her toy. Doesn't McKenna know the dog's going to pester her forever to keep playing? Before I can take control of the situation, McKenna barrels into my chest.

"Oh! I'm sorry! I didn't see you there."

I wrap my arms around her and inhale her unique fruity scent. Mouth watering, I say, "I knew I'd get you to forego the professionalism eventually."

At my feet, Bans barks and McKenna jumps. Keeping the woman snug to my chest, I address my dog. "Go lie down." The golden retriever whimpers, but turns and goes to her bed. I better remember to give her a treat for making me look good in front of company.

McKenna tilts her head up so she can look at me. "I didn't realize you were done getting ready."

Dropping both my voice and my head, I suggest, "I can get out of these clothes in no time. I remember when you preferred me like that." I nuzzle her hair. "And I'll not say 'no' to you joining me."

With a dry voice, she steps back and retorts, "Let's go to the living room and finish our conversation."

I let her go and follow her into the room, watching as she gives Bans wide berth. I grab our now empty glasses and refill them. Handing her the bubbly, I consider crowding McKenna on the sofa but opt for the chair. I'm going to need the distance to spill my guts.

McKenna directs all of her attention to me. Why did I think this was a good idea? Right—I need to break the cycle somehow. I clear my throat. Where to start? "So, when all of the songs for my first album were written, I was living in Puerto Rico. Where I was born. It took a couple of years to get each song the way we wanted them."

"We?"

I inhale. "Yes. We. If you check the record sleeve, you'll notice I co-wrote all of the songs with Luis Garcia. He used to be my best friend."

"You wrote the music and he wrote the lyrics, or vice versa?"

"Good question. Actually, we both did everything. He'd come up with a riff and I'd add the words. Or, I would hum the melody and he'd put lyrics to it. It was a real collaboration."

"Why don't you call him up now and do it again?"

My hands go cold. "It's not that easy." No way am I telling her about him screwing Teresa while I was being faithful to her out on tour. Apparently, he thought the nature of our collaboration extended to my wife.

She takes a sip of her drink and asks, "Why not?"

"When Platinum discovered me, my band was playing at clubs in San Juan. Selling out, actually."

She smiles. "I believe it."

"Yeah, well, I was the lead singer and guitarist, while Luis played keys and couple of other buddies rounded out the group."

"Are any of them still with you now?"

I shake my head. "No."

She cocks her head. "Why not?"

How do I explain what happened all those years ago? "Platinum happened."

"Your record label?"

"Yes. You see, they came up to me after one of our shows and told me they'd been following me for the better part of a year. They wanted to sign me. I was so excited. This was my big break." Turned out to be an empty victory. I stall by taking a swig of the prosecco, not even tasting it on the way down.

"Go on."

"Platinum only wanted me. They said they had other musicians who would form my band."

"How awful. What did you tell Luis and your other friends?"

"I explained everything to them. My drummer and bass player were cool with it—they both had kids on the island and didn't want to go out on tour."

"But Luis?"

I try to take another swallow, surprised to find my glass empty. "We had several rounds of discussions. I wanted to make sure he got credit for co-writing our songs, which he did."

"I don't understand. If you and Luis were sort of a package deal, why did Platinum want to break you up?"

"In a word? He didn't have 'the look.'" I make finger quotes around the term that Platinum used to justify leaving Luis out of the bigger part of the deal.

"The look?"

"Yes." I shift in my seat. "Let me paint a picture. Luis is short, a little underweight and doesn't work out. He always wears bandanas or hats to cover his thinning hair. Ladies weren't exactly throwing their panties at him on stage."

"So you're, well, you, and Luis didn't add to your mystique."

I roll my eyes. "I guess you can put it that way."

"But, you said Platinum gave him writing credit on the album. So why can't you collaborate together, like Bernie Taupin and Elton John?"

I chuckle. "We're no Bernie and Elton."

"You are in your own way."

Her belief in me shocks me. "Aw, McKenna, I didn't know you cared."

"I've always enjoyed your music."

"And here I thought you were after me for my other talents." I rock my hips.

"C'mon, Ozzy. Be serious. Why don't you just call up Luis and start to collaborate again?"

Because the fucker jumped in bed with my wife the first time my back was turned. But I'm not about to share that with her. So I offer another truth. "I haven't talked with him since I signed the contract with Platinum. It was his decision." I run my hand through my hair. My writer's block stems from my lack of a partner, but it's more than that.

"Oh. I'm so sorry. I know what it's like to lose touch with a best friend. Rose and I went our separate ways after college and, even though we didn't have a falling out like you two did, I know how difficult it was for me."

"At least your story has a happy ending."

She beams at me. "It's all because of you, you know."

I quirk my eyebrow. "Come again?"

"One night in Vegas a year or so ago, you had finished up your concert where Cole jumped on stage and previewed 'No One to Hold.' I was in your suite for an afterparty and went into your bedroom to, ah, to look for the bathroom." She shakes her head. "Anyway, Rose was in there, crying her eyes out. That's when we got reacquainted."

I remember Rose coming to my room, her luggage trailing behind her, looking like a wet cat. "And the rest is history."

"Yeah."

Silence descends.

"Well, I sincerely doubt I'm going to end up at a party with Luis." No. Fucking. Way.

"You could call him."

"No." More like no-fucking-way-am-I-ever-going-to-talk-to-that-asshole-ever-again. But "no" will suffice.

She sighs. "Alright. If what you did before isn't an option now, what ideas do you have to get your writing back on track?"

I laugh. "If I knew that, I wouldn't be in this situation, would I?" I start to drop the word "babes," but stop myself. Somehow the nickname I always use with women is starting to ring hollow when applied to McKenna.

She smiles. "No, I guess not."

While she takes another sip of the prosecco, my alarm goes off. "It's dinnertime. Want to join me?"

"Dinner?" She checks her watch. "It's barely even afternoon."

"With my performing schedule, I prefer to eat my big meal midday. Gives time for digestion before I get up on stage. Plus, I'm over at the Jade around normal dinnertime anyway, practicing and getting ready."

She stands. "I don't want to intrude."

I snort. "Says the woman who broke into my backyard."

Shrugging, she says, "I was motivated."

"Speaking of which, who do I have to fire for giving out my home address?"

She raises her hand and makes a zipping motion across her mouth. "I'm no tattletale."

"I'll get the info out of you one way or another. C'mon." I stand. "I'm making dinner and you're helping."

Seven

MCKENNA

Ozzy's KITCHEN IS BIGGER THAN MY childhood house, including the basement. It has all the newest gadgets and appliances. Frankly, it's my dream.

I slice lemons and oranges as garnish for the halibut. Who has fresh halibut in their refrigerator? It's over thirty dollars a pound! Ozzy puts the finishing touches on the pan sautéed fish.

"Can you give me the platter over there?"

I hand it to him, careful not to make contact with his skin. "Did your mom make this for you growing up?"

He chuckles. "She would cook fish if we had a good day with our rods, but usually we were a chicken and rice type of family."

"I seem to recall you're from a big family."

"I have one sister and two pain in the ass younger brothers. Plus, plenty of aunts, uncles and cousins." He starts to assemble the salad. "How about you? Do you have any brothers or sisters?"

I shake my head. "No. It's just me." Because I don't want him to delve any deeper into my family, I deflect. "What's your favorite dessert? I enjoy cooking, but I love making desserts."

He pauses. "My favorite is this Puerto Rican cake called 'Tres Leches,' which means 'three milks.' It has evaporated milk, heavy cream and sweetened condensed milk in it and it's so damn good." He rubs his flat abs. "I don't see it much around here, which is a good thing. I'd have to add another mile to my laps in the pool if I had easy access to it."

My mouth waters at his description. "I'll have to look it up. I've never heard of it. Maybe Grandma Gertie has."

"That woman could turn a sinner into a saint with her cooking. I swear she makes the best blueberry muffins I've ever tasted." He plates the fish and spoons some of the pan juices over each filet. It smells divine.

"Yeah, they're pretty awesome." Ever since she shared her recipe, I've been making them at least once a week. No doubts where my extra pounds came from.

He points to the citrus I cut. "Can you squeeze some of the lemons and oranges over the fish while I dress the greens?"

I do as I'm asked while he expertly finishes up the salad and stirs something in a smaller pot. Man, he eats healthy. And he doesn't even have a pint of ice cream in the freezer—not that I checked or anything. When the meal is ready, I help him bring the platters to the eat-in kitchen table I had set before. "This is fun."

He tips his head. "I do enjoy cooking a good meal with a beautiful woman."

Heat warms my cheeks, but before I can reply, he asks, "More prosecco?"

Trying to hide my reaction to his compliment, I keep my head down and reply, "Sure, thanks."

He points to the feast he whipped up and says, "Help yourself." He disappears into the bar area while I make a plate for each of us. All of the fresh herbs dance in my nose.

He hands me my glass and puts two down for him, but neither are bubbly. "Water?"

"And tea. Better for my vocal cords."

I didn't realize how serious he was about his singing. Of course, I know that's what he does for a living, but I guess I've never seen him in "work mode" before. Huh.

We dig in. The halibut is cooked perfectly. "Wow. If your writer's block continues, you could make a name for yourself as the tatted chef. This is fantastic."

"Thanks. I may need to take you up on it. Will you give me a good recommendation?"

I swallow the quinoa broccoli side dish, and smother a groan. It's delicious—and I don't even *like* broccoli. "Without a doubt."

He smiles, but I can see the hurt in his eyes. His writer's block weighs on him. I finish off my prosecco and ask, "Seriously, have you tried looking for another collaborator?"

"No way. I'm done with that." His utensils clatter to his now-empty plate. He adds agave to his tea.

"Okay. I didn't mean to upset you." I just need to light a fire under him so he can give me some songs to design my graphics around. "Maybe I can help?"

"Ever write a song before?"

"Well, no, but—"

His tone takes on a sharp edge. "But what? It can't be *that* hard?"

I sigh and place my fork onto my plate. "That's not what I was going to say at all. Your songs are all so personal. They make me feel your joy, your happiness. Maybe we can take time to do something that makes you happy. Get you out of your head."

His eyes slant in the way they used to before he stripped me naked. My core tightens. "Anything but that."

"Aw, now you're taking all the fun out of it."

Bells go off in my head. That's it. He's not having fun. How can he write about happiness and joy when he doesn't feel them? His songs told of being free in the sun and sand and surf. In a near whisper, I ask, "Is this the problem? Do you not want to write about upbeat things anymore?"

"Now I think you're getting too deep there. I'm just having an off time. Sophomore slump and all that. Don't go psychoanalyzing me."

He stands and brings his plates to the dishwasher. I know deflection when I see it. After all, I've gotten my Master's in it. Although, he might have his Ph.D.

Joining him by the sink, I enjoy his strong profile, gages in his ears and tattooed, muscular sleeves. A flash of him sweating over me in Rose's apartment the night she and Cole got back together pops into my head— which I quell. Damn my libido.

Clearing my throat, I ask, "Tomorrow? Are you free to get together tomorrow?"

"What do you have in mind?"

No water here in Vegas, but sun and sand I can do. I offer a beguiling smile. "You'll see. Are you man enough to trust me?"

He stands and looks down at me. Running a finger down the side of my face, he replies, "We both know exactly how much of a man I am."

I bite my lip and step back. "So we're on?"

"If it'll make you happy, fine, but I can't promise to be inspired to write again simply because you take me to pet some pretty unicorns or sprinkle wildflower seeds or whatever you have up your sexy little sleeve. And I have to be at the Jade by six, in case my schedule cuts your plans short." He puts my plate into the dishwasher. "Since I agreed to what you want, now you have to do me a solid."

Oh, the possibilities. None of which I would take him up on, however. I tilt my head. "What?"

"Come to my concert tonight."

I swallow. Mom's day nurse leaves after dinner and I'm responsible for her at nights. Maybe I could slip away? I'd have to tuck her in early and ask Becky to keep an eye out for her. I've avoided going to see him perform since his residency started, but now it's sort of my job. And I did go to all of the other artists' shows.

"I didn't ask you to commit to fly to Europe—just come to see me perform tonight."

It should be fine. I can handle this for one night. "Deal." I stretch my hand out.

He grasps mine in his, the rough callouses on his fingertips reminding me of his profession.

And the way they used to feel running over my nipples.

ELAINE FINISHES HER shift and hands me a letter before she leaves. I sit with Mom, watching television. An old rerun of *Golden Girls* makes her laugh. Like it did when she saw the same episode a month ago. I guess losing her memory is a type of blessing—she'll never see a rerun again.

Idly, I open the envelope. It's from the battered women's shelter that I volunteer at, asking for donations. I sigh. While I'd love to give them money, I'm too strapped right now. I grab a pen and circle the option for "time." My therapist recommended the shelter to me as part of my healing after Matt's abuse, and I'm glad she did. I enjoy the monthly visits I spend with the women and children there, I only wish I could do more. If I win the national competition, I'll be able to make a donation, and afford around-the-clock care for mom, and get my own apartment again, and… the list was too long to contemplate. In order to make any of it happen, though, I need to start with Ozzy.

"I'm going out to a concert tonight." I stand. "Work stuff."

She nods. "Sounds like fun."

Yeah, well, something like that. "It should be good." I spot her knitting needles and yarn on the side table and bring them to her.

"Thanks, honey. I'll knit you a hat tonight."

"I'd love it, Mom." I kiss the top of her head and go to my room to change for the concert. I flip through my clothes. Nothing says "professional" *and* "cool" to me. My hand stills on a red, high waisted skirt that runs to mid-calf. I pair it with a thin, black see-through blouse. Holding up the pieces in front of my floor-to-ceiling mirror, I decide this is slutty, not sensational. But if I put a black tank under the blouse and knot it at my nonexistent waist, it might do the trick.

I slip into the outfit and turn around to view it from all angles. When I tie the top, I look rounder than before so I button a few buttons and leave it undone. Tomorrow, I'll start walking on the treadmill that's been collecting laundry.

Sighing, I find a pair of black booties to finish the ensemble off nicely. I put large hoops through my ears, which sort of remind me of Ozzy's gages in reverse. After adding a funky bracelet and a red cocktail ring, I'm ready to do my makeup and hair.

Twenty minutes later, and one phone call to Becky, I emerge from my bedroom. Knitting needles clack away. "Please don't wait up for me. No leaving the house, alright?"

Mom looks at me and smiles. "Sure thing, McKenna."

Relieved that today's been a pretty good day for her, I head toward the front door. Mom's voice stops me. "You look terrific. Now, go show them what you've got!"

I give her the thumbs-up and lock the door behind me. Soon, I park my Civic in a compact car spot in the garage of the Jade. I'm going to watch Ozzy perform to try to get ideas about how to trample his writer's block. He has a little over a month to write at least thirteen songs. I have no idea if it's even possible, but I'm going to do my damndest to get at least three songs out of him so I can complete my presentation. I refuse to let anyone stand in my way.

Even Ozzy.

With all his tats, piercings and abs. Not to mention his "V." And his new cock piercing—no! Stop it, McKenna. Professional. That's what tonight is all about. Not his body. Or how he cooks for me. Or how he takes care of his voice for his performances.

I repeat my mantra as I trek through the lobby to the box office. At a special window marked "Industry," I wait behind a group of three women.

The tall, skinny blonde one says, "I hope he gives me the towel tonight. I brought him a gift."

Her friend, a reed-thin, shorter blonde with enough makeup on that I could carve my initials into her cheek without drawing blood replies, "Are you sure you're not just returning his vibrator?"

Her other friend, a wispy red-head, says, "We're all going to get lucky with Ozzy again tonight. His penthouse is ours. I can feel it."

At the mention of Ozzy's name, my breathing hitches. I know he's a total manwhore, but three? Obviously, this won't be the trio's first time together. The green-eyed monster that has nothing to do with the name of the casino threatens to snark out at them, but I tamp her down. Professional. I'm here for professional reasons only. It doesn't matter to me who he sleeps with.

Right?

Right.

Right!

The triumvirate get their tickets and giggle their way out of line. I give my name to the agent, and he hands me an envelope. I take a couple of steps away from the window and open it. A front row ticket and a backstage pass. I hope I'm not seated by those three slutty groupies.

Walking past the counter, I see a vendor selling all things Ozzy, from T-shirts to programs and even shot glasses. I stop and take a good look at the inventory. Most every one features Ozzy's face except for the back of the T-shirt, which is a rear view of him playing guitar. No other band members are shown.

I guess this makes sense given what he told me this afternoon about leaving his bandmates behind when he was signed. Lonely, though. Not so much upbeat and fun. And random, nameless sex has to get old—even with three.

I walk down to the front row and take my seat in the center. Man, this is an incredible view. Better, by far, than any of the other concerts I've attended while working on the Project. I bet this ticket sells for hundreds. Ozzy sure knows how to treat a woman. At least, one he wants in his bed, even for one night. My resolve starts to dip until I catch a glimpse of his unholy trio half a row away and put my barriers back up again. He's everything I can't want in my life.

I promise, Daddy.

The lights dim and the extravaganza that is the Ozzy Martinez residency starts. High flying trapeze artists, gymnasts on trampolines, dancers on individual high stages, lighting galore. High intensity doesn't even scratch the surface of his show, which features all of his older hits and covers of some current pop tunes.

My favorite song, though, is a traditional Puerto Rican ballad honoring his homeland. In Spanish. Everyone quiets and breathes in his soul. His heart's ripped open. When the song ends, the audience explodes.

On stage, Ozzy wipes the sweat off his face with a towel. Hmm. Much smaller towel than the one covering him at his pool this afternoon. Don't think about that, McKenna. *Especially not what was under the towel.* He takes the mic and starts talking, effectively diverting my wayward thoughts.

"Thank you all for coming tonight!" He rubs the towel again over his wet forehead and locks eyes with mine. With a wink, he tosses it.

Catching my prize, I hold it over my head, giving the trio from the Box Office a side glance. I shouldn't go so petty, but it sure does feel good. And the applause from the crowd doesn't hurt.

On stage, Ozzy walks to his band members and talks to them. Then he comes back to the mic. "Okay, Vegas, we have one more song tonight for you! Are you ready to blow the roof off this place?"

I scream, "Yes!" with everyone else around me. The buzz of the crowd is electric and being this close to the band has every sound vibrating through my body.

Ozzy cups his ear. "I didn't hear you. Are you ready to blow the roof off?"

I jump up and down, screaming, "Yes!"

"I'm still not convinced. Stan, are you?"

The spotlight goes to the drummer. He twirls his sticks and shakes his head. "Nah, Ozzy, I'm not."

The crowd now goes wild. Three bras float up on stage. I slant a look to the three slutty women, who are waving at Ozzy. *Geez.*

Ozzy bends down and picks up the bras. "Maybe I was wrong. Looks like at least three of you are ready to party." He holds the bras up to his chest and laughs. Attaching them to the end of his guitar, he says, "Let's get ready to 'Hit the Streets!'"

The first strains of his most popular hit bounce off the walls. Thumps from everyone jumping *en masse* pulse through my body. Smiling, I bounce up and down with the rest of the crowd. He plays the upbeat guitar solo like he does everything—with total abandon. The song ends but the musicians keep playing, riling up the audience even further. Damn. His show is honed to perfection.

Ozzy takes the mic one last time. "From here at the Jade, I thank you, Las Vegas, for partying with me tonight! You all rock!" He sings the last verse of the song again, takes his bow and disappears off the stage.

About a minute later, the house lights come up. My heart races from the high-octane energy of the show, and my ears ring from the sudden silence. Around me, people gather their things and talk about how incredible the show was.

A couple sitting next to me points to the towel. "Lucky girl."

I smile. "Thanks." Maybe I can use this time to do some recon. "Did you enjoy the show?"

The guy of the pair wraps his arm around his girlfriend's shoulder. "It was great."

His girlfriend agrees and adds, "I agree. Just wish he had some new stuff."

I nod and let them exit. His old stuff—and by "old" she meant from two years ago, when his last single hit number one—is great. The void is in the here and now. I sigh. I really need to get him back on track.

Making my way backstage, a throng of people wait outside an unmarked door. A huge guy in a security uniform steps outside and bellows, "Only those with backstage passes can enter."

Ahead of me, the trio elbow their way to the guard. I can't hear what's being said, but they show him something and walk inside. Great. Others follow suit, while a few are turned away, grumbling. When it's my turn, I show the guard my pass and join the somewhat smaller group inside.

A Maroon 5 song plays, which released last month. They seem to be able to write and put out songs regularly. When the song ends, a Cole Manchester hit starts. His latest album is amazing. Even though he's on his honeymoon now, I know for a fact that he's been writing new stuff. The pressure to produce hits me, and I'm not even a musician. How much harder must it be for Ozzy?

I glance around the room but I don't see the man of the hour yet. Walking to the side table, I pull up next to Aiden. "Hey," I say, holding a beer up to him.

"Hey." He grabs one for himself. "Everything alright?"

I don't pretend not to know what he's talking about. "Yeah. Didn't give you up."

He bends his head. Opening the bottle, he brings it to his lips. "I see you got the towel tonight." He reaches into his back pocket and offers me a keycard from the Jade. "Take this up to the penthouse. 8H."

What? Now I know what the trio meant about wanting to get the towel. Do he and Ozzy have a secret handshake that the woman he throws his towel to is his bedmate for the night? My stomach clenches as my heart speeds up. No matter what my heart wants, my brain is winning this argument. "Keep it. We're not sleeping together." My voice is higher pitched than normal.

His eyes widen. "Sorry. My mistake." He stuffs the keycard back into his pocket.

Leaving a sheepish looking Aiden behind, I make my way to a relatively uncrowded part of the room. As I walk past the tall and leggy blonde of the threesome, she puts her hand on my arm. She stares at the towel Ozzy tossed to me and crows, "You may have caught the towel, but just so you know, *I'm* the one who'll be sharing Ozzy's bed tonight."

My stomach tightens. "Is that so?" I snap the material between my hands.

"That man is a beast, and I need my fix. Besides," her eyes travel my full length, "I think I'm more his *style*."

This bitch is getting under my skin. It's not like I'm sleeping with Ozzy, but if I were, she'd be no competition. I tap my foot. "Don't you think Ozzy should be the judge?"

"What do you want me to judge?"

Ozzy appears at my right, causing me to jump. The blonde next to me smirks. Two can play this game. I shrug. "This *lady* called dibs on your penthouse tonight."

Ignoring me, the blonde bimbo reaches out and traces his tatts with a manicured fingernail. "I know what turns you on, Tiger."

He places his finger under her chin. Since they both are so much taller than me, I have to crane my neck to take this all in, no matter how revolting. Ozzy chuckles. "Jenna, you're one insatiable piece." He kisses her lips. "Why don't you go grab us both a couple of beers, babes?"

"Be right back," she says in a sickeningly-sweet voice. She throws me a triumphant look before heading toward the bar area.

"Did you enjoy the show?"

My spine bristles at his use of the name "babes" for another woman. A reminder that I'm strictly here for business. Professional. It doesn't matter to me who he sleeps with, especially since it won't be me. "If you're talking about the one that just went down before my eyes with—what was her name?" I snap my fingers. "Jenna." Rolling my eyes in the direction she went, I continue, "I have to say, I wouldn't pay for a ticket. However, if you're talking about the show you did on stage, then yes. I have to admit it was a great performance."

He grabs a lock of my hair, wrapping the white around his finger. I'm going to dye it purple tomorrow, the color I'd like his face to be as I'm strangling him. "Performance has never been a problem for me."

I flip my head, knocking my hair out of his reach. "I suppose not. I'm sure *Jenna* will enjoy the benefits tonight."

"Jealous?"

"As if," I scoff.

"It could be you in my penthouse tonight."

"The room would be awfully crowded. *Jenna* has two friends she plans on bringing with her." His eyebrow raises, then he shrugs. Before he can make another crude remark, I continue, "Look, thanks for the ticket. We can discuss the show tomorrow. I'll be at your place—your *house*—at nine o'clock sharp. Be ready." I turn on my heel.

As I walk away, Jenna and her two friends sidle up to Ozzy. Behind me, he calls out, "Keep the towel."

I stop in my tracks, flip it over my shoulder and continue straight out the door.

Eight

OZZY

I STUMBLE DOWNSTAIRS AND POUR myself a cup of coffee. The clock on the stove says eight forty-five, so I have fifteen minutes before McKenna will be here.

At least I got to bed at a relatively decent hour last night, much to Jenna and her friends' dismay. I stayed at the party until midnight and then told them I had to leave. For some reason, getting up early for McKenna was more appealing than rolling around in the penthouse with those three. Not that it wouldn't have been a good time. Just wasn't into it.

I sip my coffee and walk outside, Bans at my heels. I toss her ball as I make my way to the chair and place my steaming mug on the table. Bans brings the ball back and I toss it again. We continue this way until I hear a car door slam shut. With one last throw of the ball, I rush through the house to greet McKenna, ignoring the tightness in my chest. Why am I rushing?

Opening the door, I look down at the woman standing there. The only woman who knows where I really live, versus my fuckpad at the Jade. Still don't know how she found me, though. I place my arm on the doorjamb. "Hey."

She looks me up and down. "Good, you're ready. Thought I'd have to go to the Jade and pry you out of bed from your playmates."

My eyebrow quirks up. Hell hath no fury, as they say. "You *are* jealous?"

"Ha. You wish." She pushes past me and I detect melon, peach, apple and another scent I can't place. It's spicy, though, like her current attitude. I follow her through the foyer and into the kitchen, where she pours herself a cup of Joe.

"Help yourself."

She doesn't hesitate. "Sugar?"

I point to the cabinet. She retrieves the sugar bowl, then opens the silverware drawer and grabs a spoon before fixing up her coffee with both sugar and milk. "We have to leave in ten."

"Where are we going?"

"You haven't earned the right to ask questions."

I smile as I crowd her against the counter. Lowering my voice, I reply, "Oh, it's a surprise. I like surprises. Especially when they're accompanied by a beautiful woman. More often in bed." I run my fingers over her now-purple streak of hair. "Purple?"

"Yeah. Thought it was appropriate for today," she says, dipping her face deeper into her mug.

"Because you're with rock royalty?"

She nearly spits out her coffee. "Think what you want."

She tries to move away. I have the urge to grab her by the hips and keep in her place but, instead, I step back. Something about her demands more from me. She finishes her coffee and says, "Ready?"

"Sure. Let me get Bans."

Her eyes grow wide and she says, "I'll meet you outside." She turns on her heel and disappears toward the front door.

I'm going to have to do something about her fear of Bans—what kind of woman doesn't love dogs?—if she's going to be sticking around. Whoa. Not going to happen. I don't need *any* woman in my life outside my bed. Thank you, Teresa.

After making sure Bans has everything she'll need for the day, I meet McKenna by her car, her keys in her hand. A little Honda Civic. No way in hell can I fit half my frame in there. I shake my head. "Sorry there, McKenna. I'm driving." I walk over to the garage and plug in the numbers on the keypad. The door slowly opens to reveal my motorcycle.

"Don't you own a car?"

I chuckle. "Afraid?"

She snorts. "You wish. I thought you'd have your choice of vehicles since you have a three-car garage."

"Yeah, well the Jade provides transportation for me to and from my performances if I ask, so I don't really need anything else." I walk to the side and grab my extra helmet. Instead of handing it to her, I plunk it down on her head and pull the strap tight. Knocking on its top, I put my helmet on, visor up, and swing my leg over Shirley.

"Hop on behind me."

The helmet shakes and she hands me her purse. A quirky contraption in a patchwork of colors. Sort of like her. I put it in the storage compartment and look at her. She hasn't moved. "Are you a motorcycle virgin?"

Her mouth purses but she doesn't say anything.

"Don't worry, I'll be gentle."

She gives me a dirty look and throws her leg over the seat. "Do your worst."

I tap the shiny chrome. "Shirley and I go way back. You'll be fine."

"Shirley?"

I shrug. "Seemed like a good name at the time. Now wrap your arms around me and give me the address." She tells me an address in the nearby town of Jean, and I plug it into my GPS. I close my visor and she does the same, then her arms snake around my torso. I place my hand on hers intertwined on my ribs and give them a squeeze. The feeling of this woman wrapped around me short circuits my senses.

"I'm waiting," she says.

Pulling my head out of my ass, I focus on giving her a great ride. The only type of ride she'll accept. *For now.* Throttling up, I leave the garage and press the pre-programmed button to close the garage door. Soon, we're on the open road. I take the turns easy but she leans into me with perfect balance. I revise my initial thought—this certainly is not her first time on a bike. As I'm heading for the unknown address, I don't try to talk. Rather, I relish the feel of her tits against my back, her helmet-covered head on my shoulder and her arms around my middle. Fuck. This feels too good. I speed up.

After nearly twenty minutes, I turn into our destination—a parking lot with a "Ride the Dunes" sign. I cut the bike and raise my visor. "A dune buggy ride?"

She untangles herself from me, causing me to miss her lush body against mine. Her words distract me. "We're going to have some fun!" She hops off the bike and hands me her helmet. Seems like her mood smoothed out over the ride. I secure the bike and follow her toward the front of the building.

As I walk in, the weight of every eye is on me. Fuck. I didn't bring a disguise. A rack of hats with the "Ride the Dunes" logo is off to the side, so I make a purchase and quickly plop it on my head. Not much, but I can breathe easy again.

I join McKenna at the registration counter. "That'll be four-hundred dollars for the both of you."

I swallow. She's commented enough on her money issues so I reach for my billfold, but she's already handed her credit card to the clerk. She looks at me. "I've got this."

Making a mental note to have Aiden send her a refund, I kiss the top of her head.

The clerk hands McKenna back her card and motions for us to go into another room, where a lanky dude in a "Ride the Dunes" T-shirt welcomes us and about ten others. He gives everyone a crash course in how to handle the souped-up dune buggies and what to expect on the course. Gotta hand it to McKenna—this does sound fun.

We're all given lockers for our personal items, where I have to leave my newly-purchased disguise. Next, we're herded into another room to get our gear. I slink to the back of the room and keep my head down until I receive a helmet, goggles and driving gloves—each marked with a logo. They've got their branding down, for sure.

As a group, we walk to a bunch of multi-colored dune buggies, following our guide's instructions. McKenna stops in front of a purple one, and I help her into the two-seater. I can't resist. "Matches your hair."

She gives me a secretive smile and nods once. "I hope you have fun out here, Ozzy," she offers before strapping in.

"You, too," I say, then choose a black one, placing my helmet and goggles on my extra seat while I get situated in it. Once we're all set and have given our guide a thumbs-up, we head off for the dunes of the Mojave Desert.

The power of the vehicle surprises me, and we race around the sand. I chase McKenna's purple buggy, letting her cut me off, laughing my head off. Setting my sights on another one being driven by a guy around my age, we leave interweaving tracks all over the desert.

All too soon, we pull behind the main building. How fucking exhilarating! I loved every single second of the ride, especially when we went balls to wheels. Reminded me of Go-Kart races when I was growing up—only on steroids. I rip my helmet off my head, jump out of the dune buggy and rush over to the purple one where McKenna sits fiddling with her hair. I grab her under her arms, pull her out and swing her around.

"That was the most fun I've had clothed since I can't remember when. Thank you!" I kiss her lips before putting her feet to the ground.

She looks up at me, a big smile across her face. "I'm glad you enjoyed it. I had a blast, too." She bends over to retrieve her helmet and goggles—giving me an excellent view of her ass—and together we walk back to HQ to turn in our gear.

One of the ladies in our group approaches me. "Excuse me. You're Ozzy Martinez, aren't you?"

Some of the joy of this morning starts to evaporate. I put my finger to her lips. "Shh."

Crimson moves its way up her neck. I remove my finger and she whispers, "Could I get a selfie with you?"

Seeing no way out, I motion for her to step out of the way of the others in our group. "Sure thing. Where's your phone?"

She hands it to me, but McKenna pipes up. "Here. Let me take it of the two of you." The woman nods, so I give it to McKenna and the ordeal is over in three clicks.

After putting my new baseball cap and sunglasses on, I lead McKenna back to my bike. "Honestly, I loved this. I had no idea this was even here."

"Leave it to a resident to show you to all the really cool places."

"I think I will." My stomach rumbles. Checking my watch, I notice it's lunchtime. Since she did something so nice for me, I want to return the favor. "Lunch?"

"I'll never turn down a meal."

I ruffle her hair before she puts her motorcycle helmet on. "Let's go grab a bite. Know any good places out here?"

"There's a steakhouse nearby. Sound good?"

I pat my toned stomach. "Sure thing. Nothing a few more laps in the pool won't overcome." She gives me the address and we take off.

Walking into the wood-paneled restaurant, I silently give thanks it's the lunch crowd and not the dinner crowd. It also hits me—I haven't been out to dinner at a restaurant in forever. While I enjoy my fans, I've been sticking to either the Jade or my rental. Why have I become such a hermit? Only one answer comes to mind—Teresa.

Fuck her. It's time I took back my life. I like this mantra.

The hostess does a double-take at me, then leads us to a table in front by the windows. I'm uncomfortable being so exposed, even with my new grip on life. McKenna pipes up. "Do you have another table we could have? Perhaps, more in the back?"

The hostess looks to me, then my lunch companion, and takes us to a much more private table. When she leaves us, I say, "Thanks."

"I thought eating in a fishbowl might not be so pleasant. This is a nice table, though."

We order drinks and enjoy the goodies in the bread basket. As we wait for our entrees, it hits me for the second time today. I'm having pure, unadulterated fun. No expectations. No strings. And we're both fully clothed. I pick up my Cuba Libre.

"A toast. To the best day I can remember in a long time."

She touches her mojito to my glass. "To having fun!"

When she puts her drink down, a bit of salt clings to her lower lip. Instead of telling her, I reach out and remove it with my finger and hold it up for her to see. Latte-colored eyes zero in on my fingertip before traveling to meet mine. "Oops!"

As I wipe my finger on my napkin, she says, "So, tell me when you knew you wanted to be a musician."

Visions of Tío Miguel, my dad's brother, and his guitar cloud my memory bank. "I always loved music. Growing up in a Puerto Rican family, there always was music around. We'd get together with my aunts, uncles and cousins at the farm, make a roasted pig and dance all night long. My uncle always had a guitar."

She takes another sip of her drink, her pink tongue swiping her lips to make sure no salt was left behind. "Sounds like a great time."

"It was." I break off another piece of the multi-grain bread and dip it into olive oil. I'll pay for the carbs later. "Tío Miguel had a band, and played at small clubs and bars on the island. Traditional Puerto Rican stuff."

Her hand stills. "Like the ballad you sang last night?"

I smile. "Yeah. It was the first song he ever taught me to play."

"I loved it. I could really feel that your heart and soul were in it, and now I know why."

Our conversation is cut short when our waiter brings our meals. I dive into my porterhouse, while she enjoys her filet mignon. Once our meals are devoured, we sit in the restaurant and talk about everything and nothing. We laugh. We joke around. She makes fun of my empty three-car garage while I tease her about being afraid of Bans.

The server interrupts, holding a tray filled with desserts. "Would you like something sweet?"

Of course, my mind travels down a non-food path. McKenna's eyes, however, devour the dessert tray like it's Christmas morning, straying to one particular item. I ask, "Is that crème brulee?" When he nods, I say, "Great. We'll take one—two spoons—and I'll have a tea with agave if you have it, while the lady would like a coffee, sweet with cream."

"Very good, sir." He walks away.

McKenna clears her throat. "How interesting."

"What?"

"You ordered my favorite dessert without even asking me."

I tap my forehead. "I know things." She giggles, the sound sending a thrill throughout my body.

"I guess I should ask you how you enjoyed your after-after party last night."

"Slept like a baby." I'm tempted to leave her dangling, amused by her curiosity, but she deserves clarification. "Alone. At home."

A huge smile creeps across her face. "Really?"

Our conversation doesn't get any further when the dessert is placed between us. We pick up our spoons and dig in. It's sweet and creamy, exactly the way I remember her tasting. I sit back and drop my spoon.

"Don't you like it? I think it's great."

"It is."

She swallows another spoonful. "Well, you better get your next taste before it's all gone." Her spoon hovers above the ramekin. I grab mine again and tap hers away and take another, large spoonful.

"Hey! Leave some for me!" She shoves my spoon to the side and plunges hers into the dessert. Within minutes, it's gone. Enjoying her passion for it was almost erotic. She excuses herself to go to the ladies' room and I check my phone while paying the tab. Five missed voicemails and ten texts, mostly from Ginger and Aiden. Sighing, I respond to them all, some of the joy of the day diminishing.

When she returns to her seat, I stand. "Ready?"

"Did you pay?"

"Yes. It was the least I could do after everything you did for me today. Plus, I should get home and let Bans out." I place my hand on the small of her back—relishing her tiny shiver—and lead her out of the restaurant. She's not immune, just protesting.

I throttle down Shirley as we pull into my driveaway. Maneuvering to the side of her Civic, I hit the kickstand and pull my helmet off. Behind me, McKenna does the same. Before she swings her leg off the bike, I swivel my head to her. "Not your first time on a motorcycle, huh?"

She runs her hand through her hair to remove the helmet-head. Without meeting my eyes, she replies, "There's plenty you don't know about me." Then she hops off and extends the helmet to me.

Her answer makes me want to dig. "But you like them, right?" I take the helmet from her and hook it onto the bike.

She shrugs. "I like my Civic. Steady and reliable. Can you please hand me my purse?"

Bending over, I retrieve it. "Here you go. Do you want to come inside? I have some time before I need to get ready for the Jade." I surprise myself with this question, but it's too late now.

"Oh. I, uhm." She looks at her car, then at the front door. "Sure. Thanks."

Together we go into the house and Bans comes racing over. McKenna jumps behind me as the golden retriever jumps on my front. A smile snakes across my face—not quite the lady-sandwich I'm used to, but I like it.

I accept Bans's kisses. "Okay, girl. I'm home. Let's go outside." I point toward the back patio, and she takes off like a shot.

Once the dog's gone, McKenna appears at my side. "She's well trained, I'll give you that."

I chuckle. "Hours of obedience school." Wish others would be as amenable. "She's really sweet and super friendly, I promise."

McKenna gives me a sideways glance, then forces a smile. Rather, her lips move upward and some teeth show, more like a baring of teeth. "I'll remember that."

"Would you like something to drink?" My standard question.

"Nah, I'm good."

With her response, we bypass both the bar and the kitchen and head to the back patio, where Bans waits patiently, a chew toy in her mouth. I go over to her in the grassy area while McKenna takes a seat. As I proceed to play with Bans, McKenna asks, "Do you have a guitar here?"

"Of course. What self-respecting rockstar would be without his instrument?" I pull on the chew toy, Bans tugging back.

"I wasn't sure if you left everything at the Jade."

"Nope." I win the tug of war and throw the toy for her to fetch. "I have two here—my very first one that's more sentimental than anything, and one I use…" For writing. Not much call for it lately.

McKenna crosses her leg, but she's so short that her other foot dangles rather than being planted firmly on the ground. She uncrosses it and swings both feet. I'm not sure she even knows what she's doing. I chuckle at how cute she is. Bans barks to get my attention and I play tug-of-war with her again.

"Why don't you go get your sentimental guitar? I've only ever seen you with a shiny electric one onstage."

Her question throws me so much I lose my grip and the golden retriever wins this round. She races around the pool, doing her victory lap as I struggle to respond to my guest. "I really haven't taken it out in a while."

She cocks her head to the right. "Where'd you get it?"

Immediately, my mind goes back thirty years. "Tío Miguel—the uncle I told you about—gave it to me when I was eight."

She smiles and I swear the two clouds in the sky part.

I return her smile as memories of my uncle wash over me. "Tío Miguel was something special." Tuckered out, Bans plops down by the bushes, so I join McKenna at the patio table.

"Was?" When I take my seat, she places her hand on top of mine. "What happened to him?"

"About six years ago, he had just finished playing a set with his band when he had a massive heart attack. He died instantly. He didn't suffer."

She squeezes my hand. "But you did."

I nod, my eyes latched onto her hand on top of mine. "He was a good man. The best."

"And he gave you your first guitar. He must have been so proud of all your success."

I get lost in her expressive eyes. Something tells me she knows about losing someone close. "He came to quite a few of my concerts. I didn't get really big until after he passed, but he supported everything I did. It was his advice that I missed when Platinum came to me with their offer for me alone. He would have known what to do."

She pats my hand, then clasps them in her lap. In a low voice, she asks, "Would you get out his guitar? I'd love to hear you play the Puerto Rican ballad—the one he first taught you—with only it accompanying you. I bet it would be amazing."

My chest constricts. Can I do it? Yes, I play the song every night at the Jade, but it's with the full band, lights, the works. Here, it'll just be me and the guitar. Exposed. Before I make up my mind, I'm already heading toward the music room. Guess my decision was made.

When I return to the patio, McKenna claps. "Oh, it's such a pretty guitar. The little dings and scratches tell its story. And I love acoustic."

I smile at her and run through some chords. Unconsciously, I play the first part of my warm up that I do at the Jade. When I realize what I'm doing, I slow down and strum the strings. Swallowing over the lump in my throat, I say, "This is what Tío Miguel taught me how to play."

I start singing the Puerto Rican ballad, but have to close my eyes. I can't look directly at her and sing the words about love of country and family. With my eyes closed and singing outside, I'm transported back to Puerto Rico—jamming with Tío Miguel under the stars. I finish the song with a traditional flourish, like he taught me to do. Not the way I do it in concert.

When I open my eyes, McKenna's hand is over her mouth. "Ozzy. Oh my goodness! How gorgeous."

Inclining my head, I say, "Gracías."

Replacing her hands on her lap, her smile is genuine. "Tell me what the words mean."

"It's a story, really. About the hardships my people have endured but how they overcame them with love for each other. How Puerto Rico will always be a positive place so long as we have love. That's our strength." Perhaps true love isn't such a farce? I shake my head. No—not for me.

"So beautiful."

A melody suddenly pops into my head. One I've never heard before. Looking down at my guitar, I start strumming the notes, translating what's in my head. When I stop, McKenna asks, "That's pretty, too. Is it from another song Tío Miguel taught you?"

I lift my head up as if coming out of a daze. "What?"

"Did Tío Miguel teach you that song, too?"

I shake my head. "No. He didn't. I, ah, it just came to me."

Her mouth drops open. I don't have time to process her reaction as more of the music starts to flow. As I explore the notes, she rushes into the house. I ignore her quirky behavior and continue to play. When I've finished, she takes her seat again, a sheaf of paper in her hand.

"Here. I found this in your living room." She hands me blank music sheets and a pencil. I've left piles of these sheets all over the house in frustration, when nothing was coming to me.

Without a word, I start scribbling down the music. She watches me as I play on the guitar and then commit the music to paper. When I finish with what I've created so far, I play the unfinished song. I like it. A lot.

"Awesome!" She does a little jig, throwing in "Whoop! Whoop!" for good measure.

Her excitement is contagious. I place the guitar on the table and hug her around the waist for the second time today. She grabs my shoulders and I look directly into her eyes. She says, "You did it!"

"I did." Before I can stop myself, my lips meet hers for a scorching kiss. One she returns.

The words I sang in the Puerto Rican ballad replay in my head. *Love.* My eyes open and my mouth disengages. What the fuck am I thinking? I lower her to the floor, still man enough to enjoy the feeling of her soft body pressed against mine.

She steps back, running her hand through her purple hair. "Congrats, Ozzy. I mean it."

I may have gotten lost in the moment, but I remind myself that no woman can be trusted. Including McKenna. "Thanks, *babes*." I emphasize the nickname for my sake. Reaching for her again, I'm sure pounding into her body for a quick release will make all those other crazy feelings disappear. Love, ha.

I can see the excitement drain into something like disappointment at the use of the nickname. She steps back and opens her purse, taking out a car key. "I'd better be going. You have to start preparing for your performance, and I have things to do."

"Sure." I clear my throat. "Want to come to the show again tonight?"

She shakes her head. "No, but thanks. I've seen everything I need to see."

Because she's a woman, I tell myself. She only sees you as a meal ticket. I write the songs, she does the graphics so the Project and her company—more importantly, she—get recognition. Remember this, buddy.

At the front door, I say, "I had a really good time today. The dune buggies were fun."

"I did, too. Knock 'em dead out there tonight. And make sure you use a clean towel." With those parting words, she walks out of my rental.

Oh, I'll use a clean towel alright. Tonight, I'm throwing my towel at some willing chick and cleansing my system of McKenna for good.

Nine

OZZY

I WAKE UP IN MY RENTAL AT EIGHT in the morning and flip on the television. An exposé about Puerto Rico following the disaster of Hurricane Maria relives the horror of those days. Even after all this time, the island is still recovering.

I turn off the TV and pick up my cell. "Hola, Mamí, how are you doing?"

"Much better now that I've heard your voice, hijo."

Hearing her say "son" in Spanish soothes my soul. "I was just watching some old news coverage of Hurricane Maria."

"Díos." I spent some serious cash moving her and my younger brothers and sister to a safe area before the hurricane hit, but they still have to deal with fallout like rolling electricity outages from time to time. I'm glad I did this before Teresa cleaned me out. "Did you hear Jorge made the baseball team?"

"Sí, Pablo texted me." My younger brother couldn't wait for the baby of the family to call before he told me the good news. That's how it works in my family. "I'm excited for him. How's Papí doing?"

"Oh, you know. He's still working and driving everyone crazy at the shop."

I'd love to tell him to sell the auto body shop, but I know he loves it too much to stop. "At least he's out of the house and not driving *you* crazy."

She laughs. "Well, that's true. So, have you had any word about your divorce?"

Never fond of my ex-wife, she asks me this every time we speak. I should've listened to her—would've saved me a boatload of dinero. "Actually, yes. Signed the papers the other day. It's over."

"Gracías a Dios. Good riddance." When I don't respond, she says, "So, tell me, hijo, when am I going to see you again? We can celebrate—it's been too long. I have to resort to YouTube to catch glimpses of you."

I close my eyes. I miss my family, but Teresa and Luis are back home and I don't want to risk seeing those two ever again. Not to mention my commitments here. "I'm not sure. My contract with the Jade runs through the end of the year."

"Well, hopefully, in January then. Maybe for Three Kings Day?"

Her hope springs through the phone. With everything so up in the air right now, I can't commit. "I'll try."

Noise in the background like someone just entered her house filters through her cell. "Oh, Letzy is here with her little ones." She says something to my sister, who pops onto the phone.

"Hola, big brother. How is life in Sin City treating you?"

"It's great," I half-lie. McKenna's making life interesting. "How are my niece and nephew?" I don't ask about their deadbeat baby daddy.

"They're great. They're growing like weeds and miss their Tío Ozzy. When will you come visit?"

This steady refrain—coupled with my desire to be as far away from my ex-wife and ex-best friend—is the reason I don't call home much. Mom's voice filters through—she's playing with the kids. "I'm not sure yet, but I'm working on it. Listen, I have to go. Tell Mamí I'll be in touch soon."

The call disconnects and I flop onto my back. Last night's show was good, probably one of my better ones in a while. That is, if I discount the night before, when McKenna was in the front row. I bet Mamí would love McKenna. She's nothing like Teresa. *Fuck.* What is this woman doing to me? Despite my intentions, I didn't have the desire to hook up with anyone after last night's show either.

Hopping out of bed, I make my way to the kitchen where I down a protein shake. Then I strip and dive into the pool. Swimming laps always clears my mind. After one-hundred, I swim as far as I can go underwater and break the surface. I get out of the pool in roughly the same spot as two days before and check to see if anyone has joined me.

Well, hello there.

McKenna holds my towel out in front of her. Dripping wet, I saunter over to her, where she wraps the towel around my waist since I wasn't about to do so.

"Fancy meeting you here."

A light shade of pink stains her cheeks, but her chin goes up. "Thought I'd stop by to see how everything went last night."

My pulse picks up and I run my index finger down her cheek. "And by that you mean you want to know how many chicks I hooked up with?"

"No. Not at all." Biting her lip, she steps back. "I was actually wondering if you wrote any more of your new song."

I chuckle. "Yeah. Keep telling yourself that."

Turning, I make my way inside. "C'mon in. I'll go change while you make us coffee." I take another couple of steps and toss, "And the number was zero." For some reason, I had to tell her the truth. I don't look back and go straight to my bedroom. In minutes, I'm showered and downstairs again, led by the aroma of freshly-brewed coffee.

I pour myself a mug. Next to the coffeemaker is a plate of muffins. "Are these Grandma Gertie's blueberry muffins?"

In a sing-song voice, she responds, "Maybe."

I take a bite. Heaven. "Damn, woman, they are. Are you trying to fatten me up?"

She giggles. "I know you like them and I had some extras, so I brought them over."

I finish the muffin in one bite and grab another. "For this, you deserve a reward."

All sorts of rewards pop into my head—all of which involve us both, naked. Deferring to her protestations of not being interested in going another round, I opt for her reaction to the reason I slept alone last night. "I wrote the bridge to the song I started yesterday. With some lyrics. Want to hear it?"

She squeals. "Yes! I'd love to!"

Her exuberance feeds my ego. I motion toward the living room. "I left my guitar in there last night."

She sits on the sofa and I take a spot on the chair, guitar in hand. I strum a few chords, more nervous now than I've been for a very long time. I glance at McKenna and take a deep breath.

"The working title for this song is 'Take Me.'" I lick my lips and start the melody I wrote yesterday. I still don't have lyrics for this part. When the time comes, I play the bridge, with the few lines I jotted down last night.

Tonight I'm all yours—Take me all the way
Make me forget and I'll do the same
Your screams will drown out the noise
And mine will bring us to a higher plane

As I complete the bridge, additional parts of the melody form and I continue playing. When I reach the end of what I have, I do one final fast strumming of the strings.

After a second, she jumps up and runs to me, her arms coming around my neck. "That was hot," she says, kissing my cheek. "It's so fresh and different from anything you've done before. Just the sort of thing I need to let my imagination fly!"

She returns to her seat and rummages through her bag, pulling out her computer. "Can you play it again?"

"Sure." I do, adding even more of the melody to the end. Finished, I grab the sheet music and scribble down the new notes. "What do you think?"

She's clicking away on the keyboard, deep in thought. After a while, she places her laptop on the coffee table and turns the screen toward me. It's a rough graphic that goes with the lyrics to the bridge, showing what looks to be El Yunque, the rainforest in the center of Puerto Rico with panoramic vistas of the ocean. Superimposed on a waterfall is a couple in skimpy bathing suits, kissing. It's like she was there, in my head with me, seeing what I was seeing as I wrote the song.

My eyes travel to hers. She runs her hand through her hair, her feet shuffling on the rug. "It's rough, of course. It's what came to my mind while you were singing."

My throat constricts. Blood rushes through my veins such that every molecule pings against my skin. "No one has ever done something like this for me before."

Her eyes return to the graphics. "But do you like it?"

I can't form words.

"It's silly. Let me erase…"

"NO." I startle her with my exuberance. "I like it. A lot. In fact." I grab my guitar again and start playing the introduction to the song, lyrics falling from my lips as if they were crafted for the music. Well, I guess they kind of are.

When I finish, she says, "Ozzy, this is fantastic."

Smiling, I grab my pencil and write down the lyrics before they disappear. When the last word tumbles from the lead, I toss the paper onto the coffee table next to her computer and collapse back into the chair. Placing my guitar on the floor, I stare at the ceiling.

"You think so?"

"I know a good song when I hear one. It's like you've written a story around the couple in my graphics. You've given them a whole life."

My lips tick upward. Without moving my neck, I reply, "Thanks."

She picks up her laptop and resumes her clicking. I remain looking up at the ceiling for a good minute until my curiosity gets the better of me.

Standing, I walk around and sit next to her. She refines the graphic, changes out the couple a few times, and plays with the colors. Makes it more vibrant.

"There. I think it's better now. Still rough."

"McKenna, it's really good." Lyrics jump into my brain and I pick up the sheet music and add the words to the song. We continue like this—she plays with the graphics and I compose—in silence. The only soundtrack being her keys clicking and my eraser changing words here and there.

Lost in the process, I have no idea how much time has passed when my creativity ebbs. But the song is basically finished. "I think it's almost done."

"Really?"

I nod. As I stand to get my guitar, Bans races into the room, knocking me over, slobbering kisses all over my face. McKenna scoots off the sofa. Laughing, I turn the other cheek to even out the doggie germs.

"Okay, down girl."

The dog's tail thumps against the back of the sofa and she barks.

"Is that right?"

She barks again. Laughing, I stand up and go over to her bowl, checking the time on the oven clock. It's nearly four—how did that happen? "Sorry, Bans. I didn't realize I missed your dinnertime." I pour her kibbles into her bowl and she starts eating before I can pull the container away.

From across the room, McKenna says, "I can't believe it got so late."

"Me either," I reply. At least we both were in the zone. "Would you like to stay for dinner? I'm not sure what's here." I open the refrigerator.

"Oh, I shouldn't."

"We have chicken and pork." I pull out the chicken. "Want some Arroz con Pollo?"

"Well…"

Her voice trails off. Neither one of us has had anything to eat since the blueberry muffins. "It'll take no time to whip up. Stay."

"What can I do to help?"

I ask her to cut up some onions and carrots while I get busy preparing our meal. It's going to be a shortcut version and not the authentic one Mamí makes, but still good.

Her hand steals one of the blueberry muffins and brings it toward her mouth. Grabbing her wrist, I tease, "Don't mind if I do," and take a bite of her delicious muffin. The blueberry kind.

"Hey." She giggles. "Get your own."

As we continue preparing our meal, Bans enters the kitchen and runs in a circle around us. While I'm amused, McKenna drops her cutting knife at least three times, her shoulders nearly at her ears.

Taking pity on my dinner companion, I send Bans outside. McKenna's shoulders immediately drop into their normal place. "She's really a sweetheart."

"I'm sure you're right. I'm just not a dog person."

"Kinda picked that up."

"But what an unusual name. Is it short for anything?" She places her elbows on the island.

"Yeah. For Banshee."

"Oh." She bounces off the island. "Why'd you name your dog *that?*"

No matter what's happened today, I'm not ready to admit all the shit that went down with my ex-wife. So I give her a sanitized version. "I got her a few years ago when things were going pretty bad." Not that things have gotten much better, but at least I'm free of that bitch forever. "I needed a name to express how I was feeling at the time, and 'Banshee' seemed to fit."

I tense. I'm not sure how she's going to react. So, I'm not prepared when she throws her head back and laughs. I can't help myself and chuckle. "Damn. Well, that about sums everything up, huh?"

"Pretty much."

"So, are things better, now you've got *Bans?*"

"I think they're turning around." Because I wrote my first song, solo, ever. And McKenna's here.

"Well, then, good."

It dawns on me that I've been a crappy host. "Would you like something to drink? Our coffees went cold ages ago."

"Tea would hit the spot."

While I pour the water into mugs and put them in the microwave, she excuses herself to go to the bathroom. I haven't been this creative since I can remember. Well, truth be told, I never was this creative. Luis and I would often go off for a weekend hiking and drinking and sometimes smoking, then come back with a couple of tracks. This song, the one I wrote all by myself, only needs a tweak here and there, and it'll be ready for Ginger.

What changed?

McKenna returns to the kitchen and I have my answer. And neither of us is naked. *Yet.*

I wink and serve our simple dinners. We eat in silence for a bit. When her plate is almost finished, she removes the fork from her mouth and points it at me. "This was a productive day, huh?"

Swallowing my last mouthful, I reply, "Yup." I place the tines of the fork onto my empty plate and ask, "Any chance you'd like to come over tomorrow and do it again? I got a lot done when you were here." That didn't make me sound too much like a pussy. Right?

She takes another bite and chews, leaving me hanging in anticipation of her response. I focus on breathing in and out in a steady rhythm. Finally, she responds, "It was interesting to watch you work. Like my own private show."

Air rushes out through my nose. "Was it now?"

"Oh, you know. As in, I've never watched another creative mastermind at work before." She smiles and a little piece of cilantro is stuck at her gumline. Adorable.

"I'm no genius, that's for sure." I indicate she has something in her tooth.

She closes her mouth tight and I can see her tongue going over her teeth. She smiles at me. The cilantro is now stuck in her bottom row. I laugh and shake my head. Walking over, I use the tip of my napkin to remove the green bit. Still up in her face, I say, "There. All gone."

"Thanks," is her throaty response.

We stay like this for a couple of beats, her lips looking plumper by the second. The pulse at her neck pounds in a staccato rhythm. I grab her shoulders, squeezing and releasing them in time with her body's reaction. Faster and faster.

She emits a small gasp.

With deliberate slowness, I close the gap between us. Not once does she protest what's about to happen.

My lips cover hers, and I taste the Arroz con Pollo and the tea, plus something uniquely McKenna. Her arms come around my shoulders and I pull her upward, aligning her body with mine. Extending my tongue to her lips, she opens for me. Her hands climb into my hair.

She moans softly and I wrap my arms around her back, her tits slamming into my chest. I groan at the impact. Pulling my lips away from hers, I trail kisses down her throat. Her fingers rake through my hair, scraping my scalp.

Biting the shell of her ear, I return to her mouth. My hand slides around and cups her tit through her blouse. My cock strains against my shorts.

All of a sudden, Bans barks, jumps up and licks my face, breaking our embrace. McKenna races for safety around the island.

"Bans, down!" I look over at McKenna, who's hiding her beautiful face behind her hands. "I swear, she's never like this." Maybe because McKenna's the first woman I've brought here—Ginger doesn't count.

Bans obeys and sits at my heel. McKenna heads to the living room, where I hear the zipper on her bag close. Commanding Bans to stay, I join her there.

"I have to head over to the Jade in a few minutes. Want to come with?"

She shakes her head. She repeats a similar excuse as last night. "I can't tonight. But knock 'em dead."

I smile and run my hand through her hair, playing with the purple streak. "You didn't answer my question from before. Want to set up shop here while we're working on the Project? You can get a pipeline to my new songs." I don't confess she's my new muse, but I suspect she already knows it.

"So long as that's the only pipeline I'm getting, sounds good. I'll see you tomorrow, Ozzy."

Ten

MCKENNA

THE NEXT MORNING, I WALK OUT OF MY bedroom and bump into Mom. "Oh, sorry! I didn't see you there."

"It's okay, McKenna. I heard you up and was coming to see what you'd like for breakfast."

I check the clock. Ozzy didn't ask me over for a specific time, and I want to share a good morning with Mom, since it looks like she's herself for now. Besides, Elaine doesn't come for another hour.

"What are you having?"

"I was thinking scrambled eggs. You know, the ones you like, with the cheese in them."

My mouth waters. She hasn't made these in so long—and no matter how hard I try, I can't replicate her recipe. "Sounds good to me." I place my laptop case by the door and join her in the kitchen.

We talk about all sorts of topics, like we used to do. Before Mom's memory started failing. Before Daddy was killed. Placing those awful thoughts back into their proper mental compartment, I engage about her plans for the day.

"So, I was thinking about going shopping for a new dress."

I blink several times. She doesn't get out much anymore—only to doctor appointments. "Oh?"

"Yeah." She motions to the blue dress she's wearing. "I like this one, but I need something new. Maybe in purple." She picks up my hair. "Like this."

"Sounds good to me."

"I can wear it tomorrow. It's Thanksgiving, you know. We still need to go grocery shopping."

How could I have forgotten? It's my favorite holiday—but Ozzy's been taking up so much space in my brain that there's been little room for other things. Not even Mom. Better right this train, pronto. "You'll look beautiful. I'm making us a turkey." Thank God I ordered it a month ago. It's been brining for a few days. "And I have a grocery delivery scheduled."

She nods. "Great! I'll make the side dishes today, so all we have to do is heat them up tomorrow." Yes. Just like old times. Only now Elaine will be here to ensure there's no mishaps.

Plating the scrambled eggs and bacon, she tells me to set the table then joins me with the plates. We both dig in. "This is the best, Mom," I say between mouthfuls.

"I agree," say says, enjoying her breakfast. "So tell me, what's your new project all about?"

"I'm finishing up the graphics for the local charity that fosters art in schools. Working with a musician who's writing new songs for it." I take my last bite of my eggs. "I think it's my best work."

"Sounds great, McKenna. You're going to have to show it to me when you're done."

Once we finish and clean up, I pick up my laptop case. Since she's doing so well, I think it's safe for me to leave before Elaine gets here. She'll be here soon anyway. "I'll be home around the same time as the past few days, around six or so. I might eat while I'm out, though. I have a lot of work to do."

"Have fun with Mateo!"

I stop as if I hit a brick wall. With deliberate movements, I turn to face Mom, whose eyes have taken on a cloudy sheen. I remind myself she doesn't know what she said. She doesn't remember what my ex-boyfriend did to Daddy and to me. But I do for the both of us.

Inhaling air instead of gulping it, I reply, "Matt's away." Hopefully I'll never have to see his face ever again. He still has years to go. Forever's too short. Needing an escape, my hand reaches out for the doorknob. "I've got to get to work."

"Oh, right. Of course, dear." She smiles and sits down on her chair in front of the television.

Placing my work bag on the floor, I move to kneel at her feet. "You know, on second thought, work can wait for a little bit."

"I don't want you to get in trouble with your boss."

"Everything will be fine, Mom." She forgot I was fired and started my own freelance career, and I'm sure she's forgotten our breakfast conversation already. I stroke her hair. "Would you like to do some knitting?"

"Sounds delightful." She looks around for her yarn and picks it up. "What would you like me to make for you?"

"Anything you make would be wonderful."

"I think I'll make you a hat. I've never made one before, so it might be a little funny, but you'll like it, I hope. You'll need something to keep your head warm since the weather's changing." She smiles and the knitting needles clack.

I have an entire drawer full of hats she's made me, including one from a couple of nights ago. Stroking her hair, I reply, "I look forward to seeing the finished product." Why can't they find a cure for dementia? Closing my eyes, I count backward from ten.

The front door opens and Elaine pops in. I stand and greet her, motioning toward the kitchen. "Mom had a great morning, she even made us breakfast and knew tomorrow's Thanksgiving. I was getting ready to leave when her mind flaked out."

Elaine glances toward the living room. "She looks involved in her knitting. I'll make sure to keep her engaged and hopefully this episode passes."

"Thanks. Having you with her is a godsend." I hug her, kiss Mom's forehead and leave for Ozzy's, my mind mourning the slow loss of the woman who used to be my rock.

Before long, I pull into his driveway and shut off my car. It's later than I've come here before, so hopefully he's done with his naked morning swim. Not that I minded the view. Damn, the man is hot. Scorching. I shake my head—get your head out of the gutter, girl.

No matter the kiss between us yesterday. He was just excited to have written a new song. Maybe now he sees he doesn't need Luis. What a terrible position Platinum put him in, though.

Today has to be about creating graphics for his new song. No more kissing. No more wanting to rub my hands—and more—all over his perfect body. No more remembering how well he knows how to use his huge cock. *No. More.*

He's reckless and only out for fun. And I've had enough fun. Look where it landed me.

My vow to Daddy resurfaces. Mom's slow descent away from me is all the ammo I need to refocus.

I ring the doorbell and Ozzy answers. I muster some lighthearted wit to keep the darkness from taking hold. He certainly doesn't need that. "And you're dressed!"

He wraps his hand around his neck. "Yeah. Happens sometimes." He opens the door wider. "Come on in."

I walk down the tile floor toward the living room. His hand encircles my elbow, causing my breath to hitch. "No, wait. I want to work in the music room today." He points to a different hall.

Tamping down my body's reaction to his, I remind myself this is his gig. Wherever he feels comfortable writing is good with me, so I follow his directions. He leads me into a cavernous room, larger than the living room, which I thought was huge. His guitar is there, together with another, electric one. Keyboards and a small drum set also are set up. A round table covered in sheet music is off to the side. It easily could seat eight, maybe ten people. Recording equipment is across the room from the table. A sectional and other cushy chairs complete the room.

I wander from instrument to instrument, and run my fingers over his acoustic guitar. "Impressive, Mr. Martinez."

He waves his hand. "It's a music room."

"I've only ever been in Cole's, and I think yours is bigger."

He smirks. My core tightens. Traitor. "That's what all the girls say."

I shake my head. "Not anymore."

He snaps his fingers. "Rose. Right."

Needing a break from his intensity, I walk over to the bank of windows overlooking the pool. Without turning my head, I ask, "Did you swim today?"

"Yeah. Wasn't as much fun without you waiting for me, though." His last words skim across my ear.

Closing my eyes, I remind my body who's in charge. *Me.* I'm the one who needs to tamp down her feelings and overrule my urges. Swallowing sawdust, I reply, "Gotta keep you on your toes." I turn my head, almost bumping into his nose. Taking a step backward, I say, "So, let me hear what you've got."

"Right to work, huh? You know what they say about all work and all that jazz."

"I'm excited to hear what you did to the song last night." I pause. "Assuming you put finishing touches on it?"

He backs away from me. Good. I didn't want him so close anyway.

Riiight.

He offers a shy smile. Shy, ha! Ozzy doesn't have a shy bone in his body. *Bone.* Crap. I did not go there. His next words cut my thoughts off.

"Actually, I did work on it after the show.'" He retreats from me and picks up his guitar.

Smoothing my already straight hair with shaky fingers, I proceed to sit in one of the chairs. It swivels and rocks. Nice. I turn and give him my singular attention. "Can't wait!" I smile and urge him to start singing. To take me away from the voices inside my head.

"Well, here you go." He plays the now-familiar melody and then his baritone wades in. The hard-hitting song draws me in and I lean slightly forward in the chair. He stands in the middle of the room, eyes closed, performing for one. I breathe when he does. It's like I'm hypnotized, under his sexy spell.

Finished, he moves his guitar to his side. Then he opens his eyes and seeks mine. The dark brown of his eyes appears deeper.

He stands in silence. Waiting.

"Ozzy, that was incredible!" I jump up but stop myself from racing into his arms. "I loved what you did, the changes you made. The amped-up Latin beat. It's really, really good."

"You think?"

"I know. I bet you'll hit the top of the charts when it's released."

He makes a sound, somewhere between a chuckle and a snort.

I reach down and take my laptop out of its case. "Would you mind playing it again for me? I want to see what other graphics I can come up with to go with the song, now that it's basically finished."

As I power up the computer, he strolls right behind me. Yesterday's piece pops up, which I analyze. It captures something intangible. The routine pieces I've been doing for clients over the past years fall away as sparks from Ozzy's new music takes hold.

"This one's pretty good but something's not quite right." If the couple were positioned differently.... Because the Project is a non-profit on a tight budget, I can't hire a photographer to take pictures of models in poses I request, so off to stock photos I go. When I find a couple on a beach I like, I download it and then play around with the background and other stuff. Flip the models around. Add lighting streaks. It's nearly there.

"Wow. You're really good at this. What a great image to go along with the song. Like you're taking my music and making it artwork."

I jump, forgetting Ozzy was standing behind me while I was working. "Oh, thanks."

"Want to hear it again?"

I nod. He starts the song and I keep refining this graphic. As I'm working, I glance at Ozzy, who saunters over to the keyboard. He plays some notes and writes down the music. We continue like this for a long while. It's the most erotic experience I've had with my clothes on.

I've now created several graphics to go along with the feel of the song. I'm not sure what was going on inside of his head when he wrote it—I can guess but certainly am not going to probe—but these graphics tell a great story. I'm not done, but I'm starting to see a novel storyboard come together.

Holding up my cell phone, I ask, "Would you mind playing 'Take Me' once more so I can record it? This way, I can continue working on it tomorrow."

Thanksgiving.

Before I can stop myself, I ask, "Do you have plans for Thanksgiving?" Brilliant move, McKenna. It's not like I can invite him over to Mom's—what if she has an episode while he's there?

"Yeah. Aiden invited me over to his family's."

My body relaxes. Close one. "Oh. Good. I wouldn't want you to be alone on the holiday."

He nods, his eyes searching mine. Does he want an invitation to my house? Well, that's not happening. I incline my head toward his guitar. "The song?"

"Oh. Right."

I press record on my phone while he sings the brand-new melody. Each time he sings it, he tweaks it a bit to make it even more perfect. When he finishes, I say, "That was the best yet."

"Thanks." He puts his guitar down. "Want to take a break?"

I peer over my laptop screen at the man who's haunting my days and nights. A couple more weeks and I'll be finished with this part of the Project. I won't have any reason to spend more time with him. I can hang onto my sanity for that long.

"It's not lunchtime yet."

"Not everything revolves around food."

Ha! He obviously doesn't know me too well. I press Save. "What do you have in mind?"

"Well, you took me on a dune buggy ride, so I was thinking—how about we up the ante and go skydiving?"

"I'm not an adrenaline junkie like you," I squeak.

He chuckles. "Not from a plane. The indoor one, at the Jade."

"Oh. I've heard good things about it." When the Jade was built a few years ago, they put in one of these attractions.

"I have passes."

I'm not the type of girl who hangs on Ozzy's arm in public. Besides, I don't want to be. *Keep telling yourself that, McKenna.* "As much fun as that sounds—" I stop myself. *Fun.* That's what he needs in order to create. It worked yesterday, after all. I guess I have to suck it up if he's going to write more songs. And I'm going to finish the Project. This is for work. "On second thought, sure. Why not?"

"Great. I'll go put in a call and be back in a sec."

While he's making arrangements, I putter around his music room. Funny, it's both lived in yet impersonal. It doesn't have any personal touches. No photos, no knickknacks. I look over the sheet music, featuring scribbles and cross-outs. It's a good song. A really good song. I can already hear it on the radio. See him performing it onstage to screaming fans. Tossing bras.

"Ready?"

Ozzy pops his head into the room, now in low-slung jeans and a Jade T-shirt straining over his broad chest and arms. His nipple rings protrude. Man, he's too hot for his own good. And mine.

"Yup."

We head to the garage and he backs his motorcycle out. I point to my car. "I'll drive myself and meet you at the Jade. That way, you can stay there for your concert tonight. I have to prep for Thanksgiving, so I can't make it."

His jaw tightens, but he acquiesces and hops on his bike. Trailing Shirley, my eyes roam over him. He's sexy as fuck. And creative to boot. My hands tighten on the steering wheel. Remember your priorities, girl.

Soon, we arrive at the Jade. We go into a side entrance, through the bell captain's office. "Hey, Bobby," Ozzy greets one of the workers.

"You're here early," he replies.

"Going to enjoy some of what the Jade has to offer before the show."

Bobby nods and opens a door leading to another back hallway. At the end, we turn right and Ozzy knocks at a door marked "Concierge." So this is how Shelia pops out of nowhere.

As if my thoughts conjured her up, Shelia opens the door. "Ozzy, come on in." Her eyes seek out his guest. "Oh. McKenna!"

I give my friend a hug and whisper, "I'm working with him on the Artist Adventure Avenue Project." Can't have her thinking I'm his latest bedwarmer. Because I'm not. My eyes travel to his fine backside. *Definitely not.* I follow Ozzy into the office.

Shelia explains that we have to walk through the casino to get to the elevator bank, which will take us to the "Skydiving Extravaganza." She says she'll take us, but he'll be exposed, so we need to move quickly. The skydiving people will call her when we're through and she'll return to escort us back down to the lobby.

Seems like a lot of cloak and dagger stuff to me, but then again, Ozzy is the resident star of the Jade, so he needs to be protected.

"Thanks, Shelia," I say, earning a swift look from Ozzy. To him, I explain, "We've known each other forever."

He nods. "I'm ready when you are." He puts on his dune buddy baseball cap.

Soon, we're crossing through the casino, the familiar bells and rings and dings of gamblers on the machines providing our playlist. We move at a good clip—not too fast so as to garner attention, yet by no means are we strolling. Actually, I need to do a jog every fifth step or so just to keep up with their longer strides. A group of people head our way and Ozzy keeps his head down. His arm extends toward mine and he entwines our fingers, pulling me close. I land at his side on a half jump.

My head knows he's using me as a human shield. After all, no one would think *the* Ozzy Martinez would be out and about with a short, curvy girl like me. His ruse works as we pass by them without incident.

I try to release my hand, but his tightens around mine. Like he wants to hold it. I focus on maintaining my pace to keep up with theirs.

Finally, we arrive at the elevators. Ozzy's hand goes from holding mine to wrapped around my shoulders. The bill of his cap hits the top of my head. He's got this hiding in plain sight thing down really well.

The elevator cab arrives and the three of us hop on. Shelia presses some keys and the doors close before anyone else can get on with us. I step out of Ozzy's one-armed embrace and try to hide my labored breathing over such a quick race through the casino. Of course, neither he nor Shelia are breathing heavy.

"You did great, Ozzy," Shelia says. "When the doors open, turn left and we'll be at the registration desk for the Skydive Extravaganza. You're already checked in, and Kacey will take you from there."

"Thanks so much, Shelia," Ozzy says. He reaches for my hand again. I'm too focused on my breathing to register what he just did. "We appreciate it."

We?

The elevator doors ping open and we turn left. A beautiful, tall, thin blonde—of course, why is everyone tall, thin and blonde in this town?—greets us. Not wanting to give Shelia the wrong impression, I catch her before she pops back onto the elevator.

"Seriously, Shelia. This is business-related."

"Listen, if I could get that man to so much as wink at me, I would. You go enjoy...your business meeting." She kisses my cheek and disappears.

Sighing, I trudge back to the skydiving reception area, but it's empty save for some tourists filling out paperwork. I find Ozzy and the blonde around the corner.

"There you are," Ozzy says, handing me a clipboard. "We have to fill this out."

I make quick work of the paperwork and both of us hand it in to Kacey the Blonde. She looks everything over, her eyes halting on my response weight. I guess NOYB—None of Your Business—isn't what she expected.

Her pen taps on my papers. I jut my chin, not giving an inch. She writes something and then says, "Follow me."

We're brought into a small room with a video explaining what we're going to experience and gives us instructions about what position to maintain while we're "skydiving." Then we have to practice holding the "superman" pose.

"I'll go first," Ozzy volunteers. Maybe he'll get a passing grade and can go gear up while I attempt to get into this embarrassing position.

Ozzy hops on the wooden table-like thingy and gets into "Superman" without any issue. His lithe form stretches into the pose like he was built for it. Damn. Kacey walks around him and declares, "Perfect."

I'll say.

Smiling, he stands and rubs his hands together to announce, "Your turn, McKenna."

Great. I look around but the door to the room remains closed. No way out. Sighing, I flop like a beached whale onto the bench and stretch my arms and legs out. Kacey adjusts all of my limbs, puts her hand under my chin so I'm looking up, and places her hand on my lower back. I feel like pretzel dough getting ready to be rolled out.

"Now take a breath," Kacey instructs.

Like anyone can breathe in this position. I try to force some air through my nose. Kacey moves my arm up, then my leg. I struggle to maintain the arch in my back while tipping my head up.

"Head up, McKenna."

I close my eyes. Maybe this was a worse idea than I thought. And I wasn't all that into it before.

Kacey says, "Okay, you're good."

I collapse onto the wood bench, my hands and feet hitting the floor and my chin resting on the hard surface. Seriously? How am I going to be able to do this?

"It's much easier when there's a fan pushing you ten feet up," Kacey says.

I guess there's that.

Ozzy chuckles and taps my back. I turn my head, still not ready to relinquish my position oozing over my bench. "Let's go get our gear. I can't wait to see you all bundled up like the Michelin Man."

No worries about being mistaken for sexy here. I try to dismount gracefully, but my foot catches on the wooden leg and I fly forward, the bench turning over.

"Oh!"

Ozzy grabs me by the shoulders and pulls me upright. "Gotcha!"

I throw my head back and look into his sparkling eyes, so alive and filled with excitement. This. This is why I'm here, to bring fun back into his life so he can compose songs again. And then I can finish up the Project and get paid. *Nothing else.*

I smile and hold onto him while I regain my equilibrium. "Thanks."

He doesn't let me go, just holds me like he needs me to survive. I can't move a muscle, I'm so enthralled. Kacey clears her throat and we disengage.

She hands us puffy suits, helmets, goggles and even boots and brings us to an office to change. "Normally, you'd get suited up in the lockers but because of your celebrity," she looks directly at Ozzy, "we thought you'd be more comfortable in here," Kacey explains.

"Appreciate it," he responds and starts getting into the gear.

"Yeah, good call," I say. Not seeing any other way around this, I put the jumpsuit on over my clothes as well.

Soon, we're both dressed in the most unflattering suits ever. We both look like Weebles! I start laughing. I bet Ozzy's never been compared to a Weeble before. Me, on the other hand, well…

Ozzy joins my laughter and grabs my gloved hand, twirling me around. He chest-bumps me and I go flying backward. He catches my arms and brings me back to him. "You look adorable."

"And you look like a Weeble," I manage to get out.

We're laughing when the door opens and an unsuited Kacey enters, followed by a guy in a similar suit. "This is Brian, and he's going to be your guide in the skydiving room. Have fun."

Fun. There's that word again. Yes, we are having fun.

We follow Brian into a padded room with a huge fan in its center. Brian shows us what to do and I generously let Ozzy go first. He flies up in the air like a pro, whooping it up. When he lands, it's my turn. I dive into the Superman position over the fan and lift my chin upward like I was told. Brian yells instructions to me from the floor, and I self-correct, but I'm doing it. I'm weightless and flying through the air like Superman.

As I flutter near the ceiling, all of the weight of my worries falls away. I'm free! I wish I could stay up here forever. Thoughts of Daddy cheering me on bring a smile to my face, replaced by sadness that he's gone. And my role in his death. I lose my balance and tumble to the floor. When it's my turn again, I banish all bad thoughts and sail away.

After two more turns each, Brian cuts the fan and ushers us back into the office. My cheeks hurt from smiling so much. We hand him our goggles and helmets and he closes the door for us to take off the rest of the gear.

"How fucking amazing," Ozzy's baritone booms. He unzips the jumpsuit and it falls to the floor. He kicks it to the side and takes off the boots, standing in stocking feet.

"I had a blast," I respond. I unzip my jumpsuit and peel myself out of it.

Before I can stoop down to take off my boots, he picks me up and hugs me to his lean body. "Thank you."

My arms go around his neck and I hold onto him, my booted feet dangling. "You're welcome, crazy. Now let me get my boots off."

He leans back, his eyes bouncing from my feet back to my face. No, not face. Lips. Oh no.

I shake my head. "Ozzy—"

He growls. "I'll help you get something off, that's for sure."

His lips crash down on mine, his tongue seeking entrance right away. I keep my lips shut, so he traces them instead.

Sensations of feeling sexy and wanted ricochet through my body. Discounting our kiss yesterday, I haven't felt like this since, well, the last time I was *with* Ozzy—over a year ago at Rose's apartment. Maybe I can indulge him here for a minute. Let myself feel. I open my mouth a fraction and his tongue swoops in, punctuated by a low groan.

Still holding onto his shoulders as my feet haven't touched the floor, I maneuver one hand upward to the thick curls at the top of his head. Our kiss deepens and he slants his mouth over mine to get a new angle.

Then the door opens.

"Oh, excuse me. I didn't realize—"

The door closes, but our moment is over.

I pull my lips from his. "Put me down," I whisper.

Bending at his waist, he lowers my feet to the floor. Once I'm on steady ground, I pull away from his embrace, my heart going faster than the huge fan in the other room.

Am I already in too deep? Being with Ozzy is starting to feel a lot like jumping out of a plane and into thin air, all the damn time.

Eleven

OZZY

I DIG INTO THE HOMEMADE APPLE PIE. "This was awesome, Siobhan. Thanks for such a great meal. Aiden here is lucky to have you as his mom." I reach out and thump my assistant on the back.

Her cheeks pinken. "Why, thank you, Ozzy." She turns her attention to her son. "And Aiden would do well to remember that."

Aiden gives me a dirty look before popping more pie into his mouth. I decide to let the good-natured banter slide, and we enjoy the rest of the Thanksgiving feast. When we finish, I offer to help Siobhan clear the table but she shoos me out of the kitchen.

Grabbing a beer, I join Aiden and his sister and her kids in the family room. They're gathered around a large television where the football game plays. The kids are too young to really participate, but the older one is learning the rules of the game from his dad.

This scene reminds me of how things were with my family in Puerto Rico, with my cousins and extended family. We'd watch the game and then head outside to party all night long. Usually with Tío Miguel playing on the guitar.

I sigh. Everything's changed now.

Aiden captures my attention when he says, "I've noticed you've laid off the towel throwing at your shows."

I mull over his statement. The last time I tossed a towel into the audience was when McKenna was in attendance. Ever since then, I've been too focused on writing 'Take Me' to even bring anyone up to the Penthouse. Or distracted by *her*. I shrug. "I've been preoccupied."

Aiden turns and gives me his full attention. "With what, if not pus—" his eyes stray to the kids, "uhm, the ladies?"

I take a swig of beer. Might as well come clean. "I've been writing."

"Really? Hey, man, that's totally cool."

I place the bottle on the side table. "Yeah. I think it's a pretty good song. McKenna likes it."

"McKenna, huh?"

I've had more fun with McKenna since I can't remember when. And we've both been fully dressed the whole time. Well, mainly. I smirk, remembering a couple of early morning swims that ended up more fun than I had anticipated. If you consider self-torture fun. I'm certainly not in the market for anything long-term—and something tells me McKenna might be the long-term kind.

"She reminded me what fun is." I pick up my beer again.

"I bet." He snickers. "Guess I'm off the hook for giving her your home address."

My hands knead together. So, he's how she found out where I'm staying. She has some mad investigative skills. I lift my eyebrow and warn, "I didn't say that."

He grins at me and our conversation moves on to the game. When it's over, I stand and say goodbye to the room. Specifically to Siobhan, I say, "Thanks for having me over for Thanksgiving. It means a lot to me since I'm so far away from home." And I mean it. I kiss her cheek.

She hands me a container filled with enough food for three more meals. "You're welcome here anytime, Ozzy."

Aiden pipes up, "I'll walk you out."

Escorting me through the front door and out to my motorcycle, his eyes shine. "So, when can I hear your new song?"

Aiden's a great assistant. "Stop by tomorrow at the house and I'll play it for you."

"Cool."

We shake and I hop on Shirley. On the ride back to my place, I consider my newfound writing creativity. McKenna certainly woke something up in me when she took me to the dunes. It's like I've been hibernating and now I'm wide awake. Because of her.

I shake off my last thought. No. She just took me out so I could enjoy myself again. Outside of the bedroom. I've certainly been living it up in there. By twos and threes. Then why didn't my muse return until the girl with the multi-colored hair popped back into my life?

Walking into the house, Bans races to greet me. "Hey girl." I scratch behind her ears. She's the only girl worthy of my attention. Feeling the Thanksgiving meal settling around my torso, I ask, "Want to go outside and play?"

She barks and wags her tail. I give her some pieces of turkey and laugh. "C'mon, let's go."

We head outside and play fetch for a long while. The last time I throw the ball to her, instead of dropping it at my feet, she heads over to the grassy area on the side and plops down. Even with all this exercise, I still feel restless. My gaze lands on the pool.

After the meal at Aiden's, more laps can't hurt. I shed my clothes, dive into the pool and start swimming freestyle. Around lap twenty-five, visions of McKenna on the dune buggy and flying into the air at the indoor skydiving place yesterday start playing in a loop.

This needs to stop.

I need to fuck her again to get her out of my system.

I spend the remaining laps creating all sorts of scenarios where I seduce the delectable McKenna in random places, including this pool. Yeah, exactly what I need.

When I touch the wall for the last time, I stand up instead of swimming under the water to the other side. Bans is still sleeping so I walk up the side stairs. A slight noise to my left catches my attention.

McKenna stands by the patio table.

A smile creeps across my face. Maybe we can reenact the scenes that were running through my mind. Dripping onto the concrete, I stand with my arms to my sides. "Join me in The Lambada?"

She averts her gaze. "Don't you own a bathing suit?"

I chuckle and walk over to her. "I don't wear one in my own backyard, which is supposedly private."

"I thought you'd still be at Aiden's."

"Nope." She transfers a plate from one hand to the other, and I crane my neck to check it out. "What you got there?"

"Oh." She looks down and then her eyes widen. I've come to a halt in front of her and she gets an eyeful of all of me. "I brought you a treat." She shoves the plate into my stomach.

"Oof."

"Sorry." She pulls the plate back to her body.

Deciding to give her a break, I head to the shelves and pull out a towel. Wrapping it around my waist, I return to her side. "A treat? For me?"

She nods, the newly-dyed pink streak in her hair catching my attention. I twirl my fingers in it, water dripping from my arm.

"Yes. I thought you might enjoy it for Thanksgiving. I was going to leave it on your patio table."

My lips part. "Very thoughtful."

She chuckles. "Yeah. That's me. Thoughtful." She pushes the plate forward again, careful not to make contact with my body. "Here you go."

Through the plastic wrap, it looks like some sort of cake. "What is it?"

She turns her head toward Bans. "Something I made. I hope you like it."

Even though I'm still stuffed from dinner at Aiden's, I open the wrap and break off a little piece. I give it a quick sniff. Could it be? I put the bite into my mouth and savor the sweetness. "Tres Leches?"

"I found a recipe online."

"McKenna, this is amazing. Different from what my mother makes, but muy delicioso." I reach in and take another piece, larger this time. "Did you try it?"

"Yeah. We had it for dessert tonight, with pumpkin pie. I thought it was pretty good, but I don't have a basis of comparison."

"Did you enjoy your holiday?"

"Yes."

"Great." I steal another bite. "I'd eat this whole thing, but I just came back from Aiden's and I'm stuffed. That's why I was swimming—needed to work off Thanksgiving calories." I pat my stomach.

She giggles, but it sounds self-depreciating to my ears. "You look like you could lick the plate clean and still not have an ounce of fat on you."

I moisten my lips. "I can think of something I'd like to lick all over."

Her hand plants directly on my now-dry pecs, her finger tapping a steady beat. "You."

I grab her wrist and hold it on my chest. "And you." I take the plate from her other hand and place it on the table.

"Well, I was only going to drop this off and leave, so I should be going."

Now that she's here, literally in my grasp, she's not going anywhere until we reenact my fantasies from the pool. "Stay."

She takes in a harsh breath. "No, I really have to go."

Wrapping my fingers around her wrist, overlapping my thumb and middle finger, I lean to her ear. "Dance with me."

"There's no music."

"McKenna, you're in the home of a music man." I drop her hand and pick up my cell. After tapping a few things on the screen, some seductive Puerto Rican music comes over the sound system. "Now this is music. Do you know how to salsa?"

"Not really."

I teach her the basic steps. Soon, we're moving in time with the Latin beat, hips swiveling in harmony, my towel flapping against my legs. I twirl her and she bounces around, a big smile across her face. The beats animate my hips as I keep time with the rhythm. When the song ends, another salsa comes on and we continue this way through four more songs.

Huffing, she exclaims, "No more! I need a break!"

I twirl her one last time, then pull her in for a hug. "Thank you." I move damp hair off her forehead and kiss the space between her eyebrows.

Beside me, she stiffens. Her hand slips down my shoulder. I want her much more compliant than this. Like how I remember her, all wild and freaky.

I kiss her cheek.

"Ozzy," she says on an exhale.

My next kiss lands on her lips. I move mine over hers in exploration while the playlist changes to a more sultry rhumba. My hands frame her face, thumbs skimming her cheeks.

Angling her head to the side, I deepen the kiss, offering her my tongue. She opens for me and her tongue swirls against mine. Fireworks go off inside my head. My cock stirs to life underneath the towel.

"More," I growl.

"God."

I pull back. "Nope. But I'm going to make you see heaven tonight."

She blinks, then a giggle escapes her luscious mouth. "Does that ever work?"

"Huh?"

Her hand slides down my chest, stopping above my belly button. "Keep your lines for the towel girls, okay?"

I grab her hand and bring it down over my hard cock. "How about this? Do I need to keep this under wraps, too?"

Her fingers curl around my cock so the outline of my erection is clearly visible through the towel. "Well..."

I don't wait for her to finish her sentence. My arms go around her waist, landing on her ass. Squeezing, I pull her tight against my body.

Her lips latch onto my nipple ring, which causes my balls to tighten against the fabric of the towel. Releasing the ring, she tilts her head up.

Two can play at this game—and win. My fingers reach for the bottom of her shirt and lift it up her body, over her arms and toss it somewhere on the concrete. While the fingers on my left hand play with the generous cup, my right reaches behind her. Ping! Her bra comes undone and it joins her shirt on the ground.

I flick her nipple. "Better. Now we're both topless." I bend down—way down—my mouth circling her pebbled nipple over and over. And over. Her back bends so her tit is pushed closer to my mouth. Only then do I close my teeth around it.

"Oh!"

"Like that?" I nip it again.

Squirming in my arms, she gasps, "Yes."

My hands return to her ass while my cock pushes at her stomach. Leaving her delightful tits, I return to her mouth and devour it.

Her breathing comes in rapid pants. We need to be horizontal. Or at least with some kind of surface behind us. The chaise looks perfect.

I pick her up and walk over to the chair and sit, pulling her body across my now naked one. Somewhere from there to here, I lost my towel. Whatever.

I trail kisses down her neck and return to her full tits. D cup, if I'm not mistaken. And all natural. I knead one while suckling on the other. Long pulls followed by short nibbles cause her body to writhe in time.

My hand slides downward and around her full hips. Curvy. Not all bony like some of the stick figures who have graced my bed. No. McKenna's all woman. As I reach for the zipper on her skirt, her hand closes around my cock and I lose all sense of place and time.

Collapsing back onto the lounger, I can do nothing more than watch her work her magic on me. "One of us needs to get naked. Now."

She lowers her eyes and licks her lips. "Looks like one of us already is."

I bite her pink nipple. Standing her upright, I tug on her skirt and work it down her legs, finally dropping it on the ground to take in the beauty before me. She's wearing lacy pink panties, which match the streak in her hair. "Do you match your hair and your panties on purpose?"

She bites her bottom lip. "I like to be color-coordinated."

Chuckling, I quip, "You give new meaning to matching the carpet with the drapes."

She giggles while my free hand reaches out to the elastic around her waist, but she stops me. Whatever. We'll get there soon enough. Redirecting my path, I pull her down onto my lap so she's straddling me. "I can smell how turned on you are." I inhale. "So good."

Her hips roll in a circle around my cock and her finger snakes down to play with my Prince Albert piercing. Large latte eyes meet mine. "Wow."

"The ladies love it." *Shit.* Never mention other women when you're with one, you idiot.

Her tone drops lower than the ground. "Oh."

Her face goes from sexy and turned on to closed off in an instant. The next second, she's off my lap and, in a whirl of clothing, somewhat dressed and racing away from me. At the side gate, she pauses.

"I'm glad you reminded me when to throw in the towel. Happy Thanksgiving, by the way," she says, her hand at the latch.

Then, just as unexpectedly as she blew in, she's gone.

Naked and alone, I collapse onto the lounger that was the scene of a much more fun tryst moments ago. Running fingers through my hair, I mumble, "You may not have deserved what Teresa did to you, but you sure as hell deserved this."

Twelve

MCKENNA

"WHAT WAS I THINKING LAST NIGHT?" I toss a maxi dress over my head and shake out my hair. "I'm playing with fire, and I always get burned." I step into a pair of sandals.

"The ladies love it," I mimic his tone.

Planting myself at my makeup table, I make quick work of powder, eyeshadow, mascara and blush. "I'll only get hurt if I spend any more time alone with him." I select red lipstick and blot it. I continue my soliloquy, "I have responsibilities, which don't include childish pursuits of tattooed men with piercings on all parts of their bodies. No matter how hot they are. Or how creative."

As I'm clipping my hair into a funky style, something shatters in the kitchen. Closing my eyes, I mutter, "Here we go."

I go to find out what broke. Mom stands in the middle of the kitchen, her arms around her waist. A broken crystal decanter, if I'm not mistaken, lies by her naked feet. "Mom! Stay right there. Don't move," I order and rush for the dustpan.

"I'm so sorry, Sissie. It was so pretty I couldn't help myself."

Sissie. Her sister was killed by a drunk driver when she was eighteen. Moderating my voice, I respond, "Everything's okay. I'll get this cleaned up in no time." I sweep the broken shards.

She takes a step to the right.

"No! Don't move," I bark. Tears well up in her eyes. After taking a cleansing breath, I say, "I don't want you to get hurt, okay?"

She nods. "Thank you, Sissie. You always look out for me."

I work in silence. "There. I think I got it all, but stay here for a moment while I get your slippers. Can you do that for me, Mom?"

Her head cocks to the right. "Mom's not here, right? I don't want to get in trouble."

I bite the inside of my cheek. "No, ah, Janice. Mom's not here. Now, stay put for me, okay?"

She nods. I race to her room and pull out a pair of slippers. When I return to the kitchen, Mom's not where I left her but is standing at the counter next to the coffeemaker. "Oh, there you are. I was about to make some coffee. Want some?"

Unsure of who she's speaking to, I answer with a simple, "Yes." Placing her slippers at her feet, I tell her to put them on, which she does.

Once our coffees are made, and I've scrubbed the floor, she makes omelets for us. "So tell me, what were you up to last night, McKenna? I heard you come in late."

Relieved she knows she's talking with me—her daughter—and she remembers last night, I take my last bite of omelet and stand. "I dropped off some of the Tres Leches cake at a friend's house as a Thanksgiving treat." Close enough to the truth.

As I'm putting our plates into the dishwasher, she says, "I like the dress you have on. Your hair, on the other hand, looks like a witch's nest."

I walk over to the mirror and realize she's correct. Giggling, I say, "You're right, Mom. Like usual." I remove some of the clips. "I'm going to fix it now."

With my hair in a much more becoming style, I walk Mom into the living room just as Elaine steps in for her shift. I pull the nurse to the side and explain what happened earlier.

She puts her hand on my arm. "She's back to herself now. As you know, this disease is brutal and she'll flip from decade to decade and memory to memory at the drop of a hat. My advice to you is to enjoy her while she's with us."

I look over at Mom, who is competing with the contestants on *The Price is Right*. Smiling, I decide not to go to Ozzy's today and spend the day with her, while she's still mentally here. I take a seat next to her and join the game. Mom wins both showcases and gloats for five full minutes.

"Well, loser makes the winner pastries. How does that sound?"

"Oh, yeah. Can you make me the ones with the cheese inside?" She licks her lips.

Laughing, I agree and start toward the kitchen. A knock at the front door derails me. "I'll get it."

Our neighbor Becky stands at the front porch. "I was hoping Janice would be okay today. I miss her. Just wanted to drop in and say hello like old times."

I nod. "She had a rough morning, but she seems to be perfectly fine now." I open the door wider. "Come on in, she's in the living room."

"Great," she says, breezing by me to join Mom, who adopts her polite mask that I know hides her inability to remember the person in front of her.

I jump to her rescue. "Isn't it great Becky, our neighbor, came over to visit with us today, Mom?"

Mom keeps her polite smile on her face while she greets Becky who, apparently, doesn't pick up on Mom's confusion. After the two exchange pleasantries, Becky points to the wingback chair, "I'll take my usual seat."

"Of course," Mom replies and then her face morphs with recognition. "I swear, I should have your name engraved on the chair!"

Exhaling with relief that Mom's back, I head back to the kitchen. Soon, their voices rise, punctuated with laughter.

I roll out the dough for Mom's win, the way Grandma Gertie taught me. Forming the pastries onto a sheet pan lined with parchment paper, I insert jelly in some and cheese in others. Once the oven is up to temperature, I wash my hands and go in search of my phone to call Grandma Gertie about my recent baking exploits.

I pick it up from my bed and am greeted by three missed texts. Wonderful. I open the first, from Rose. It's a photo of her and Cole enjoying their honeymoon. Greece, if I'm not mistaken. They look tanned and so very happy. My stomach twinges.

Typing a quick note back to her, I move onto the next text, this one from Felicia at the Project. I reply with a quick update, saying I'm working on the final set of songs now. Not a lie. If only Ozzy would finish up his songs, I could bang out the graphics and move on with my life.

Bang. Mental images of Ozzy banging me in all different positions around his house pop into my mind. Stop. It.

I go to the final text. Speak of the devil. Shit. My finger hovers over the icon to open it. After an internal debate, I decide to read it.

I'm an idiot. I'm sorry about last night. But, I started another new song and I'd love your opinion. Please.

When the pain in my jaw captures my attention, I release my clenched teeth. If I'm going to finish the Project and get into the running for the national competition—earning enough money for around-the-clock nursing care at home for Mom—I'm going to have to listen to this song. But that doesn't mean I have to work at his house all the time. I respond:

Sorry, I'm busy today.

Why did I look for my phone in the first place? Oh, right. Grandma Gertie. Before I can pull up her contact, the oven timer beeps. I return to the kitchen and pull the cookie sheets out, scrutinizing each pastry to ensure they're properly cooked. Satisfied, I place the cooked ones onto a rack to cool and stick the last of the batter into the oven.

As I pick up my phone to call Grandma Gertie, a text pings. Ozzy. Again.

Are you sure you can't stop by the house? I promise not to take up too much of your time.

My shoulders droop. He did apologize for being an ass. And I know how protective he is of his new work, especially since he's been in such a dry spell. Creativity-wise, that is. And before him, so had I. Reluctantly, I reply:

I'll try.

I'll be there when I'm there. And I'll keep my clothes *on*, thank you very much.

Checking the timer on the oven, I place a quick call to Grandma Gertie, telling her I'm making her pastries. "Girl, you go and enjoy them. They're one of my favorite recipes."

"Ours too."

"How's your Mama doing?"

She's the only person on earth who I've told about Mom. "She's doing really well now. This morning, she thought I was her sister for a while."

She clucks. "I'm so sorry. Dementia is an awful disease, stealing yourself right out from under you."

"Don't I know it." The timer goes off and I remove the last batch from the oven. Inhaling their delicious scent, I tell her they're done and end the conversation. Short and sweet. Like her.

Smiling, I load some of the cooled pastries onto a tray and bring them into the living room. "Mom, you get first pick."

Her eyes—clear and excited—light up. I point to the cheese one and she bites into it. "Oh my, this is truly decadent."

Becky and Elaine take theirs and offer similar praise. I grab a jelly one and return to the living room, where Elaine is setting up a game of Scrabble. I look from Elaine to Becky, and then to Mom who's rubbing her hands together, declaring she's going to wipe the floor with them, and smile. Scrabble's a great game for the memory. I mouth thanks to Elaine and smile as I enjoy my jelly-filled pastry.

I'm the first one out. "Geez, you guys are sharks."

Laughter ensues. I head into my room and grab my laptop. Today's turning out to be a good day for Mom, so I decide to bite the bullet and head to Ozzy's now. Returning to the kitchen, I place a few pastries onto a paper plate. Even if I'm not going to sleep with him, he might like these. Besides, if I keep them here, I'll eat all of them by myself, which won't be good.

Waving to the women in the living room, who are in the middle of a heated debate over whether "THYZE" is a word, I stuff another pastry in my mouth and head out the door.

Once I arrive at Ozzy's place, I give myself another pep talk about staying fully-clothed and head to the front door. Ozzy, dressed—thankfully—in a dark blue polo shirt and khaki shorts, with sandals on his feet, answers.

I hold up the plate of pastries. "Brought you something."

His eyes light up like a child's and my stomach flips. Why is he so beautiful? I know he's a guy, and men aren't usually beautiful, but he is. He really is. *Remember yesterday.*

His baritone beckons me inside. "Thank you, McKenna. First Tres Leches and now this. You're spoiling me. What do we have here?"

"Pastries. Some are jelly filled and others have cheese."

He selects one—jelly—and takes a huge bite. About half of the pastry disappears. With crumbs and jelly stuck to his face, he says, "Amazing." He looks at the remainder. "Grandma Gertie's recipe?"

"Yup."

"Dayum, I love that woman." He motions for me to go to the music room, while he detours into the kitchen.

I hurry down the hallway and choose to sit on a chair at the table. Not the sofa, where he could crowd me. And his scent would envelope me. Not. Going. To. Happen.

I'm booting up my computer when Ozzy enters. He nods at me and walks over to his guitar. Looks like he has the same idea as me. What happened yesterday was a mistake that won't be repeated.

Then why has my chest tightened?

I busy myself by focusing on getting my graphics program up while he plays a few notes on the guitar. My program opens but I continue to stare at the screen rather than look at the rock god next to me. Finally, the strumming ends.

"So, it seems I now have two new songs."

Bracing myself for the impact of him with a guitar strapped around his torso, I glance at him and smile. "Great."

He nods. "Let me play you 'Take Me,' and then I'll be ready to let you be the first person to hear my new one, 'Honesty.' It's not done yet, though."

I bite my inner cheek at the song title, but I remain silent. Knowing he needs my encouragement—and I need his songs—I force my voice to be light and clap. "Can't wait!"

He plays his first song and I note the changes he's made. I bet he'll continue tinkering with it until it's recorded. And even afterwards, he'll tweak it for live performances. His imagination is inspiring.

When he finishes 'Take Me,' I smile. "That was great. I like what you did at the end."

"Gracías." He strums the guitar hard and fast. I cross my ankles and recross them, trying to stifle the shivers coursing through my body at the way he makes love to his instrument. Oblivious to my inner turmoil, Ozzy says, "Here's what I have so far for my next song. I'd like to know your opinion before I continue."

He values my opinion. Bowing my head, I give this honor the weight it deserves.

He clears his throat. "Here goes." He begins playing and the vibe in the room immediately changes from the hard-pounding sex beat of 'Take Me' to a power ballad. He sings of love and betrayal and pain and loss. Of being blindsided. And needing honesty.

Not complete, the song stops. I meet his eyes and see the turmoil behind them. This is raw. Clearing my throat, I say, "Wow. Ozzy, that is so, I don't know. It's real."

He takes his guitar off his shoulder. I continue, "I can hear it sung in a huge open-air stadium, with everyone holding up their cell phone lights." My voice drops, and I give him my honesty. "And wanting to give you a huge hug."

He opens his arms wide and, without thought, I jump up from my chair. My arms encircle his trim waist as his come down on my shoulders. He pulls me into the solid wall of his torso. With my flat sandals, I barely reach his collarbone.

I inhale the scent of his cologne, mixed with his natural musk. When I flex my arms, he reciprocates by kneading my shoulders. With all my senses heightened, I close my eyes and absorb his breathing. After a minute, my eyes open and I step back from his large body, my neck tilting upward.

I ask, "Care to talk about it?"

His hands caress my shoulders and move down my arms. I'm not sure he's even aware of what he's doing to my body because he seems locked away inside himself somewhere. If I'm going to be able to help him, though, being inside his embrace isn't the best option. "Let's sit down."

I turn toward the sofa, his hand sliding down my arm until our fingertips part. We sit. Half-turning to face him, I bring my leg up and under me. His gaze is on the floor.

Silence. I'm not sure if he's ever going to say anything, but I'm not going to be the one to break the quiet. Besides, he started it with his song.

"I'm not sure where to begin."

I place my hand on his forearm. "Wherever you'd like. I'll catch up." I offer a slight smile, which he returns.

He inhales, his chest expanding by half. "I think I'm ready for you to know about this. I'm not sure why."

I maintain my posture, afraid if I move a muscle wrong, he'll be scared off. "You don't have to tell me, if you don't want."

He chuckles. "Believe me, I don't want. But I have to, if I'm going to complete this song."

The way he's talking unnerves me. What does he have to share with me? I give him a slight smile of encouragement.

Stormy eyes meet mine. "I appreciate you, McKenna."

My tummy somersaults at his admission.

"I'm ready to let you in."

I swallow over his choice of words. I don't want to know. I'm not deserving of them—Matt made sure of that. Before I can voice my protest, he begins,

"I already told you about Luis, my ex-best friend and writing partner for all of the songs on my first album."

Because I can't form a syllable, I nod.

"What I didn't tell you is—" He clears his throat and chuckles. "This is more difficult than I thought it would be."

I place my hand on his arm, my index finger tracing the intricate tattoos there. "You don't have to."

"I do." He removes his arm from my fingers. I mourn the loss, until he continues. "You see, before this all started." He gestures toward the inside of his house. "It was just Luis and me. We wrote songs together. Hell, we went all through school together. Got into trouble. Shared women." He glances at me.

I shrug. His sexual past doesn't impact me. *Right*, keep telling yourself this, McKenna.

He continues, "We put a band together with a couple of guys from the neighborhood and picked up gigs around the island. Our songs were well received. And there were plenty of groupies."

He rubs his arms and sighs. "One night, I hooked up with this young woman. Teresa."

His words stop. A buzzing starts in my belly at the way he says her name.

"A few months later, Teresa and I became exclusive."

The buzzing travels up through my torso and lands somewhere around my heart. I place my hand there, unsure of what it is but not wanting to interrupt his story.

He clears his throat. "She was in her second year in college, and came to all of our gigs. That summer was the best. Even though my mother didn't approve, I asked Teresa to marry me—because no thirty-one-year-old wants to listen to his mother. We did the deed on the beach a month later."

The buzzing turns into needles piercing my heart. So what if he's married? I haven't slept with him. This time. Oh God, I slept with a married man!

My thoughts are cut off when Ozzy says, "We were living large. The band had gigs all over the island and we were gaining a following. Teresa and I were inseparable. Luis and I wrote new material. Life was good."

"Sounds idyllic," I whisper.

He nods. "It was. Then, a year or so later, a guy from Platinum Records asked to see me backstage. I didn't know who he was at first, but when he gave me his business card, my eyes nearly bugged out of my head. He said he wanted to sign me."

"And only you."

"Sí. Only me. I told you this part. The other guys in the band were okay with it and Luis said he was, too. Teresa had decided to change her major at The College of Puerto Rico to business. She was going to become our business manager."

He falls silent. My heart continues to beat, somehow, over the pain. His words, his tone, scream bad things happened.

I don't have to wait too long before he continues, "You know I took the contract and went out to LA to record. The label thought it best if I didn't wear my wedding ring because they wanted to play up my image as a single, available party guy. Of course, I did what they told me and Teresa said she understood. During this time, I flew home a couple of times to see my wife." He chokes on the last word.

I'm dying to know what happened, but need to keep my mouth shut. Besides, I have no right to know anything about his personal life. So what if we hooked up before? He's not mine and never will be. He belongs to *Teresa*.

"Then the tour started. I couldn't get back to Puerto Rico often, but I talked with Teresa every night. Calls with Luis became less and less frequent, though. I wanted to go home, but now I had obligations. When there was a break, I hopped onto a plane and had Teresa meet me in a hotel by the airport. We didn't surface until I had to leave a couple of days later. That's how things went." He stops talking.

I wrap my arms around my middle, unable to believe I slept with a married man. And nearly did it again. "Tell me the rest." I can't bring myself to say her name or her title.

"At that point, my life consisted of touring and trying to connect with Teresa. I didn't go to after-parties longer than I had to." His voice drops. "I didn't sleep with anyone but her."

My mouth falls open. I do a quick calculation—he's talking about years ago. I hooked up with him for the first time a couple of years back.

"Finally, I got another three-day break and headed to Puerto Rico, expecting a repeat performance from the last time. I wanted to lose myself in my wife."

He shakes his head and the needles attacking my heart turn into little hammers of warning.

"I caught an earlier flight and got to the hotel sooner than anticipated. I rushed into the room, only to find it already was occupied. By Teresa and Luis." He stops talking.

I tap my fingers together. "They were friends from the early days."

"Not like this they weren't."

"Oh!" My hand flies to my face. My heart breaks for him.

His voice turns hard. Like the shards of glass at mom's feet this morning. "Turns out, he'd been screwing my wife behind my back for months."

Thirteen

OZZY

MY EARS POUND AS VISIONS OF THAT moment replay in my head. Bare-assed, Luis jumped out of the bed yelling "Ozzy!" He searched for something to cover up his little dick while Teresa yanked the sheet up to her neck.

"Nothing I haven't seen before," I'd growled at her. Then I looked over at Luis, now wearing a white robe and sporting a smirk. The fucker.

A soft hand lands on my tense forearm. "Ozzy," a light voice says, bringing me out of my misery from over three years ago.

Blinking, I turn to the woman next to me. "I'm okay." Needing her touch, I place my hand over hers, keeping it in place.

"I can't believe they did that to you," she whispers.

A sad chuckle escapes. "Yeah. Took me a couple of minutes to get my head back together." I fall silent, remembering the fallout.

"What did you do next?"

I slant a glance toward McKenna. "I went down to the hotel bar and got shitfaced. A couple of people recognized me. I chose two of the women and went back to their room. Fucked them both for a day, and then flew back and rejoined the tour."

She doesn't say a word, but her cheek tightens. "I understand."

I release her hand and try not to miss the comfort it gave me. We sit in silence for a long while.

On a whisper, she asks, "When did this happen?"

"Three years ago." Three years, one month, five days; not that I'm counting. "I threw myself back into the tour with a vengeance. Partied harder. Hooked up."

"I remember."

I turn to her and run my fingers through her hair. "I know."

Her eyes close and she pulls away from my touch. "Did you ever find out why she did this to you?"

"She told me she was lonely."

She snorts.

Ignoring her, I go on. "Said college was hard and she needed someone on her side. Plus, she was taking care of her aunt who had a stroke."

"Not that I'm making excuses for her, but that's a lot of responsibility and she was young."

I nod. "Eleven years younger than me." Shrugging, I continue, "I think Luis did it to get back at me."

"You're probably right. That was a shitty thing Platinum did, breaking you guys up the way they did."

"He didn't have 'the look.'" I use air quotes around the phrase. "I did."

She smiles and ruffles my hair. "Still do. Even at your advanced age."

I laugh. How could this woman get me to laugh when I'm spilling my guts to her about the worst time in my life? Getting myself back under control, I say, "Yeah, well, it's all over now. Signed, sealed and delivered."

"You got divorced?"

I nod. "Day before Cole's wedding."

She flinches. "That took a while."

"Things can get dragged out if one party wants them to." I rake my fingers through my hair. McKenna knows the person dragging out the proceedings wasn't me.

"I'm amazed nothing about this hit the tabloids."

"Shari's good. She put a blackout on the story. No one outside my family, Cole and the label knows I was ever married, much less divorced." No reason to delve into the fact that Teresa cleaned me out and if I don't come up with some more songs quick, shit's really going to hit the fan. "Among Shari, Platinum and Aiden, I've been able to keep everything under wraps."

"I'm so happy Shari is taking care of you. Rose's partner is super nice and obviously excellent at publicity."

"She is."

McKenna rubs her arms. "Do you believe her?"

"Teresa?" She nods. "I guess so. Makes sense."

"If I had a guy like you, I don't think I'd ever be lonely, even if we weren't physically together." Her hand clamps over her mouth. "I didn't mean that the way it sounded. What I meant to say is her excuse seems a bit thin to me."

I like the sound of the first part. Maybe she does want to be with me? Smirking, I consider the second part of her statement. "Well, we got married and then I was off to the mainland while she was at college. We weren't together very often."

"But you spoke every day on the phone."

"We did. However, Platinum was playing me up as a party-goer, so there were photos of groupies. Even though I didn't touch one at that time, the tabloids needed some fodder. Between Cole and me, we put all of the paparazzi's kids through school."

She smiles. "It's good you talked daily. I bet you got to experience college with her, just like she got to virtually go on tour with you."

I consider her words, remembering back then. "Well, I did share a lot about touring life with her. She never seemed to want to talk about college, though."

"Really? My college days were quite something. That's where I met

Rookie—Rose. Changed majors a couple of times. Things were wild then. I'm surprised she didn't want to share her experiences."

"Well, I guess she tried a few times."

Her head tilts. "And?"

My mind goes back in time. "I always let her talk, but somehow things came back around to the tour. I guess it was more exciting."

She rubs her knees. "Sounds to me like neither of you were ready to be married."

I was the wronged party in this scenario. Never once did I consider anything otherwise. My anger bubbles up. "Well, I didn't go fuck any of the groupies who threw themselves at me at the time. I kept it in my pants."

"I believe you. But, a relationship is about more than physical fidelity."

I jump up. "Spoken like a girl who's never been cheated on. When you have, we can talk."

She gets to her feet next to me. "God, you're such a self-centered prick. I'll let you stew in your selfish indignation. Think about what I said. You're mad because you know I'm right." She grabs her laptop and purse and stalks out. I don't follow her.

What the fuck does she know about my relationship? If Teresa wanted to tell me about her college life, she could have. I wouldn't have stopped her.

Fragments of conversations with my ex-wife pop into my head. Her telling me about a campus party and me getting mad about the guys around her. Her talking about a male professor while I trampled over her story with my own about roadies.

Fuck.

Maybe McKenna is right and I've always been more concerned with my own life than anyone else's.

No fucking way. Teresa and Luis were sleeping together for months before I found out. I was faithful to the undeserving bitch.

The front door opens and I stomp out to the hallway. "Did you forget something?"

My assistant's thumb points to the driveway, where McKenna's car zooms away. "What's that about?" At his voice, Bans comes barreling into the front hall, demanding his attention. Aiden reaches down to pet her.

"Believe me you don't want to know." I turn on my heel and stalk into the house.

"Uhm, okay." The front door snicks shut. "I have some paperwork to go over with you."

My temper cools a fraction. "Drink?"

"Iced tea, if you have it."

I head off to the kitchen to get his drink and pour a glass of water for myself. While I want something stronger to take the edge off, it's getting too close to the time I have to leave for the concert tonight. Walking outside, I watch Aiden toss a stick for Bans.

"Here you go." I place his glass down on the patio table.

"Thanks. What'cha been up to?"

He's fishing for information about McKenna. Not going there. "I've been busy." I take a sip of the water and put my glass down next to his, my temper cooling by degrees.

"Writing?"

I nod. "I completed one song and am a good way through a second."

He plays with the ice in his glass. "Can I hear the one that's done? You kinda said I could yesterday."

Music soothes my soul. "Sure. Let me go get my guitar." I head inside as my assistant and my dog continue to play.

When I return, Aiden's on the phone. He mouths, "Ginger," and points. *Great.*

"Ozzy just came out. I'm going to put him on speaker."

I force a smile. "Hey, Ginger."

"Hey there, Ozzy. Aiden tells me you're writing again."

No need to hide the fact. "Yup."

"Glad to hear it. We need your new songs soon."

"I was going to play my newest one for him. Want to hear it?"

"You know I do."

I chuckle. This business is nothing but predictable. I can practically hear the dollar signs racking up in her head over the phone. "Okay. It's called 'Take Me.'" I begin to play the guitar and Bans lies down on her bed. Aiden sips his iced tea. When I finish, Aiden whistles. "That's hotter than the hinges of Hell."

I salute him with my glass of water.

"I love the bridge," Ginger praises. "And the Latin beat is different for you. I can already hear a full band behind you. With some work, this should blow up the charts."

My chest feels lighter at her praise. "I hope so."

Aiden gets to his feet. "I think this is your best song. Better than any of your previous hits, and they were hot."

"Thanks, dude."

Ginger clears her throat. "And I have a surprise for you that'll really kick everything up."

My stomach cramps. "Oh. What's the surprise?"

"Now what's the fun if I tell you? You'll have to wait and see. Do you have any other songs written?"

My mind goes to 'Honesty,' but it's not ready. "Nothing so far."

"Well, you may want to add 'Take Me' to your setlist. You can really gauge how well the song'll do by playing it live."

I consider her suggestion. "Makes sense. I have rehearsal in," I check my watch, "an hour. I'll introduce the song to the band."

"Great. I'll let you go—talk with you later." The line goes dead.

I look at my assistant. "What did she mean that she has a surprise for me?"

Aiden shrugs. "No idea." He points to a stack of papers. "Let's get through all this so you can make it to your rehearsal on time."

Rehearsal's finished and I'm out of sorts. The band likes 'Take Me' and even collaborated on some new musical licks for it. It felt good to play something new—which I wrote. All by myself.

Then why am I at odds with myself? I wander backstage and grab a turkey, stuffing and cranberry mayo sandwich—Thanksgiving leftovers—and hot tea. I didn't have time for dinner today thanks to Aiden, so this will fuel me for the night.

As I bite into the sandwich, a couple of female hotel workers pass by and give me "the look." I glance at the time—I could take one, or both, of them to my penthouse and squeeze in a quick fuck. The girls are cute and I could use the diversion.

Before I can make my move, a text chimes. McKenna. My anger resurfaces. Do I want to read what Miss Know-It-All has to say? Shaking my head, I return to my dinner, but the girls have moved on. My temperature rises at McKenna, who is now an effective cockblocker. I finish my sandwich with one bite.

My phone chimes again, reminding me I have a missed text. Fuck it. I open her message.

I apologize for how I left things today. I shouldn't have told you what I was thinking. I don't know everything about your relationship...your marriage.

Damn straight. All of my anger leaves my body at her words, though. She admits she was wrong. I can't seem to hold a grudge against this woman. Before I can think better of it, I reply:

Come to the concert tonight. I'm going to debut 'Take Me.' I'll leave your ticket at the Industry line.

Why did I ask her here? Maybe I want to show her she was wrong about me. That I wasn't an arrogant asshole with my ex-wife, and was only interested in himself. Doubt niggles at the outskirts of my mind. Still, I was faithful.

McKenna's response is one word: *Alright*

After calling Aiden over and instructing him to leave McKenna a ticket, I go backstage to perform my pre-show ritual. One-hundred decline diamond push-ups. A run through the scales. Sing 'Lamento Borincano,' a traditional Puerto Rican song made popular by Marc Anthony. One last mug of tea.

Checking the clock, I have ten minutes before the curtain goes up. I jog in place to get rid of the nerves that always attack before showtime. The stage manager instructs us all to get to our places. With one final swallow of tea, I strap on my guitar, go behind the stage and wait at my mark.

The band starts to play the intro music to the first song. The audience claps and I shake my fingers, still jogging in place. My stomach feels like a bunch of bats have taken up residence. Inhaling and exhaling slowly, I clear my mind of everything except the first note I'm going to hit.

The light show begins, illuminating my band up on the stage. The musical overture strikes a higher note, and the sold-out audience shouts. Finally, it's time. The hydraulic lift I'm standing on starts to rise slowly into the center of the stage. I close my eyes before the spotlight hits me—learned that trick the hard way.

Breathe.

I begin strumming my guitar, open my eyes and walk toward the mic. "How you doing, Las Vegas?"

My question is answered by the full house shouting and clapping and stomping their feet. It's going to be a great show. Smiling, I sing the first line of the song.

After the first half, I walk over to the drum set and grab a bottle of water. I down most of it and pour the remainder over my head and toss the empty to Aiden offstage. Shaking my head, water droplets rain down on the audience. Screaming from the ladies shows their approval.

"Are you having fun?"

The audience shouts, "Yes!"

Smiling, I ask, "Can I have the house lights? I want to see you!"

The lighting guys comply, and I am able to make out the first few rows. Walking up to the edge of the stage, I scan the upturned faces. I reach out, clasp some hands and tap others. Scanning the crowd for the one doe-eyed brunette with a pink streak in it—unless she's already changed it—who has captured my interest.

There. She's smiling at me, waving her arms in the air. I wink at her and all the tension of the day drains to the floor. What is she doing to me?

Deciding to fuck with the band and crew, I sit down on the edge of the stage, my feet dangling, and pick up my acoustic guitar. "Hi, ladies," I say to the first few rows, off mic. They squeal and fan themselves.

My eyes lock with latte ones and I lick my lips. Into the mic this time, I say, "So, I've been working on some new stuff." I strum the guitar. "Want to hear?"

The wall of sound that responds to my question is overwhelming. My fingers continue to play basic chords. I nod. "Guess that's a yes."

More applause.

"Listen, we didn't rehearse this and the song isn't quite perfected yet, but I'd love to know what you think." I swivel around and tell the band to take a break. When they're off stage, I say, "So, now it's just you and me and this guitar."

I wait for the crowd to calm down a little before continuing. "I'd like to play you all a little song called 'Take Me.' I hope you like it."

Sitting on the edge of the stage, with only a mic and my guitar, I start to play the intro. The notes fly from my fingers in a hard-pulsing beat. I wink at McKenna and sing.

When the song ends, I look at the one person in this audience who means more than any other. She's on her feet, jumping up and down. I can't hear her, but she's screaming something. Judging by the smile on her face, I did good. I mouth "Thank you" to her, then look around at the rest of the crowd. They're all clapping wildly. Guess 'Take Me' might be a hit.

And I did it all by myself.

Smiling, I jump to my feet and make my way back to the center of the stage as my bandmates return. Stan, the drummer, says, "Way to go, man. We're going to take that one to the top of the charts."

Tim, the keyboardist, slaps me on the back. "Couldn't wait for the rest of the band, huh?"

A bottle of water halts on its way to my mouth. "I wanted to get feedback. Raw and stripped down."

He smiles. "And you did. It's a great song."

When everyone's back in place, I turn back to the front and continue our show. I enjoy the female dancers as they fly through the air on their trapezes made out of ribbons while others dance—or rather gyrate—all around me. The final indoor pyrotechnics signal the conclusion of the show.

After we all take our bows, I run off-stage and grab yet another bottle of water from Aiden.

"Great job out there, boss. You had them eating out of the palm of your hand with your new song."

"Thanks." I finish the bottle of water in one gulp. Damn. This show is a workout.

I'm soon surrounded by all of my bandmates, congratulating me on the debut and offering some suggestions about how to change up the music and even stage it. To say I'm pumped is an understatement. It couldn't have gone any better. Better than the Molly I took to get through Cole's wedding, for sure. To know that my effort, *mine*, was so well-received. Now that's what they call a natural high.

We make our way backstage, where McKenna stands in the hallway outside my dressing room. She's wearing a dress that has a funky bottom to it, with a bunch of multi-colored layers. The top is a simple scoop neck, in black, showing off her tits nicely. My palms itch to touch them.

Reaching out, I grab her by the shoulders—even with her high heels, she's still short. Her chest rises and falls fast. I like it. "Did you like the show?"

She nods. "I did. 'Take Me,' was fantastic. The crowd loved it as much as I do."

"Awesome." My band surrounds us and I step back and introduce McKenna to them. She shakes their hands like the capable woman she is. When they leave, I turn toward my dressing room. Time to get out of the crush of people backstage.

I bend down to whisper in her ear. "Let's have a private celebration."

She shakes her head, eyeing all the people milling around. When she focusses on one person in particular, I follow her gaze to Shelia, the concierge. McKenna calls, "Shelia! Here I am."

The concierge waves and joins us. "Ready for our girls' night?"

Well, shit. I guess McKenna has plans for a private party that don't involve me.

Fourteen

MCKENNA

SHELIA AND I SIT IN THE BAR, sipping margaritas. We were lucky to snag a table in the back, away from the crush at the front. A girls' night out is just the break from Ozzy's magnetic pull I need. I'm so happy she reached out to me today.

I lost touch with Shelia after high school, only reconnecting with her after everything went down with Matt. She doesn't know what happened during those intervening years—no one does since Matt and I were living in a different county and the local press here didn't pick up the story—and I intend to keep things this way. Despite what my therapist told me, I know it's my burden to bear.

She puts her glass down. "So tell me—did you two have fun skydiving?"

The thrill of that day floods my body. "Yes. It was really fun."

"You two looked great together. When did you start dating?"

I lean my head on the wall at my back. "I already told you. We're not dating. I'm helping him out with his new songs."

She gives me a hard stare. "I know what I saw, and that wasn't a platonic outing."

I swivel my head against the wall and sigh. "Honestly, we've only fooled around a little. Haven't even gotten to second base." At least within the past year. Not for his lack of trying, though. What's wrong with me? He's great in bed and he obviously wants me. His dedication to his craft rivals my own. Why am I fighting this so hard?

Because Matt not only took Daddy from me, but also crushed any hope I had at love.

"Goodness, why not? I'd jump him in a second if I had the chance." She fans her face.

"He's a player."

"Well, true. You know about his towel tossing, right?"

"Yep."

"Word is his Penthouse is well-used every night. I'm not saying you should marry the guy, but I can't imagine what it would be like to have him for one night."

"He is pretty terrific." I push my hair back. Time to change the color again. Bright red feels right.

"So you *have* slept with him." She nudges my shoulder. "Spill."

My cheeks inflate, but the rest of my body feels heavy. "We've hooked up a couple of times over the years. No strings."

"Lucky girl."

"I guess." Why don't I feel lucky? "It's hard to consider yourself lucky when Ozzy spreads the luck around."

We spend the rest of the evening catching up—she discusses her mostly unfulfilling dating life and I tell her about the Project. When the clock strikes midnight, like Cinderella, I leave and return home. My thoughts repeatedly return to the man who sang his heart out sitting on the stage tonight.

Pulling into the driveway, the house is lit up like a Christmas tree. Shit. Not a good sign. I *knew* I shouldn't have stayed out so late. I try the front door, but it's locked. "Thank you," I whisper and let myself in.

Mom stands motionless in the middle of the floor.

All of my thoughts about Ozzy disappear as I rush to her side. "Mom! Mom, are you alright?"

In what seems to take forever, she turns her head and points to the shabby carpet. "Don't you see it?"

Adrenaline oozes out of my body. At least she's not hurt. "See what?"

"The crater. It's getting bigger all the time!" She shakes her finger.

Nothing's amiss in the room. I shake my head. Using a soothing tone, I respond, "No, Mom, I don't see it. Your mind must be playing tricks on you."

Her eyes round. "Really?"

"Yeah." I place my hand on her arm. "Here, let's get you to bed, alright?"

She moves her toe across the carpet, making circles, and then brings her other foot to join it. Our slow trek across the room takes twenty minutes. When we reach the threshold of her bedroom, her footsteps pick up to their normal speed and soon she's tucked in for the night.

Entering my own bedroom, I wrap my arms around my middle. Tears overflow their banks. The doctors told me spatial perception can be distorted due to her dementia. At least she was inside the house and unharmed. This scary episode, along with the sexual tension from Ozzy, plus our earlier "discussion" about his ex-wife, slam into me all at once.

I miss Daddy.

After allowing myself five minutes to cry, I put my emotions away. No more time for self-pity. And no more late nights. Mom has to be my number one priority. I slip off my high heels and change into my nightshirt. After washing all of the makeup off my face, I collapse into my bed. What a shitty day.

My ALARM GOES off at seven-thirty. I pry open my eyes and turn over. The sound of someone in the kitchen brings me out of bed. Tossing on a robe, I go into the kitchen to find out who Mom is this morning.

Mom chirps, "Good morning, McKenna. Did you sleep well?"

At least she's back. Score one. Forcing a smile, I lie, "I slept okay."

She hands me a coffee. "Great! I was going to make waffles this morning for Daddy and me. Do you want any?"

My heart plummets. I don't have the strength to keep up the charade. "Mom, Daddy's been gone for years now."

She stops her puttering and looks at me, her head tilted. "Oh. Right. How silly of me." She plays with her sleeves.

I sip the coffee but my stomach roils. She doesn't remember—she's covering. Classic signs of her disease. "It's okay, Mom. Go ahead and make yourself some." I hold up my mug. "Just coffee for me today."

Mom looks at me. "Are you trying to lose weight?"

A swarm of bees run up my spine. I know I've gained weight lately, but I don't appreciate having it pointed out to me. Even if Mom doesn't know everything she's saying anymore. "I'm not hungry."

Shrugging, she says, "Suit yourself." She takes out the waffle maker and I return to my bedroom. Can't I catch a break?

Standing in front of the full-length mirror, I survey my nude body with a critical eye. Shoulders drooping, I trudge upstairs and hop onto the treadmill. Halfway through the cycle—sweat-soaked and panting for scraps of air—I shut it off. I'm done for today. Tomorrow, I should be able to do a little more. If I care enough.

Before I shower, I check my phone. One missed text, from Ozzy.

Can you come over to my place today? I'd like to do something fun with you. :-)

At the word "fun," all of my thoughts freeze. I should stay away, but I can't. After everything that happened with Mom last night and this morning, I deserve what he's been offering. The sex will be good. He'll make me forget. Ignoring my head pleading me not to go, I text that I'll be there.

As I tuck a shirt into my capris—my last-ditch effort to fend off Ozzy— Elaine arrives for her shift. I put on red lipstick to match my newly dyed hair and grab my purse. Elaine and Mom talk about going for a walk to the park, which would be good for her—maybe getting out of the house would help clear her head. With a word of warning about Mom's status, I head out, laptop in hand.

Driving toward Ozzy's house, I turn on the radio and give myself permission to allow Elaine to provide Mom with the comfort she needs. She's trained to do so. And my therapist convinced me I'm not a failure because I simply don't have the skillset.

I search for a release valve from my emotions surrounding Mom's condition, and consider what Ozzy's been offering. Maybe I need to run a pro/con list?

PROs—he's great in bed, creative, funny, fun, intense, sexy, hot. Oh my God! I need to move on to the...

CONs—he doesn't do serious relationships (neither do I), he's a player, he'll leave Vegas at the end of the year when his residency at the Jade expires

The "pros" have it.

As I'm feeling confident with my decision, the DJ comes over the radio, saying, "Here's Ozzy Martinez with 'Hit the Streets,' his first Top Ten smash. Word has it he debuted a new song last night in concert at the Jade, which is good news for fans. Can't wait to hear it! If you were at the concert, call in now and let us know your thoughts."

'Hit the Streets' starts to play as my mind goes back to last night. To memories of Ozzy sitting on the side of the stage, singing his new song with only his guitar. It was ... magical. Pride wells up in me. He created it all by himself, from start to finish. I even had a tiny role in helping him with it.

The song ends and the DJ comes back on. "So, here we have Dana, who was at Ozzy Martinez's concert last night. Tell us about his new song, Dana."

A new voice comes over the radio. She gushes, "It was awesome. He sat down on the edge of the stage with his feet dangling. Just him and his guitar and he sang 'Take Me.' It was hot! I wanted to crawl over all the other audience members and do him right then and there!" Both she and the DJ start laughing.

Well, there you have it. I put my blinker on to turn into his driveway and shut off the radio. When I shift into park, I relax my head against the cushioned headrest. Before I can get out of my car, Ozzy bounds out of the front door and jogs down the steps, helmets in his hand. I step out as he approaches, arm extended.

"Here you go. Put this on. We're going out." His eyes shine.

Taking my helmet from him, I say, "Wow. You're clothed and ready to go for once. What exactly do you have up your sleeve?"

He turns both arms—which are bare save for his tattoos—over. "Not a thing." He winks and heads off toward his motorcycle.

"I could drive us there!" I yell to his back.

I'm greeted by his chuckle. "C'mon. You know you like my bike."

Well, damn. What's not to like about the hottest guy you've ever seen on a motorcycle? I put the helmet on and hop on.

"Ready to rock?"

"Where are we going?"

He revs the engine. "You're going to like it."

With that, we take off in an opposite direction from the Strip. I close my eyes and allow my body to yield into his. Being with him is so different from getting on a bike behind Matt.

I shake my head to clear it and take in our surroundings. What is out here? The only thing I can think of is Edie Z's. My mouth starts to water. When we turn into the chocolate factory and botanical gardens, I almost leap from the bike.

"I love it here! Daddy used to take me here every Sunday!" He'd let me have one—"only one, McKenna!"—piece of candy. Then, we'd stroll through the gardens. After about an hour, we'd head back to the house. Good memories.

I do a little jig while Ozzy secures the motorcycle and our helmets. "And here I thought I was doing something novel."

I smile. "I always see something new here. No matter how often I visit, no two times are the same. Plus, I haven't been since Daddy—" My voice trails and I grab Ozzy's forearm to ground me in the present. He doesn't notice my change in mood, but bends over and takes out a long-sleeved shirt and baseball cap from the storage area. "Come on!"

We go through the factory tour. People give Ozzy the side-eye because he's such a tall and imposing figure. However, his dune buggy hat obscures his face. Plus, his button-down shirt, even though open, hides his tattoos. No one would think "the" Ozzy Martinez would be on such a tour.

After it ends, I grab *two* pieces of candy—because I'm an adult—and lead Ozzy to the gardens, filled with desert plants. Various types of cacti and other flora entice us through. Soon, we're in a remote area of the gardens, deviating from the main pathways while nibbling on our chocolates.

I pop the final piece into my mouth. "Mmmm. So good."

Ozzy laughs. "If I knew chocolate would put that look on your face, I'd have bought out the store for you."

I shake my head. "Not just any chocolate. It has to be Edie Z's."

He licks his index finger. "Come here, Dulcita Mía. You have some chocolate on your lip."

I tilt my head. "'Dulcita Mía'? What does that mean?"

"It means 'my little sweet.'" The corner of his eyes crinkle.

I can live with that. "Oh." My tongue reaches out to capture the missed goodness, but he says, "Nope."

Stepping forward, his finger rubs against my bottom lip and he holds it up for me to see. I grab his hand and bring his finger into my mouth, licking the sweet stuff off.

All of a sudden, I realize what I'm doing. Ozzy's finger is in my mouth. My eyes travel upward to his, which have turned smoky. Instead of pulling his finger away, he inserts a second one between my lips.

This is what I want. What I need. My breathing hitches as my tongue swirls around the second digit, our eyes never faltering from the other's. His thumb rests against my chin as he pumps his fingers back and forth. Feeling unsteady on my feet, I drag my hand down to hold onto something for balance, ending around his waist.

He bends down and says in a throaty baritone, "Let's get out of here."

Removing his fingers from my mouth, he grabs my hand and marches me out of the gardens and to his bike. "Get on Shirley," he commands while exchanging his cap for the helmet. After he passes my helmet to me, we're zipping out of the parking lot within seconds.

We drive farther away from the Strip. The landscape turns from buildings and commercial spaces to desolate. The first sign away from civilization says "panoramic vista" and points to the right. We turn. Driving to the very back of the almost empty lot, he motions for me to get off and to give him my helmet. Soon, he ushers me into the wooded area.

After walking for a bit, he stops and looks around. A grouping of boulders is off to one side. We're all alone. My heartrate picks up its pace.

Ozzy takes a step toward me. I know what he wants. I need what he's offering. He's better than chocolate.

He puts his hand on my hair. "Red. Fiery. Just like you."

His hand snakes to the back of my head and draws me toward him. Our lips meet in a frenzy of teeth and lips and tongues. Not a gentle exploration. This is the culmination of the past few days of his confessions and my emotional rollercoaster. I'm helpless to stop it. We both need this.

He pulls back. "I haven't had sex with anyone since you barged into my backyard."

A fluttering erupts deep in my belly at his words. I've only slept with *him* since Matt, and that ended six years ago. Wrapping my gooseflesh-speckled arms around his neck, I whisper the only word in my brain, "Please."

He picks me up, making me feel as if I'm tiny, and carries me to the boulders. Taking his button-down shirt off, he lays it over the rock formation. My feet touch the ground and then I'm leaning against his shirt as his body covers mine.

Ozzy growls into my mouth. "Fuck. Too many clothes." His hands reach for my waist and he pulls my top out from my capris and up and over my head.

His large hands cover my breasts and squeeze. Over and over, he molds them. He flips the cups down, exposing me to his gaze. Without pausing, his mouth descends on my nipple and he sucks. Hard. My core clenches when he bites down.

"Oh." I wriggle my hips and reach for his belt buckle. It comes undone with a click and my fingers open the fly of his shorts.

Without moving away from my body, he shucks all of his clothes. He's sculpted—lean and ripped. And all mine. At least for now. As I reach to trace the V on his torso, he unzips my capris and pulls them—together with my red panties—down my legs. One hand drops from my breast to my pussy, and he rubs my clit.

Putting his finger in his mouth, he says, "Damn. You taste good. Better than chocolate in my book. Up you go."

He lifts me onto the boulder and my legs fall open. When he steps into the breach, I barely register the rigidity of the rock beneath me. Both of his hands mold and tweak my breasts, which are at an obscene angle since they're pushed up by my bra. I can't help myself and tilt my hips into him. A second later, his head descends between my legs. I want to explore the new jewelry adorning his cock—and I will—but for now, I rest on my arms and watch him perform his magic.

His tongue circles and sucks and nips, causing me to swivel my hips in response. I drop my head backward. "Ozzy," I breathe.

He inserts one finger into my center and licks me from front to back. "Like that?"

"More."

He chuckles. "Only too glad to oblige."

While he circles my clit, the shimmer of an orgasm starts to build. Immobile from the waist down, I latch onto his hair and tug. My body clenches and I scream, pulling his head forward, begging him not to stop. Ozzy continues to attack my clit as wave after wave crashes inside me.

I fall limp and look down at the man who gave me such a violent orgasm. His head comes up from between my legs, mouth smeared with my juices. I need to wear the same look.

From somewhere deep inside me, I rumble, "My turn."

He smiles and stands up. I toss his shirt at his feet and drop to my knees onto it. Tilting my head up, up, up, I take in the full length of this amazing man. Tattoos, piercings, hard muscle.

"You're gorgeous."

"You're going to make my head swell." He bucks his hips toward me, his cock glistening with pre-cum.

I run my finger over the new piercing. "I like this."

He smirks. "You're going to like it a whole lot more when it's inside you."

My mind blanks. I raise my eyes to him, desire blazing. I just had a crazy orgasm—my first from a man since he gave me some back at Rose's apartment over a year ago—but it's like it never happened.

He must've read my mind, because his hands go under my armpits and he hauls me up his body. Turning me so my hands are on the rock, his knee goes in between mine from the back. My mouth goes dry.

"Don't move," his baritone grumbles.

He bends down and fishes something from his shorts' pocket. I turn my head to watch as he carefully smooths a condom over his pierced cock. Sheathed, he turns feral eyes to me.

"Ready?"

Still staring at his oversized cock, I can do nothing but nod. "Good answer." He places his hand on my lower back and guides himself to my entrance by way of sliding down my butt. My skin is on fire where we touch and my body screams for his.

I don't have to wait another second. He bites my neck and pushes into me at the same moment.

"Oh!" I shout, absorbing his cock in one long stroke.

"Yes!" he exclaims as he covers my entire back with his front.

I can't move. I'm caught between a rock and a hard place, literally. His hands snake around me and grab my breasts as he pulls back and slams into me over and over. He swivels his hips and his piercing hits me at the right spot.

"God," I hiss.

He does it again and I moan. "Told you you'd like it better inside."

I can't speak, my body is one big nerve ending that starts and stops with his erection. He controls my body. His fingers pinch my nipples, sending bites of pain directly to where he's pounding into me. His teeth latch onto my earlobe. What this man does to me.

"Come for me now," he orders.

I push back as much as I am able, keeping our relentless rhythm going. He bites me again and I scream as fireworks shoot throughout my body. The piercing moving within me prolongs my ecstasy for longer than I've ever felt before.

Behind me, he stills and then lets out a harsh cry of release, his fingers digging into my breasts. He collapses on my back. We remain like this until our breathing slows down to a mere gallop.

"Damn. That was better than I remember." He nips the back of my neck. "Knew we'd get here again."

"It was something else."

His hands slide down my sides, stopping at my hips. He pulls out of me and steps back, and ties off the condom. Turning, I stare at his cock which, although depleted, is not flaccid. I want him. Again. His shirt is still on the ground, so I slow-walk him over to it and drop to my knees.

Grinning at him, I say, "I got interrupted."

He runs his fingers through my hair like I've seen him do to himself several times. A smile crosses his face. "Have at it."

That's all I need to hear. I lick my lips and his cock bounces, already recharging before my eyes. Sticking my tongue out, I run it up one side of him and down the other, weaving past his piercing. I pay close attention to the vein on the underside of his shaft and drop lower, sucking on one of his balls.

"Feels so good. Don't stop."

After giving the same attention to the other one, I return to his shaft and work my way up and over and back down to the base.

"Suck me." His hand fists my hair, but he doesn't push. "Please."

I sit back on my heels. "Since you asked so nicely." Opening my mouth wide, I envelope his cock, the piercing teasing the back of my throat. He continues to grow bigger as I suck harder, hollowing my cheeks.

His hips get into the act, pushing back and forth as he fucks my face. He's coming undone in my mouth, and I love it. Owning this man, even if it's for a little while, is a heady experience.

I make figure eights with my tongue until he throws his head back and moans. Then, I bring my hands to his balls and run a fingernail over one.

"Fuck. I'm almost there."

That's the idea. I continue working him over in the rhythm he sets with his hands on the back of my head. He swells, stills, then releases his essence down my throat. I make sure to lick every last drop before letting him fall from my lips.

Looking down at me, he says, "Home. I want to get you to my home. Now."

In no time flat, we're both fully dressed and back on Shirley, speeding through the streets of Las Vegas. My mind races faster than we're traveling. After everything that's happened, I deserve this break from my reality.

He scoots around my little Honda and stops the bike. Shaking his head as if arguing with himself, he says, "McKenna, I want you to hear what I did with 'Honesty.' It's done. And I started another song." He takes off his helmet and admits, "It's you. You're my muse." He nips my earlobe. "In more ways than one."

With those words, he hops off the bike and leads me into the music room. I'm his muse now? Is that a good thing? Well, yes. He's writing more songs, which means I can do my job and finish up the Project. And get paid.

A nagging thought tells me he means more to me than a simple paycheck. Much more.

Fifteen

OZZY

STILL BUZZING FROM OUR TRYST—one that blew me away on every level—I say, "I've been working on 'Honesty.' Let me play it for you."

At her assent, I steer her into the music room. She takes a seat as I strap on my guitar. "Here you go. Be honest." My lips curl at my play on the title. But the sentiment behind my request is valid.

When my fingers play the final note, I open my eyes for the first time. I needed to let the music take over my body, so closing them was the best way to block everything—including McKenna—out. I swallow and allow myself to look at my audience of one. She's wearing a goofy look on her face. "Well?"

"Ozzy, I love this song so much. Don't get me wrong, 'Take Me' is a powerful, sexy song but this one reveals something more about you."

She tilts her head the way she did by the boulder before taking my cock into her extremely talented mouth. My lower half starts to stir. "I'm glad you like it." I start to remove my guitar, but McKenna comes up to me. "Keep it on."

"Okay," I elongate the word. Without warning, I flip the guitar to my back and pull her into my body. "You're so tiny."

She laughs. "Short. I'm short. I'm certainly not 'tiny.'"

I take my time looking from her hairline to her toes and back up. "Let me amend. You're tiny in stature but with real curves. I like everything you are." I take her lips with mine, molding and sucking on their fullness. Her hands reach out for my stiffening cock. How long ago did I have her? Less than an hour ago? Damn.

I start walking forward, causing her to retreat in equal measure. When she reaches the conference table, I sweep off all of the papers and put her on top of it, my hands reaching for her zipper. I want to take it slow, but she kicks her shoes off and rips her shirt over her head. My resolution evaporates. "Lift your hips for me."

She does and I skim her pants and panties off her body. She unclasps her bra and tosses it aside. Stepping back, I survey all that's mine. Real hips, real tits. I reach out and flick her nipple. "Perfect."

"Ozzy."

"I love how you say my name. Say it again."

"Ozzy." Her hands reach for my waist, and pull my T-shirt out of my shorts. "Off." I reach to take the guitar off my back, when her hand stops me. "No, keep it on. Just your shorts."

Chuckling, I say, "You want a music man now?"

"Nope. Only you. And your guitar is an extension of you."

I don't stop to ponder her words. Pulling my shorts off, I grab a condom from my pocket before they hit the floor. As I open her legs wider, I ask, "What do you have for me?"

"You tell me."

Damn. This girl is so right for me. I take my index finger and trail it from her chin, down her throat, between her tits. Past her belly-button, I end up in her pussy. When I'm circling her clit, her hips swivel.

She throws her head backward. "Yes. Please."

My other hand joins the first, and I insert a finger into her wet warmth.

The fingers on my other hand continue circling her clit. She drops her head onto the table, her hips moving. I know what she needs to get off, but I don't want to give it to her just yet.

Her head thrashes from side to side and my cock swells to a painful level. Abandoning her body, I roll the condom on to the sound of her whimpers. Before I'm fully sheathed, her fingers slide downward. Mesmerized, I watch as she plays with her sex. Without warning, her body bows and she cries out.

I nearly come at the sight. "That was seriously one of the most fucking erotic things I've ever seen."

Unfocused eyes meet mine. She licks her lips. "I couldn't wait."

"And now I can't." I pull her arms away from her body, extending them to either side of her to form a "T." Positioning my hips, I enter her with one single hard thrust and still, savoring her tightness around me. Her tits bounce with the force of our joining.

As I push in and out, my guitar hits my ass with each beat. The stimulation is mind-blowing, although I much prefer how she's milking me for all I'm worth than the tapping on my ass. I continue my onslaught until she constricts around me.

"Come for me again."

She explodes and I can't hold back any longer. I wanted to make her come at least twice more, but my balls tell me otherwise. I pound into her a few more times and let go into her body.

Once I've recovered my ability to move, I remove the guitar strapped to my back and toss the condom. Returning to the table, I look down on the beauty who's still spread eagled there, feeling ten feet tall at putting that look on her face.

"What you do to me, Dulcita."

She snaps her legs closed. "Feeling's mutual."

Damn, she's good for my ego.

I help her dress, which finally happens after much more kissing, and we spend the rest of the afternoon working on music. She shows me her graphic ideas and I share snippets of the new songs.

When my cell phone alarm goes off, I stand. "Dinnertime."

Her fingers drop off the laptop, her eyes zeroing in on my crotch. "I know what I'd like for dessert."

Her eyes catch mine and the lust blazing from them makes me suck in my breath. Is it possible I've met my match? My libido has always been strong but she's as insatiable as me. I wrap a lock of her bright red hair around my finger. "You're as horny as me. I like it."

Chuckling, I grab her hand and we walk into the kitchen. I pull out some leftover rice and beans and a few chicken breasts. Together, we cook up a delicious meal that reminds me of home. I have *her* for dessert, though, served on the kitchen counter.

"Let's head over to the Jade."

"I'd love to but I can't tonight. I have a meeting with one of my clients."

I place a kiss on her neck. "Cancel."

Her pulse pounds beneath my lips, but her next words dash my hopes. "I wish. This meeting already has been rescheduled three times."

Something about the way her eyes dart tells me she's not being truthful. She *is* different from all the rest. Right?

AT THE JADE, I sip my tea and reflect on the turn of events from today when Aiden walks in, interrupting a particularly vivid memory of McKenna against the rocks.

After dumping a folder on the table, he asks, "Is McKenna here?"

I shake my head. "No. She has a client meeting tonight."

"Oh." He pops a handful of M&M's into his mouth. "Then do you want me to make sure the Penthouse is set up for you?"

My stomach cramps at the thought of bringing anyone there. "No."

"Sounds like the little graphic artist is getting under your skin."

Not wanting to admit the depth of my feelings yet—even to my PA—I retort, "Now don't go getting your panties in a bunch there, Aiden. She's a hot piece. Nothing more." My words sound hollow to my own ears. A knock at the door diverts my thoughts. Welcoming the distraction, I call, "Come in."

My dressing room door swings open and my band filters in. Sticks banging on his thigh, Stan says, "Hey, we thought we'd go over some of the new music with you before tonight's show." For the next half-hour, we jam to the new stuff I've been writing, making changes that kick the songs up.

Aiden enters the room fifteen minutes before showtime. "Hey, guys. I'm your fifteen-minute warning." He hands me another cup of tea.

"So, we're definitely adding 'Take Me' to the lineup tonight." We discuss final changes to the setlist and everyone files out to head for the stage.

As I wait backstage for my cue, I realize I'm not as nervous as I usually am. The bats are still there, yes, but not in the full-on swarms like before. Before McKenna.

She's only a diversion.

Remember that.

Sixteen

MCKENNA

I TURN OVER IN MY BED, A SORENESS between my thighs. *Ozzy.* A smile creeps across my face and I start to hum his new song, 'Take Me.' I shake my head. Keep things to the "just sex" level, girl, and stop trying to read more into the situation than what's there. My smile fades and I toss off the blankets.

An hour later, I'm dressed in leggings and a yellow long-sleeve peasant shirt, with both my hair and makeup done.

Before I can leave my bedroom, my cell phone rings and I nearly drop it in anticipation of Ozzy's wakeup call. My smile dims when I see it's Felicia from the Project, but I force it back, answering with a jaunty "McKenna James."

"Hey, McKenna. Hope you had a nice Thanksgiving. I'm checking in with you about where you stand with Ozzy."

My mind races with all sorts of inappropriate responses. Stifling an inappropriate retort, I reply, "Hi, yes, my holiday was great. I'm making some good progress with Ozzy, to answer your question."

"That's what I was hoping to hear. We had a meeting last night at the Project to get ready for the Big Reveal party on December fourteenth. You remember your graphics are due next week, right? All of the other candidates have already submitted theirs."

Bully for them. My mind races. Tugging on my sleeves, I say, "I'm working on Ozzy's stuff now." My eyes close. I know hers isn't a question and she expects only one answer. "So, uhm, sure. I'll make the deadline."

"Perfect. Just drop by the office with a thumb drive when you're ready. I can't wait to see everything you put together."

"You're going to love it." This presentation is, by a yard or a mile or a missile-launch, my best work. All because of Ozzy.

Disconnecting the call, I look at the blank cell screen. I need to push Ozzy to finish up at least one more song—and create the graphics for everything—all in a week. This is going to be insane.

Trudging into the kitchen, I put leftover waffles into the toaster. Luckily, the water in Mom's shower is running, so she must be feeling herself today.

When my waffles are heated, I plop down into the chair and mechanically start eating. How can I push Ozzy to finish his songs? Creativity can't be forced, but I need to nudge him somehow.

As if he knew I was thinking about him, he texts me.

Missed you last night. Got something big waiting for you right now.

Especially when he texts me stuff like that. Maybe sex will make his songwriting skills go faster? I don't pause to consider what I'm writing and respond to him with:

As long as it's pierced at the end, I'm in.

The front door opens and Elaine pops into the kitchen as I'm cleaning up. "I heard the shower shut off a little while ago. Haven't spoken with her this morning."

"Don't worry. I'll take care of her."

"You're so good with her. Thanks."

She takes out a mug and runs water in it for tea. "Don't be so hard on yourself. What you've done—giving up your condo and moving back in—is a lot. And you're not a trained caregiver."

Her words echo those of my therapist. Shouting into Mom's bedroom that I'm heading out for work, I drive to Ozzy's. The ride over consists of me trying out different ways to get him writing. From telling him the truth to sexing him up. Maybe both.

At his front door, I press the doorbell and wait. And wait. I press it again and Bans barks from the other side, but the door remains closed.

He must be in the backyard. Hopefully swimming in the buff. I turn and skip down the steps and around the side yard to the gate. Opening it, I stroll into his backyard and check out the pool. Empty. My shoulders droop.

The French doors open and Ozzy strolls through carrying two glasses. After putting them onto the table, a closed-off look crosses his face for a second. Then, all smiles, he opens his arms wide. Discarding his unexpected initial look as my mind playing tricks, I can't stop myself from walking directly into his invitation.

He kisses me with a thoroughness I've never felt before. "I missed you last night."

"Me, too," I mumble, stealing more kisses.

He breaks our contact. "How was your meeting?"

A made-up meeting was the white lie I gave him so I could stay home with Mom. Is it the cause for his look? Nah. Get a grip. There's no need for my worlds to cross. What I need to do is care for Mom and protect her as best I can. No one—especially no man—will ever come between me and my family again. Ozzy's only a much-deserved stress-reliever. I step back and force a sunny smile.

"Oh, you know, boring." I run my fingers down his forearm. "Besides, have to keep you on your toes."

His heels rise off the concrete. "Here I am." Reaching out, he grabs me by my waist and pulls me close.

See, no worries. "Yes, you are." My hips rock toward his.

Maybe one more round before getting down to business? I grab the rounded globes of his ass beneath his shorts. He's commando. His mouth covers mine and my thoughts scatter. I rub up and down against him, his cock jutting into my torso. If only I were taller.

"Damn," he growls and walks us to a chaise lounge. Stepping back, he kicks off his sandals, glides his T-shirt over his head and pulls his shorts down his legs. Naked, he sits.

Looking down at him, my eyes travel from his hair to his sexy feet, feasting on his various piercings. Especially the one pointing at me. I swallow and he chuckles.

"Are you going to stand there and look, or are you going to make us both happy?"

"I vote for option B," I reply, my voice throaty with desire.

He pats his thighs. "Good answer."

Stepping out of my sandals, I place one foot next to the chair and swing my other one over him, then sit down on his powerful thighs. His arms come around me at once and pull me to his body. Our lips devour each other while his hands play with my breasts, then take off my top and bra.

Leaning back, I place my hands on his knees and arch upward. His strong hands make their way to the waistband of my leggings, which he shoves down. I move so he can toss them, together with my panties, over his shoulder. His mouth finds my boob while his finger swirls around my pussy.

My nipple falls from his mouth with a pop. "So wet for me. So perfect."

Perfect. He thinks I'm perfect. His finger rubs my clit. "Oh."

"I need to be inside you now." He points to a foil packet so conveniently located on the table. Guess I was a foregone conclusion.

Jumping off his body to get the condom, he takes the packet from me and sheaths himself. His cock looks huge and angry and so ready for me. I want to ride him.

Turning my body to give him a view of my ass, I sink onto his cock with a groan. Behind me, he grunts, "Ride me."

I give him a cheeky grin. "You read my mind."

I raise and lower my body in a steady rhythm, one that drives us both wild. My body urges me on faster, but I keep this pace, enjoying the way he fills me to almost bursting. Looking back at him, his face is scrunched up with the effort my speed—or lack of it—provides.

His hands come to my waist and I face forward again. He pushes me faster, faster, faster and I willingly go. Soon, I'm racing toward the finish line. His hand comes around and twists my nipple, and a tingling buzzes from my center outward. I explode with a loud "Fuck."

A strained laugh comes out of his mouth as he thrusts into my body. Squeezing my boob, he stiffens and then shouts, "Fuck, yes!"

His mouth contacts my back, kissing from one shoulder blade to the other all the while his fingers remain on my boobs. I squeeze him from inside since I don't have access to any other part of his body.

"What are you doing to me, woman?" He collapses back onto the chair.

I stand and face him, knowing a goofy smile covers my face. "I could ask you the same question." Taking in his relaxed features and hard body, heat travels up my neck and cheeks. I put that look on him. *Me.*

"Damn. If you don't want a repeat performance in about five minutes, you'd better get dressed."

Before I can consider my words, "Sounds good to me" tumbles out of my mouth.

He chuckles and in one swift move, comes to his feet, picks me up and tosses me into the pool. Spluttering to the surface, I shout, "Ozzy!"

Standing by the side of the pool, he laughs. Before I can do anything with my now wet hair and ruined makeup, he cannonballs in to join me. A wave hits me from the force of his entry, causing me to giggle like a schoolgirl.

Ozzy swims over to me and grabs my waist, pulling me into the deep end. Not ready to let reality interfere for another few minutes, I wrap my arms around his shoulders and hang on.

Leaning in, I whisper into his ear, "Think you can do a repeat, old man?" I roll my pelvis toward him.

"Who are you calling old?"

"Well, you are eight years older than me. If the shoe fits…"

His hands drop to my ass. "I'll show you what fits."

Re-dressed, we make our way into the music room. I excuse myself and go to the bathroom to try to fix the mess of my hair and makeup. With only limited supplies, I do my best and return carrying two iced teas.

He takes his cup. "Thanks, Dulcita." While he begins playing 'Take Me,' I set up my laptop.

Truth.

I promised myself I'd tell him the truth about my deadline. Here goes. "Felicia from the Project called me this morning. She wants to have my submission ready by next week." I suck in my breath.

"How many songs do you need?"

"Three. Maybe four." I keep my eyes trained on booting up my computer.

"Okay."

My eyes snap to his. "Okay?"

He nods. "I have 'Take Me' basically done, and 'Honesty' is in pretty good shape. I've been kicking around some new melodies. Let's get to work and see what we come up with."

The next three days flash by in a blur. He writes, I create graphics. Sometimes my graphics change his songs. We work together and have sex. Good sex. Like really, really good sex.

But, I always come up with an excuse as to why I can't go to his concerts. How many more times can I can pull shit out of thin air before he starts questioning me? It's not that I want to return home every night—alone. Yet it's easier to hide the truth than to let him in.

Because if I did, there's no chance he'd be able handle it.

Seventeen

OZZY

My muse is in high gear. I don't ever remember feeling this creative before. Every day McKenna comes over, I'm inundated with new music or lyrics. Sometimes both.

But it's not only that she unlocks this part of my brain. She's my sexual match, too. I love that I can be writing a song one second, then throw her over the sofa the next, and then go back to the song afterwards. And she's always so responsive.

Plus, she's a great cook—especially pastries. Damn. I've swum more laps since we've been together than I can remember. The only issue is she's skipped my recent concerts and never sleeps here. It's starting to get on my nerves. I can understand not coming to my concerts all the time, but I've asked her over every night and she always has an excuse.

An unscheduled meeting at the Project.

An emergency with a client.

She forgot a change of clothes. I tell her she might as well be naked.

Aside from that, she's perfect for me. And honest. Right? Ignoring a niggling doubt, it hits me—I've never felt like this, even toward Teresa. It's like she's in my bloodstream, feeding my organs.

I'm in love.

The thought rips through my brain, causing me to jump up off the sofa. "Bans, come!" I put her leash on and we go for a long, rapid walk around the neighborhood. By the time I return, my heart has resumed a normal pace. *Love?* Ha! I don't think so.

A while later, the doorbell rings and I rush to answer it, my fingers itching to sink into her body. "Hey, Ozzy."

My shoulders drop. "Hola, Aiden."

"Don't sound so excited to see me."

Closing the door behind him, we make our way through the house. "Thought you were Mckenna."

"Sorry, dude." He detours into the kitchen, pours himself an iced tea and heads toward the patio.

Choosing to stick to a non-alcoholic drink, I do the same and follow him out. "So, what's up?"

"I got a call from Ginger, and she's coming to tonight's concert. Says she's bringing the surprise she mentioned."

She's been dangling the idea of a surprise over my head. I have no idea what it could be—more Molly, maybe? Not that I've needed any "extra" help since I've been with McKenna. "Sure. Whatever."

He shrugs. "'Take Me' is going over really well. I'm sure Ginger will be very pleased."

I take a sip of iced tea. "Yeah. And I've been working on some more new stuff, too."

He rubs his lip. "It's great you're back in the game." He drinks and places his cup down on the table, then produces a stack of paperwork.

"Don't you ever come here without a shit-ton of papers for me?"

He grins. "That's why you pay me the big bucks." He points to the first one in the pile and we start slogging through all the business. When we finish, he says, "So, McKenna, huh?"

I lick my lips. "Yep."

"Do you want me to pick up anything for her from you? Clothes, handbag? Jewelry?"

His question brings me up short. "Oh shit. We've been so focused on writing and," I slant him a look, "other things, that I haven't even gotten her a present. Well, other than the skydiving experience. Thanks for arranging that, by the way."

He nods, as if it was no big deal. I guess for him, it wasn't. "Okay. Let me know if I can get anything for your girlfriend."

I can't have my PA buy my girlfriend a present. Whoa. *Girlfriend?* "No, I'll take care of her."

He scoffs. "I bet."

I give him a dirty look, then break out in a grin. The doorbell rings and I jump to my feet. "That's going to be her. Are we finished?"

He chuckles. "Yeah. I'll clean all this up while you go greet your *girlfriend.*"

"Dick." Walking through the house, I wipe suddenly damp hands on my shorts. Since when did I get nervous around women, especially one I've been screwing? When do I offer a woman repeat performances daily? I place my hand on the doorknob and take a calming breath. Opening it, I look at the sprite waiting for me. "I was just talking about you."

She smiles and my cock rises to bask in her sunshine. "All good, I hope."

I wink. "Come on in." I take her laptop case and bring it into the music room.

In the foyer, McKenna nods and says something to Aiden, which makes him laugh. That's what she does. She brings light and laughter wherever she goes—all good things. Minus the staying overnight part. Regardless, she's the real deal. And I've begun to crave her.

I break up the pair by kissing McKenna on the lips. Not one to be embarrassed, she kisses me back, Aiden be damned. He clears his throat. "Well, I'm going to leave you two. Remember that Ginger will be in the audience tonight." My mouth seeks hers again as the gentle click of the front door sounds.

She giggles and steps back. "You're so bad."

"What? I hadn't seen you in hours. I had to say hello."

She shakes her head. "So, who's Ginger?"

"Jealous?"

Her hands go to her hips and her foot taps. "Nope." The "p" pops as she says it, reminding me of the same sound she makes when my cock leaves her mouth. I grab her in my arms and kiss the shit out of her. "I think you've earned your answer. Ginger's my rep from Platinum."

McKenna's finger trails across my cheek. "Then I guess you need to be in tip-top shape for tonight."

I wink. "Want to help me get there?"

HOURS LATER, MY bandmates surround me at the Jade. Mark, the bassist, says, "Listen to what Jazz came up with for your newest song."

Caught up in their exuberance, I motion for the lead guitarist to play. He modified the bridge and chorus somewhat. Clapping him on the back, I say, "I like it, Jazz."

"Thanks, man. I thought the riffs would really go well in there."

Strapping on my own guitar, I ask him to play it again and then copy him. A thought filters into my mind and I try it out. "What do you think of that?"

Jazz copies what I just did and adds some more beats. Soon, we're rocking out to a new and improved version of the song. Mark joins us with his bass while Stan pounds out a beat on his leg, the table and whatever else is nearby. From across the room, Tim hits some keys on the portable keyboard.

Aiden appears in front of me. "Guys! Guys! Save some for the concert, okay? You have fifteen minutes."

Where did the time go? Grinning at each of my band members, we high five each other and they head to their dressing rooms before going backstage.

When my dressing room is empty, one person claps. I whip my head around to find McKenna grinning at me, her long skirt flowing freely around her calves.

Swinging my guitar to my back, I open my arms. "I'm so happy you made it. When did you get here?"

"I slipped in about five minutes ago." She wraps her arms around my waist. "That was awesomesauce, Ozzy."

Nodding, my chin bounces off the top of her head. "It felt pretty great."

"Tonight was the first time I saw you guys really rehearse together as a band. It was cool." She leans back and smiles.

Stealing a kiss, I reply, "It was. I've never worked together like that on a song before."

"Another notch in your belt. I'm so happy for you."

"Me, too." I kiss the top of her head.

Aiden walks into the room. "Sorry to break you two up, but you need to take your mark, Ozzy. And don't forget, Ginger will be here with your surprise afterwards, so definitely be out to impress tonight. Break a leg."

Squeezing McKenna, I say, "See you on the other side, Dulcita."

"Knock 'em dead."

With a kiss, we part ways. Tonight's going to be epic.

AFTER THE CONCERT, which went great, I grab the bottle of water from Aiden's hands. "That was the best performance of 'Take Me' yet. Good job!"

"Agreed." I down the bottle and hand the empty back to Aiden. "Felt great out there tonight."

As I'm heading down the hallway toward my dressing room, Aiden calls out. A note of caution in his voice makes prickles run up my spine. "Ginger's in your room already. She has—"

Tamping down my body's odd response, I continue on my journey. "A surprise. Yeah, I know." My stride lengthens as I picture myself in the shower. With McKenna.

"Ozzy!" Aiden's voice can barely be heard above the din of backstage.

Sometimes he can be such a worry wart. I wave my hand and continue toward my dressing room. McKenna's standing in front of the door, waiting for me to get to her.

"Super show, Ozzy!" She says as she jumps up into my arms and wraps her legs around my hips. Her nose wrinkles at my stage sweat.

Catching her lips in a kiss, I find the door handle, open it and slip us inside. She laughs while our mouths devour each other. My balls tighten at the sound and I squeeze her tighter.

A cough penetrates my mind. It's followed by a masculine chuckle. Ginger says, "Surprise!"

Great timing. McKenna releases her legs from my middle and I lower her to the floor. Turning, I greet my rep. "Ginger, may I introduce you to McKen—"

My voice stops mid-introduction. Ginger, blonde and skinny and dressed in a mini skirt-suit stands next to Luis.

Luis.

Ex-best friend and homewrecker extraordinaire.

I go rigid. Next to me, McKenna places her hand on my arm, rubbing her fingers up and down. "Ozzy?" she whispers.

The asshole extends his hand. "Long time no see."

I remain motionless. A huge part of me wants to beat the shit out of the asshole. A very small part wants to hug my former best friend. I've fantasized about what I would do if I ever saw him again, but now I'm overcome with emotion and can't make a move.

Luis drops his arm. Ginger looks between us. "Ozzy, your concert was great. I really liked 'Take Me.' And the audience did too." She pauses. When no one speaks, she continues, "Since you've vetoed ghostwriters, Platinum wanted me to bring Luis back to help you finish out the album. He's my surprise."

Beside me, McKenna repeats, "Luis."

He's not my collaborator any longer. Keeping my eyes locked on the asshole, I give a curt nod to Ginger. McKenna's now rubbing my arm in small circles.

My body temperature rises the longer I look at the man I used to call friend. I note the changes in his appearance since the last time I saw him. He's thinner, if that's even possible. His clothes hang loosely off his skeleton-like frame. His bald head is covered in a fedora, as usual. His beard is longer than I remember, scruffier and ungroomed.

Ginger pushes Luis toward me. "You two need to get reacquainted."

Luis extends his hand again. "Looking good, Ozzy."

I retreat a step. "Can't say the same."

A cell phone rings. Knowing it's not mine—I always leave it turned off in here during a concert—I ignore the sound, and remain staring in disbelief at Ginger's surprise. How could Platinum possibly have thought this was a good idea?

"Well, I'll see you both at the after-party. Enjoy catching up." Ginger picks up her bag with logos all over it and walks past McKenna, who, I now realize, is on the phone.

Luis begins, "Listen, Ozzy. It's been years. I'm ready to leave the past behind and start writing together again. We produced some great hits. We used to be hermanos."

I brush out a harsh laugh. "Says the man screwing the bitch who just got a ten-million-dollar payday."

At his side, his hands fist. "You don't know what you're talking about."

"Fuck you." I step forward and bring both of my hands to his chest and push. He falls two steps backward before catching himself.

From off to the side, McKenna's rising voice captures my attention. I ignore the loser in front of me and focus on the one person in the room who matters. "Everything okay?" I whisper.

Keeping her eyes on the floor, she shakes her head and turns. Well, fuck. Since I can't talk with her right now, I turn my attention back to Luis. "How are you spending my money? Buying a house? What about a yacht? I know she always wanted one of those."

He flips his hat in a way I used to think was cool. When it's back on his head, he shrugs. "We're not together anymore."

I laugh. A full-on belly-laugh. "Karma's a bitch, isn't she?"

The corner of the room goes silent. McKenna picks up her bag off the floor and says, "I'll leave you two to sort things out. I have to go." And just like that, she leaves. In the moment I need her the most.

"McKenna, wait—" My words float into nothingness as she closes the door behind her. What the actual fuck?

Whirling on my former best friend, I snarl, "I don't know what caused you to think this was a good idea, but you can go crawl back under the rock you came from. I don't need you." I turn and follow McKenna, blood coursing through my veins like a fast-moving stream on its way to the ocean.

The bright red stripe in her hair is already halfway to the lobby. Since I know where she parks, I bypass the main lobby and take the backway to the parking garage. Sure enough, she's getting into her Honda when I enter the deck.

Still fuming that Platinum thinks I need Luis, I grab my helmet, hop on Shirley and follow her. Where is she going? Is she meeting up with another man? Why am I torturing myself with such thoughts? Seeing Luis has scrambled my brain. She's not anything like Teresa. But I didn't think Luis and Teresa could double-cross me, either.

Amid traffic, I follow her to the driveway of a small-ish house with a slightly-overgrown lawn, and park the bike on the street a few houses down. McKenna gets out of her car but, instead of going into the house, she rushes in the opposite direction. Dismounting from Shirley, I keep pace with her from two blocks away. Up ahead, an older woman in her pajamas is the only other person on the sidewalk. Several cars pass.

McKenna reaches out and touches the woman on her shoulder, causing her to spin around. Her arms flail and it appears as if she's going to fall, but McKenna catches her. Why didn't she walk around her?

Stopping, I watch as McKenna wraps herself around the woman and then jumps back as if scalded. She says something to the older woman—seemingly trying to comfort her—but the other woman shakes her head.

I stand, transfixed, watching the exchange and ready to intervene if McKenna needs me. Even though she just bailed on me. She turns and points down the street, directly at me, and her mouth falls open.

Shit. Caught.

When in doubt, deflect. I raise my chin and walk toward the two women, one of whom is shooting daggers at me from her eyes while the other starts fluffing her hair. "McKenna."

I look at the older woman, who starts at my voice, her latte-colored eyes meeting mine. Eyes that match McKenna's exactly. I take a wild guess. "Mrs. James."

The older version of McKenna looks confused. "Mateo, we're way past such formalities."

Mateo?

McKenna springs into action, wrapping her arm around her mother's shoulders. "Excuse me," she says as she navigates past me.

What is going on? Who the fuck is Mateo? I follow the pair down the sidewalk, which takes a surprising amount of time considering her mother stops to examine every thing—some flowers, a sign, rocks. What's wrong with her? Is she on drugs?

At her driveway, McKenna turns and addresses me. "Good night, Ozzy. I think you've seen enough."

Oh, *hell* no. This does not end here. I've let this woman into my home, my life, my heart. No way is she going to get away with locking me out of hers.

Eighteen

MCKENNA

I N MY DRIVEWAY, I HOLD MY BREATH and wait for Ozzy to leave. Please leave. Of course, he doesn't. Instead, his chin goes up a couple of notches.

My heart pounds. Realizing I'm going to have to tell him some version of the truth, I sigh and turn Mom and me toward the red front door. "Come on, Mom. Let's get you inside."

We shuffle up the short front walkway to the door, which I open and motion for her to enter. Once inside, she plants her hands on her hips and says, "Aren't you going to invite Mateo inside?"

From behind me, Ozzy agrees. "Yeah, McKenna. *Mateo* would like to come in."

Cornered, my whole body droops. There's no getting around telling him about Mom. Or about Matt. Unless I can pull an invisibility cloak from somewhere. "Fine." I usher both of them into the living room.

He's so big, he dwarfs the size of the room. His eyes bounce from family photos to our neat but aging furniture. Not wanting to offer him a drink but knowing that Mom, even in her fugue state, will do so, I ask, "Iced tea?"

"I'd love some," comes his instant response.

Leaving him alone with Mom is my only option, so I make quick work of pouring the drinks. The opened letter from the parole board catches my eye, and I shove it into the junk drawer, in the off-chance Ozzy walks in and sees it. When I return with two glasses, Mom's deep in conversation with Ozzy. However, her words jump, making her sound like a crazy person.

Which, in a sad way, I guess she is.

"Here." I pitch his glass toward him and put mine down on the coffee table. "It's time for bed, Mom. Say goodnight." I close my eyes, hoping she doesn't put up a fuss, especially since she was out roaming tonight.

Obediently, she stands and kisses Ozzy's cheek. "So good to see you again, Mateo. McKenna hasn't been herself since you stopped coming around. Now, you kids kiss and make up, and I'll see you both in the morning." She pecks my cheek and leaves for her bedroom. I'll check in on her once I get rid of Ozzy.

Pursing my lips, I look at my unwelcome visitor. "Happy? You can go now." I pluck his untouched drink out of his hand and use it to point at the door.

Ozzy's face blanks. It actually changes from the open and loving man I know, who was being so patient and understanding with Mom, into one I barely recognize as his. "I think not." He settles deeper into the couch.

I stand, holding his glass for a minute before giving up and returning it to him. Collapsing into Mom's chair, my butt slants forward when a knitting needle stabs it. I pull the offending needle away from my body and toss it onto the table, where it lands with a soft clunk. Crossing my arms like a disobedient child, I say nothing, daring him to speak.

"What's wrong with your mother?"

Delaying, I reach out and take a sip of my own drink. Should've put rum in it. Or skipped the tea altogether.

His dark eyes follow my every move. "She's." My mouth clamps shut and

I look out the window into the dark evening where Mom was wandering around in her pajamas. Thank God Becky called, but I can't rely on her to keep tabs on my mother any longer. She's my responsibility and I've been slacking.

My hand rubs the back of my neck. Exhaling, I complete my sentence in a rush, "She has early onset dementia." My face falls to my hands clasped in my lap.

When he remains silent, I look up at the man who has made the past few weeks better than any others in my life. He studies his glass. After taking a drink—his Adam's apple bobs in the masculine way that makes my heart skip a beat—he looks at me. "What can I do?"

His words both humble and infuriate me. Comfortable anger takes precedence. My words come out in a shrill tone. "Do you think I can't take care of my own mother?"

He places his glass on the coffee table. In a calming tone, he replies, "I didn't say that at all, McKenna. I want to help you."

"I don't need any help. She's my responsibility."

"Yes, as her only child, she is. And what you're doing is very honorable. But, everyone needs help sometimes, right? Look what you've done for my music."

I swallow over the baseball trying to come up through my throat. Averting my gaze from the man occupying not only my living room but also too much space in my heart, I reply, "I've got it."

He nods. "You know what's best. I'm here for you, if I can do anything." He runs his hand through his hair.

"Thanks," I say, knowing I cannot accept his help. Daddy passed the responsibility to me and I will never dishonor my vow. Plus, Ozzy has his feet out of Vegas—his residency ends in a few weeks and he'll be gone.

"So." He clears his throat. "Who's Mateo?"

My stomach clenches at the sound of the name spilling from Ozzy's lips. My eyes stray to the kitchen, where the letter now resides in the junk drawer, screaming out like a beating heart. Why did Mom have to confuse him with

Ozzy? Okay, they're both Latino, but that's where the resemblance ends. They couldn't be more opposite if they tried. For one, Ozzy's free to roam the streets. "He's no one."

"McKenna."

He doesn't say anything else. He doesn't have to. Scrambling to come up with a description that will satisfy him enough not to pursue this line of questioning, I pick up the knitting needle and reply, "I dated Matt. Years ago. Mom confused you with him. She wasn't in her right mind tonight." A tear leaks from my eye, which I swipe away.

In that instant, Ozzy appears at my side and pulls me into his embrace. I melt into him, rejecting my prior anger and accepting his comfort. Ignoring the letter and all it means, my focus returns to Mom. She's deteriorating and I don't have the funds to hire a nurse to stay with her twenty-four hours a day. If I make it to—and maybe even win—the consortium's national competition, I'll be able to hire a second shift. But, for right now, I'm stuck.

He rubs my back, which I find comforting. "I knew you were keeping something from me. I wish you had told me sooner."

I shrug into his embrace, not trusting my voice.

He leans back. "Anything else you want to share?"

I shake my head. I certainly have nothing else I want to come to light. *Ever.*

He kisses my forehead, then puts his hand on the back of my head, pushing it into his body. I inhale his comforting musky scent. "You're so strong," his baritone whispers through my ears.

"Hardly. I'm barely keeping it together." I laugh, which ends with a hiccup.

"Do you have any help at all with your mom?"

I nod. Since my head is against his pecs, my forehead bounces off his shoulder. "I sold my condo so I'm able to have a nurse here one shift a day."

"Oh, McKenna."

The two-word sentence brings tears down my cheeks. "I did what I had to do." What I vowed.

He rears back and wipes my cheeks with his thumbs. "You're special. Not many people would give up their independence to take care of a parent."

Sniffling, I can't force any more words out of my lips. I don't have to, as his cover mine in a soft caress. Sharing our breaths, I allow him to comfort me. Soothe my frustration and sadness over how things are turning out.

"Can I stay?"

I'm shaking my head before my brain registers his words. "I don't know who Mom will wake up to be tomorrow. It's best if you're not here in the morning."

"She's the reason why you never stay at my place? Why you've skipped my concerts."

"Yes."

He kisses my forehead again. "We'll figure this out."

I close my eyes against the tender gesture. He gathers to stand up, but I need him too much to let him go. I pull him back down and wrap my arms around his shoulders. His knees hit the floor as my mouth seeks his. I kiss him with my whole heart, pouring my gratitude for his words and happiness at being with him into the kiss. He returns my passionate kiss with his own.

When we separate, I remember what happened at the Jade—what feels like years ago. I suck in my breath. "Oh my God. *Luis.*"

His eyes slam shut. "Don't worry about him. You have enough on your plate. I'll handle it." He gives me a half-grin. "He's my responsibility." He kisses my nose. "And so are you."

Nineteen

OZZY

THIS MORNING'S SWIM FELT BETTER than the previous ones. I did my mile in record time. Must have been my conversation with McKenna last night. She explained so many things—why she never sleeps here, why she misses my concerts, her preoccupation with money, even an ex-boyfriend. It's not like I've never had women before. Fuck, she knows all about Teresa.

Clearing the air between us fuels my morning positive attitude.

Humming my newest song, I tie my sneakers. When I get all the songs written for my new album, I'll use my check from Platinum to help McKenna with her mother. She seems to want to keep her at home, so I'll look into adding another nurse to the cycle. Maybe even a live-in nurse—so McKenna can move in with me.

Whoa.

Sitting on the bed, I let the realization that I want her to move in roll through me. Followed by another—I'm not going to be here past the end of the year, when my residency at the Jade ends. I'll be in LA, then on tour.

McKenna'll have to come out with me. Since she's a graphic designer, she can work anywhere with an internet connection. And if her mother's being taken care of, there's no reason she can't be at my side. So different from Teresa's having to stay behind.

Smiling at the easy resolution, I go to the kitchen and start a late breakfast. Picturing McKenna in here with me.

As I'm washing out the blender from my protein shake, the doorbell rings. I need to give McKenna a key. Rubbing my hands on my T-shirt, I race to the front door, eager to hold my girl. Bans joins me, barking. "Sit," I order, knowing how nervous McKenna is around my dog.

"Morning, Dulc—"

My voice cuts off when I open the door to Ginger and Luis standing on the step. I hold it partway open, my knuckles turning white. "Ginger." At my side, Bans doesn't move a muscle, but growls. I don't correct her.

Ignoring my obvious omission of acknowledging her guest, Ginger pushes past me and crosses the threshold uninvited. "Ozzy." Not addressing her, I lock eyes with my former best friend. Ginger calls over her shoulder, "Luis, please come in."

I step to the middle of the doorway, Bans at my heel. Smart girl, she can smell a rat when she sees one. "You're not invited."

Ginger's footsteps return to my side. "Ozzy, let him in. We need to talk. Platinum's orders."

Feeling the walls closing in, I say in a hard voice, "In the office."

"Fine." Ginger turns and leads the way, followed by Luis. I bring up the rear with Bans, imagining all sorts of ways I can kill him and hide his body. Bans would be an innocent accomplice. When we're all in the room, Ginger nods at Bans. "Can this be humans only?"

Seeing no way out, I point toward the door. Bans barks but follows my command. I leave the door open in case I have a change of heart and decide to let her tear his guts apart.

Ginger begins, "Listen. I don't know or care what went down between you two. All Platinum cares about is that Ozzy's next album is in the recording booth come January. Meaning twelve new songs. Eleven more than you have, Ozzy."

I hate letting Luis see me in a position of weakness. I didn't want to share about the progress I've made writing, but seeing no other option, I state, "I have three more written, and more in the works."

She blinks. "Well, that's good." Pointing at Luis, she continues, "But you wrote your first album with Luis, which included six number ones. He's here to collaborate with you to ensure the magic happens again."

"No."

Ginger plants her hands at her waist.

Luis taps his hat. "Listen, bro—"

"Don't 'bro' me, you asshole." I don't care if Ginger's here or not.

He plays with his fedora. "We were a great writing team. Our songs lived at the top of the charts for months. We can do it again."

"No."

"Platinum's not asking, Ozzy. We need you to get your next album to the studio in a few weeks. Luis can make this happen."

My eyes swing to my rep. "My band has been collaborating with me. He," I nod toward the asshole standing in my office, "isn't needed. Or welcome."

Ginger huffs. "You two need to work whatever this is out." She motions between the two of us. "I'm going to leave. This isn't a request." Before she reaches the door, Ginger pulls a pill bottle out of her purse and tosses it to me. "This should help ease the tension." She walks out of the room.

Bans barks and Ginger yells for her to stay down. Luis watches as I play with the pill bottle, neither one of us uttering a word. After a minute, the golden retriever returns to my side, growling at Luis.

"Sit."

Luis drags his eyes away from the drugs. After a long moment, he walks over to a chair and slouches down like he owns the place, while the real object of my command sits at my feet. I smirk. Patting her head, I praise, "Good, Bans."

Remaining where I stand, I look down on the weasel. "I don't need you. Go."

He gives the drugs another hard stare, then stands. Which doesn't raise his stature much. "You heard Ginger. Platinum wants me here."

"Need the money?" I snap my fingers. "I guess you do since the bitch dumped your ass."

"Royalty checks keep me flush." He pauses. "Your new girlfriend could be her gringa carbon copy, you know. Although, fatter."

I'm on top of the asshole before he takes his next breath. Grabbing his shirt and twisting, I say, "Keep McKenna out of it. You don't deserve to hold her purse." I continue twisting my fist under his chin, cutting off his windpipe. Bans barks at my feet.

He raises his hands in surrender, and I drop mine. Bans keeps guard. "Even you have to admit that she looks a lot like Teresa," he says between wheezes.

I never consciously compared the two women. And I won't now. "They're nothing alike," I grit out.

Straightening, he reaches into his pocket and pulls out an envelope. "Look, even though Teresa and I broke up, we're still friends. She wants you to have this." He extends his hand.

I don't move.

He drops the envelope onto the desk. "Read it. Or not. I don't give a fuck. You're nothing but a lowlife who rode my coattails to success anyway. Without me, you're nothing. Just look at the position you're in."

"Now the true Luis comes out. Was wondering where the shithead was."

"Yeah, well, while you're singing the songs I wrote, I'm back in PR working my ass off." He fluffs his blazer and looks around. "Nice digs, by the way. It wouldn't hurt you to show me a little respect since you wouldn't have any of this if it weren't for me, bro."

I can't resist. "Yeah, well, maybe if you didn't look like a strung-out slob all the time, Platinum would have been willing to sign you. But you're too busy scrounging around for scraps to give a shit. And it shows. If you're looking for respect, *bro*, maybe you should try asking yourself for some."

He's on me this time. Or tries to be. Bans latches onto his leg and won't let go. I laugh at the unlikely sight. He shakes his leg. "Get off!"

Bans hangs on as if he were a chew toy, causing me to laugh even harder.

I cross my arms. "They say dogs are excellent judges of characters. Looks like she has you pegged." I watch for another few seconds, then call her off and send her out of the office.

Alone with Luis, we stare at each other. For the second time, I take in his skeletal appearance. "Here's your first test." I walk over to the pill bottle Ginger left behind and toss it to him. He catches it and rolls the container between his fingers.

Popping the top, Luis peers into the cylinder. "Molly. More your speed. And here you are lecturing me about how to live my life." He throws it back to me and I put it on the desk.

We remain at a standstill.

Luis sighs. "We're not going to write any songs, are we?"

"No."

His body turns in onto itself. "Fine. I'll see myself out."

"Hell no. I'm tossing you out." I escort/drag him out of the office and through the front door. Slamming it shut, I rest against it. Bans races up to me and I bend down to thank her for protecting me. In return, she licks my cheek off.

After washing my face, I go out to the patio with her and throw the ball, working off the nervous energy left behind by my ex-best friend.

My mind drifts to the office where Teresa's letter awaits me. Why should I read more of her poison? McKenna's words float through my head, about how I didn't listen to her when we were married. Sure, I was physically faithful, but did I give her my attention?

My feet lead me into the office, where I take her letter out of its envelope. Her penmanship is unmistakable. I pour myself some whiskey and return to the patio, placing the letter onto the table and taking a sip of the amber liquid.

A breeze picks up and the notebook paper blows, causing me to clamp it down. Fine. I'll read what she has to say. Then, I'll burn it and be done.

Ozzy,

I've started writing you several letters, but always got stuck. When Luis told me Platinum is sending him to you to write more songs, I knew I had to finish this one. It might be my last chance to communicate with you.

We got married when I was young. You weren't there to share college with me. When we talked, I brought up what was going on in my life, but you never seemed too interested. If I mentioned a guy ~ even my professor ~ you always got so jealous.

And I was so hurt that you didn't wear my wedding ring when you were away. I know it was Platinum's idea, but all the photos of you at parties gutted me. But that's no excuse for what happened.

Luis was on the island when you weren't. He listened to me. He encouraged me to pursue my dreams. I never meant for you to find out about us the way you did.

My life is different now. I got a job in the government and Luis and I are just friends. I hope someday we can be friends, too.

I did love you. If nothing else, please believe that.

I truly wish you all the best.

Fondly,

Teresa

Well, shit. My brain transports me back and I go through our conversations again. Teresa's not wrong. McKenna pointed this out right away. But, still—I never cheated on my wife.

I'm brought up short. I haven't referred to Teresa as my wife in years.

Mind in disarray, I reach out for my lifeline and text McKenna. Not my usual smartass line, but instead I ask if she can come over. Her response is immediate and affirmative.

Standing, I bring the now-crumpled notebook paper into the office and drop it on the desk next to the clock, which reads noon. Maybe I'll show it to McKenna. Maybe not—no need to prove I was a total jerk. Best to let her only *think* I was, no confirmation needed.

I'm in no mood to cook so I pull out a takeout Mexican menu and place an order for our dinner to be delivered later. Then, I pull two bottles out of the fridge. McKenna rings the bell less than an hour later. Bans beats me to the door, growling.

"Bans, no. The bad people are gone." She seems to understand what I say as she turns and walks to her bed.

I open the door and the sunlight hits McKenna as if it were a spotlight. Pulled forward, I wrap her in my arms. "You're a sight for sore eyes."

She returns my embrace. "I wasn't sure you wanted to see me again, after last night."

Looking down at her, I shake my head. "No way. Only made me more intrigued. Come on in." As she passes, I inquire about her mother.

"She's much better this morning, thanks for asking. Elaine, her day nurse, is with her now."

When we reach the patio, I hand her a Mexican cerveza. "I ordered Mexican for dinner, hope that's okay?"

She clinks the necks of our bottles together. "More than okay."

We smile and enjoy the relative cool breeze and drink our beers. We discuss her mother's condition, and how much Elaine takes some of the burden from her shoulders. I'm impressed with my girl's resilience.

She puts her bottle down on the concrete. "What's wrong?"

I finish off my beer. "That obvious?"

Her lips curl upward, into a half-smile. "I'm getting to know Ozzy-isms."

"Yeah, well." I cross my leg over my knee. "Ginger brought Luis here today. She expected us to write the rest of the album together."

She gasps. "I hope you told them to pound sand."

A small chuckle escapes, despite my mood. "I kinda did. I told Ginger I've written a few songs and don't need his help. I let her know my band is my new collaborator." I pause. "I should've said I have a super-sexy and inspiring new muse, too."

I reach out and grab her by the middle and drag her onto my lap. Both of her legs dangle off the side of my right one. Tracing her leg with my fingertip, I say, "Because I do."

She giggles. "I've never been a muse before." Her eyes get wide. "Do I have to do anything special?"

All thoughts about Luis and Ginger and Teresa and songs flee, as images of how McKenna can "feed my muse" overtake them. Over a harsh intake of breath, I lean into her ear, "Oh, yes. There are several things you have to do to keep my muse pumping out songs."

A shaky hand runs through her hair. "Really? Like what? I mean, I want you to keep pumping." Her fingers trail down the center of my chest, stopping at my belt buckle.

My cock strains against my zipper. Grabbing her hand and abandoning it on top of my hardness, I kiss her neck. "I'm sure you'll think of something."

She squeezes and I nearly jump out of the chair. Groaning, I encourage her. The buckle opens and she pulls my cock out, her hand running its length. At the top, she stops and swirls her thumb over the drop of pre-cum that's leaked. She brings it to her mouth.

"Mmmm."

The doorbell rings.

I drop my head backward. "Fuck. Dinner's here."

She giggles and jumps off me. "I'll get it. You better stay here and take care of him." She points to my cock, which is pleading for her to continue what she was doing.

While she gets our dinner, I take off my sneakers. I want my dessert before the main course today. Besides, I'm not sure I could stand unless it was to plow into her tight body.

Rustling of bags snags my attention. McKenna asks, "Want to eat out here?"

"I definitely want to eat you out here."

She squeaks and drops the bags onto the table. "You're not dressed."

"But you are. Let me change that." And I do.

Much later, we sit with our feet in the swimming pool, all of our appetites fulfilled for the moment. My eyes roam over McKenna's body, for the first time noting the similarities between her and Teresa. While Teresa was short and skinny with huge tits, brown hair and brown eyes, McKenna's curvy. More to hold onto, in my book. Plus, her hair is more imaginative, if that's the word for it, since she's always changing up the color streak. It's part of her style and flair. And her eyes. Brown, yes, but more of a latte that change with her mood—blazing when she's feisty, darker when she's horny, dancing when she's happy. No. She's all woman with deeply-held responsibilities where Teresa was a girl.

"Penny."

"What?"

She taps my forehead. "A penny for your thoughts."

I smile. "I was thinking you're all woman, and I'm really glad that you're all mine."

Her teeth overtake her bottom lip. "You sure know how to woo a girl." She stands. "Let's get some work done before you try to get in my pants again."

We both get to our feet and head inside. Instead of heading down the hallway toward the music room, McKenna turns toward the office. "Let's work in here for a change, okay?"

I shrug. Doesn't matter much to me so long as I have McKenna and my guitar with me. In that order. Smiling as I make my way to the music room, I gather my guitar, sheet music and a pencil. For a day that started out like shit, it sure has turned around. All because of McKenna.

Entering the office, I stop as if I hit a brick wall. McKenna's expressive eyes now are nearly slits and she's holding out the drugs Ginger left for me.

"What's this?" she demands, shaking the container. The pills clink inside the bottle.

I reach for it but she pulls away. "Just something Ginger left for me and Luis. Thought it would help us write better, I guess."

For each step I take toward her, she takes another backward. Abandoning our dance, she holds her ground. Eyeing me up and down, she asks, "And did you?"

"Partake?" I shake my head. "No." Her expression remains the same—all jerky movements, quick breaths and rigid posture. I grab for the pills again. "What's up?"

She swallows, and her throat expands and contracts. She seems to weigh her responses, finally saying, "I don't want drugs near me. Anything stronger than an Advil is forbidden."

Forbidden? "Listen, it's not like I do them all the time."

"You were high at Rose and Cole's wedding."

"Well, yeah, but I needed the escape. I had just signed the divorce settlement." And made a ten million-dollar wire transfer.

"Not an excuse."

I grab the pills from her and toss them onto the desk. They land on top of Teresa's note. Wonderful. "Can't go back in time, McKenna. But, I didn't take any of these."

Her eyes roll. "Flush them."

"What?"

She crosses her arms across her chest and nods to the pills. With McKenna, I haven't felt like getting high—probably because she gives me a natural one. I shrug and head to the bathroom. Tossing the pills down the toilet, I flush them good-bye.

When I return to the office, McKenna sits on a chair, her head in her hands. Going onto my knees next to her, I rub her back. "Want to tell me what that was all about?"

Without lifting her head, she shakes it. "Suffice it to say I had a bad experience and can't stand the sight of drugs now."

I squeeze her shoulder. "Fine. I don't do them often, so it's not a big deal." Her head pops up, tear tracks left behind on her cheeks. I want to know why she's reacting like this, but now's not the time. Trying to lighten the mood, I quip, "Now, if you had something against rum, we'd have to talk."

A reluctant smile crosses her face. "No. I'm good with rum." She swipes her cheek.

I tip her chin upward. "The only thing I want from you is honesty. If drugs make you," I search for the right word. Settling for "uncomfortable," I continue, "There won't be any in the house. So long as you're here with me, I'm good."

"What did I do to deserve someone like you?"

I look around. "Someone? Hello, you have the real thing." I pound on my chest.

She taps my pecs, then eases her arms around my neck. "I am one lucky lady."

"Are you sure you can't come to my concert tonight? I always perform better when you're in the audience."

She shakes her head. "I really can't. I've left Mom home alone at night too often and, well, you saw the net result last night. I want to stay with her to make sure she's safe."

Can't argue with her but, damn, I'm going to miss her. Her next statement leaves me flabbergasted.

"Oh, and I have a meeting tomorrow, so I probably won't be able to make it over here at all."

Oh, hell no. "What's more important than working on the songs for the Project? I thought everything hinges on that." I pause. "For both of us."

Her lips purse and her eyes drift to the side. "I need," she blinks, "I have to bring Mom to the doctor and it usually takes hours. I'm sorry."

I can't argue with her about her mother. Yet, something in her stance leads me to believe there's more to it than she's telling me. "Want company?"

She puts her laptop into its case. "No. I've got it. You work on your songs." She walks toward the door.

"Hey, McKenna."

Halting midway through the office, she swivels her head. "Yes?"

I open a desk drawer, pulling out an extra key. Handing it to her, I say, "Here. I want you to have access to me anytime."

Her fingers close around the symbol of my commitment to her, even if she doesn't recognize it as such. "Thanks, Ozzy. This means a lot to me." She returns to my side and gives me a very thorough kiss.

Once she's gone, a contentment I haven't felt in years—if ever—washes over me. McKenna's really taking up residence in my life.

And I like it.

Twenty

MCKENNA

I CROSS AND RE-CROSS MY LEGS ON the hard bench. Of their own volition, my fingers strum the beat to 'Take Me.' Air in the windowless room is stuffy and smells of stale cigarettes. The table on the dais has five chairs, each with a tag in front of it. The warden. The case worker. Other officials.

I close my eyes and try to still my rampant heartrate. This is the first parole hearing Matt's been granted and the prosecutor told me it's merely a formality. Inmates hardly ever get released the first time they're eligible.

Considering Matt's in for manslaughter, I can't imagine he'll be set free. But I came to be sure of it.

The prosecutor sitting at the table in front of me sets out his stuff—legal notepad, pens, a big folder with several files in it. This is going to be okay. All I have to do is tell my story and leave. I won't have any interactions with Matt. If only he wasn't going to be in here. I don't want to see him ever again. The trial was enough.

A side door opens and Matt—wearing an orange jumpsuit but no handcuffs—shuffles into the room. I drop my head and refuse to look at him, even though his eyes burn into my skin. He doesn't deserve to see me cower. Lifting my head, I focus on the table on the dais. In short order, people take their seats and the proceeding begins.

After a bit, I'm called to make my statement. Wishing Ozzy were here for moral support, I remind myself he's not a part of this nightmare. I take a deep breath, stand and look at the prosecutor, who indicates I can speak from here since it's not a courtroom.

Clearing my throat, I begin. "My name is McKenna James, and Harry James was my father. Matt—Mateo Lopez—killed him when he caught Matt beating me. Matt was mad because I refused to do what he wanted in order for him to score more drugs. Heroin, to be exact."

My eyes drop to my feet. I can't look at anyone as I dredge up the details of the worst day of my life.

Seeing as no one asks me any questions, I force myself to form words. I start with some background. "I met Matt when I was twenty-two. I had moved back here after graduating college, and we moved in together within a couple of months. At first, it was great. We went to parties and did things normal twenty-two-year-olds did. Soon, he started taking drugs and I"—I play with my hair—"I joined him. I worked for a graphic design firm at the time, so I'd go to work, come home, get stoned. Pot. That was my life. Matt worked as a handyman, so he worked odd hours and often was paid in cash."

Wanting this to be over, I rush through the next part. "Unbeknownst to me, Matt started shooting heroin. He kept asking to 'borrow' money from me. When I didn't have any to lend, he got upset. He hit me, but I kept it quiet, not wanting anyone to know things were going badly at home." Besides, when he did that, he'd get me high and things evened out. Or so I thought.

I cross my arms. "It didn't stop. After a really bad beating, I gave in and reached out for help. I called my father, who came over right away."

Rubbing my arms, I will tears not to fall as I speak the last part. "When Daddy was helping me pack my things, Matt came home. He started yelling and throwing things, and he knocked me against the wall. I blacked out.

When I came to, Matt was holding a knife to my father, telling him to stay out of our lives. My father stood up for me and Matt plunged the knife into him." Turns out Daddy brought the knife from home as protection. While I was out cold, Matt must've gotten control of it from him.

I tell of screaming and rushing to his side, but omit my promise to take care of Mom. That's no one else's business. Tears flow.

Sucking in my breath, I continue. "Matt's assertion of self-defense was rejected by the jury and he was sentenced to ten years for manslaughter. He's only served five years of his sentence. He is a drug-addicted, cold-blooded murderer who never deserves to see the light of day. I do not believe jail has changed him at all. If anything, I can only imagine it's made him worse. He's never shown any remorse for killing my father, or for beating me." I toss in the last part, even though what he did to me pales in comparison. "In fact, while my father lay dying, his only reaction was to tell me, 'Look what you made me do.' He's a twisted, heartless monster, and he never deserves to be set free."

One person on the panel, a woman, asks, "Have you visited Mr. Lopez while he's been in jail?"

Is she fucking kidding? "No."

She follows-up. "Have you communicated with him at all?"

"No."

"Has he reached out to you since he's been in here?"

"No."

"Okay. Thank you for your testimony. You're free to leave."

I nod and collapse back onto the bench. I want to run far away from here, but need to hear what's being said. I have to know he'll stay behind bars for the entire length of his sentence. If not longer. Forever and a day wouldn't be sufficient.

The prison guards testify about Matt's time in jail. Apparently, he's been a model inmate. So what? Doesn't change what he did. The loss my heart feels every day only grows heavier.

The proceeding wraps up when the warden says they'll take everything under advisement and render a decision soon. I wish they had said "denied," but I guess I'll have to wait for that bit of good news.

Together with a few others in the room, I stand and collect my things. Against my instincts, I lift my head and lock eyes with the man who changed my life forever.

Murderer.

The attorney for the prosecution touches my arm and brings me out of my head. He says, "Thanks for speaking up. I know how tough it was for you, but you did well. You were very brave."

There's that word again. I don't feel very brave today. Ignoring Matt as he's being escorted out of the room, I manage to utter, "Appreciate it."

"I'll be in touch with the decision when I receive it. Don't worry, this was only his first time up for parole. I'd be surprised if they make any changes."

"I hope not."

With that, the attorney returns to his paperwork and pulls out another file. Guess it's parole day.

Gathering my purse, I lift my chin and walk out of the room. With every step I take, the weight of today's hearing lifts. By the time I'm at the car, I've nearly convinced myself Matt can't get an early release. And I almost believe it.

Inhaling a deep breath, I enjoy the smell of freedom. Something Matt won't be feeling for five more years, God willing. Putting my key into the ignition, the key to Ozzy's house clicks against the various storetags hanging on the keyring.

Ozzy.

He's much too good for me. What does he have in his background? An ex-wife? Ha! I'd take his baggage any day. I know he's into me—but for how long? Not even he can lift the burden of my vow from me.

Even if all I want to do is run into his arms.

I don't realize I've driven to the battered women's shelter I volunteer at until I pull into the parking lot. Years ago, my therapist recommended I spend time with others who are healing. While I'm here to inspire others, I always get re-energized with each visit. With today's hearing behind me, I throw my shoulders back and spend time with some of the most amazing women on the planet.

Hours later, I park in our driveway and make my way into the house. Even though I told Ozzy I would try to go to his concert tonight, I'm not feeling it. Walking into the house, I give Mom a kiss. "Hi, Mom."

"Hi, McKenna. Hope your meeting went well."

She doesn't know where I went. The trauma of losing Daddy sped up the dementia, so I keep everything related to Matt well-hidden from her. And no need to share about my time at the battered women's shelter, either. "It did." At least the second part of the day. I rub my hands together. "Want some cookies?"

Her eyes light up. "Chocolate chip or Nutella?"

I force a laugh. "Your pick."

"Hey, Elaine," Mom calls out. "McKenna's making cookies today. What kind do you want?"

Looks like Mom's having a good day. Score one. At least today isn't a total loss. From the laundry room, Elaine says, "Snickerdoodles!"

I can't stop myself from embracing Mom. "How about I make all three?"

"You won't hear me complain."

After dropping a kiss on her cheek, I go to the pantry and pull out flour, Nutella, chocolate chips, sugar and cinnamon and lose myself in baking.

A few hours later, I pull the last batch—chocolate chip—out of the oven. Mom hands me a glass of milk. Using a spatula, I offer her a hot cookie of gooey goodness. We both inhale the delicious, chewy cookie.

"I swear, if you weren't a graphic designer, I would beg you to become a pastry chef."

"Thanks, Mom."

Elaine strolls into the kitchen, purse slung over her shoulder. "Well, I'm out of here. See you tomorrow, Janice."

"See you then," Mom says, giving her another Snickerdoodle for the road.

Mom and I stay in the kitchen, laughing and talking while chowing down on the cookies. The old clock chimes seven.

"Shit! I didn't realize the time."

"Language."

"Sorry, Mom. We didn't have dinner. What would you like?"

Mom pats her flat stomach, something I envy every day. "I'm full up on cookies. We can skip dinner this once." She leans in. "But don't tell your father."

My heart plummets. Spending time with her was so fun that I almost forgot about her condition, and about seeing Matt. I place my hand on top of hers. "Don't worry. I won't." Standing, I survey the damage in the sink. "Why don't you go watch TV while I clean up in here?"

"Boy, I really got the good end of this stick." She smiles and leaves me alone. Even when I'm with her, sometimes, I'm alone. Trembling hands start the process of cleaning up the mess.

When all the dishes are cleaned and put away, I remember to turn on my cell phone. Ozzy's left me several texts. He has about a half-hour before he takes the stage. My thumbs hover over my phone and I text him back:

Sorry, I missed you all day. Time ran away from me with all the docs. I'm spending tonight with Mom, I hope you understand.

I reread the text a couple of times before pressing "Send."

He replies instantly:

Glad to hear from you. I'm really missing you, but I get it. Hope all is well. Can I do anything?

A smile plays around my lips, but I shake my head. No. As much as he wants to be involved, he can't make this go away.

No, but thanks for the offer. Knock 'em dead tonight!

I add a "kissy-face" icon and tap "Send." Suddenly exhausted, I drop the phone onto the counter and walk into the living room. *Jeopardy!* is on the television and Mom's asleep in her chair. She looks so peaceful. Deciding not to wake her, I lock up, turn the alarm on in case she decides to go out for a stroll later on, cover her with a blanket and head to my bedroom.

Tomorrow has to be a better day. Right?

Twenty-One

OZZY

AFTER MY MORNING SWIM AND SHOWER, I pull on my usual outfit of T-shirt and shorts and lay back on my bed. Feeling restless, I turn to my side and pick up my phone. Not wanting to seem like a pussy and text McKenna again, I choose a different contact.

"Hola, Mamí."

"Ozzy! So good to hear from you. How are things going out in Las Vegas?"

"They're … interesting. I've been writing new songs for my album."

"That's great. Write any songs about your dear old Mamí in Puerto Rico?"

I chuckle at her question. "Well, the whole vibe is much more Puertoriqueño than my last album. Tío Miguel would love it."

"I bet I will, too."

I turn my head on my pillow. "So, Mom. I wanted to run something by you. Teresa sent me a letter." Via Luis, but I don't share this piece of news.

Her voice takes on a hard edge. She spits, "She did?"

Gotta love a momma bear looking out for her cub. Even if this cub is now thirty-eight-years-old. "Yeah. Among other things, she said I didn't listen to her when she wanted to share news about her college life."

"Well, sounds like sour grapes to me. You're a huge star now. I think she's trying to make you feel guilty."

"And do what? Take her back?"

"Oh, she was a master-manipulator. I saw that right from the start. I wouldn't be surprised if she didn't want to get her hooks back into you. You're well rid of her."

"She's ten million bucks richer now, 'cause of me. I'd never look twice at her again."

"Money well spent."

The note of finality to her tone shifts my focus from my past to my future. "Besides, I've met someone out here."

"You have? Tell me about her."

I play with the pillowcase. Sucking in a breath, I admit, "Her name's McKenna and she's a graphic designer. She's working on the Artist Adventure Avenue Project that some of my songs will be featured in."

"I remember your telling me about the Project. She sounds smart."

I push back against the headboard. "She is. And she's funny. Plus, she doesn't let me get away with anything."

"I like her already. When can you bring her here to meet the familia?"

My eyes go wide. "Slow down there, mamacita. We've only started dating."

"You're still planning on coming here in January, right? Maybe then?"

I roll my eyes. Why did I think calling Mamí was a good idea? Oh yeah, because McKenna's not here. Deciding to ignore her last comment, I ask about my brothers and sister, which takes her down a different path. Once I'm all caught up, I promise to call her again soon, and hang up with an "I love you."

Bans barking at the front door brings me down the stairs.

"Down!" McKenna points to the floor, juggling her laptop. "Ozzy!" she yells in frustration.

The golden retriever only wants to lick McKenna's face, but I can't convince her of that. "Bans, come."

Immediately, Bans turns and sits at my heel. A smile works its way across my face as I drink in the frazzled beauty in front of me. Giving the dog a hand command to stay, I approach McKenna, take her laptop case and put it on the floor. And proceed to join my lips to hers. "A day was too long away from you."

She runs her fingers through my hair, then down to brush against my stubble, her finger ending up on my bottom lip. "You're a sight for sore eyes."

Not letting her move out of my embrace, I ask, "How's your mom? Did the docs give you some good news?"

She breaks our eye contact. "She's doing alright."

Bending down, I wrap my arms around her waist and lift her off the floor. "Glad to hear it," I whisper into her ear.

Giggling, she arches her back. "How's the song writing biz?"

I deposit her back on the floor. Grabbing her laptop case in one hand while interlocking our fingers with the other, I lead her to the music room. "Going well. The band and I worked late last night at the Jade—since you weren't coming over—and we started a few more songs."

She claps. "Awesome! I'm so happy for you. Let's hear what you've got."

Grabbing my guitar, I say, "I hope all my fans are as excited as you for new songs." I play a few chords. "Oh, and did I mention I'm thrilled you used your key today?"

"Yeah, well, Bans had other ideas." She cocks her head. "Maybe if you gave her another name, she wouldn't be so angry all the time."

"What? She loves her name." I strap the guitar around my body and pull out the sheaf of sheet music I've been working on.

Booting up her laptop, she eyes Bans, who has walked into the room.

"Come here." I stretch out my hand, motioning for her to take it, which she does. I lead her over to the dog. "She's very friendly to people she likes, and I can tell she likes you. Why don't you pet her?"

"Dogs make me jumpy," she whispers.

I go on my haunches and Bans's head comes up. Looking into McKenna's eyes, I incline my head toward the dog. Taking McKenna's hand in mine, we both pet the dog, whose tail wags with all the attention.

"She's soft."

"Aiden took her to the groomers yesterday for me."

We continue petting her together. When she rolls over, I scratch her belly and stand. McKenna joins me. "See, she's really a pussycat."

Next to me, McKenna snorts. "I wouldn't go that far, but she's sweet." Bans goes over to her bed and lies down, her tail wagging.

Once we resume our positions—McKenna at the table with her laptop and me by the instruments—I proceed to play all of my new songs. McKenna records them on her cell phone and scribbles notes onto a stray piece of sheet music. She offers her opinion on some of the songs and then goes off to work on her computer while I continue to play around with the notes.

My mind keeps straying to the letter Teresa sent me. I need her take on it. Without interrupting her work, I go into my office and pick up the notebook paper. Sitting next to McKenna, I offer it to her to read.

She holds it up. "What's this?"

"Teresa sent it to me. Had it hand delivered, actually, by Luis. I'd like an outsider's perspective." I push it back so she can read it.

She bites her bottom lip. "Okay." Her eyes skim the words, her eyebrows forming a frown. When she finishes, she places the paper down. Running her tongue over her lips, she asks, "What do you think about what she said?"

"You sort of nailed it. I didn't take her life into consideration," I reply. "But, I like to think I've changed."

"Life makes change happen, one way or another. I'm sorry you had to go through this." She kisses my cheek.

"I missed you yesterday."

"And I missed you, too. But, I'm here now."

She embraces me. I don't care about anything but showing this woman how much she means to me. Now. "Dulcita."

She doesn't move. "Yes?"

My hands reach for her waist and pull out her shirt from her pants. "Off."

Her hands fly up and I skim her blouse over her head. For her part, she unbuckles my belt and my cock stirs in anticipation. Like every other time, we're naked in no time flat. Standing up with her, I grab her hand and head toward my bedroom.

Not having the patience to walk even another step, I bring her over to the stairs. "I need you hard and fast," I growl in between kisses.

"Please," she mewls.

I dip my fingers into her center, greeted by wet warmth. "Always so ready for me."

Her lips play at my nipple rings while my finger circles and circles her clit, working her into a frenzy. I urge her up one stair so we're now almost equal height. Rolling a condom over my length, I put my leg between hers, which she rides.

"Like that?"

"Mmm, hummm," comes her response.

I grab her ass, and tilt her body into mine. I don't allow my cock to slide home, but rather for the friction to heighten our senses. My mouth latches onto her nipple, and I bring my teeth together, causing her to cry out.

She continues to hump my leg while her hands grab my ass and squeeze. "God, Ozzy. What you make me feel."

In response, I let her nipple fall from my mouth and take her lips in mine, my tongue swirling to mimick the rhythm of my fingers now inside her warmth. Her body clenches and then she cries out as liquid coats my fingers.

"One."

I want to hear her scream at least once more before I pound into her right here on the stairs. Spinning her around, I rain kisses down her spine. My hands find her hips and dig in—I can dig in because she has some meat on her bones. And I like it.

Stepping forward, I thrust my cock between her ass cheeks, rubbing myself all over her. "Ever been taken back here?"

"What? Oh." She thrusts back at me. "Uhm, yeah."

"But never by me."

Her head shakes from side to side. Damn. Where's the lube? It's upstairs in the bedroom, a whole long flight of stairs away. Continuing my onslaught on the outskirts of her ass, I bring my fingers forward and play with her pussy. "Next time."

A long moan accompanies her next thrust backward. Her hands reach forward and she folds onto the steps, catching herself by her hands, ass in the air.

"Two."

Taking my cock in my hand, I position it at her entrance and enter her with one thrust.

"Oh my God!" She pushes back, absorbing all of me.

Standing over her body, sweat pouring off both of us, I ram into her over and over, each thrust better than the last. "I would fuck you forever, if I could," I manage.

She pushes backward. "And I'd love every second of it."

Wrapping her hair around my hand, I tug. Her neck extends, her tits bouncing before her. "When you come next time, I want you to scream my name so that the neighbors all know who's screwing you."

She pants out a "yes."

I continue the punishing rhythm until I feel her walls closing in on me. My balls tighten and I pull on her hair as I shout, "Fuuuuck!!" I keep thrusting until she screams, "Ozzy!"

When the last tremors run through our bodies, I skim my fingers up and down her torso from her hips to her tits. Placing kisses on her neck, my lips make their way up to her earlobe. Biting it, I whisper, "You make me insane."

Her lower half shifts. "Right back at you."

With her on the first step, she's a lot taller than usual. I enjoy the feel of her body against mine.

As I'm pulling out of her, she asks, "What's up here?"

"The bedrooms." For as many times as we've had sex, it's never been in a bed. My cheeks inflate against her neck. "Gotta make you earn admittance."

Her hand sneaks around and grabs the back of my head. She turns and kisses me full stop. "Game on."

Stepping around me, she breaks our contact and scoops up her clothes. I watch as she puts one foot, then the other, into her panties and pulls them up into place. When she picks up her bra, I snatch it from her grasp. "Please, allow me."

"I'm glad you're able to come to the concert tonight." She even brought a change of clothes.

McKenna puts the strap of her dress into place. It's a yellow confection—hence the hair color change—rhinestones glittering all over it. "Our neighbor promised to look out for Mom."

I play with the skirt that's higher in the front than the back. When she produces red, high-heeled sandals, my mouth waters. "Damn. You're fucking hot."

Once her shoes are on her feet, she marches up and down. "Gotta keep up with my tatted and pierced man." Her fingers trace the sleeve of tattoos on my right arm. "Tell me about all these."

I bark a laugh. "We don't have time for all the stories."

She points to a mermaid. "Okay. This one."

I smile. "My sister loved Ariel, the Disney mermaid. Got that one for her."

"Nice." She kisses it.

"Not as nice as these." I kiss her tits through her dress and she giggles. "C'mon, let's go. The guys wanted to practice 'Honesty,'—we're going to debut tonight."

After a quick ride on Shirley, we're inside my dressing room at the Jade, surrounded by my band members. Stan's drumsticks play on the coffee table while Tim plays the portable keyboard. I join in and sing the first verse, then Jazz and Mark add in their instruments during the chorus. Our first run-through of the song ends with all of us at full-throttle.

Our audience—consisting of McKenna and Aiden—yells their praise. McKenna's heard my solo version of the song, but never with my band, and this is Aiden's first exposure. The band's stoked about it, but I'm happy these two like it, too.

Aiden stands and claps. "Guys, this is phenomenal."

For her part, McKenna runs to me and kisses my lips. Then, she turns and gives each one of my band members a kiss on their cheeks. The guys, to a one, blush and look at their feet. I grab her around the waist and plant a sloppy kiss on her.

Clearing my throat, I say, "Thanks. You're our first test audience."

After shooting the shit for a while, Aiden says, "Okay. It's time to take your marks, guys."

I turn to McKenna while everyone leaves for the show. "Watch backstage tonight. It'll be our first time."

She touches my pecs and leans in. "I like it when we do firsts together."

My mind immediately goes to taking her ass, but I shake my head to clear it. I have a concert to give and I don't want to be hard to start it. "You're a menace."

"And you like it!" She giggles and walks to the backstage area, leaving me with barely enough time to bury my sex thoughts and mentally prepare for tonight's show, complete with 'Honesty.'

"Thank you, Las Vegas! You rock!" I shout into the microphone as my band members join me in the front of the stage and we take our final bows. The curtain closes in front of us and we high-five each other.

"Super gig guys," Jazz says.

Stan chimes in, "They love the new stuff."

"Thanks to you," I add. Turning, my eyes land on McKenna, who's talking with Aiden. I stride over to them, stripping off my wet shirt as I go.

Aiden hands me my bottle of water, which—as usual—I down and pour the remainder over my head. Droplets spew over him and McKenna when I shake it. Aiden rolls his eyes, but McKenna jumps backward. Some of the water seeps through the top part of her dress. All right.

Laughing, I grab her hand and bring it to my lips. "Let's shower, then we can join the afterparty."

She nods. Hand-in-hand, McKenna walks down the hallway with me when a guy wielding a camera turns the corner. "Great show, Ozzy," he offers, snapping photos of us.

"Thanks, man."

"Who's this lovely lady?"

I glance at the woman on my arm for direction about how she wants to handle this. Her torso inflates as if she took a huge breath. Not waiting for me to respond, she says, "I'm McKenna James." She extends her hand.

Gotta give my girl credit. Yep, she's fearless.

The reporter writes her name down in his notebook and leaves us. I wrap my arm around McKenna and usher her into my dressing room. "You're not afraid of anything." Closing the door behind us, I amend, "Except Bans."

She smirks. "I'm afraid of taking a shower alone."

Smacking her ass, I reply, "No worries there."

Twenty-Two

MCKENNA

When I enter Ozzy's house, Bans rushes to me, tail wagging. My body stiffens, but I force air through my lungs and say her name, followed by "Sit." She does, looking up at me with those soulful eyes—begging to be pet.

I reach out and pet her head, then drop a bit lower to scratch behind her ears, earning a lick on my cheek. Maybe she isn't so scary after all.

"Come on, Bans. Let's go find your owner."

My heart constricts. Can I have him and still handle all my responsibilities? My mind returns to the parole board hearing, for which no decision has been rendered. If they were going to let Matt out, I'm sure I would've heard already. Right?

Passing the stairs leading to still-unseen bedrooms, I remember Ozzy's prodding at my back entrance. The images I pushed away yesterday float through my brain—Matt and I having anal sex a handful of times. Because he raved about it, I gritted through the pain. Being high helped. Now clean, I wonder if even Ozzy can turn my experience around.

Shaking out those old memories, I pop my head into the music room, but Ozzy's not here. In fact, he's not inside the house at all. I check out the patio and no, he's not in the pool either. I settle in the living room and cue up the graphics for the Project. I puff up. I'm about finished, and need his approval to make the final touches.

Ozzy's baritone bounces off the walls. "Bans!" The dog races from her spot at my feet to greet her true owner at the front door. Strolling into the living room, he carries a bunch of packages, which he deposits onto the couch when he sees me. He opens his arms wide and I walk straight into him, inhaling the musky scent that's one hundred percent him.

"Been here long, Dulcita?"

I shake my head against his chest. "About an hour."

I tilt my head back and his finger smooths the crease between my eyebrows. "What's this frown for?"

Not wanting to reveal anything about Matt and the parole hearing, I incline my head toward the bags. "Shopping?"

He gives me a searching look, to which I smooth my features, and he sighs. "I went to check out a tattoo parlor nearby but got sidetracked by the Harley shop. Got you a new helmet." He releases me and holds up a badass helmet.

"A bald eagle?" I ask, referencing the picture depicted on it.

"Fearless. Independent. Like you."

"Well, when you say it like that," I reply, a huge grin stealing across my face.

"And you're going to need to be." He pulls out a magazine and flips it open, then holds it up for me to see. It's a photo of Ozzy and me after his concert the other night—Ozzy's shirtless and sweaty from performing and I'm smiling up at him.

I take a deep breath. "Oh."

His finger taps on the caption. "They spelled your name right, at least."

I read the short text that, indeed, does spell my name right and calls me his newest flame. "Our relationship was bound to come out."

"Yeah. I'm surprised it took this long."

How do I feel about it? It's relatively innocuous. So long as I keep him compartmentalized in my life, this can work. I hope. "So, I'm your flame, huh?"

He touches my shoulder and makes a sizzling noise. Shaking his finger, he teases, "Hot."

Then, he unveils another bag. This one is from Edie Z's Chocolates. Forgetting about the magazine, I snatch the candy from his hands and wave a peanut butter confection under his nose. "I'm certainly fearless enough to steal your candy." I pop the chocolate into my mouth, punctuating its utter perfection with a moan.

Ozzy takes the bag out of my hands. "Enough. The only time I want to hear that sound coming out of your mouth is when I'm deep inside of you." I moan again for good measure. "Which I will be in less than a minute if you don't stop."

Glancing at the clock, I see it's still early. Plus, it's been too long since we've been together—at least twelve hours. Swallowing the last bit of the candy, I give him an exaggerated moan.

"That's it."

He grabs me by my waist and proves he's a man of his word.

DRESSED AGAIN, WE sit on the couch and Ozzy watches the presentation I designed for his songs. I take notes while he absorbs it, in full, for the first time. When the last song finishes, I press stop.

I don't have to wait long for his evaluation. "That was award-winning."

"You like it?"

"I really do. I never would have come up with such concepts, but they work. The way you see through my music and make it both personal and universal. You're a freaking genius." He pulls me in for a bear hug.

"Thank you." I hold up my notes. "I need to make these changes, but so long as your songs stay as they are, it's almost done."

"You know what? The band was talking last night about hitting the recording studio to lay these first tracks down."

"Really? When?"

He pulls me close. "Starting tomorrow. So, I'm not going to be able to spend my days with you."

"That's okay. I need to put the finishing touches on this." I gesture toward my laptop. "The Project set up a meeting on the seventh, so it'll be good for me to focus on polishing it up, without any distractions." I poke him in his chest.

A rumble of laughter greets me. "I'm a distraction, am I?"

"You know you are." I kiss his lips.

His arms come around me. "Then I better get in all my distracting while I can."

THE NEXT FEW days whiz by. Ozzy records during the day and performs at night. While he's recording, I put finishing touches on the designs for my presentation to the Project. We sneak in sexy times when we can. Overall, life is good. So long as I keep any thoughts about Matt buried.

"You better hurry up, McKenna, or you'll be late for school."

And keep a lid on my worries about Mom. Her bad days are starting to rack up, although she still has more lucid days than not.

"Be right out." I give my hair a shake and put on some funky bracelets before packing up my laptop and heading out of my bedroom.

"I made French toast," she calls from the kitchen.

"Thanks, Mom." I grab a plate and pour my coffee before sitting down at the kitchen table.

"Did you do all your homework?"

I force a smile. "I have a big deliverable, I mean, uhm, test, today. I'm prepared, so I think it'll go well."

"I'm sure it will." Mom places another piece of French toast on my plate. "Here. Eat this for good luck."

No wonder I use food as comfort. However, another slice does sound good, especially since they're truly mouth-watering. "Thanks."

Elaine comes in and I fill her in on Mom's mental condition for the day. "She usually pulls out of it by midday, don't worry. Now, you go and do your presentation. Good luck!"

I give her a quick hug, kiss Mom's cheek and head out the door. Nervous energy overrides my worries for Mom, and I tap the steering wheel as I drive to the Project's offices. I hope they find my designs as good as all of the musicians said they were. They're certainly my best work ever. By far. Thanks to Ozzy.

Stuck in traffic, my fingers continue their tapping until a call comes over my Bluetooth. It's the prosecutor from Matt's parole hearing. Good. I can go into the Project meeting knowing he'll be behind bars for years to come.

"Hello," I answer the phone.

"Hi, McKenna." He clears his throat. "I just got the decision from the parole board about Mateo Lopez." Papers rifle in the background. "It seems his motion has been granted. He's being released today."

I slam on my brakes to avoid hitting the car in front of me. "What?" I garble.

He sighs. "I'm sorry. We put our best case forward, but apparently he's been an exemplary inmate. With the overcrowding in the jails…"

He continues talking but I can't make out any of his words. Matt's being released. Today. Oh. My. God. This can't be happening.

In the middle of his sentence, I blurt, "He can't get near me, right?"

"I'll put in a petition for a restraining order against him on you and your mother's behalf. I'm sure it'll be granted right away."

"Thank you. Please let me know as soon as it's been processed. I need that security." Disconnecting the call, I sag against the seat and turn into the Project's office.

How can this happen? He killed my father and only had to serve five years in prison? Frustrated tears course down my cheeks, which I dash away. Smacking the steering wheel, I scream, "fuck you," over and over again.

When my anger runs its course, I check the clock on my dashboard. At least I planned to arrive early, so I have time to collect myself before presenting my finished project to the powers that be. All I need to do is set up my laptop and press play.

Matt has to be mentally put far away again. No way will I let him destroy this shred of hope I have for turning around my future, and my mother's. I worked too damn hard to arrive at this moment for him to continue ruining my life. A restraining order will be filed against him, and he'll never be able to hurt me or my family again.

Focus on the Project. I need the money. I have to be advanced to the national competition.

Gulping air, I picture a bald eagle and thrust my shoulders back. Fearless. That's who I am. Who I need to be.

I walk into the Project's offices and am greeted by Felicia, who looks me up and down. "Why are you so pale? You're going to do great," she whispers.

If only she knew. Tamping down the emotions threatening to push their way out, I force a smile and go with the lie she provided. "Just a case of the nerves."

She wraps her arm around me and gives me a one-armed hug. "Don't worry, McKenna."

At her words, I freeze the smile on my face and walk into the conference room on wooden legs. Felicia makes idle chatter with me as I set up my computer.

"Caught that photo of you with Ozzy Martinez in the magazine," she notes, fanning her face.

"Yeah, well, don't believe everything you read," I say as I hook up the computer to the projector.

"Photos don't lie. He had his shirt off and—whew!—those abs." She leans in. "Not to mention the nipple rings."

My tongue tingles at the remembrance of swirling around his nipples. And then his piercing lower....

I'm jetted out of my thoughts when Felicia continues, "Please, please, please give me a little bone. Something."

"I don't kiss and tell. He might, though." I offer her a wink.

"I knew it! I'm jelly." She taps my shoulder and leaves me to set up.

Finished preparing for my presentation, I steal a bottle of water. More to have something for my hands to hold than to drink. My mind is a blur, and it's definitely far from where it should be, which is here, at this conference table, about to make or break my future.

Members of the board and other workers at the Project soon file into the conference room. The president of the Artist Adventure Avenue Project, Peggy Laswell, takes a seat at the head of the table. Next to her is Greta VonStein, the PR woman for the Project. My eyes skip over her, knowing what she did to Rose and Cole at the beginning of their relationship. *Bitch.* I have to appease her, though, as she has the power to make or break my presentation.

Once everyone's seated, the president wastes no time in asking me to turn on the video. Felicia dims the lights. Taking a deep breath, I press "play."

An hour later, the lights come back up. This represents a year of my life's work. I met with and got approval from all of the artists, but none have affected me as much as Ozzy. None unleashed my creativity like he did. I placed his segment at the end.

Everyone in the room claps once the video has ended, taking my last breath with them. Once things quiet, Peggy says, "McKenna, yours was an amazing piece of work. I need to watch it a few more times so I can offer you some suggested changes, but I want to let you know I'm thrilled with what you put together for us."

"Thank you so much." My mind swirls with whatever changes she may want me to make.

"Don't forget the Big Reveal is next week, on the fourteenth." I nod. "Speaking of which, when you submit the final, make sure to include your invoice."

"Will do." The money will relieve some of my problems. I might need to set aside a little bit to handle any legal issues from Matt's release, though.

The meeting breaks while I dismantle my computer hook-up. "Great job," Felicia gushes.

"Glad you liked it."

"It was so fresh. A different take on all of the songs that we know so well. And a few new ones, too." She elbows me in the ribs.

Knowing she's fishing for more information about Ozzy, I place my laptop into its case. "Ozzy's been working on the new songs featured in here. Some of the other artists also wrote special songs for the piece."

"I'll make sure to get the suggested changes to you by tonight. We're going to need the finished product, plus a highlight reel, by the day before the event."

I place my laptop case on my shoulder. "Ozzy and his band are recording the new songs this week."

Felicia grabs my arm before I can leave. She whispers, "I think you're the frontrunner to move to the national competition."

My eyes close. "I hope so," I whisper. I need this win. Mom needs it.

From the table, Greta stands and her assistant distributes a packet to everyone assembled. As I leave the room, she begins, "This details all of the PR coming up over the next week for the Big Reveal…"

Back in my car, I rest my head against the headrest. I'm so happy they liked my work. The possibility of making it to nationals dangles in front of me like a tantalizing chocolate from Edie Z's.

My mouth waters and my fingers reach into my bag to call Ozzy. Then I remember he's in the recording studio today and drop the phone. I should call Rose and let her know that Greta got this gig, but she's still on her extended honeymoon and I don't want to bother her. I'll email her when I get home.

Surprised at how long my meeting ran, I drive into an In and Out Burger for a very late lunch. Munching on their delicious fries, I bask in the president's words. All of my hard work is finally paying off.

My mind returns to the prosecutor's call, which cuts into my glow. How can Matt be a free man again? My stomach twists. Tossing the remainder of my food into the trash, I return to my car and pull into my driveway an hour later.

Bone tired, I grab my laptop and trudge into the house. Between the news of Matt's parole and Ozzy's keeping me sleep deprived, I need to sleep for twenty-four hours straight. But before I can even get my key into the front door, voices waft out to me. Doesn't sound like Elaine. *Great.* Mom has visitors to whom I now have to be polite.

Shaking the exhaustion from my body, I tip my lips upward and walk through the door. "Hi, Mom," I say, hanging my keys on the hook by the door.

"McKenna. I'm so glad you're back from school, just in time."

My smile slips. She still thinks I'm in high school. Guess Elaine was wrong about her snapping out of it. "Yeah. It was a rough day."

"Well, I have someone here who can make it all better. He brought flowers and everything."

He. Maybe Ozzy got out of the studio early? On butterfly feet, I walk into the house and turn into the living room.

Where I bite back a scream.

Matt stands up from the couch, causing every one of my extremities to clench. "Your Mom offered me some of your cookies." He raises his cookie-filled fist and, involuntarily, I shrink backward. "Good to see you again, Kenna."

His use of my nickname. Eating my cookies. Inside of my house. It's too much.

My instinctive recoil to seeing him morphs into deep-seated hatred. Standing in front of the bay window, I point to the door. In a deadly-calm voice I barely recognize as my own, I order, "Get the fuck out of my house." I dig through my purse, fumbling for my cell phone. "I'm calling the police."

From across the room, Mom asks, "What's wrong? Mateo and I were having a lovely chat. Why are you being so rude?"

"Yeah, Kenna." He mimics, "Why are you being so rude?"

Abandoning my search for my phone, I focus on getting him alone so I can kick his ass out of my house. Mom simply can't understand what she's saying. I take a deep breath. "Mom, why don't you go make some coffee to celebrate"—his name can't leave my lips—"his release."

Mom frowns. "Release?"

Shit. I shouldn't have said that word. Now's not the time to jog her memory. "Football season's over. He's released from practice," I improvise.

"Oh. Well, sure." She gets to her feet and leaves me alone with the *animal* who murdered my father. When I'm sure Mom can't hear me, I hiss, "Last time I'll say it. Get the fuck out of my house."

He saunters toward me. I stand my ground, hands on my hips and raise my chin. "Is that any way to greet your *high school* boyfriend?" He mocks, his hands clasping my shoulders.

My body tenses—I refuse to be cowed by this lowlife asshole. "There's a restraining order against you. You're violating your parole." A smile stretches across my face. "You'll be back in jail before you can say 'breaking and entering.'"

He squeezes my shoulders. "One, there's no restraining order. Two, you owe me five years. But for your testimony, the jury would've believed my self-defense story. Your father brought that knife."

"Yet you took it from him. He was unarmed. You killed him."

Ignoring me, he barrels forward. "And three," he points toward the opened magazine on the coffee table, "you're mine. Stay the fuck away from that Ozzy Martinez guy or he'll join your father in Hell."

My blood runs cold. I swing at his smug face—how did I ever think he was handsome?—but he catches me by my wrist and pulls me into him. He got stronger in jail. I guess not being on drugs and working out every day will do that.

Before I know what he's about to do, his lips cover mine.

"No, no, no!" I scream and shake and shove at this monster. "Get off of me!"

Distracted by some street noise, he releases me. Taking advantage, I jump back and wipe my mouth with the back of my hand. Just then, Mom walks into the living room, coffee service on a tray. He lopes his arm around my shoulders.

"Here are our coffees," she says in a singsong voice as she deposits the tray onto the table.

He smirks and guides us over to her. Bending down, he takes a mug, all the while knowing I can't do anything in front of Mom. Taking a seat on the couch, he pats his lap. "Kenna."

Oh, hell no.

My eyes travel to Mom, who wears a sappy smile on her face as if this piece of shit didn't ruin our lives years ago. Years she doesn't remember.

"I wish Harry were here to see you two." My heart flips when she mentions Daddy. She looks at the clock. "He should be home in half an hour." She addresses Matt. "I do hope you can stay."

No fucking way. I jump up. "He can't stay, Mom. He has to get to his job. *Now.*" I wrench my face in his direction. "You don't want to be late, do you?"

Apparently decided he's made his point, he stands. "Kenna's right. I need to get going." He gives her a crocodile kiss, then wraps his arm around my shoulders in a punishing grip.

Before he can close the embrace, however, I stride to the front door and open it. I say under my breath. "Never darken my door again. You will never see me or my mother. Ever. Again."

He gives me a feral smile. "We'll see about that, won't we?" As soon as he exits, I slam the door shut. And turn the lock.

Twenty-Three

OZZY

I PULL UP OUTSIDE McKENNA'S HOUSE, excited to hear how her meeting with the Project went. I bet she kicked ass.

After today's recording session, I did something I swore I'd never do again. I walked into a jewelry store and checked out some of their pieces. I decided on a bracelet that I know she'll love. It has interchangeable gems she can match with her dyed hair—and panties.

Shutting Shirley off behind her little Honda, I put the kickstand into place. I flip open the visor of my helmet and direct my eyes into the little house. McKenna crosses the living room in front of the bay window. I sit like an idiot in her driveway and breathe in all that is my girlfriend. The woman who has taken my heart and given it new meaning.

As my hand comes under my chin to release the strap, McKenna stops moving. A guy appears in front of her, his hands on her shoulders. Who the fuck—my thought is cut off as he takes her into his arms and kisses her.

They're *kissing*.

What the fuck is going on?

They turn and he puts his arm around her shoulders. She's looking up at him but I can't make out her expression.

Like I need to.

I know what her expression says. It says "I got that schmuck Ozzy to fall for me" and "We're going to milk him for all he's got."

Too bad she doesn't know I'm not worth much anymore.

I flip down my visor, release the kickstand and roll out of her driveway. How could I have been taken for a fool *again*? Gotta give it to her, though. She's a superb actress. My lip curls upward. Maybe the dickwad she's really with can't get her off like I do.

Somehow on the freeway, I gun Shirley. Eat up the miles. After driving aimlessly for at least an hour, I pull into my driveway. My empty driveway. What did you expect? A little Honda waiting for you?

Walking through the front door, Bans races to me. I drop a couple of pats on her head on my way to my target—the bar. There, I pour a double shot of whiskey and tip my head back, savoring the burn on its way down my throat. I slam the shot glass back onto the counter, picking up the whiskey bottle to pour another, when the doorbell rings.

She seriously decided to come here now? Right after sending her other boyfriend on his way? I join Bans at the front door and swing it wide.

"Hi, Ozzy. You left some paperwork at the studio, so I thought I'd—"

Aiden's voice trails off when I leave him at the door and head back to the bar. "Want anything to drink?"

"I take it tea's not on the menu?" Aiden asks when I don't turn into the kitchen.

"No."

Since he doesn't reply, I pour my second shot and down it.

"Woah there, boss. Where's McKenna?"

"Not here." She's with her *other* boyfriend.

"Oh." He shuffles some papers. "Well, ah, I brought your notes from the studio. And, I have some other things we need to go over to prepare for the end of your residency."

A sound somewhere between a snort and a laugh escapes my lips. Of course my residency is ending. I have a quarter of a new album recorded, with other songs in various stages of draft. Luis's words haunt me about never being able to finish up the album without him. His words are followed by McKenna's saying she loves the songs and urging me on. I wonder if that was an act, too.

Aiden takes my silence as acceptance and spreads the paperwork over the coffee table. As if I care. I can sell my house in LA and rent a one-bedroom. Or I can fuck my way through LA and never need a home base—or an income. He talks about turning in the Penthouse at the Jade and this house, but I'm beyond caring.

Bans, as if sensing my unease, rubs her head on my leg. I pet her silky coat and she lays down on her back, wanting a belly rub. As I'm obliging my dog, I realize she's like every other bitch in my life. Only, once I make her feel good, she still wants to be with me.

"I should stick with dogs, right Bans?"

She barks as Aiden drops his pen on the documents. "You haven't been listening to a word I've said."

"Nope."

He sighs. "Did something happen between you and McKenna?"

"What a loaded question." I run my fingers through my hair and eye the whiskey. I have a concert to give in two hours, so I better lay off. Well, one more can't hurt. Striding over to the bar again, I respond to Aiden while pouring another shot, "She had a meeting today about the Project."

He smiles. "Oh. Well, I wouldn't be nervous if I were you. I bet she kicked ass. That one's a real fighter."

I swig the shot. "She's a real something, for sure."

Aiden takes the shot glass from my hand. Walking toward the kitchen, he says, "C'mon, let's get some food into you. You guys didn't break for lunch so you'll need some fuel before tonight's show."

I move to follow him, but stumble. Shaking my head, I check to see what I tripped over, but don't notice anything out of place. Moving more deliberately, I sit at the kitchen table while Aiden puts some food onto a plate and turns on the microwave. "You have quite the choice in the fridge."

I shrug. What can I say? McKenna and I ate well. While it lasted.

He places the dish in front of me and I choose to eat rather than engage in any conversation with my assistant. It's none of his business anyway. As I'm finishing up the rice and beans, my phone pings. Maybe it's McKenna telling me she had a slip up. Maybe she'll have the decency to come clean.

I take my phone out of my back pocket. Sure enough, it's a text from McKenna:

Meeting went well. I'm going to be wrapped up with finalizing my submission until the Big Reveal on the 14th. I'll try to get out to see you, but I'm really swamped.

What the fuck is this? I toss my phone onto the table. "Take some advice from me, Aiden. Stay away from women."

He sits next to me, a glass of iced tea in his hand. Sighing, he asks, "What happened with McKenna?"

I force a laugh. No way am I going to reveal that I was played—again. It's bad enough he knows all about Teresa and Luis. No money has to be exchanged this time, so he doesn't need to know all the gory details. "She was a diversion. She kickstarted my muse so I could write the album, but I don't need her anymore."

His eyes bounce around the room, but he remains silent. Smart guy.

"She fulfilled her purpose," I mumble more to convince myself than Aiden. I reach for my shotglass, only to realize I left it in the bar.

He clears his throat. "So, then, do you want me to get you some towel girls tonight?"

Every molecule in my body stills. I should return to screwing all of the groupies, but my heart screams no way. "You know, not tonight. I haven't been getting too much sleep lately, if you know what I mean?" Since when did I let my heart rule my cock?

He nods. "Okay. Let me know when you're ready. I'll make sure the Penthouse is in good shape."

I shrug. "Well, I'm going to shower for tonight's concert. See you there?"

He gives me the once over and taps his lip. "Sure."

BACK IN MY dressing room after the show, I take a shower. It wasn't a great concert, but the audience seemed to enjoy it anyway. All of the whiskey from this afternoon wore off before I took the stage, yet I couldn't get my mind off of McKenna in some other guy's arms. Who the fuck is he?

Throwing on a pair of jeans and a Jade T-shirt, I head to the afterparty. Jazz is the first to see me.

"Hey, Ozzy! You haven't been back here for a while."

I grab a beer off a table. "Yeah, well, I think it's high time I corrected that."

"Is McKenna with you?" He looks around.

"Nah. I'm done with her. Got what I wanted and it's time to move on." I wiggle my eyebrows for effect, hoping he'll see that rather than hear the dull tone of my voice.

"Sorry, dude. Sucks." His hand stills for a moment, beer hovering midway between his chest and lips, then continues its ascent. Swallowing, he says, "Plenty more out there, my man."

I clink the neck of my beer with his and chug about half in one gulp. Looking around, I reply, "Don't I know it."

Three more beers in and I'm surrounded by a bevy of tall, willowy blondes. I made sure not to include anyone under five-foot-two or brunette in the group. Similarly, each of my band members has at least one girl on his arm—or attached to his face. This is the way things should be.

I smile at the women surrounding me. None of whom grab my attention, even the one next to me who's rubbing her fingernails up and down my thigh. "You know what, ladies? I'm getting tired."

The one with the fingernails coos, "I can wake you up."

I force a smile. "I bet you can, babes." As soon as the familiar nickname falls out of my mouth, McKenna's gorgeous face materializes in my mind's eye. Mi Dulcita. All the alcohol in my stomach turns sour. I can't do this. "I think I need to go to bed to *sleep* tonight. Hopefully you all can catch me again tomorrow, when I'm more rested."

The women, as one, sigh. I turn my back on them and call for the limo. They don't matter to me, and I don't matter to McKenna. Fine fucking life I got going on.

Night turns to day, which turns to night again. Concerts come and go. Women throw themselves at me but I still can't bring myself to seal the deal. All because of McKenna, who texts me less and less frequently. Not like I ever start an exchange.

I bring up our last conversation.

McKenna—*Super busy with everything ~ How are your new songs going over with the audiences?*

Me—*Everything's going well.*

My finger traces her name. We've gone from sexy flirting to all business. I guess that's what I was to her all along anyway—a job.

I spend most of my time drunk. Aiden pops over sometime around three in the afternoon to sober me up enough to perform. Then he's smart enough to let me resume my drinking for the night. Tomorrow's going to be different, though. Tomorrow's the Big Reveal for the Project. Ginger made it perfectly clear I have to attend. And *she's* going to be there.

At least Aiden helped me pick out two chicks to accompany me.

I down another whiskey. I'm going to need it to get through the next twenty-four hours.

Twenty-Four

MCKENNA

A S SOON AS MATT LEFT THAT DAY, I called my attorney and made sure the restraining order was put in place. But, as many women know, a piece of paper isn't necessarily an effective weapon. So Matt's shown up at places I've gone—like the grocery store—and stays just far enough away that I can't do anything about it. He's haunted my steps, which has made me more and more of a recluse.

But not today. Today, I have to go to the Project's Big Reveal. It's the day the finalists for the national competition are announced.

And Ozzy will be there.

I lace up my shoes and stand. Grabbing my phone, my finger hovers over Ozzy's name. Matt's threat forced me to keep my distance from him and it's been torture. It's taken all of my willpower not to drive over to his house and throw myself in his arms, dumping all my problems—and Matt's threat against his life—on him.

No.

This is my fight. He's already seen me struggle to keep my mom under control—I can't let him know I also have my father's life on my conscience, and a psychotic ex-boyfriend on my tail. I'm supposed to be his muse, not a woman who can't keep her world in check. I toss the phone onto my bed and add more concealer under my eyes. Yes, retreating from Ozzy is for the best. But, it's killing me by inches.

Straightening the sheer sleeves of my blouse, I give myself the same pep talk I've been using all week. He's better off without you. You're doing him a favor. It's better he's alive and with someone else than with you and dead. And, above all, this is my responsibility to resolve. The law did its part, now it's my turn to keep everyone safe.

"Are you almost ready?"

A smile crosses my face. Mom's been having a really good week, never once forgetting time. That could be because I've been home these nights on a reliable basis, as opposed to flitting through her life and throwing off her sense of normalcy. She's what matters. I need to stay grounded for her above all else. "Almost, Mom!"

I put on some eyeliner and mascara, flip my full head of brunette hair—no color appealed—and place a printed copy of the graphics into my bag. I set up the entire display yesterday on the Project's computer system, but grab a thumb drive with it on just in case. Can't be too prepared.

Walking into the hallway, Mom motions me over to the living room's bay window. She twirls her finger in a circle, and I obey, giving her a three-sixty of my outfit. She laughs. "I don't know where you got your sense of style, but you always look spectacular. Your work is going to be adored today."

I kiss her cheek. "I hope so." No need to let her worry about the monetary aspect if I don't make it into the national competition. I can tell her the good news later. Hopefully.

"I wish I could go to the party with you. But my mind sometimes leaves me." Clearing her throat, she continues, "Know I'm there with you in spirit, cheering you on."

It's as if someone punched me in the chest. That she's still aware—on any level—of what's happening to her is tragic. I force a sunny smile. "Thanks, Mom. Honestly, I don't think I'll be gone too long."

She pats my hair. "Now stop trying to play this down. It's a big deal." She hugs me. "You're my big deal."

I blink back tears and check the clock. "Well, I better go. I'll let you know all about it when I get home."

"Knock 'em dead!" She picks up her knitting and starts another new hat. She sends me off with the same words of encouragement that I gave Ozzy before he did his shows—thoughts of the man send a pang through my heart.

I walk out of the house and gulp some air. Ozzy's going to be there. I haven't seen him in over a week and our texts have become more perfunctory as the days passed. Sometimes he didn't even respond. It's all for the best. If Matt sees us together—and he's always around me somewhere—he could kill Ozzy. I can't be responsible for another death. I can't.

Swiping the tears away from my cheeks, I hop into my Honda and head off toward the venue for the party. As I drive, more tears course down my cheeks. I miss Ozzy so badly.

Getting my emotions in check, I wonder if he'll come to the event alone. I can't imagine he's met someone else. Who am I kidding? He's probably met several someones. After all, it's been *days*. When it comes to Ozzy and sex, that's like dog years. I sniffle as I turn into the parking lot.

Once inside the party, I plaster a fake smile on my face and greet the members of the Project. Felicia comes over. "Hi, McKenna! Great turnout, huh?"

Forcing an upbeat tone, I reply, "Sure is. Everyone's excited to see the newest attraction at the Strip."

"Your presentation is going to be the highlight, for sure." She winks. "Can you believe it's finally seeing the light of day?"

I grab a champagne flute from a waiter as he walks by. "I know. The year flew by." Does she say this to all of the graphic designers here tonight?

Other members of the Project join us and we all marvel at the press in attendance. "Greta did a super job with PR." I nod. I bet Rose would've done better, but keep my thoughts to myself.

Felicia's index finger points into the room. "You got to work with him, huh? Man, your job didn't suck."

Proverbial red lights flash. I brace for impact as my eyes travel the distance to where Felicia is pointing. It's one of the artists I worked with—not Ozzy. My body relaxes. "Yeah, I had it easy. His songs were hard to create graphics for."

"But you did a great job."

"Thanks."

I sneak an avocado toast point off a tray and leave Felicia to walk around. I need to keep moving, otherwise I'll jump right out of my skin. A waitress approaches. "Gazpacho?"

"Sure." I take a shot glass filled with the chilled soup. Smiling at various luminaries, I nod and keep moving.

The air changes and I know, without turning, that Ozzy's here. Late, which suits me just fine. Placing a now-empty dish on a high-top table, I suck in a breath and turn around slowly. He's across the room from me, looking as hot as ever. Sunglasses, a white T-shirt, bracelets around his wrist and ripped jeans—the quintessential rockstar. And hanging off of him are two bimbos.

I blink.

He has his arms around each of the tall, skinny blondes. He laughs, living large. My scalp prickles and I make my way to a quiet corner. Knowing I can't keep staring at the blank wall forever, I turn around and look at the floor. Maybe I can remain out of the way until they announce the finalists for the national contest. And then escape without having to interact with him at all.

Ozzy's belly laugh brings my head back up. On their own accord, my eyes travel in the direction of his laugh, and land on the trio, who now are talking with the President of the Project. He stands with his legs apart, and one of the women has her hand on his abdomen. *Bitch.*

I stifle the urge to run over to the trio and scratch the bimbos' eyes out. Well, he's the one encouraging them, so I add Ozzy's name to my shit list. How could he do this to me? He of all people knows how important this night is to me—how much rides on it not only for myself, but for my mother.

"Looks like he's having a good time," Felicia notes, her eyes filled with pity.

Jumping at her sudden appearance, I cover my reaction with a nod. Wanting to disabuse her of the need to pity me, I say, "Do you know when Peggy's going to speak?"

She glances at her watch. "I think the President's Address is within the next half-hour or so."

How am I going to endure thirty more minutes of this torture? Maybe I can hide out in the ladies' room. "If you'll excuse me, I need to find the restroom." Not waiting for her response, I head in that direction.

Once inside, I plop down in the little seating area and take several deep breaths. Wanting to appear busy in case someone should enter, I fish out my lipstick and hold it in my hand. Cover story in place, I rest my head against the wall. No sooner do my eyes close than the door opens, so I sit up. In walk the two bimbos who complete Ozzy's outfit. *Great.*

"I felt his nipple rings," one giggles.

The other replies, "I heard he has his junk pierced, too. Can you imagine?"

Cackling, they head into the stalls. Ignoring the belly flops occurring in my stomach, I mutter, "Why, yes. I can imagine." All too vividly.

Their chatter carries to the anteroom, but I can't make out their words. Knowing my sanctuary has been invaded, I drop the lipstick back into my purse and escape.

Straight into a broad chest.

"Oh!" I bounce back.

A very familiar musky scent—combined with the sharp aroma of whiskey—invades my nostrils and I know, without looking up, who that chest belongs to. With slow movements, my eyes run from his boots, up his legs and straight to sunglass-covered eyes. Who the hell wears sunglasses at night? Oh, I know. Some douche nozzle who needs to cover up the fact that he's drunk at the biggest event in my career in years.

"You're drunk."

"Not enough, apparently."

Biting my lip, I say, "Excuse me." Because, what else can I say?

In response, his stance widens and he flips his sunglasses to the top of his head. His pupils are pinpricks. I close my eyes against the evidence that he's high as well.

"I thought you were different, but I was wrong." He bends down, the pungent smell of whiskey almost making me gag. He slurs, "You're just like Teresa. Since you don't have the balls to break up with me 'cause you're in love with another guy—not that we ever were really dating, only fucking—I'm doing the honors. Have a nice life."

Each one of his words hits its target, directly on my heart. He doesn't know the threat Matt poses, or the pressure I'm under. Not understanding his reference to Teresa or another guy—and tamping down my desire to go postal on his drugged-out ass—I remain silent. This is for the best.

Giggling precedes the sound of the door opening and the two bimbos head toward their prey. I don't say another word and scurry as far away from him as I can get, but not before I hear him smack their asses and their responding sexy squeals.

Safely ensconced back into a corner, I check the time and pray for this to be over. The lights blink, indicating the speeches are about to begin. An announcer asks everyone to take their seats. I scan the room until I find Ozzy and his blondes, and find a chair as far away as possible.

Felicia stands up at the front and, when her eyes light on me, she motions for me to join her. *Crap.* Plastering a smile, I walk over to her and sit. "Thanks, Felicia."

"Couldn't have our star graphic designer hiding in the back." She nudges me in the side, wearing a grin.

I should say some witty retort, but my brain is fried. I want to throw myself into Ozzy's arms *and* beat him upside the head at the same time. Instead, I nod and open a program I didn't design.

Sighing, I force myself to look forward and not to glance to my right where *he's* sitting. Finally, the President takes the podium. "Hello, my name is

Peggy Laswell and I'm the President of the Artist Avenue Adventure Project. I want to thank you all for coming here today to see the three wonderful presentations we have for you. You're definitely in for a treat, I can tell you that."

I join in the applause, although not really caring what she's saying.

"So, without further ado, we're going to run the three programs for you, back-to-back. Each feature well-known Las Vegas musical artists, and showcase some wonderful graphics by really talented local people."

The highlight reels begin to run. The first is well done, if not a bit traditional. The second one has a unique take on the music. Mine runs third. While the other two receive polite applause, the ovation for mine is longer than the others combined. Please let this be a good sign.

The lights come back up and the applause lasts for another full minute. When it quiets, Peggy says, "I'd like to introduce you to the three graphic designers behind these wonderful presentations. Please stand when I announce your names— Penelope Miller, Stefan Leonard and McKenna James!"

Forcing a smile, I stand. Two other people in the audience join me.

The President continues, "Let's give all three of the designers another round of applause!"

Shifting from foot to foot, I endure the spotlight. Can Ozzy see me? Is he even looking? As soon as the applause dies down, I slink into my seat.

From the podium, Peggy says, "Well, I have one final bit of housekeeping before this part of the program concludes—the announcement of the finalist who will go on to represent the Artist Adventure Avenue Project in the Youth-Art Consortium's national competition."

This is it. What I've been working toward for this past year. The exposure alone should keep Mom in nursing care twenty-four-seven, even if I don't win. I need to be the finalist. I cross my fingers and Felicia puts her hand over them.

The President holds up an envelope and rips it open. "The person going on to represent the Project in the national competition is …"

I try to quell my rapid breathing, but my chest rises and falls in unmeasured beats.

The President looks around. "McKenna James."

I sag as my name is called, my eyes now filled with tears. I made the cut. Felicia shakes me and I smile. I'm one step closer to keeping Mom at home, and honoring my vow to my father.

On their own volition, my eyes skim over heads and land on Ozzy's curly one. Two blonde ones surround it. I wring my hands.

The President clears her throat. "Congratulations, McKenna. Remember, the winner of the national competition will be announced next month in Los Angeles. Now, everyone, thank you all for coming and please enjoy the rest of the party!"

Felicia hugs me. "I wanted to tell you that you made the finals before, but I was sworn to secrecy. I'm so happy for you!"

I force my leaden arms to wrap around her. "Thanks. I truly can't tell you how excited I am."

She laughs as we stand. "I'll email you your plane ticket and information for the event in LA. I'm rooting for you."

"Thanks."

Ozzy's laughter floats into my ears, which forces me to walk in the opposite direction. He made it perfectly clear I'm no longer a part of his life. And judging from his behavior, I'm well rid of him.

Keep telling yourself that, McKenna.

I'm swarmed by a bunch of people offering their congratulations. I spend the next hour or so meeting and thanking them, all the while trying to track Ozzy's movements. I know the exact moment when he leaves, his hands full of his blonde companions.

"Please add my congratulations to the pile you received today." An attractive guy about my age, although somewhat scrawny, holds out his hand. When I shake it, his piercing hazel eyes capture mine. "I'm Jeremy Davis, and I write for the *Record News*. The Project asked me to write a profile about you."

"Oh. I didn't know about the publicity."

He smiles, his longish blond hair brushing against his shoulders. "I think Greta set it up."

"That makes sense."

"So, can I interview you tomorrow? I'm on a tight deadline." He glances toward the projector. "I really enjoyed your work."

I laugh. "You don't have to butter me up, you already got the interview."

He shrugs. "Simply telling you the truth." We set up a time to meet tomorrow morning at a local coffeeshop.

Back in my car, my whole body deflates from the effort of the ruse I just put on. I need to tell Mom the good news—if she even understands.

And cry myself to sleep.

Twenty-Five

OZZY

I SLAM BACK ANOTHER SHOT OF whiskey. Why did McKenna have to look so fucking fantastic yesterday? Her outfit was super funky, yet no one else on earth could pull it off but her. And all I wanted to do was rip it off of her and make her scream my name.

But I didn't.

And she didn't.

Despite everything, I'm proud she won. All her hard work paid off. *Too bad that's all you were to her—work.*

Thankfully, last night was dark. I was so drunk off my ass I wouldn't have been able to perform anyway. Partied with the women I took to the Big Reveal but wasn't in any shape to fuck them. I sent them home and went to the Penthouse to sleep it off.

Good thing the bar is always stocked here. I eye another shot, and glace at the clock. My concert's several hours from now. I toss it back and collapse onto the sofa.

Knocking on the door wakes me. I stroll over to it and look through the peephole. Opening the door for my PA, I mumble, "Hey."

"Hi there. I've been looking all over for you. Took care of Bans."

How could I have forgotten about my dog? "Thanks, man." I make my way to the bar and hold up a glass. "Whiskey?"

"No, thanks."

Aiden watches as I pour myself another and do the shot, his eyes boring into me. "What? It's only a shot." I won't tell him about the others.

"I wanted to let you know Ginger called again about your album. I told her you're working on it with the band."

I nod. "Yeah."

"She's stopping by your place tomorrow for a sampling."

Her demand doesn't shock me. I pour another shot and, fingering the rim, reply, "Fine. The songs are good. I'm sure Platinum will be happy."

"That's good news." He steps up to the bar, tapping his lip. "Why don't you go down to your dressing room to get ready for tonight's show? It starts in an hour."

Where did all the time go? I grab the shot and do it, using my fingers to wipe my mouth. "K, let's go."

An hour later, I'm waiting for my cue. The music flows around me but it's as if I'm not a part of it. I shake my head to rid all thoughts of *her* and step onto the platform that lifts me onto the stage. The swell of the audience raises me higher and higher throughout the night. Who needs one woman when you can have the adoration of thousands every night?

I forget the lines to a song, but then cover up my flub by holding the mic out to the audience, which supplies them for me. Close call, but maybe I'll add it into my routine. When Jazz asks if we're going to do 'Take Me' tonight, I tell him no. I can't do anything new right now.

The concert ends and we all head backstage. I avoid going to my dressing room, instead heading straight for the afterparty.

Tim bumps my shoulder. "What's up? You were off tonight."

"Sorry. Shit on my mind." Time to deflect. I look around. "Any hot chicks in here tonight?

"Aren't there always? It's Vegas, baby." He grabs a beer and hands one to me.

Walking over to a group of women, I start chatting up a redhead. Her hair reminds me of the time McKenna dyed some of her locks the same exact color, so I move on to a blonde. No—she's the same exact height as McKenna. After talking with several women, all falling short of the bar set by McKenna, I decide to head home. Alone.

Hopping on Shirley, I race down the Strip, cutting some cars off, feeling reckless. All too soon, I find myself on a residential street. A familiar Honda is parked in a driveway. The lights are off inside the house. Is she with him in the bedroom I've never seen? I gun the engine and scream down the street. Why did I come here anyway?

Johnnie Walker is my preferred companion tonight.

THE NEXT MORNING, I wake with an awful headache. "Having too many whiskeys will do that to you," I mutter as I dive into the pool. The cool water slaps me upside the head, and I punish my body with an hourlong swim.

Finished, I hop onto the patio, my eyes drawn toward the gate. Of course, McKenna's not there. She never will be again.

After toweling off, I shower and get ready for my meeting with Ginger. It's now or never for the songs, all of which have McKenna's imprint on them in some way. Shaking my head as if that would make all visions of her fall out of it, I slip the button through the final hole on my shirt and secure my belt. The doorbell rings and I head for the front door.

Opening it, I welcome Aiden and Ginger into the house. "Would you like a drink? Iced tea or something stronger?" My stomach revolts at the thought of adding more alcohol to it, so I go with the iced tea.

Handing the same to Aiden and a water to Ginger, I escort us outside, picking up the music and my guitar on the way. Once we're all seated at the patio table, Ginger asks, "How many songs do you have for me today?"

"Four are done, and another five are in different stages of completion, but all are ready for you."

She inclines her head and goes over the sheet music for the new songs. After giving some suggested changes and listening to what we recorded, the two go back and forth about logistics and recording time in LA next month. I'm content to let Aiden carry this meeting. While I'm proud of my new songs, this whole process feels like a farce somehow. Actually, more like hollow.

Ginger turns to me. "This is quite the body of work you created. I love the new vibe. Different. And your lyrics are much more evolved." She huffs out a strangled laugh. "Here I was worried Luis was the real talent."

I had wondered the same thing for a long time, but Luis was more of a crutch. We were good together before Platinum came knocking. Now I realize, though, that he smothered my creativity. Writing these songs was more freeing. More *me*. "These songs better represent me. Plus, I did have help from my band. They're a great group of guys."

"Do you want to stay together for this next album?"

Nodding, I answer, "I do. They need to be listed as co-collaborators because we've been tweaking what I wrote. And I want to tour with them, assuming they're okay with leaving Vegas." I never asked them if they'd go on tour with me, but since we're all single, I doubt there would be an issue.

Ginger scribbles some notes down on her pad. "We'll make it happen." Standing, she gathers her papers. "We've been at this for three hours and I have to head back to LA." She places her hand on my shoulder. "Keep up the great work. I'll schedule more recording time for you in LA in mid-January." She looks at Aiden. "I'll let you know the exact dates."

I should be more excited. Yet, I'm empty. "Sounds good. Come on, I'll walk you out."

Returning to the patio, I drop down into the chair next to Aiden. "Your album is hot AF. You're going to rule the airwaves."

I take a sip of my remaining iced tea. "I hope so. I need to pay the mortgage."

He laughs. "I'm pretty sure you don't have to worry about that." Bans runs through her doggie door and drops a drool-covered ball at his feet. Without flinching, he picks it up and throws it to the far end of the yard. "So, McKenna's really history, huh?"

The unexpected mention of her name halts my hand from returning my glass to the table. "Yeah," comes out in a strangled tone.

Bans barks and he tosses the ball again. "Too bad. I liked her."

"Boy, can I pick them. She was just like Teresa. All women are the same."

He places his glass down with a thud. "No way? I didn't get that vibe off of her. She seemed so real."

Running my fingers through my hair, I watch Bans as she scampers back to us, ball in her mouth. Snapping my fingers, she alters course and brings her toy to me. Throwing it in a different direction, I reply, "I thought she was."

Silence, except for an occasional bark from Bans, descends on the backyard. After two more throws, Aiden stands. "I've got some errands to take care of for you before the concert tonight. I'll see you at the Jade in a couple."

"Sounds good."

He lets himself out, leaving me alone with sheet music that tells the story of falling in love. I pick up my pencil and start crossing out some lyrics. What do I know about love anyway?

Twenty-Six

MCKENNA

I DISCONNECT THE CALL AND WRITE down the names of the nurses from Elaine's agency who will be coming here to be interviewed for the second shift position. Even though the decision about the national competition isn't for another month, I want to be ready to jump if the exposure itself brings in new clients.

Wandering into the living room, Mom's watching the soap she's been hooked on ever since I was a kid. "Monica looks so old. Why did the makeup people do that to her face?"

I glance at the screen. "What do you mean? I think she looks the same."

Mom shakes her head. "No. It's like they aged her at least twenty years. And why isn't she with Rick? Who's this guy? I don't understand."

But I do. My body sags, recognizing her mind has regressed decades. I've been spoiled for the past week, when she didn't have any "incidents." Guess she's about due.

"You know how these soaps go, Janice," Elaine says, placing a cup of tea on the coffee table. "They always have to mix things up to keep people interested."

Mom sips her tea and sighs, "Yes, you're right. Have to keep us viewers on our toes, I guess. But, I don't like her makeup one bit. If I were the actress, I'd complain."

Elaine sits in a chair opposite, watching Mom as she drinks the hot tea and replaces the teacup onto the saucer. "I bet you would," she chuckles. Elaine's been a godsend. When Mom retreats into herself, I don't know how to handle her. Elaine never flinches.

"Thanks," I whisper. In response, the nurse smiles and nods, then turns her attention back to Mom.

A jogger catches my attention and I walk to the bay window. He's wearing a pair of shorts and nothing else, and both of his arms are tatted. His abs are cut just like Ozzy's, yet neither of his nipples is pierced.

I picture Ozzy jumping out of the pool, naked. His tattoos and piercings on full display. My body yearns for him, but I know that part of my life is over. My eyes follow the jogger as he turns a corner and only then do I realize I've been holding my breath. Exhaling the stale air, I close my eyes and let the raw feeling of loss shower over me.

He seemed to be well over me, by the looks of him yesterday. Two bimbos on his arms, drunk and high, yet able to express exactly how he felt about me. He was so wrong. I would still be with him but for Matt. All I meant to do was keep him safe.

Opening my eyes, I notice Matt driving by, stopping in front of my house. When he sees me looking at him, he honks the horn and waves, then takes off leaving squealing tires in his wake.

"What's that racket?"

I turn around. "Some jerk driving like a maniac, Mom. He's gone now." If only he'd stay gone, for good. Or, stick around long enough for me to get the police here.

"Don't know what's wrong with your generation. When your father gets home, I'm going to have a talk with him about what we can do."

My eyes meet Elaine's. I say, "You do that, Mom," knowing full well she'll forget her outburst within the hour.

Sighing, I leave the two of them and return to my bedroom. My journal catches my eye and I pick it up, opening it to a random page. One that's filled with all sorts of amazing details about a tryst with Ozzy. When I wrote it, I knew we wouldn't last, which is why I wanted to capture every single moment. So I'd never forget. As if I could, even if I become like Mom.

I flip the pages, skimming over memories of being taken by him in all sorts of places—the stairs, the patio, his music room—and open up to a blank page. Picking up a pen, it stands poised to take down my innermost thoughts. Only, I don't have any. I'm as blank as these pages.

All because of Matt. Everything flows back to him.

The doorbell sounds, followed by Elaine's voice. "McKenna, there's a gentleman here to see you."

Ozzy! Dropping my journal on the bed, I rush out to the front door. My shoulders droop when the lanky journalist from the Big Reveal stands in the open door. Shit! I forgot all about him.

Tucking my hair behind my ear, I welcome him into the house and usher him to the kitchen before Mom engages. "Would you like something to drink?" I motion for Jeremy to sit while I prepare his requested cup of coffee.

"I hope you don't mind, but Felicia gave me your home address. When you didn't show up at the coffeehouse, I figured our meeting had slipped your mind."

I purse my lips, mentally berating myself for forgetting such an important interview. "I'm so sorry, Jeremy. With all the fuss from yesterday and, uh, things, I totally forgot all about it." I put his coffee down in front of him, in a mug that says *I'm Silently Judging Your Font Choice*.

Jeremy takes out a notebook. "No harm done. Is it okay with you if we run through the questions here?"

Not really. "Sure thing." I grab another mug—this one says *I'm a Graphic Designer. What's your Superpower?*—and set my coffee to brew. "Give me a sec, okay?"

He nods and I take my time walking out to the living room. Can't let him see I'm panicked. Smiling at Mom, I bend down to Elaine and whisper, "The guy's a journalist. I was supposed to meet up with him but forgot, so he came here to do the interview. Can you please keep Mom out of the kitchen while I do it? I'll try to be quick."

"I'll do my best. Sometimes she gets a thought in her head and I can't control her, but I'll keep her entertained out here. Or, maybe we'll go for a walk."

I dart a quick look to Mom. "Don't disrupt her rhythm." With that, I return to the kitchen, praying Mom stays put.

Forcing a smile, I get my coffee and add creamer and sugar. Stirring the brew with a spoon that I drop into the sink, I say, "So, what do you want to know?"

He smiles back. "Oh, everything."

His quip makes my heart flip. No way will I tell him anything more than about my work for the Project. And even that will be censored. "Then it'll be a very short interview." I offer a half-grin.

After pressing a few buttons on his phone and giving me a questioning look that I accept, he turns on the recording and flips open his notebook. "So, tell me, why graphic design?"

Exhaling at his softball question, I launch into my spiel about what brought me into the industry. From there, the interview goes on a rather predictable course and I find myself relaxing in his presence. Jeremy's a very good journalist, judging by how he gets me to open up and share slightly more than I anticipated. But still in the safe zone.

"Rose was right about you. You are a bundle of energy," he quips as he writes something down.

"Rose?"

Hazel eyes meet mine. "Yes. I met her, I don't know, a year or so ago."

Everything clicks into place. He was at Rose's big introductory party after the Billboard Music Awards. "You're *that* journalist! I knew you looked familiar but I couldn't place you."

His hand moves across his chest. "Guilty as charged. Rose calls me up from time to time with some scoops and stories of interest. She pointed me toward the Big Reveal, and talked you up. When you were named as the finalist, I knew I had to interview you."

"Well, I'm flattered. Rose is a great friend." The best.

He looks down at his notes. "Where were we? Oh right. Please tell me how you got inspired for each of the musicians who you created designs for. Starting with Ozzy Martinez."

All of the good will we created dissipates. Standing, I dump the rest of my coffee down the sink, all the while trying to come up with some plausible tale. Rinsing the mug, I put it into the dishwasher, then retake my seat.

"He was the most difficult of the musicians to work with because he was in the process of writing new music. All of the other acts mainly used older stuff, but he wanted to introduce new songs."

When I stop talking, he presses, "Go on."

And he didn't have a muse, until me. Until his lips covered mine and his body made mine scream in pleasure. Shaking my head, I reply, "So, I got to see him not only as a performer, but also as a creator. It was fascinating, really." Inhaling, I continue, "It was fun to see how another creative-type works. Of course, he's in a totally different medium." I take us down the rabbit-hole of performance versus design. We move on to discuss the other musicians in my presentation.

"McKenna, I have only one more question. I'd be remiss if I didn't ask you about your relationship with Ozzy. Would you like to make a comment about it?"

I force out a laugh, hoping I don't sound like a deranged Christmas elf. "Don't believe everything you read in a tabloid. You, of all people, should know that."

"Gotcha. Well, I think I have everything I need. I really appreciate your taking the time to meet with me—and for letting me crash your place." He offers a wry smile while adjusting his glasses. He really is very cute.

"I'm sorry you had to hunt me down."

He stands and rubs his hands on his thighs. "I hope you don't think I'm out of line, but I really enjoyed talking with you. I'd love to take you out and continue our conversation."

Before I can stop myself, the words, "Like on a date?" fly out of my mouth. I slap my hand over my lips.

His eyes fall to the floor. "Yeah. Like on a date."

He's a really good guy. Not the typical bad boys I've been with—well, Ozzy is the only guy I've been with since Matt, and both of them could win awards for being bad boys. Although, Ozzy's great in so many respects and nothing like Matt. I shake my head. For his own good, I need to let him down gently. "Jeremy, I would like nothing else, but I'm getting over a really bad break-up. Maybe another time?"

His cheeks flush. "Sure. I get it." After clearing his throat, he says, "Your article should be in this week's magazine." He turns his head. "Oh, and the magazine got photos from the event, so you don't have to worry about anything."

"Great," I croak. "I really did enjoy meeting you."

Mom shuffles into the kitchen, Elaine at her back. Time to usher Jeremy out. Pronto. "This is my mother and her ... friend, Elaine. Jeremy's just leaving now."

Mom nods at us and walks to the cupboard. I almost push Jeremy out of the room. "Sorry about the interruption," I say as I urge him to the front door.

He stops and turns to face me, then hands me his business card. "In case you change your mind, my personal cell is on the back. Feel free to use it."

I take his card. "Thanks."

After he leaves, I toss the card into the trash. I bet he's a great guy, but I'm not in the market for one. No. I need to focus on my responsibilities. I can't get sidetracked ever again. Every time I do, someone gets hurt. Especially me.

DAYS GO BY, which I spend interviewing potential evening shift nurses. I click with Mandy, and go through all of the paperwork associated with hiring her. Tossing my pen onto the kitchen table, I clap twice. "I really like her."

Elaine replies, "It'll be good to have your mother with full-time care. You'll be freed up to live your life without worry."

"Mom's my responsibility. I just need some help with her." I make a neat pile of the paperwork. "Besides, it's not like I have a life," I mutter.

Elaine puts her hand on my shoulder and walks toward the living room. "Good things are about to happen. I can feel it."

Rolling my eyes, it's all I can do not to laugh out loud. Elaine believes the best for everyone, but I'm a realist. Looking at the holiday cards adorning the kitchen walls, my mind roams to the upcoming holiday. I already got presents for everyone. Except Ozzy. I snort—no need to get him one now. The past few days proved that to me. Not to mention an online photospread of him at his concert last night. He had some red-headed slut hanging off his arm. I really have to stop torturing myself by googling his name.

Pulling out the flour and sugar, I start baking some more Christmas cookies. Everyone enjoys them, and it usually calms my nerves to bake. But not today. Every cookie reminds me of what I had to give up. Rather, who. Thanks to Matt and the bad decision to date him I made all those years ago. Not to mention calling Daddy to be my knight in shining armor that fateful night.

Elaine walks in as I'm mangling a Nutella chip cookie. "These were just dropped off for you." She hands me some magazines.

"Thanks." I wipe my hands and open Jeremy's, the *Record News*. Sitting down, I flip the pages until I find the one with the headline, "Local Graphic Designer Finals in Competition." There's a photo of me at the Big Reveal.

Taking a deep breath, I start reading. Jeremy's words jump off the page and paint a picture of me I don't recognize. Of a woman in charge, taking control of her career and putting her best foot forward. Well, I guess that's me. I certainly put everything I had into the presentation.

I finish the article and toss the magazine to the side. A supermarket tabloid is underneath it. Looking on the cover, my heart cramps at a huge photo of Ozzy, half naked and walking backstage at the Jade. I trace his torso with my finger, wanting it to be real. But, it isn't. The caption under the photo catches my attention next: "Rockstar Dumps Murderess!"

What?

I flip the pages and land on a huge photospread—of me! The photo of Ozzy with me taken by the paparazzi now sports the headline: "Ozzy's ex tied to her father's murder."

I can't catch my breath. "Oh my God," I say to no one. My eyes greedily read the words, trying to make sense of the story. The writer focused on my testimony at Matt's trial. It paints me as a total party-girl who was into drugs and alcohol with Matt. They even dug up some old photos of me out on the town with him, which they must have scored from an old Facebook reel or something. I deleted my account in the aftermath of the case.

"It seems that James's father caught wind of the extreme partying his daughter was doing and drove over one night to stop it. A fight ensued, at the end of which her father was dead. During the trial, the defense argued that Lopez acted in self-defense, and that Ms. James herself provided the knife that killed her father. Lopez was convicted of manslaughter, based on James's self-serving testimony. Seems to us that Ozzy is well rid of this modern-day Lizzie Borden."

I scream, "No, no, no!"

Mom rushes into the kitchen. "What's up, McKenna?"

Wiping the tears streaming down my face, I pick up both magazines and jump to my feet. Not wanting to share this horrible story with her, I lie, "I thought I burned the cookies, but they're all good."

"I'm sure we'll love them." She nudges me and winks. "Your father loves everything you cook, even if you burn a couple. You know that."

I suck in my breath. It's too much. I toss the oven mitt to Elaine as she enters the room. "Can you get the cookies out? I'm suddenly not feeling well and have to go lie down." I don't wait for her response but rush into my bedroom and close the door.

How could the magazine print such lies? What can I do to stop this story? The tabloid is dated today. I hop online and the story is plastered all over. I'm too late to do anything about it. Even if I asked Rose to intervene, there's nothing she could do.

I didn't give Matt that knife. I didn't want Daddy dead. How could they print utter lies? I put my face into my pillow and cry, sobs making my whole body convulse. The whole world knows my secret—even though it's all wrong.

My cell phone rings. Out of habit, I check to see who's calling. It's the President of Project. "Fuck."

Sniffling away the tears, I croak, "Hello?"

"McKenna, this is Peggy Laswell."

I lift my chin, trying to stifle my sobs. "What can I do for you?"

"I just finished the most disturbing article about you. The other board members read it as well, and we'd like to give you the opportunity to come in to the Las Vegas office tomorrow to explain before we send the second place finisher to the national competition."

I suck in my breath. This can't be happening. "Peggy, it's all lies."

She cuts me off. "Save your explanations for the full board meeting. You'll be there, correct? We start promptly at ten."

I clear my throat. "Yes, of course—" Before I can get the full sentence out, the call disconnects.

Another sob escapes, followed by countless more. I try to catch my breath—I have until tomorrow to get my thoughts in order for the meeting of my life.

Twenty-Seven

OZZY

"**O**zzy!"

Aiden's voice carries up the stairs and into my bedroom, where I'm still lying in bed. Haven't slept for hours, but haven't moved either. I turn my head away from the door.

"Ozzy!"

"Go away," I whisper. I'm in no mood to play nice. It's been days since I've seen McKenna, and each one gets harder to get through.

"There you are."

I turn onto my side, away from him, grumbling, "Can't you take a hint?"

"Come on, wake up." He shakes the bed, followed by Bans's barking from down the hall.

"Great. Now you've woken her up."

The golden retriever jumps onto the bed and puts her doggie breath all up in my grill. Backing away, I say, "It's too early for this shit."

"But not for this." Aiden tosses a magazine on top of me.

Flicking it to the side, I say, "Whatever. Don't you have something else to do besides bother the piss out of me?"

"Nope."

The rustling of pages being flipped reaches my ears. Sighing, I turn over and throw my arm over my face.

"Here it is." Aiden makes a weird-ass sound in the back of his throat.

And, nothing.

Moving my arm to the side, a huge photo of me is on the front cover. "Great. What did that rag print about me now?" I sit up, resting my back against the padded headboard. Listless, I look out the window, my mind blank. Empty. Like my life.

"Ahem." Aiden brings me out of my musing.

Waving at him, I instruct, "Go ahead. Let's hear their lies."

He shakes the tabloid. "It's not what you think." He shows me the photos and reads a lurid tale about McKenna and Matt, ending with her father being killed. "Seems to us that Ozzy is well rid of this modern-day Lizzie Borden." He finishes and looks at me.

My mind is everywhere and nowhere all at once. "She never mentions her father. I assumed he wasn't in the picture." A fragment of a conversation rises to the top. "No, wait. That's not true. She did mention he used to take her to Edie Z's for a chocolate every week."

Silence falls over the room, the only sound being Bans's snoring. Ignoring the fluff-ball, I shift in the bed. Anger overtakes me. "Why the fuck didn't she talk to me about this? Oh, right. How was she going to tell me that she killed her own father?" I adopt a high-pitch tone. "By the way, I happened to hand my boyfriend a knife, which he stuck into my father."

Aiden drops the rag onto my bed.

I shake my head. None of this meshes with the woman I know. "This doesn't add up."

"Maybe they got it wrong. Fuck knows, they mess stuff up all the time."

The need to get to the bottom of this gnaws in the pit of my stomach. I can't believe she killed her own father—she doesn't have it in her. But then again, I didn't think she had it in her to cheat on me either, so what do I know? When I can't take all of the unanswered questions ramming my brain, I toss the blankets off my nude body and stalk into the bathroom. "Can you take care of Bans for me today? I have to find out what all this is about."

"I thought you might say that." Aiden holds up her leash. "C'mon Bans, let's go for a walk."

I shower and dress in shorts and a Las Vegas T-shirt. Stopping in the kitchen, I make myself a protein shake. Each whirl of the blender fuels my anger toward the woman I thought I was falling in love with. Ha! What a freaking shit-show that would be. Maybe I should send some flowers to the tabloid for doing me a favor. She makes Teresa look like a saint.

But that's not the McKenna I know.

Shoving my head into my helmet, I hop on Shirley and barrel toward her house. She better have a good explanation about all this. And, more importantly, why she didn't she tell me about it ages ago?

Something's really off.

I pull into her driveway and ring the bell. When no one answers, I knock loudly enough to wake the neighborhood. A woman I've never met answers. She looks me up and down. "Can I help you?"

I widen my stance. "I need to talk with McKenna right now."

From inside the house, another woman's voice sings, "Who's that?" The woman in front of me half-turns and replies to McKenna's mother, "A man looking for McKenna."

"A man? My little McKenna's too young to know any men. Send him away."

The woman at the door shuts her eyes, steps outside and closes the door behind her, forcing me to take a step backward. "Now's not a good time. Ozzy, right?"

I blink. I never introduced myself. Yeah, but it's not like all of Vegas doesn't know who you are, dude. "I need to talk with McKenna. Send her out to me."

The middle-aged woman shakes her head. "She's not here."

I cross my arms across my chest. "I'll wait."

Not a shrinking violet, this woman puts her hands on her hips. "I don't know how long she'll be gone. Why don't you leave and I'll tell her you visited when she returns?"

I laugh. "Yeah. I'm sure you will. Who are you, anyway?"

Her posture shifts. "Elaine. And might I add that I have more right to be here than you do."

Maybe I can take advantage of my charm with the ladies. "Well, Elaine, it looks like we're at an impasse. I have some unfinished business with McKenna. So, let me in and I'll happily wait until she gets back. Okay?" I wink at her.

"I can't let you do that."

Frustration rages through my bloodstream. "Listen, Elaine, I'm working on a short fuse. If McKenna's not here, where the hell is she at," I consult my watch, "eleven in the morning?"

The rumbling of a car pulling into the driveway diverts our attention. A man steps out—I recognize him from the tabloid photospread. Matt.

Next to me, Elaine sucks in her breath.

When he sees me at the front door, he puts his head down and rushes up the sidewalk, yelling, "You. You've been fucking my girlfriend." Stopping half a foot away from me, he pushes against my chest.

"What the fuck?" I push him back.

The front door opens behind Elaine. McKenna's mom stands in the open doorway, wearing a bathrobe. "What's going on here?"

"Let's take this inside," Matt says and pushes me toward Elaine. I catch her before she and McKenna's mother fall over, and Matt rushes by us. Once all four of us are inside, he slams the door shut.

Ignoring the two women, Matt turns his attention to me. "Thought after your stunt at the Big Reveal that you two were over." He looks me up and down. "Guess I was wrong." He cracks his knuckles. "Looks like I'm going to have me some fun."

McKenna's mom shrieks, "Who are these strange men! Get out of my house!" Neither Matt nor I turn our heads in her direction. Elaine hushes her and pulls her into the interior of the house.

"Come here, pretty boy." He makes a "come hither" motion with his fingers.

Notching up my chin, I refuse to let him get the best of me. If my boyhood fights in Puerto Rico taught me anything, it was how to keep my wits. "You first."

My stillness on the outside belies the blood surging against my veins' walls. I'm pissed at McKenna—pissed at the world—and this guy might provide me with a much-needed outlet.

Matt lunges at me, but I duck and he misses. His next three punches score my face in rapid succession, which only enrages me further.

Weaving to avoid his next two attempts, he hits nothing but air. Spitting blood onto the carpet, I gloat, "Missed."

He roars and rushes me again, pushing me backward and over a table. A lamp crashes to the floor.

A female voice screams.

On top of me, Matt pulls his arm back. As if in slow motion, it screams toward me, but I wrap my legs around his waist and twist at the same time.

His hand punches the carpet and I take advantage of his momentary discombobulation, arching my back upward to dislodge him. I jump to my feet a second before he stands in front of me. We're both breathing hard, focused on taking the other out.

He does a roundhouse swing at me that narrowly misses. I step forward into a right hook and connect with his jaw, sending his face flying to the left. I follow it up with a left jab and he stumbles backward.

Seeing as to how we don't have much room, and aware of the women somewhere inside, I put my head down and run him into the wall by the torso. Stupefied, he blinks. I grab his wrist, wrap it up high behind him and pull. Hard. His only response is a grunt.

His foot contacts my shin. Not letting go of his wrist, I step to the side before he can try a second kick. And push him downward.

Sirens screech down the street. Elaine rushes by us and opens the front door, pointing to us. "Him! That's him. The one bending over."

I look down at the man gulping air and pull on his arm once again. The cop approaches us. "We'll take it from here, sir." He clinks a pair of metal handcuffs.

Twenty-Eight

OZZY

"THANK YOU FOR WHAT YOU DID out there," Elaine says as she offers me ice for my eye and knuckles, after the cops took our statements.

"Looks like I'm not playing tonight," I mutter, noting the bruises starting to form. Withdrawing the towel from my lip, I fish out my cell and gingerly text Aiden.

McKenna's mom walks into the kitchen. "Oh, my." She looks at my hands. "Keep ice on them, it'll bring down the swelling." She takes me in, her eyes cloudy. "I'm sorry, do I know you?"

Elaine sighs. I force my lips to tick upward. "I'm a friend of your daughter's."

"That's nice," she says. She pats my shoulder and leaves the room.

"Today's not a good day," Elaine explains. "And I'm sure all of this excitement didn't help matters."

"Dementia's nasty."

"Sure is. It'll be much better for her, though, when McKenna can add a second shift nurse. Assuming everything gets straightened out."

I try to piece together what she's telling me. Elaine is Mrs. James's day nurse?

She busies herself in the kitchen. Placing the towel over the handle of the oven, she says, "Thank you for protecting us from Matt. Needless to say, he's done this family enough harm already."

"I got that."

She moves to stand next to me. After starting to speak a few times, she manages, "Listen, I shouldn't be telling you this, but I think it's important for you to know. McKenna's wanted to hire a second shift nurse for her mother for a while now. She sold her condo to pay for my salary, but it can't cover another nurse. If she wins this national competition, she'll be able to hire someone. Heck, being named to the competition is drawing more interest in her business. She's been interviewing nurses in anticipation."

"If the other presentations from the Big Reveal party are any indication, McKenna's got it in the bag."

"I hope so." She crosses her arms across her chest and takes a deep breath. "McKenna's not here because she got called to an emergency meeting of the board."

My one eyebrow furrows. "But she owns her own company and doesn't have a board."

She shakes her head. "No. The board of the Artist Avenue Adventure Project. Did you see the article in the tabloid?"

I swallow. "Yeah. I came over to talk with her about it, actually." Maybe I'm overstating things. I did want to scream and yell and get to the bottom of the story.

"Well, so did the board. They called her in today before deciding whether to pull her name from consideration for the national competition."

"What?" The legs of the chair scratch against the tile as I stand. "What do you mean?"

"Exactly what I said. They called an emergency meeting this morning."

I stalk around the kitchen, walking from the mixer to the fridge and back to the table. Elaine watches my progress in silence. "There's no way she killed her father."

"Of course she didn't. She was involved with that guy, Matt, and wanted to it break off with him. When he gave her trouble, she called her father to help. He came to bring her home and Matt killed him in the process."

I let her words sink in. "I believe you. I need to find McKenna." I turn on my heel and resume my pacing. Each step is like a thud on my heart, trying to tamp down my feelings for McKenna. Ones that keep resurfacing—of her laughing and challenging me and making me venture outside of myself. Of us on the dune buggies and at the skydiving experience. Singing to her from the stage. Making love with her.

I stop as if I hit a wall.

Making love. That's what I did with McKenna. It was so much more than having sex. Realization that I'm in love with her crashes over me. "I love her."

"Glad to hear it. Maybe you should stop making her life so much harder than it already is, then."

I reach into my back pocket and pull out my phone again. "What's the night nurse's name McKenna wants to hire?" Elaine gives me a name and her agency's phone number. Nodding, I call Aiden this time.

"What do you mean you're canceling your concert tonight?"

I don't have the patience for this. "I'm going to text you a nursing agency and an employee there. I need you to hire this woman, staring immediately, for McKenna's mother."

"McKenna? I thought you said that she—"

Before my ill-chosen words are spewed back at me, I jump over Aiden's response. "Fuck what I said before. I want you to do as I'm saying right now. I expect her to be paid, in full, through the end of the year. Tell them to send me the bills from now on. Got it?"

"Loud and clear. Is she why you're you ducking tonight's concert?"

My bruised knuckles throb. "No. I'm not getting into this now, but I'm in no shape to perform."

I kill the call and look at Elaine, who's smiling from ear to ear. "Well, that's certainly a start."

Buoyed by her positive response, I state, "I'm only getting started. Do you have the address for the Project's office?"

"Wait here." She leaves the kitchen and I toss the frozen packs into the sink. "Here you go." Elaine hands me a piece of paper.

I skim the contents. It's an email from the Project with their office address at the bottom. McKenna scrawled today's date and ten a.m. on it. "I'm going to straighten them out first. McKenna's next."

"I have no doubts."

I kiss the woman's cheek. "Thanks for being such a friend to McKenna and helping her with her mother."

"It's my job, but I love that girl, too. Now go and take care of business."

I leave her in the kitchen. McKenna's mother waves at me from a seat by the television, signs of the struggle between me and Matt still littered around her. I need to get to the Project's office. Calling over my shoulder, I say, "Don't clean up in here. I'll have someone come and do it."

Elaine responds, "You've done enough. I'll take care of it. Now, go."

I offer them both a nod and race out of the front door. The cops left Matt's car here, but it's not a problem for Shirley.

Pulling into the parking lot, I release the kickstand and hop off the bike. It's after noon. They better still be here. Looking around, I notice McKenna's Honda is nowhere to be found. *Shit.* I cross into the small reception area and ask the receptionist about the board meeting.

The young girl's mouth drops open when she realizes it's me. I don't have time for any fangirl bullshit right now and repeat, "Where. Is. The. Board. Meeting?"

Her mouth pops closed. She swallows and says, "They're in the back conference room, but they're meeting behind closed doors." Ignoring the rest of her sentence, I brush past her and stride to the back of the building. "Hey, wait, I said you can't go back there. You're not on the agenda." An Exit sign leads outside and I turn away from it to the closed door that will lead me into the conference room.

I inhale and twist the doorknob, the receptionist hot on my heels. Leaving the door open, I enter the room.

"I'm so sorry. I tried to get him to stop, but he wouldn't listen," the receptionist worries behind me.

A tall woman with a brunette bob stands. I recognize her as the President from the Big Reveal and address her. "Peggy, so nice to see you again."

Peggy lifts her hand, stopping the yippy receptionist in her tracks. "Mr. Martinez, to what do we owe this pleasure?" Her voice is disapproving, probably as a result of my being wasted at her party.

Shrugging off her disapproval, I approach the round table. I'm here for my girl. Nodding at each one of the people I saw at the Big Reveal, I reply, "I heard there was a meeting about McKenna, Ms. James, and I have some things to share."

Peggy motions for the receptionist to leave us and looks at me. "We're all still here. What do you want us to know?"

That McKenna's one-of-a-kind. That she's sacrificed so much for her mother. That I wouldn't have an album or probably a glimmer of a future if not for her. That she deserves to stay in the competition.

I swallow and take my time, looking at each board member. "When I first got together with Ms. James about the Project, I had no new music. Nothing."

I let my words sink in. "I had been trying to write new songs for so long, but didn't have anything to show for it. The stuff I did have was absolute crap." I place my hands on my hips. "Ms. James changed everything. She taught me how to get outside of myself and reconnect with music. She listened to me— really listened—and challenged me to try something new. And it worked."

I walk behind Peggy and place my hands on the back of her chair. "Isn't this what your organization promotes? Challenging the youth to look at things from another angle and daring to be different?"

The board members look among themselves, murmuring.

Not letting them take the floor from me, I continue, "I know Ms. James met with you earlier." I pause and observe heads bobbing in agreement. "I'm sure she explained whatever that stupid tabloid printed was lies, distantly related to the truth. So what that she made a bad relationship decision in her past? Who hasn't?" I chuckle. "I know I have. But this time, I'm hoping to turn all that around."

A few of the board members drop their heads. Taking their response as silent assent, I say, "What matters is how you deal with your mistakes. If you're me, you run and hide and stop living your life. That's not how Ms. James handled things. No. She took over her family's responsibilities, all the while building her graphic design company from scratch. And she's a fantastic designer. You know that. You *saw* her work."

I walk across the room. "I know you're deciding whether to allow her to represent you at the national competition. I also know you're afraid to take a chance on someone who might not have a squeaky-clean reputation. But I was at the Big Reveal and I know what I saw. Ms. James's presentation stood out above the others. And I'm not saying this because my music was featured in hers or because I would never have produced another song if not for our collaboration."

I smile and garner strength from the chuckles around the table.

"I think you need to choose the one artist for this award who created a visual masterpiece out of songs. The one who made you want to celebrate life and living. Because that's what Ms. James does. She makes you experience joy through her work. She brought me out of a place of darkness to a place of creation, and I'm a much better man for having her in my life."

I stop. What else can I add to change their minds?

Peggy stands, "Thank you, Mr. Martinez. We appreciate your words and will take them—"

Before she can cut me off, I blurt, "We all know she owns this competition. But she also owns my heart." My next words tumble from my mouth.

Twenty-Nine

MCKENNA

I DRIVE PAST THE JADE WITHOUT TURNING my head. Barreling down the Strip with so many others, I stop at traffic lights and move forward when they turn green. Visitors mix with locals on the streets, but I don't pay them any attention.

Driving past one of the "Welcome to Las Vegas" signs, I turn left and then hang a right. Before I know it, I'm at the cemetery. Leaving the air conditioner on, I stare blankly forward.

Peggy Laswell's parting words to me ring true. "Thanks for your time, Ms. James. We'll take everything you've said under advisement and get back to you by tomorrow as to whether your candidacy will be continued. I have to say that I, for one, am sorry your story came out this way and put such a big, black mark on you. We'll be in touch."

If only I didn't need the positive press—and money—from the national competition so badly, I'd tell her where she could shove that big black mark.

I only want to help Mom. I smack the steering wheel. Is that too much to ask?

My anger is replaced by tears of frustration. Exiting my car, I take faster and faster steps on my way to the grave, clear away some leaves and fall to my knees in front of his tombstone. "I know I promised you, Daddy, that I'd take care of Mom and never put her into a nursing home. I'll keep my vow, somehow, even if I don't make it into the national competition." Tears drip onto my skirt-covered legs.

"Get a grip," I admonish myself while playing with the green in my hair. Somehow the color of sickness felt right today. "Everything's on me. Like always. If the Project decides to go with someone else, I need a backup plan."

"If." I shake my head. "Ha!" I have no doubts in my mind at all that the board has already tossed my presentation into the circular file and have contacted the runner-up.

I take a deep breath and try to remember the name of the newest casino that's being put up. Maybe I can call and get into their management before someone else scoops up the graphic design contract. Assuming, of course, they didn't see the article and think I'm a murderess. I trace Daddy's name in the granite. Matt is ruining my life without even having to break the restraining order I got against him.

"It's all on you, McKenna. You need to figure this out. No one is going to come to your rescue," I say aloud to no one.

The one and only time someone came to my rescue, Daddy ended up here.

I close my eyes as pain washes over me. If only he were with me right now. He would tell me to "Buck up, buckaroo. Things are never as bad as you think they are. Just remember to tell the truth and goodness will win out."

My eyes pop open. I forgot to tell the board that I recently got the restraining order against Matt. This has to be considered evidence that I wasn't in on the crime with him! Placing a kiss on the marker, I say, "Thank you, Daddy."

Feeling like everything could work out for the first time in weeks, I blurt,

"I can do this. I'm going to take care of Mom." Standing, I tuck my hair behind my ear. "After I get this sorted out with the board, I'm going to talk with Ozzy. I've mucked things up with him, but he's a fantastic guy, and I need to come clean to him. About everything. I want to live again. You'd want that for me."

Soon, I pull into the back of the Project's office. Determined to share what I forgot to tell the board earlier, I park and enter through the backway.

The door to the conference room stands ajar. I hope they haven't left yet. Crossing the hall, I stop before getting to the threshold when Ozzy's voice reaches my ears.

Ozzy? What's he doing here? My heart skips a beat. I shove my fist into my mouth and lean in, careful to keep my body out of sight.

Ozzy stands with his feet planted wide, hands on his trim hips, his words running together. "We all know she owns this competition. But she also owns my heart. I've never met a more kind, giving and optimistic woman. She showed me I was a self-centered asshole, too caught up in my own shit to see what was going on right in front of me. And you need her to do that for you. You need to get out of your own way and let her soar. Because believe me, you will gain national acclaim if you let her submission move forward. Not only that, but her work has the potential to change the lives of so many people, the same way it did for me."

I squeak. Everyone turns and looks at the open door.

Thirty

MCKENNA

WITHOUT THINKING, I STEP THROUGH the open doorway, my eyes focused on the only person in here who matters to me—Ozzy. He draws in a breath.

"Ms. James, we're in a closed session," Peggy Laswell announces.

Without moving my eyes from the larger-than-life rocker standing before this group and singing my praises, I say, "I came back because I forgot to tell you something."

Peggy waives her hand, either in frustration or welcome, I'm not sure. "Come on in, McKenna."

McKenna. Not Ms. James. I take an unbalanced step toward the conference table, still looking at the man who stole my heart. Before I can process his black eye and split lip, he rushes toward me, tattooed arms open. I step into his strong embrace.

"Ozzy," I say as he whispers, "McKenna."

I tilt my head back, our lips a breath away from each other. I want to ask what happened to him. More importantly, I want to close the gap and kiss him for all I'm worth. My eyes stray to the conference table, where Peggy smiles at me.

Returning to look at Ozzy, I confess, "Nothing matters to me if I don't have you." My mouth bridges the small distance between us and I peck his upper, non-split lip. I whisper, "Let's get out of here."

"What about why you came back here in the first place?" His baritone seeps into every crevice of my body.

Sighing, I recognize that he's right. I need to correct the record before the board. And then get the hell out of here—to someplace where Ozzy and I can be alone. I steal one more look at his bruised face. "I'll make it quick."

I disengage from him, immediately mourning the loss of his arms. Turning toward the table, the members of the board look a lot more relaxed than when I was before them this morning. Knowing Ozzy's on my side, and obviously wants to work things out, I gulp some much-needed air.

"Thanks for letting me speak to you again. Before, I told you all about what happened that night years ago and my testimony at the trial. However, I forgot to let you know that I testified at Matt's parole hearing a couple of weeks ago, arguing against his early release. When I learned that—for whatever unknown reason—he was granted parole, I got a restraining order against him for my mother and me. He's violated it several times already and I'm sure he'll be back in prison soon. You can check all this with public records, if you want. I just wanted you to know about this."

From behind me, Ozzy says, "Actually, he's back behind bars as we speak."

I suck in my breath and swing around. "What?"

Ozzy shrugs, my eyes landing on his swollen knuckles for the first time. I grab both of them in my hands. "What happened?

Looking down at me but responding so that the entire room can hear, he says, "I went to McKenna's house today and he showed up. The police came and took him away."

The nervous energy coursing through my body since Matt was released dissipates all at once. He's no longer free. He's not a threat anymore. "Oh,

Ozzy!" He smiles down at me, his left eye nearly shut. "Please tell me he looks worse than you do."

A smirk crosses his face. "Oh, yeah. Believe me, Dulcita."

I need to get out of here. This room is not the appropriate place for me to tear Ozzy's clothes off. Although Peggy might enjoy the show, considering how she's looking at him.

Smiling, I turn to the board and say, "That's everything. I hope to hear my candidacy is still in place." Placing my hand around Ozzy's forearm so as not to injure his hands any further, I push him toward the doorway.

Peggy's voice stops our escape. "McKenna, we had already decided to keep your name in the competition before Mr. Martinez came in and spoke on your behalf. But his certainly was a heroic performance."

Her words ring in my ears. I did it! I spin around and say, "Thank you."

She shakes her head. "No, thank you. You both reminded us about why we love the Artist Avenue Adventure Project, and what's so inspiring about it. It's made up of wonderful people like you both, who always strive to do their best. We look forward to seeing you in January in LA for the awards ceremony."

I nod as Ozzy grabs my hand. Together, we race out of the room to the sound of chuckles from the board. While hearing my chances to stay in the national competition is a relief, I need to reconnect with the man at my side now. In the hallway, I point to the side entrance, "I'm parked out here."

He nods. "Shirley's out front. And she missed you."

We change course, pass the receptionist and out the front door. Shirley gleams in a nearby parking spot. When we reach her, Ozzy opens the storage area and hands me my helmet. Not caring that I'm in a skirt, or that the bald eagle helmet will screw up my hair, I buckle the strap and enjoy the show as he hops onto the bike. Wrapping my arms and thighs around him, I hold on as he peels out of the parking lot.

Laughing, I squeeze his chest and enjoy having his hard body in front of me. We zip through the streets of Vegas, and soon pull into his driveway. Instead of going in through the front door, he leads us to the side gate.

The pool glistens in the afternoon sun. The patio furniture is inviting. Standing about four feet away from me, he turns. All I want to do is jump into his arms again.

"I can't believe you went to the board on my behalf."

"Yeah, well, kinda surprised myself, too. When Aiden brought me the article, I was pissed at you. Why didn't you tell me anything about this?"

I swallow over the huge lump lodged in my throat. Looking at Ozzy, it hits me that I have to share my burdens with him if our love is going to flourish. And I so desperately want it to. In a quiet voice, I confess, "I don't share personal things I should be able to handle on my own."

His chin ticks upward. Taking a deep breath, I continue, "I'm not sure how much you know."

"I need to hear it from you."

I tell him about getting together with Matt and then how it went into a downward spiral when drugs got involved. How he abused me, and I didn't leave. Shame washes over me, but I keep going. Through that awful night and what happened to Daddy.

"Daddy made me promise I would take care of Mom. I loved him so much. I wanted it to be me who bled out and not him. I feel like I've had a gaping wound ever since." I end my story with a sob.

Ozzy wraps me in his embrace, his chin on top of my head. "Shh, it's okay now. I've got you."

He rubs my back as my tears flow. Tears about Daddy. About what happened afterwards. Knowing my story doesn't end on that night, I force myself to say, "The trial was awful. Mom was too broken to go to most of it, but she did hear me testify. I think that was a turning point for her. Her early-onset dementia ramped up about then, but I was too wrapped up in my own misery to really notice. I took my inheritance and bought a condo in town. I had to start my own graphic design business because I was fired after I stopped going to my job when everything went down with Matt."

I swipe the back of my hand over my nose. "My graphics were rote. Uninspired. I didn't land great clients, but picked up enough little projects to keep the lights on."

Ozzy continues to rub my back, remaining silent. Encouraging me to share. "I stopped my party-girl ways, Ozzy. I did. I stayed inside. I volunteered at a battered women's shelter. Still do."

His arms still for a moment, then continue their soothing movements. "I'd like to make a donation," he murmurs.

"They'd appreciate it." I suck in a breath and continue, "Every once in a while, though, I would let loose, simply because I had to. Sometimes I would go out with Shelia to concerts at the Jade, but I would always keep the banter light between her and me. I didn't open up. To anyone."

"We hooked up back then."

I nod, my forehead hitting his chest. It's now or never. "You were, you were the only guy I hooked up with after Matt. When you took an interest in me once, I thought it would be a one-time fling. And I really needed the validation. When you came back to town, I'd try to catch your eye."

His arms run up and down mine. "I always saw you, even back then. I felt something pulling me toward you and wanted to be with you, but fought against it. Sometimes, I'd cave and get another fix. Most times, I picked another woman so as to show myself you didn't mean that much to me."

My lips lift at his admission. "I thought you wanted variety. But, I always wanted to be on the menu."

He kisses the top of my head. "Tell me more about your mother."

Closing my eyes, I recount her continued downward spiral. "A few months ago, I received a call from Becky, our neighbor, that she was roaming around the neighborhood. It was then I knew I had to put her needs above mine. I looked into home nursing care, since I had promised Daddy never to put her into a nursing home. I guess he recognized something in her even back then." My voice trails off.

"And then you moved."

I clear my throat. "When I found out how much the care would cost, I put my condo up on the market and started staying overnights at the house. I closed on the condo right after Rose's bridal shower. I immediately put the funds into an account and hired Elaine. She's the best thing to come out of this whole mess."

"She was pretty great today."

I tilt my head back, and he tells me about his fight with Matt. I kiss his knuckles, lip and eye. "I'm glad you're okay." I pause. "And that Matt's back in jail."

One dark brown eye bores into me. "McKenna, who have you shared all this with?"

I force a smile. "You."

He shakes his head. "That's today. I mean, who's been helping you with all of this?"

"I saw a therapist for years. She helped me sort through all my emotions, and to place blame where it belonged—on Matt. She didn't let me off the hook, though, and together we worked through the abuse."

"I'm glad you got the help you needed."

My eyes stray to the pool. "And, Elaine knows most of it since she's been taking care of Mom. We talked about you."

His eyebrows raise, highlighting his black eye. "Why didn't you tell Rose? You two seem close."

I shrug. "Not her responsibility."

He pulls me tighter, squeezing the air out of my lungs. "Didn't your therapist tell you that you need to let people in?"

On a hiccup and pressed against his warmth, I respond, "Yes."

He takes a deep breath and I feel his body shake. "I want to help you. Forever."

His last word hangs in the air for a second before coating me from head to toe. The graphic of the word melting over me, then locking me in its cocoon dances in my mind's eye. *Forever.* "I'd like that. Forever."

One of his bruised knuckles tips my chin upward, so that we're looking directly into each other's souls. "I took care of the second shift nurse, starting tonight."

I should be outraged at his high-handedness. Or feel like I shirked my duty to Mom. But, I don't. No, I'm relieved this burden has been lifted and Mom will get better care. I'm also overjoyed that he would do this for me.

"Ozzy. I don't know what to say, other than thank you. And those words are so inadequate." Tears cling to my eyelashes.

"You can thank me by staying here overnight. I don't have a concert tonight."

Overnight. Without worry about Mom for the first time in over a year. My body begs me to jump into his arms and never let go, yet my head knows we still have one major issue to discuss. I place a kiss on his chest. "Why did you show up to the Big Reveal high, with other women on your arm? You knew how important that night was for me. It was like you were trying to ruin it."

His hand skims over the stubble on his chin. "Yeah. That." He steps back. Once. Twice. My body protests the loss. "I saw you."

My eyebrows form a "V." "When?"

"I drove to your house after recording with the band"—his eyes light up and dim almost simultaneously—"and when I pulled into the driveway of your house, you were standing in the bay window. In Matt's arms."

All the air leaves my lungs. "And you thought I was playing you like Teresa did," I whisper.

"I should've asked you about it. I was going to, but then you texted me and essentially pushed me away."

His reaction clicks into place for me. "I was afraid Matt was going to hurt you. He saw our photo in the magazine and threatened to kill you." I take a step toward him but stop. "I should've told you, too."

"I'm not proud of what I did during those times. I performed a concert drunk. I partied. But, I never took anyone to the Penthouse. I couldn't."

I process his words. He was faithful to me like he was faithful to his wife—even if he thought I was cheating on him. Yet he's been so open with me, I need to do the same. "It hurt to see you at the Big Reveal with those two blonde bimbos." He smiles at my characterization of his dates. "But, you were high. You knew what that would mean to me."

He nods and drops his head. "I wanted to get back at you and I knew that by hurting myself, I would hurt you. It was stupid, I know." He raises his head and looks directly at me. "Never again."

I erase the distance between us. Placing my hand on his chest, I say, "We've both done stupid things." I screw up all my courage. "I've lived with feelings of guilt and shame over my bad judgment with Matt, which caused me to shut down. No more. I believe in you. You're not perfect, but neither am I. But, together we make one hell of an amazing pair." I blow air through my mouth, causing my bangs to fly upward.

Because I'm touching his chest, I feel his pulse flutter. "I love you, McKenna James."

My heart spirals out of my chest at his three words. "I love you so much!" I wipe yet another tear from my cheek. "Will you kiss me now?"

"You better believe it."

His mouth crashes down on mine in a kiss that obliterates every other one I've ever had. His hands land on my hips and pull me forward while his lips explore mine. His tongue reaches out to mine and together they dance. Tingles ripple throughout my body, centering in my core. We may not be perfect, but we're perfect together. I trust him with all of my secrets, and know they're safe. And I'll do that for him.

He trails his lips across to my ear. "McKenna, will you stay with me tonight? And every night?"

My muscles go weak. "Yes."

While I expect him to strip me on the spot, he bends down and picks me up. Walking toward the French doors, he says, "That's it. You're mine now."

"Sounds good to me." He enters the house and crosses the living room, walking toward the front foyer. "Where are you taking me?"

A smirk crosses his face, marred by damage inflicted by Matt. He's still the sexiest man I've ever seen. "To bed."

My eyes widen. "I've never been to your sanctuary."

He places his right foot on the first step. "Probably because I had to get inside you so fast that I couldn't wait to go up the flight of stairs."

I loop my arms around his neck and arch my back. "I like the sound of that."

He hesitates on the third step, then shakes his head. "Good try. I want you in bed. I want to hear you scream my name all night long. I want to fall asleep connected to you and wake to do it all over again."

"You can't say stuff like that." I wiggle my hips. "You make me all sorts of achy."

He stops at the landing and kisses me. "That's the point."

Taking the next set of stairs two at a time, we turn into a massive bedroom. I barely have time to admire the grey walls, large windows with blue curtains before I'm dumped on top of a crisp, white bedspread covering a humongous bed. Ozzy flings himself on top of me, bracing himself on his elbows.

"I love you," he says as he rains kisses all over my face, ending on my nose.

Crinkling my now well-loved nose, I reply, "And I love you, rocker man."

He rears up. "Rocker man?" He bites his battered lip in an exaggerated way. "I can live with that."

I roll my eyes. "Oh, boy." Pulling him down to me, I say, "Let me do something productive with that big head of yours."

We kiss for what seems like an hour. Who knew kissing could be such a turn on, even if we have to be careful about his injury. I want to rip the clothes off my body and his, but he has both of my arms outstretched and holds them down on the mattress by his hands.

"I need you naked," he says in a gruff voice.

"Finally."

His hands go to my waist and he pulls my top out of my skirt and over my head. The sound of my skirt's zipper bounces off the walls, followed by it hitting the floor somewhere. My hands make quick work of his T-shirt and shorts, his shoes having come off before we hit the bed.

All that's between us is his underwear, my bra and panties and my shoes. He stands and strips off his last piece of clothing, his pierced cock beckoning me. Wasting no time, I sit up and lick all around the head, playing with the metal ball.

He groans and his head falls backward. His hips begin to thrust toward me, pushing him down my throat. I grab his ass to keep him closer, but he makes a strangled noise. "No. Not like this."

Pulling out of my throat, he drops to his haunches and removes each one of my shoes, placing little kisses on my arches before tossing them over his shoulder. Returning to his feet, he looks down on my body. One that isn't tall or skinny, by any means. I can tell from the expression on his face, though, it doesn't matter to him at all. Which makes me feel like the most beautiful woman on earth.

Smiling, I tip my chin upward and lick my lips. "What's next, rocker man?"

"Oh, you're going to like it. A lot."

He places one knee onto the bed next to my hip and reaches one arm around me. With a quick flick, my bra sails off my body. His lips devour each nipple in turn, nibbling and sucking so hard that I almost forget my name. Only when he's given both boobs equal attention do his hands slide downward to my hips. He tugs and my panties slide down my legs.

I sigh into his mouth as he looms large over me. "Four corners."

His good eye crinkles at the corner. "Come again?"

"I hope to," I reply, winking. "We have to take advantage of all four corners of this bed."

A wolfish smirk crosses his face. "Plus the center. Be ready, Dulcita."

He pushes me forward so I'm in the dead center of the bed and nudges his knee between my thighs. "I'm going to like this game." He kisses my inner thigh. "And so are you." He kisses the other before his mouth moves upward.

His tongue contacts my clit. "Oh!"

He licks. "Oh, what?"

I wriggle my hips. "Oh, Ozzy!"

"I like my name on your lips." He licks and nibbles on my clit until the rush of my orgasm screams through each of my limbs. I swear the whole room turns white with stars flickering.

He rolls a condom over his magical cock. "I can't wait another second." That's all the warning I receive before he pushes into my body with one hard thrust.

"You're mine, McKenna."

"Back at you, Rocker Man."

He thrusts hard and fast, then slows to an almost painful pace. I wrap my legs around his waist and put my heels into his ass, urging him to move faster. I'm rewarded by a throaty chuckle and he picks up his pace once again, to an almost punishing rhythm.

A tingling in my toes lets me know I'm going to come again for this man. And I want it. Pushing my hips upward as he thrusts downward, I'm overwhelmed by the sheer force of my climax.

"Ozzy!" I scream.

"Louder."

I repeat, at the top of my lungs, "Ozzy!"

He responds, "McKenna!" Then, he pumps into me. With a groan, he collapses on top of my body, our sweat mingling.

After a long while, he moves off of me and out of the bed. I admire the dimples on his ass as he walks to what I presume to be the bathroom. When he returns, he's wearing nothing but a very satisfied smile. Bending down, he grabs me by the ankles and pulls me to one end of the bed. Flipping me onto my stomach, he says, "Corner number one, coming up."

I giggle. "I bet I'll be coming first."

"Count on it."

I didn't know how creative Ozzy is. And I'm not talking about his music. He's a beast, taking me in so many different ways—positions I've never even heard about. We're both a sweaty mess when he hauls my exhausted yet energized body to the last corner of the bed. He quirks his eyebrow up. "Ready for this?"

"Bring it!"

He shakes his head. "God, I love you!"

He brings his index finger into his mouth and flips me over again. After smacking my butt, he lets his finger trail between my cheeks down there. He inserts it inside. The idea of anal—with Ozzy—makes me shift under him.

"Is this okay? I remember you said you've done this before."

"I have." Shunting out memories from my prior experiences with Matt, I *need* to feel what it's like with Ozzy. To know how my body should respond. I push my butt back a little.

He chuckles. "Thought your pussy could use a break."

I turn my head on the mattress. "She is kinda sore."

He bends down and bites my ass, never once removing his finger from there. A second digit joins the first and he scissors his fingers inside me.

An entirely different feeling from before races through my bloodstream. "OH!"

"Like that, huh?"

"Mmm, hmmm." I can't get any real words to form.

"Then you're really going to like it when my pierced cock is buried inside."

I swear a mini-orgasm shakes me at his words. "Oh, God."

Ozzy rubs his condom-covered cock against my pussy, the piercing hitting my clit at just the right angle. "You got my cock all lubed up, Dulcita. Ready?"

Am I ready for him to invade my backdoor? When I did it before, it hurt. But Matt was never gentle with me. Something tells me it's going to be much different with Ozzy. Quashing the butterflies, I nod.

Ozzy pulls his fingers out of my butt and they're replaced with the tip of his cock. He swirls it around, pushes in a fraction and then out. Over and over. Each time he does it, he goes in deeper. I don't feel any pain. The longer he goes, the more pressure builds inside of me. It's different from my other orgasms. Instinctively, I raise my butt. I want more.

He smacks my cheeks, then brings his hand around and down so that his fingers play with my clit. He keeps pushing into my ass, little by little, until he bottoms out. Standing still, he bends over me and kisses my neck. "Feel good?" he asks directly in my ear.

"God, yes." He never hurt me. And I'm almost out of my mind with the fullness of him.

"Good. Cause we haven't even begun."

I can't process his words before he moves forward, then pulls back. Not all the way out. And then he's pushing forward again. Without warning, his finger enters my pussy. I'm at his complete mercy, and I love it. He thrusts and plays me like I'm one of his guitars.

A clenching of my body like I've never felt before starts at my calves and arms and rushes toward my center. In a fury of sensation, it explodes from my center, blanking my mind for anything except one word. "Ozzy!"

My climax continues through his repeated thrusts. When he stills and shouts my name, I break all over again.

Once he takes care of the condom, he returns to the bed and eases me under the covers. Wrapping his arms and legs around me, I can do nothing more than close my eyes in his safe cocoon.

Thirty-One

OZZY

Pins and needles in my arm wake me. McKenna's on top of it. Not wanting to arouse the beauty with the streak of green in her hair, I take my time and twist my arm until the rush of blood circulating in it catches my breath.

The pain doesn't matter.

All that matters is the woman in my arms. Last night's epic sex marathon replays and I know, without a doubt, she's mine. Forever. I told her I love her, but it goes so much deeper than a four-letter word. I breathe her deep in my soul. Music exists because of her.

I stroke her hair off her forehead. She looks so peaceful—carefree even—in slumber. My heart starts to sing a new song about wanting to hold still in this moment forever. I can hear the guitar playing and the drumbeat. I have to capture McKenna's song.

She turns onto her side and I stare at her naked back for a moment.

Dropping a kiss onto her shoulder blade, I reach over and pick up some sheet music and a pencil from the side table and start scribbling.

Two hours later and 'Hold Still' is complete. This is one song I'll refuse to let the band collaborate on. No. This is my song to my girl.

Next to me, McKenna stirs. Stretching her arms over her head, she turns her face toward me. "Morning," she says in a sleepy voice.

I smile at the beauty in my bed. "Hey. How'd you sleep?"

She giggles. "Like someone who's been well-loved." Her hand reaches out and smooths down my chest. I watch its descent, my dick starting to warm up to the idea of yet another round.

Before she wraps her fingers around me, I grab her wrist. "You must be sore."

Her legs move under the blankets. "Maybe a little."

Sighing, I push her hand upward instead of down. "Let's get you into the bath. There's a jacuzzi tub in there."

"I'd expect nothing less."

It dawns on me that she thinks I own this house. Picking her up because she needs to be in my arms, I walk us into the bathroom. "Actually, this isn't my house. Platinum rented it for me for the duration of my residency."

When I deposit her onto the tile floor, she says, "Oh. That's nice of them."

I turn on the water for the jacuzzi and put a bath bomb into it. "Yeah, well, it comes out of my pay."

"Speaking of pay, I'm glad you hired the night nurse for Mom. I now have my nights available to do what we did last night." She kisses me.

"Not a problem." I eye the tub and turn on the jets. "Now, get in."

"Only if you will."

I give her a grin. "Oh, I plan on getting in alright."

Once we're settled, her in front of me between my legs, I caress her shoulders. "There's something I have to tell you."

Underneath my hands, her body goes stiff. "You have ten kids and another dog?"

I chuckle. "Nope. I have one ex-wife and that's it. I swear." I kiss the back of her neck and her body relaxes against me.

"I can handle that." She caresses my bruised knuckles, then brings my hand to her mouth and places little kisses on each one. "What's up?"

"Well, you may think because I'm a rockstar that I have a lot of money. And I do make a shit-ton for my residency. But, I have a lot of expenses. You see, I support all of my family, plus pay for everything here. The band, the crew, this house. Platinum takes a huge chunk of my paycheck." Inhaling, I confess, "And I paid Teresa ten million dollars to go away."

She shakes her head. "I'm not looking for a handout, Ozzy. I fully expect to pay for Mom's nursing care—was planning on it with the national competition. Assuming, of course, I win. Or get excellent publicity from it."

I kiss her cheek. "I have no doubt."

She turns and kisses me on the lips. "Thanks. I don't want your money. I only want you."

"I've never met anyone like you, McKenna."

Her lips curl. "I'm one of a kind."

"That is for sure."

Her hand dips below the water's surface and soon finds its way to my cock. She envelopes it, stroking its length as it grows. "McKenna," I warn.

"I'm not sore anymore."

I growl and we put her admission to the test.

WHEN WE'RE DRESSED and full from a *very* late breakfast, I bring her into my music room. "We need to talk about the future."

"Isn't that kinda soon? I mean, we just had our first overnight." She blows me a kiss from across the room.

"Our first 'overnight'"—I use air quotes around the word—"encompassed more than most couples will do in a year."

Her cheeks turn a pretty shade of pink. "Well, there is that."

I clear my throat. I need to get this off my chest. "Platinum wants me to go to LA to record the next album right after my residency ends. Which is New Year's Eve."

"Oh." She licks her lips. "So, you're moving to LA?"

I nod. "Not exactly. I do own a house there. It's nothing much, but it's in a safe neighborhood and I paid for it in cash. It was the first thing I bought, besides Shirley, when I was on my tour."

"Must've been exciting."

"It was." I don't share the conversation I had with Teresa when I first bought it. She screeched like I bought us a hovel or something. Come to think about it, though, I purchased it without consulting her first. And she never did see it, in the end. "But, now I want to sell it and buy a place with you. For us. That is, if you'll have me."

"You want to move in together?"

I cross the room and stand before her. "Yes."

Her expressive eyes take on a shine I've never seen in them before. "I'd love that. We can use the money from the sale of your house as a downpayment on ours. And, hopefully, I can contribute money from my business."

I run my hands up and down her arms simply because I have to touch her. And I need to feel her reaction to my next admission. One I've given much thought. "I've decided to tell Platinum that I don't want to do a major tour. My life is with you, and your life is here with your mother. I want us to buy a house here, in Vegas."

She stiffens. "But your career—"

"Isn't as important as you are. I know other casinos have contacted me about continuing my residency. I've told Aiden to explore the offers."

She leans back. "But what about Platinum?"

"As you've heard, my new music is less pop. I'll talk with Ginger about where I fit in the Platinum family. And I'll make sure to negotiate a couple of months off from the casino, so I can do shorter tours."

"You've really thought this all out."

I pull her into my embrace. "You're my world, Dulcita."

Watery eyes meet mine. She stands on her tiptoes and kisses my cheek. "And you're mine."

We remain locked together for a few minutes. "Let's go out to the pool. Bans needs to play." At her name, my dog pops up her head and races out her doggie door. Laughing, we join her out there.

As I toss a stick for her to fetch for the umpteenth time, I mull over some of what Teresa said in her letter to me. Thinking about moving in with McKenna has unlocked a whole host of uneasy thoughts. Knowing the importance of communication, I take a deep breath and say, "I think I was wrong about Teresa."

McKenna stops what she's doing and takes the few steps over to me. "What, exactly, do you mean?"

I close my eyes. "You pointed it out to me first. I was loyal to her with my body only. I didn't communicate with her about anything. Hell, I bought the LA house without even sending her a photo." Rubbing my bruised knuckles, I confess, "In her letter to me, she said basically the same thing. I'm not saying that we were right for each other, but I do think I owe her an apology. Although, I have no desire to see her ever again."

McKenna nods. "I understand. Why don't you do it the best way you know how?"

I consider her question. "With a song?"

"You already wrote her one. Why not change the lyrics in 'Honesty?'"

Her solution floors me. "Why didn't I think of this?" Fragments of new lyrics float out of my grasp, but I know they'll come to me. "Our divorce is final. I've paid the alimony. I'm not responding to her letter, but I can do this."

We lapse into silence, the only sound is Bans chasing the stick. After five more throws, I say, "I wrote one more new song that I want included in the album. It's about you."

"Me?" She beams at me. "I like the sound of that!" She blows on her closed fist like she's too hot to handle. I guess, in a way, she is. "When can I hear it?"

"Give me a sec." I toss the stick once more for Bans and head upstairs to our bedroom. Funny how I've changed the pronoun. McKenna and I are a "we." Smiling, I grab my notes and the jewelry box I picked up nearly two weeks ago, and return to the patio where McKenna has taken up the stick throwing duties. I love how she's come so far with my dog.

With me.

I shake the sheet music. "It's going to be my first single."

"But what about 'Take Me'?"

I shake my head. "Nope. This one. It's called 'Hold Still.' And it's for you." Without any instrument, I stand and sing the words I wrote this morning while she was sleeping in our bed:

You and I used to be
A glance, a smile, nothing more
We'd play and pass
But that was all
No reason to Hold Still

Come and go, go and come
I was cleansing my soul
And so were you
But that was all
No time to Hold Still

Chorus:
Underneath was something deeper
We both felt it but ran
No way could you be that person
For me, for you
Yet we couldn't stop — we wouldn't stop
Until we did
And you held me deep
When we both agreed to Hold Still

One day you called me on my bluff
Danced into my life for good
Challenged me to be better
But that wasn't all
Time started to Hold Still

Your smile, your genius
Your beauty, your passion
They all swept me in
But that wasn't all
I prayed for the world to Hold Still

Repeat Chorus

Now we're both letting go
Of our hurts and demons
Connecting so deep, Dulcita
But that's not all
I want this moment to Hold Still
For our love will never Hold Still

When I finish the song, I clasp the bracelet around her wrist.

Tears run down her cheeks. "Oh my, Ozzy. I love the song. And the bracelet." She throws herself into my arms. "And I love you. Forever."

Epilogue

LOS ANGELES, ONE MONTH LATER
OZZY

McKENNA AND I ENTER THE hotel's ballroom late. "Everyone's already here," she whispers to me.

"Well, you were the one who wanted to celebrate the release of 'Hold Still.'" Her cheeks turn an adorable shade of red. I kiss her blushing face. "Yeah. So we're late." I grab her hand, the bracelet I gave her now sporting an orange jewel. "Let's go mingle."

A huge banner with the words Youth Art Consortium—National Competition Awards is hung above the stage area. On the dais, the Project's logo hangs with other regional charities above the podium. I'm confident that's where McKenna will receive her much-deserved award.

"McKenna! Ozzy!" Rose and Cole join us.

"I didn't know you were coming," McKenna gushes after we say our hellos. She and Rose had a long heart-to-heart about everything, and their relationship is so much stronger now.

"How could I miss my maid-of-honor getting the biggest award of her life?"

McKenna puts her finger up to her lips. "Shh. Don't jinx me."

"I would never try to curse on you," a French-accented voice floats to us. We turn and greet Wills and Emilie.

Beaming from ear-to-ear, McKenna dances to music only she can hear. "How's wedding planning coming along?"

Instead of Emilie, Wills answers, "It's great." He squeezes his fiancée. "In less than a month, we'll all be in Paris and this woman will officially be mine." He kisses Emilie.

Not one to be outdone, Cole grabs his wife's hand and kisses it. "Glad we showed you how it's done."

The lights dim and the announcer asks us to take our seats for dinner and the ceremony. Throughout the meal, McKenna's antsy. She is lively and talkative, but I can tell it's her armor. "Party-girl McKenna." But, underneath, she's a wreck. I zip my hand up her thigh and her head swivels to mine.

"No matter what happens tonight," I kiss her cheek, "I'm so proud of you."

She changes into the woman beneath her veneer in front of my eyes. Her posture softens, and her eyes take on a darker hue. "You don't know what that means to me."

The chairman of the Consortium takes to the podium. Peggy Laswell and the other board members from the Project are in the front row. McKenna's hand finds its way into mine. It's icy. I squeeze, imparting some of my heat.

He thanks everyone for coming, talks about the Consortium and introduces the various regional competitions that brought us here. I'm impressed. McKenna will do great work for them—I have no doubt that she'll win.

"And now, the moment you've all been waiting for. It's time to announce the winner of the national competition, who'll design graphics that will introduce people across the world to the work we do. We're very excited to have all of the finalists in attendance today. Each one of you submitted stellar work, and the Consortium would be happy to have any one of you representing us. Unfortunately, only one person can be selected."

Rose beams at McKenna and nods. McKenna's response is to hold my hand tighter, but she smiles at her best friend.

"Before the winner is announced, let's see a sampling of each of their work." The lights dim and the presentations roll.

I may be biased, but hers was the best by a mile. Leaning over, I kiss my girl's cheek. "Remember to thank me for the inspiration when you win." McKenna's laugh can be heard above the soundtrack. Mission accomplished.

When the lights come back up, the chairman says, "And now, please give a round of applause for the winner of the national competition." My girl sucks in her breath. "McKenna James."

McKenna gasps and everyone around our table shouts. She and I jump up, and she wraps me in a huge hug. Having won awards before, I know how exciting this time is, and I want to make sure she enjoys every single second of it. With a big grin, I turn her toward the podium and smack her ass. She stumbles forward a step, then gives me a dirty look over her shoulder. In return, I wiggle my eyebrows.

After hugging everyone at our table, McKenna makes her way up to the stage. Once there, she turns to look out at the audience, her eyes locking on mine. "Thank you to the Consortium for this great honor. I especially want to thank the Artist Adventure Avenue Project for taking a chance on me. I know some issues arose, but I'm glad they've all been cleared up."

She beams at each board member in the front row. "I can truly share that this presentation was a labor of love for me. Working with each of these musicians was like a dream come true. Being around such creativity sparked my own, and I'm so happy you enjoyed the final presentation."

She takes a deep breath, the orange streak in her hair glinting in the spotlight. "I have to honestly admit that I wouldn't be standing here today is if weren't for my better half, Ozzy Martinez. He thinks I saved him, but the opposite is true. The music you heard and saw from him came from his heart. I should know. I was there when he created the songs. He is my inspiration. He knows everything about me and loves me anyway, and I am free to soar because of this fact."

Tears flow down my cheeks. I've never been so humbled and honored. Next to me, Cole puts his hand on my shoulder and leans over. "You deserve her." He shakes me. Knowing what's coming up later, he says, "Now, don't go all pussy on me, or I'll have to fuck you up."

I laugh and miss the ending of my girl's speech, but that's okay. Emilie motions to the waiter, and shortly we're presented with glasses of champagne. When McKenna returns to our table, Emilie stands. Raising her glass, she says, "Congratulations to the most talented graphic designer. May your star only rise from here." We all clink glasses.

A rep who Cole and I both know from Platinum stops by our table. After exchanging pleasantries with us, he turns to McKenna. Even though I try to hear what's being said, the pair keep their voices down. When he leaves, we all look at her.

McKenna holds up his business card. "He congratulated me on my win today and wants me to come to their offices while I'm still here in LA and to discuss my taking them on as a client! They want me to work with up-and-coming bands." Her excitement practically bounces off her body.

"That's my girl! I'm so proud of you," I say and pull her into my arms.

Once Rose finishes her drink, she says, "Let's go to our house for a more private celebration."

WILLS AND COLE surround me while the women are in the kitchen. "You have it, right?" Wills asks.

I pull out the ornate, old-fashioned box that Mamí gave me when McKenna and I visited Puerto Rico a couple of weeks ago. My girl was a huge success, winning over everyone in the family within minutes. And she fell for them just as quickly.

"Good," Cole responds. "Now, don't fuck this up or Rose will kill you."

I snort. "I'll try not to." I rub my suddenly clammy hands down my pants. "Were you two nervous like this?"

Cole puffs up. "Hell, no. I knew she wanted to be my wife. It was practically a mercy ask."

I squint at my friend, then turn to Wills. "How about you?"

The bodyguard-turned-gym owner says, "I asked her on my birthday. She was my best present."

"Well, shit. Today's not either one of our birthdays."

"But she did just win an award," Wills supplies, punching me in the arm.

"Damn straight she did."

The women file out of the house, each carrying a couple of platters Rose had her friend-slash-cook prepare. "Grandma Gertie's out on a date tonight, but she wanted to be sure that we all ate well," Rose giggles.

Popping a crostini into her mouth, Rose asks McKenna, "How's your Mom doing?"

"She's doing great. The doctor changed her meds, and she's responding really well."

"That's excellent news," Emilie replies.

I swipe a steak finger sandwich and lock eyes with McKenna. Her mother's new treatment has slowed down the progress of the disease. She even was able to understand when I asked her permission for McKenna's hand after our trip to Puerto Rico, which she happily granted. I wish I could've met her father, but I'm going to spend the rest of my life treating his daughter like the queen she is. Of course, if she'll have me.

The evening wears on and the platters are decimated. Mainly by the guys, but the ladies didn't do too poorly. My eyes stray to the pool, with a light show going on. Emilie yawns.

Crap. It's now or never.

"Excuse me," I say to Emilie and Wills. "I have something I have to do." Wills nods at me.

I walk straight up to McKenna, stopping mere inches from her. Cole and Rose, who were flanking her, look at each other and disappear into the background. Cole gives me a thumbs-up.

"McKenna." The word comes out strangled.

She asks, "Are you okay?"

In the background, Cole snickers. I shoot him a dirty look and try again.

"McKenna." My voice sounds much stronger. "Your words tonight from the podium honored me, but you truly had things backwards."

She looks around, as if trying to understand what's happening.

Ignoring her reaction, I continue, "You saved me. You brought music back into my life. You reminded me what fun is, because any time I spend with you—whether we're out on dune buggies, indoor skydiving, exploring new places, or simply unwinding together is fun. With you, McKenna, my life is complete."

I drop to one knee and pull out the box my abuelo offered to my abuela decades ago. My body's shaking so badly, though, that I can't keep my balance. I put my other knee on the ground and look up at my love. "I'm not on one knee—but two—asking if you'll be my wife."

She looks down at me, her head nodding "yes" before the word escapes her lips. Then they're on top of mine.

Pulling back, I slide the square sapphire ring onto her finger to the sound of applause from our best friends. "I know this isn't your typical engagement ring, but it was my grandma's. Mamí wanted you to have it. She loves you as much as I do."

Tears flow down her cheeks. She's never looked more beautiful to me.

I take a deep breath. "And I can't wait to proudly wear your ring everyday for the rest of my life."

Whatever life throws at us, we have the support around us that we need. Plus, we have each other.

I wrap myself in the arms of the woman I love, breathing her in. And I hold still.

Do you **need** to know what happened when Ozzy took McKenna to meet his family in Puerto Rico? If you want to see how this all went down, you can get the bonus epilogue for FREE by signing up for my e-newsletter **https://dl.bookfunnel.com/h3otiohshm**

Keep your eyes peeled for an entirely NEW series of hot rockers and other celebs, starting with BRAXTON HUNTE, coming in 2019!

Dear Fabulous Reader,

Thank you so much for reading Hold Still, the second standalone novel in a Hold Series Spin-off!

Ozzy and McKenna started out as such broken characters. I knew, from the first book in The Hold Series, about Ozzy's past and what drove him to be such a, well, "rockstar." It wasn't until I started working on this book that I uncovered McKenna's deepest troubles, and knew that this pairing was to be my most explosive yet. I hope you agree!

Cameos made by Cole and Rose, and Wills and Emilie, plus the other characters from The Hold Series, were like coming home. Writing the Manchester's wedding brought tears to my eyes, but I knew this was the right way to say good-bye to all of these characters. I did shed a tear at their vows, I have to admit.—And seeing Wills and Ems as they get ready for their own wedding was the cherry on top!

I'd like to share a couple of stories behind the adventures enjoyed in the book:

-Ozzy takes McKenna indoor skydiving. My hubby and I had the pleasure of trying out this exhilarating experience when we were in Canada. I highly recommend it ~ even if the training can be a bit uncomfortable. I'll never forget holding the Superman pose on that hard bench!

-Edie Z's is based on a chocolate shop that one of my great friends took me to in Chicago. My mouth waters just thinking about it!

-The imaginary crater McKenna's mother saw was inspired by a conversation I had on a train in Italy this summer with an Australian geriatric psychologist. Spatial perception is a real issue with dementia patients, so I revised this manuscript to include the episode.

This book is dedicated to my grandmother, who passed away last year at age 99. She suffered from dementia during nearly the last two decades of her life, and watching her disappear in front of my eyes took its toll on my mother and me. When I realized that McKenna's mother had an early onset diagnosis, I knew she was in for a long road, and she needed to accept help. I hope a cure for this disease is found soon. For more information about dementia, go to https://www.dementiasociety.org.

Stay up-to-date with everything I'm working on by joining Arell's Angels, my reader group on Facebook. I always share my work there first! www.facebook.com/groups/arellsangels
If you have any questions, feel free to email me at Arell@ArellRivers. com. I love chatting with readers!

Thanks for devoting your precious time to Hold Still. I hope Ozzy and McKenna gave you as many feels as they did me!

All my love,
Arell

Gratitude

Hold Still couldn't have happened without the support and encouragement of so many people!

As usual, hugs and kisses to my husband. He puts up with my crazed writing and editing stints, helps me with plot holes and supports me without question. He is my rock.

My Mom has been such an inspiration to me, especially in writing this book. Her courage never ceases to amaze me.

Noella Phillips and Michelle Bond, my critique partners, are the BEST! They were there at the plotting stage ~ in fact, you can thank Michelle for Ozzy's swimming habit!! They read this book in record time and gave me so many wonderful suggestions that truly enhanced the manuscript. I can't do it without them!

My professional team is wonderful! The following super-talented women really helped me with Hold Still, and came through under crazy deadlines, too! Editor Sarah Murphy, proofreader Virginia Tesi Carey, cover designer and formatter Cassy Roop of Pink Ink Designs. I am forever grateful to these women.

To my alphas and betas ~ Maria Dema, Gwyn Novak, Rekha Dave and Freddie Bonaire ~ you ladies absolutely ROCK. Words cannot express (even for an author) what your time and suggestions mean to me. I love each one of you so hard!!

My ARC Team is awesome!! You made me smile with your antics, found typos and gave so much love for Ozzy and McKenna! I really, REALLY appreciate your taking the time to read, review and share HOLD STILL. I couldn't ask for a better group of fantastic ladies!!!

My closed reader's group, Arell's Angels, keeps me giggling and smiling every day! I love your excitement and positivity!! Dana Fernandez, Rebecca Berland, Tracy Moyer Wilt, Vicky Bomer, Kerri Curtis, Emily Young Meador, Denice Shields, Laurie Gamble, Jessica Renee Elliston, Missy Meyer and so many other Angels really are the absolute best. A new hottie of the month, special serials where you decide the characters' fates, author takeover Sundays, games, Angel Questions of the Day and FB Live events sure put a smile on my face daily!

To the indie community, I want to say thank you. The support I receive from you every day keeps me going. Huge shout out to Maria Luis and Jessica Peterson ~ your calls, PMs and friendship mean so much to me. I can't wait to see you both again!

Hugs to the many wonderful people who provide unending support (and a reality check, when needed) to my writing journey, especially Lilly Wilde, Wendy Hamlin, WT, Candice Benson, Isabelle Peterson, the sexy ladies of the Playroom, and the amazing authors in the NJ chapter of Romance Writers of America.

And to everyone who picks up this book, *I hope Ozzy and McKenna made your heart sing*. And if you enjoyed Hold Still, please share it with your friends and write a review.

With deepest thanks,
Arell

About the Author

For as long as Arell Rivers can remember, she has been lost in a book. During her senior year in college, she picked up a romance novel ... and instantly was hooked!

Arell started writing her first novel because the characters were screaming at her to do so. The story started coming out in her dreams and attacking her in the shower, so she took to the computer to shut them up. But they kept talking.

Born and raised in New Jersey, Arell has what some may call a "checkered past." Prior to discovering her passion for writing romance, she practiced law, was a wedding and event planner and even dabbled in marketing. Arell lives with a very supportive husband who doesn't care that the bed isn't made or dinner isn't on the table. When not in her writing cave, Arell is found making dinner in the InstantPot, working out with Shaun T or hitting the beach.

Arell is a member of the New Jersey chapter of Romance Writers of America.

Want to keep up to date with Arell? Sign up for her newsletter at http://bit.ly/ArellRiversSignup. All new subscribers receive a special gift!

Connect with Arell

Facebook: www.Facebook.com/ArellRivers
Readers Group, "Arell's Angels": www.facebook.com/groups/ArellsAngels
Twitter: www.Twitter.com/ArellRivers
Amazon: https://www.amazon.com/Arell-Rivers/e/B01MT0DUBV
Goodreads: bit.ly/2h84zJT
BookBub: www.bookbub.com/profile/arell-rivers
Website: www.ArellRivers.com
Email: Arell@ArellRivers.com

Other Books by Arell Rivers

The Hold Series
Book #1: No One to Hold
Book #2: Hard to Hold
Book #3: To Have and to Hold
Prequel Novella: Hold On

A Hold Series Spin-off
Book #1: Take Hold of Me
Book #2: Hold Still

Want to see where it all began?
Read on to enjoy the first chapter of No One To Hold,
Book #1 in The Hold Series!

No One to Hold

ARELL RIVERS

One

Somehow I endure the first hour of the party.

No. Not party. Wake.

Two hours ago I placed a blood-red rose atop my mother's casket on this freezing February day. Now, I'm trapped in my parents' house, choked by a tie, listening to stories about her while pretending everything is okay. It's *not* fucking okay.

When I can't take it anymore, I collapse onto the step at the foot of the stairs, looking at all the people milling around the family room. They are eating catered food off Mom's good china. Swilling drinks from her favorite wine glasses. Photos of her are displayed everywhere, some in frames and others in the scrapbooks that she spent hours creating.

Reaching between the spindles of the banister, I pick up a frame off the closest table. It's a photo of Mom and me at the Grammy Awards a couple of years ago. She's beaming, clearly enjoying herself. I trace her beautiful smile with a calloused finger.

A bunch of Mom's high school students surround me like yipping hyenas, giving me little choice but to put down the photo, stand up and join them. They're on the cheerleading squad Mom coached. They all seem to be talking at once, making it impossible for me to follow their conversation, and a few of the girls seem star struck to be near me. Some even cast what they obviously think are flirty, seductive glances in my direction. Seriously?

One girl points her cell phone at me while the others titter. My hand flies to block my face in a gesture I've perfected after years of protecting myself from the paparazzi.

Rose Morgan, my ponytailed and bespectacled account rep with the Greta VonStein PR Agency, appears at my right. I take my first deep breath since being surrounded, knowing Rose will take care of the girls.

"Ladies, a word," she says. She's wearing what she always wears—a skirt and blazer—this time in black. Ushering the group deeper into the family room, Rose says something that I can't hear and then takes the would-be photographer's cell phone. After pushing a few buttons, she returns it to the girl, who mouths the word *sorry* to me. Quickly, the cheerleaders disperse. Rose to the rescue. Again.

Returning to my side, Rose places her hands on my cheeks. My breath catches at the contact.

In a low voice, she says, "It's all taken care of, Cole."

Behind her glasses, her blue eyes are filled with compassion and some other emotion I can't identify. They seem like they belong to someone much older and wiser than me, not to a woman who's a few years younger than my thirty-two.

I close my eyes to block out everything except the feeling of her hands on my skin and the comfort they're pouring into me. The intensity of the sensation startles me back to the present, causing my eyes to pop open. Clearing my throat, I say, "Thanks for the save. It's kinda weird being fangirled here."

Rose drops her hands and I immediately crave her soft warmth. "I'm so sorry for your loss," she finally says. "Your mom is—was—a wonderful lady. I remember the first time I spoke with her, right after you'd signed with

Greta. She couldn't believe you had a publicist." She shakes her head. "Her exact words were, 'I can't believe other people will really follow what my Cole does.'"

I laugh. It's a rusty sound. "I can hear Mom saying that."

Smiling, Rose says, "After you took her to your first Grammys, she sent me a lovely thank you note and gift basket. She was so proud of you."

"Mom never got tired of talking about when she met Adam Baret there." Mom's teenage heartthrob sent a very nice arrangement to the funeral. I'm sure she's looking down on us from above, blushing.

"Take some time and stay here with your father and brother."

My gaze follows hers to the kitchen, where Jayson and Dad are hugging. It's just us now. And Jayson's boyfriend, Carl. "I plan to."

"Family is so very important. Lean on each other." Her tone leads me to believe she's speaking from experience, although I wouldn't know. Up until now, all of our conversations have been strictly business.

I nod. Swallowing past the lump in my throat, I say, "Thanks for making the trip from Los Angeles, Rose. And I appreciate how much you've kept the paparazzi away from us."

"I wanted to be here for you." She reaches out like she's going to touch me again, which sends a flicker of anticipation through me, but her hand stops and returns to her side. My disappointment shocks me.

She continues, "And don't worry about all the cards and gifts your fans are sending to the office. We'll make sure everything receives a response, and the stuffed animals and other presents will be distributed to children's hospitals."

I shake my head at her use of "we." That idea has Rose's signature, not Greta's, all over it. "My fans are really sending stuff?"

"You mean a lot to them." Her lips quirk into a small smile, and I feel my mouth move upward in response.

"I left a card from Josh with the others over there." She motions toward the front hallway table. "I thought you'd want to see it."

"Thanks." I first met Josh four years ago at a meet-and-greet. His love of music reminded me of myself at his age, so passionate. His single mother was unable to pay for a violin coach, so I arranged for him to have private music lessons. He must be fourteen by now.

She nods, sending her ponytail swinging. For the second time today, I find myself ensnared by her blue eyes. They're an icy blue, yet they're bright with emotion behind the thick lenses of her glasses. How have I never noticed their remarkable color before?

After a beat, she says, "Let me know when you're planning on returning to LA, and we'll set up some appearances for you. In the meantime, Greta wants me to issue a release on your behalf, thanking your fans for their support and letting them know you'll be spending some personal time with your family." She gives me a quick hug and walks off in Dad's direction.

Business never stops for long.

My agent, Russell Waldock, and his wife fill the void left by Rose. At fifty-five, he's one of the most powerful men in LA, yet he's also very down-to-earth, which drew me to him. "I appreciate your coming all the way to New Jersey for Mom's"—my voice breaks—"funeral."

Russell claps me on the back. "Julie was a great lady, Cole. Always looking out for you. And she was fierce. The way she scolded me about your music video for 'Prowling' made me feel like I got caught rifling through my father's *Playboy* collection." His wife smiles at him.

I chuckle. "She always called it my 'racy' video."

"Well, she wasn't wrong there," Russell agrees. No, she wasn't.

His wife picks up a photo of Mom and Dad holding hands on a beach in Hawaii and then returns it to the side table. She asks, "How's your father holding up? This has to be hard on him."

I glance over at Dad. "He's okay. It's been . . . rough."

How *is* Dad going to handle this? Mom's touch is everywhere in this house, in his life. They were married for so long they used to complete each other's sentences. "I'm trying to do whatever I can. Of course, Jayson and Carl live nearby."

"Let me know if you need anything, okay?" Russell says.

"Thanks. I'm grateful you arranged for the label to give me an extension on recording my next album."

Russell nods. "Call me when you're ready to go back to LA. No rush."

They each give me a hug. "Thanks again for coming," I say. "Will do."

I circulate around the room, numbly making small talk with acquaintances I haven't seen in years. I'm standing in the dining room with some family friends the next time Rose crosses my line of vision. She's in the front hall, running her fingers over the framed photo of Mom holding me when I was a baby. She wipes a tear from her cheek and looks up.

Our eyes meet.

We both freeze.

After a long pause, she retrieves her coat and walks out the front door. I catch a breath as if my heart just restarted.

I continue circulating and reminiscing about Mom. Around nine, Jayson and Carl leave to take care of their new puppy. Just Aunt Doreen and her family remain. "How are you doing, Cole?"

"I'm okay," I lie. Yanking off my tie, I ask, "How about you, Aunt Doreen?"

"About as well as I can be. I want you to know you can always count on me, whatever you need."

"Thanks."

We discuss mundane things, like how beautiful the funeral was and our amazement at how many people came to the wake. After a pause, she says, "You know, I swore to my sister that I would keep an eye out for you. She really wanted you to settle down." She picks invisible lint off of my blazer.

Can't she give this a rest? Even today? I sigh. "There's no one in my life at the moment. Frankly, I'm not interested."

"I understand. But getting through tough times is easier when you have someone by your side. And celebrating the good times is better, too. I intend to hold you to the promise that you made to your mother and me before your career took off." She looks deep into my eyes. Her green gaze mirrors mine. And Mom's.

Trying not to squirm, I say, "I've kept my promise, Aunt Doreen. I don't have a bad boy reputation."

"That's true, thanks to your publicist, but we both know that running through women like tissues is not exactly living up to the spirit of your pledge." I stifle the urge to roll my eyes. "Just think about what I said. And let me know if I can help you in any way, honey. I love you." She gives me a peck on the cheek, and after another rounds of goodbyes, leaves the house with her family.

Aunt Doreen's comments remind me of my last conversation with Mom—how can it be that I won't have another one with her? I try to swallow the lump in my throat. Mom made me promise that I would settle down. And I can't deny that Aunt Doreen's words have struck a chord. At the cemetery, everyone had a hand to hold. Even my younger brother. I had Dad's, and he needed me. But it's not the same.

Taking off my blazer, I walk into the kitchen and roll up my sleeves. Grateful for something productive to do, I join Dad in packaging up all the leftover food and arranging it in the refrigerator. It looks like casseroles mated in there.

I'm exhausted, but suspect neither one of us is quite ready to face going upstairs. As has become our nightly custom since I flew back home, he pours two fingers of scotch for each of us. Tonight, I bring the stack of sympathy cards from the hallway to the dining room table before sitting down.

"Want to look at these?" I ask.

He shrugs. "Sure."

I hold up the first card and glance at the scribbled signature. "This one's from Josh."

Dad smiles at the card with the violin on the front. "You still paying for his private violin lessons?"

"Yeah." I squint, trying to read his chicken scratch. "He sends his 'condulances.'" We both smile at his attempt and clink our scotches.

Jessie Anderson's distinctive handwriting catches my eye. "Jessie and Amanda sent a card."

"Another one in the long line of ladies you've dated." He uses air quotes around "dated."

"Yeah, well that didn't end up how I expected." Jessie is gorgeous, and when Rose set us up on a publicity date, I thought we'd be in bed within hours. Shaking my head, I trace her girlfriend's name on the card. The two of them are great together. Like Mom and Dad are. Were.

Clearing my throat, I say, "Jessie's filming her TV show, so they couldn't be here. They send their love."

"Jules—Julie—your mother," his voice catches. I reach over and pat him on the shoulder while he collects himself. "She never missed one episode of Jessie's show. She had a group of friends over every Thursday night for a viewing party." He smiles. "I made myself scarce those nights. To be honest, they scared me a little."

We both laugh, then stop short as if we did something wrong. Maybe it's too soon for laughter. Dad knocks back his scotch, then stares blankly into his empty glass.

I reach out for another card, but drop my hand. I can't concentrate any longer. "Let's call it a night, Dad."

Sad brown eyes meet mine. He looks so tired. "I'll put the glasses in the dishwasher and you get the lights."

Our chores completed, he slowly leads the way upstairs. On the landing, Mom's perfume lingers. Dad pulls me in for a long hug and whispers, "Goodnight, son. I love you."

"Love you, too."

Walking to the doorway farthest from my parents' room, I enter my childhood bedroom. The room is as I left it ages ago, filled with all the stuff I once considered important. Posters of musicians—some of whom I'm privileged to call friends now. That makes me smile. Posters of models, generally glistening wet. Seems like my tastes haven't changed much over the years. Just my access.

I sit down on my old twin bed, feeling horribly alone, wishing a woman were here to put her arms around me and tell me everything will be okay. I'm thirty-two fucking years old. Shouldn't I have someone special in my life by now?

Images of Rose from today replay in my mind. The connection I felt when she touched me was . . . What am I thinking? She works for me. Besides, she's all business, all the time.

Shit, I'm living the life most guys only dream about. I have money, fame, millions of fans across the globe, houses on both coasts, people to do my bidding at the snap of my fingers and a very steady diet of gorgeous women. There can be nothing wrong with my lifestyle if it's the American dream. Right?

Looking up to the ceiling, lyrics start to form. Grabbing my trusty notebook, I scribble down the words that are tripping over themselves to come out.

Read the rest of Cole and Rose's story on Amazon ~ FREE in Kindle Unlimited ~ here! **https://www.amazon.com/dp/B01N1TKL7Z**

www.ingramcontent.com/pod-product-compliance
Lightning Source LLC
Chambersburg PA
CBHW030021180626
46810CB00001B/147